Winter i

Also by Elise Darcy

The Living Apart Together Series

Living Apart Together

It Takes 2 to Tango

Dear John

Love on the Rooftop

The Sunrise Coast Series

New Beginnings at the Harbour Inn

The Secret of the Summerhouse

The Cottage by the Sea

The Guest House at Shingle Cove

The Houseboat by the Quay

Return to Willow Tree Cottage

The Bookshop of Memories

The Beach House

A Summer to Remember

Standalone books

A Mallorcan Affair

Lola & The Man

We'll Meet Again

The Villa in Sicily

Winter in the Scottish Highlands

A Novel

ELISE DARCY

Penny Lane Press

ISBN 978-1-913147-26-6

"Your life does not get better by chance, it gets better by change."–*Jim Rohn*

1

Eleanor walked down the six concrete steps to the street, holding onto the wrought iron railings for support. She stood for a moment on the pavement, staring at the polished bronze plaque, a name, a place, embossed in thick gold lettering: *Dr Leopold, Physician, Harley Street.* She shuddered. The result was not what she had been expecting. Her thoughts turned to her husband.

She turned away from the impressive Georgian-fronted building and began to walk, heading for the nearest tube station, heading for home. The sound of a car horn gave her a start, forcing her attention to the road, where a convoy of cars waited impatiently to get past a slow-moving black Jaguar. She quickened her pace. Another car horn sounded. She glanced at the Jaguar as several cars quickly sped up and overtook it, narrowly avoiding the oncoming traffic.

She stopped. The Jaguar stopped. She stood watching as the dark-tinted driver window opened. The driver, wearing black leather gloves and a flat-topped peaked hat leaned across the seat. 'Eleanor, come get in the car. Please.'

Eleanor sighed. There were times she just wanted to be on her own; not chaperoned everywhere like a child. She was a grown woman. 'No, Edward. I want to walk.'

'You always want to walk afterwards. Come now – get in the car,' he implored. 'You do not want to get swept up amongst the crowd of commuters spilling out of their offices, heading home after work.'

Eleanor walked to the waiting Jag and bent down to look at the old chauffeur. 'I'd really like to go home by myself this time.' As with everything else in her life, Eleanor always felt compelled to ask somebody's permission.

'Each time is the same, eh?' Edward shook his head solemnly.

Eleanor made no response. She preferred to go to these appointments on her own. She turned from the car, headed down the street and started buttoning up her long coat against the chill wind. It had been sleeting when she'd arrived. Now it had turned into the first snowfall in December. Although it was not heavy, it was cold enough to leave a dusting on the London pavements.

'You be careful,' the chauffeur shouted after her.

A few moments later, to Eleanor's relief, the Jag sped off. She watched the bright red taillights turn a corner and disappear. She had thought Edward might hang around, keeping an eye out, watching her until she'd made it safely to a tube station. After all, it was already dark, even though it was barely teatime.

She didn't like putting Edward in this awkward position. It was his job, after all; a job she knew he loved, that he'd had for many years. He had worked for the family ever since she could remember, and she certainly would never want to jeopardise that. So she had always relented. But today was different. She needed time to think. Today, she didn't want to feel Edward's sympathetic gaze settling knowingly on her in the rear-view mirror.

Today, Eleanor got the tube.

2

'Mrs Campbell-Ross.' The doorman in his blue uniform was still standing in the same spot under the striped canopy outside the apartment building, as he had been when Eleanor had left that morning. He opened the glass door.

Eleanor noted the raised eyebrow as he glanced at the street. The customary Jag was nowhere to be seen. She had the impulse to tell him she was quite capable of getting the tube, like normal people – and for that matter, thoroughly enjoyed it as well. It was nice to fade into the crowds and just be Mrs Nobody.

Squeezed into the bustle of early Thursday evening commuters, Eleanor had spent her ten minutes in the real world, studying people's faces, hoping they would give her some clue as to what it was like to be normal; not rich, not poor – just average.

Eleanor walked into the marble foyer and waited for the lift. She thought of all the anonymous faces and the irony that most of the people she had seen would undoubtedly love to swap their drudgery for her privileged lifestyle. The question was, would they be able to cope with the boredom, the lack of direction, the lack of mystery about what the future held? In truth, Eleanor often fantasised about what it was like to live in such a world, with that freedom and independence.

The lift took Eleanor up to the floor below the penthouse suite. She tipped the bored porter, who was neatly dressed in a striking red uniform; her father's idea of course – the porter, the uniforms, the marble fountain in the entrance foyer. People often attempted to walk in off the street – and were stopped by Harry at the door, of course – having mistaken the building for a very grand, old-fashioned London hotel, not realising its true nature; an apartment building for executives of the Ross Corporation.

Eleanor stepped into her apartment and closed the door on her polite, self-contained public persona. Then she had a tantrum. Stamping her feet, clenching her fists, and screaming obscenities until she was red in the face.

Next, she threw her Gucci coat on the floor and her Prada bag at the door and, lifting one foot at a time, kicked off her Jimmy Choo shoes, hitting the expensive sideboard to her left with one and nearly knocking herself out with the other.

She unzipped her black skirt as she walked through the marble entrance hallway towards the double doors at the far end. She let her skirt fall to the floor and stepped out of it, nearly tripping up as she abandoned it in the hallway. She threw open the double doors to the lounge and started rolling down her tights as she headed for the other side of the room, hopping on one foot and then the other before leaving her tights discarded on a chair.

She entered the inner hallway while slipping off her blouse. She reached the bedroom in just her panties and bra, flung open the wardrobe door and walked in. One side was his, the other hers. She walked to her side and reached above the rack of designer suits, which she hardly ever had occasion to wear; it wasn't as though she worked. She stood on her tiptoes and patted her hand along the top shelf, dislodging hats, bags and shoes until the search was over.

In the bathroom, Eleanor turned on the shower and placed her favourite cosy set of clothes, the ones that she loved lounging about in, on the loo seat.

She showered. As the water cascaded down her shoulders, she sobbed.

Eleanor stepped out of the shower and wiped the bathroom mirror. She stared at her reflection. She tied her thick black hair loosely in a ponytail. Her face was devoid of make-up, just the way she liked it, showing her hazel eyes and a flurry of freckles over her plump cheeks. 'It shouldn't be happening. I'm too young. I haven't done anything with my life,' she confided to the unhappy twenty-six-year-old staring back at her. She watched the mirror steam up and her face gradually fade from view. She stood for a moment, staring at the mirror, praying that by some miracle the Harley Street doctor had been wrong.

Eleanor got dressed. The dungarees were tighter than she remembered. Her old grey college sweatshirt had turned grey with age after too many washes, and her brown suede moccasins were patchy and worn out of shape, but she didn't care what she looked like. She hadn't felt this comfortable, this at home, since she had last worn them.

She was trying to work out when that had been, but her thoughts were interrupted by the sound of the apartment door closing.

'Honey, I'm …'

Eleanor stepped out of the bathroom and cocked her head to one side at the sound of her husband's voice.

'If I find you, can I have you?' his voice rang out on a happy note. Eleanor frowned, wondering what on earth he was talking about.

The bedroom door handle turned. 'I bet the last two items are in here.' He opened the door wide, a smile on his handsome face and a pile of Eleanor's clothes, collected from the hallway and the lounge on his way through the apartment, slung over one arm. 'Ah,' he said, his smile fading as he took in Eleanor's paint-stained dungarees. His eyes dropped in dismay to her worn moccasins.

'Oh,' said Eleanor, staring at the pile of clothes and realising Jake had misinterpreted the situation. On any other occasion, any other day, she might have found it funny. But not today.

'You're not redecorating the place again – are you?'

She caught the inflection in his voice. He was not doing a good job of masking what he was thinking – that it would be a waste of time. It probably would. But, she thought, *who could blame me if I was?* There was nothing else to do. And besides, it gave her an opportunity to indulge her passion – interior design. It was what she'd studied at university. But her husband's jet-setting lifestyle, working for the corporation, meant she was never in one place long enough to put down roots and find a job. And now she had something else on her plate that was definitely going to put paid to any immediate thoughts of a career.

Jake smiled at Eleanor as he walked toward her, tossing her clothes on the bed. He stood in front of her and fingered the straps of her dungarees. 'Not quite what I had in mind, but …' He grasped the straps and gently pulled her towards him.

'No.' Eleanor pushed him away. 'Jake, we need to talk.'

'Can't it wait?' He tugged at the straps playfully.

'No, it can't.' Eleanor prised his fingers off her dungarees.

Jake sat down on the end of the bed and loosened his tie.

'From the looks of things,' he sighed heavily, well aware that she had attended her appointment in Harley Street that afternoon, 'I'm guessing you're going to tell me it's not good news.'

Eleanor hesitated. 'I want,' she began, and took a deep breath before continuing, 'I want to spend this holiday together.'

Jake held out his arms, placing his hands on her thighs. 'But of course we will,' he reassured her. He tried to pull Eleanor towards him, but she wouldn't budge from her spot.

'I want it to be just the two of us, here in the apartment together,' she reiterated, staring down at him. She took in his faded tan, his blond hair, his green eyes. His expression shifted. She thought she detected irritation in those beautiful eyes.

His hands dropped. 'Ask me any other time of the year, but not Christmas, Eleanor. It's a family tradition. You know that.'

She stared at him intently. Why do you do that?'

'Do what?'

'Revert to my full name when you're cheesed off with me?

'Who said I'm cheesed off with you?'

'So, you're not annoyed I asked that question? That I said I want us, just the two of us, to spend Christmas together?'

Jake sighed heavily and dropped his gaze, running his fingers through his hair. 'It's been a long day at work.'

Eleanor could feel her temper fraying, her frustration building. 'For goodness' sake, Jake! Did you marry me, or did you marry my family?'

Jake stood up. 'Now that's not fair, Eleanor.'

She knew it wasn't. He'd been part of the family since he was a child: a best friend to Eleanor, a best friend to her brother, Marcus. And now, he was her husband.

'Look, it's not me,' he continued. 'Think of your mother.'

Eleanor fixed Jake with a cold stare. Why did she have to think of her mother?

'Well, think of your father.'

Eleanor looked at the floor; she wasn't going to win this argument.

Jake's head was bobbing about under her nose, trying to get her attention.

He gently lifted her chin. 'He'll be disappointed if you're not there.'

She knew it was true.

'And then there's Marcus.'

'No,' Eleanor cut in, 'Marcus will be more disappointed not to see you.' She knew her brother would miss seeing his best friend at Christmas. 'And I think you'd rather spend Christmas with him than with me.'

'Eleanor, that is ridiculous! You're my best friend,' said Jake, trying to placate her, trying to reach for her hand.

'Then prove it.' She had him cornered. 'Choose to stay with me, here, for Christmas.'

Jake stared at her.

She watched his brow furrow as he wrestled with the conflicts, the divided loyalties. She stood her ground. She wasn't going to give in; she had suddenly realised just how important this was. If Jake couldn't choose her, put her first over the family just this once, she was beginning to wonder what that meant for their future together.

'I know.' His face brightened. 'We could spend a couple of days together, just the two of us.' He smiled at Eleanor. 'After the Christmas break, we could go …'

'You're not listening to me, Jake,' Eleanor hissed.

'What is so important that it can't wait?' Jake threw up his hands in frustration.

Eleanor choked back tears. 'I wanted to …' She swallowed. 'I've got something to tell …' She stopped. 'Why can't you just say yes? I have my reasons, which you'll find out soon enough. Why can't you just put me first for a change?'

Jake moved forward and took her hands in his. He cocked his head to one side, a pensive look on his face.

The sudden change in his demeanour strongly suggested to Eleanor that she had finally won him over.

Jake studied her hands as he spoke. 'I can't disappoint William.'

'I don't believe you,' said Eleanor pulling away from him. 'You see my father almost every day at work.'

'Look, can't you be reasonable?' Jake pleaded. 'You know it's a family tradition, everyone going to the house in Scotland for Christmas.'

Eleanor slowly backed away from Jake. 'I wanted it to be just the two of us.'

'Why? Tell me. I don't understand.' Jake took a step forward.

Eleanor backed into the bathroom door. She held out her hand for Jake to stop. 'You know how much I love Christmas, don't you, Jake?'

'Of course I do, darling.'

'I wanted it to be just the two of us, on Christmas Day, when I give you my present.'

'Okay,' Jake said slowly. 'I'm still not getting it. We always exchange presents on Christmas Day with the family. Look, I'm not a mind-reader. Can't you explain what's so important about this year that we've got to change our usual plans? Then I'll consider it.'

She turned away from him, the tears welling up in her eyes. Barely able to see the bathroom door, she flung it open, stepped inside and turned around to look at her husband.

'Consider this,' she screamed before slamming it shut. 'I'm pregnant!'

3

Perhaps other husbands might have guessed, but not him. Because they had been trying for so long, he'd grown accustomed to, and had even anticipated, the inevitable disappointment at another negative pregnancy test. After five years of marriage, they had both virtually given up.

He felt like retreating to the bed to sit down but instead stood on the other side of the bathroom door. Now he understood her insistence that they be together, just the two of them, for Christmas. She had wanted to savour the long-awaited news just between them.

Eleanor didn't like to be fussed over and never liked to be the centre of attention. Now she would be. And he knew she would need time to adjust to that.

'You've ruined it now,' Eleanor sniffed from behind the door.

He gently rested a hand on the bathroom door. 'I can barely believe it after all this time,' he whispered.

'It was going to be your Christmas present.' She paused. 'Our Christmas present.'

'Christmas came early.' Jake smiled ruefully. 'I can't wait to tell everybody.'

'I don't want you to do that – not right now.'

Jake nodded. He understood. They'd wait until the family gathering at Christmas. He promised, although he could hardly contain his delight. Was this how all new fathers felt? He was so excited that he wanted to tell the whole world.

Eleanor didn't respond.

'Ellie?' Jake put his ear to the door and listened to her breathing. 'Let's not keep it to ourselves this Christmas,' he said softly, stroking the door. 'We'll go to The Lake House as planned and it will be our Christmas present to …'

'You didn't listen, did you?' she said abruptly.

'I know you need time to get used to it after all the disappointments, but …'

'Disappointments,' her voice echoed.

'Yes, so I think it will do us both some good to get away and celebrate.'

There was a long pause.

'Yes, celebrate,' she said in a dreamy voice.

'Good, then it's settled. We'll give the family the news on Christmas Day. Besides, now I've got the news already, you can think of it as a practice run for the big day, when we tell the whole family we're expecting a baby. How about that?' Jake thought it was a terrific idea. Who wouldn't want to broadcast to the world that they were having a baby?

The handle of the bathroom door turned and Jake stepped back as Eleanor emerged from the bathroom.

'That's right – you come over here.' Jake guided her to the bed. 'You need to rest. It's been quite a day.'

She sat on the bed. Her hands lay limply in her lap.

Jake knelt down and took off her moccasins.

'We're not staying here for Christmas, are we?' she said.

Jake looked up into her tear-streaked face. Hadn't they just had this conversation? He didn't get why she wasn't bouncing around the room, filled with joy at the long-awaited news. Jake put the moccasins to one side and got off his knees to sit beside her on the bed. He took her hand in his. 'It must have been quite a shock today, after all this time.'

She nodded.

'I know I've ruined it for you,' Jake apologised, 'but in a few days, when we're all sitting around the tree on Christmas morning and you tell them the news, you'll be glad we decided to go. I promise.' Jake patted her hand, feeling sure they were doing the right thing. 'Besides, how would the family feel if we didn't include them?' He smiled at Eleanor.

She turned towards Jake but didn't smile back.

'Come on, you have a lie-down.' Jake plumped the pillows as Eleanor lay on her side, bringing her knees up to her chest.

'It doesn't make sense, does it?' said Eleanor, as Jake covered her with a silk sheet.

Jake had a good idea what she was talking about. 'You hear about couples all the time who desperately want a baby, and then when they stop trying, it kind of just happens, out of the blue.' Jake leaned over and gave her a tender kiss on the forehead.

❖

Eleanor closed her eyes. She felt Jake's presence hovering over her for a moment. Then she heard the bedroom door click shut. She opened her eyes wide. She was thinking about Jake's last words. She had wanted to ask the doctor how it could have happened. She had thought you couldn't get pregnant while on the pill.

Eleanor turned over and lay on her back, throwing off the silk sheet. She put a hand on her stomach, hoping to feel something – anything other than misery. She'd lied to Jake about trying to get pregnant. Deceived him. Why hadn't she been able to just admit she wasn't ready? Would he have understood, empathised with her feelings? He wanted a family of his own so very much. She just couldn't look him in the eye and tell him she felt differently. So instead, like the coward she felt she was, she had gone about things in this underhanded way.

She had put them through tests and sleepless nights, letting him believe there might be some fertility problem with one or both of them. Finally, the family doctor had advised them to forget about it, and it would probably happen. Eleanor had felt relieved because she knew when *she* was ready, then it might happen – not straight away.

But Jake had not shared her apparent stoicism. He wasn't happy with the advice, so she had still been attending family planning appointments at Harley Street when she was in London. She had insisted she attended there, because unbeknown to Jake, she had another doctor who prescribed her the pill. The appointments also gave her an excuse to spend some time in the city she loved – even if, just lately, she had mainly been seeing London out of a car window.

She propped herself up on the pillows and looked down at her tummy. There was nothing she could do about this. She ran her hands over her stomach. Popping a pill was deceitful enough, but as far as Ellie was concerned, she wasn't hurting anybody. It was just a delaying tactic, and she had felt that Jake would just have to have a bit of patience. But this was a whole new ballgame.

All she'd wanted was to spend Christmas without the whole

family surrounding her, suffocating her over the news. In hindsight, she realised she could have waited and told Jake after Christmas. But she'd delayed starting a family for long enough, and it had been for nothing – the career in interior design she'd thought she'd get off the ground hadn't materialised, and now she felt so guilty over those wasted years of not giving Jake the one thing he really wanted – a child. So, she'd decided, on the way back on the tube, that she'd give him the news as his Christmas present.

'I'm so sorry, Jake. I even ruined that,' she whispered to the empty room. She turned back on her side and closed her eyes. She suddenly felt so tired.

4

Jake circled the lounge, unable to put his mind to anything. He picked up a book and put it down. Picked up the TV controls and put them down. Picked up the telephone – bad idea – and put it down. It had to wait – he'd made a promise.

Jake picked up a glass and poured himself a drink. He took two gulps and poured another. Glass in hand, he wandered over to the sliding glass doors, opened one and stepped out onto the terrace, closing the door behind him. He breathed in the bracing December air high above the city. He resisted the impulse to check on Eleanor. Their balcony wrapped around two complete sides of the building, so he could have just walked along, turned the corner and looked in on their bedroom. But he chose not to.

Jake crossed the paved patio area and put his empty glass on the flat surface of the balcony handrail. He leaned forward to look down at the street far below, the darkness illuminated by the streetlights and the slow-moving traffic snaking along the road. Up there, he could tell the whole world they were going to have a baby; literally shout it from the rooftops without anybody hearing a single word. He had the sudden impulse to do just that.

'We're having a baby!' he yelled at the top of his voice to the people in the cars down below.

'Congratulations, Jake,' a familiar voice answered back.

Jake stepped back from the balcony, certain that he must have imagined it. There was only one other apartment on his floor, and that was allocated to Marcus, who used it when he was back in London, but just then he was several thousand miles away in America.

'It's about time, don't you think?'

The voice sounded as though it was coming from the apartment on the floor directly below rather than the other apartment on his floor. Jake looked over the balcony to see Aubrey, an older gentleman who had worked for the Rosses for years, and whom Jake had known all his life, looking back at him. Aubrey was also a dear old family friend. 'What are you doing down there?' said Jake, surprised to see him in the apartment below. Aubrey didn't live there; it was reserved for use by other employees of the Ross Corporation.

'I could ask what you're doing up there,' Aubrey answered back.

Jake looked at his watch. It was six pm; practically early afternoon as far as his office hours went. He would usually expect to put in at least another three or four hours before calling it a day, but this was one of those rare occasions on which Jake had left the office dead on five to spend time with Eleanor after her appointment – or, as was usually the case – disappointment.

He'd been surprised that day to find her back so soon, and stripping off, leaving a trail of clothes in her wake, leading straight to their bedroom. He rolled his eyes at how stupid he'd been to assume she was having some fun with him. Of course she wasn't – she'd just returned from one of those dreaded appointments. So, why hadn't she been excited, bursting to tell him the news as soon as he arrived?

Now he thought about it, it didn't really make sense. Unless she didn't want the baby. Jake's eyebrows shot up at such a ridiculous thought. Of course they both wanted a family – why wouldn't they?

Jake dismissed the thought as he picked up his glass. He smiled. He had not expected to see Aubrey in London. 'What are you doing down there?' Jake repeated.

'Mr Beale is leaving the company.'

'I see,' said Jake, thinking that it was a tough call to lose your job *and* your home. Unless he was leaving voluntarily, it must have been something serious to warrant getting the sack so close to Christmas. William might be a shrewd businessman who didn't suffer fools gladly, but he was a kind man, generous in nature, and would not have done this – not now, without exceptionally good reason.

Jake didn't know this Mr Beale personally; had never even met the man. That wasn't surprising, working for a large corporation. And Jake also travelled regularly between London and America; he wasn't based permanently in London, so he wasn't up to speed with the current employees. What he did know was that Mr Beale must have held quite a position within the company to get the apartment directly below theirs.

Apartments were allocated on merit; a promotion – or a rare demotion – would not only mean a job move within the company, but also a move up or down a floor in the apartment stakes. The higher you went, the greater square footage you acquired. The same principle applied to other apartment buildings around the world. Of course, employees could elect to live in their own accommodation, but who wouldn't choose a fully paid-up apartment in the heart of the city with a concierge, a gym, a pool and a five-minute stroll to work?

Getting an apartment in the city with your job was a great perk, but it wasn't so great when you lost your job and everything went with it. Understandably, disgruntled ex-employees were not eager to leave. Some could be a little resistant. It fell within Aubrey's remit to see to it that ex-employees like Mr Beale vacated their apartments promptly.

'Hey,' Jake called down, 'are you busy, or do you want to come up for a drink?' He'd told Aubrey their news quite unintentionally. The damage was done, so he might as well have him up and tell him all about it. Jake couldn't wait to tell *somebody*. As it turned out, Aubrey was just the person. He trusted Aubrey implicitly. He was practically family.

'Sure – why not?' Aubrey shouted back before disappearing from view.

Jake took his empty glass and went back inside. He tiptoed up to the bedroom door and listened. He slowly opened the door just a crack and looked at the curves of the silk sheet and the mass of dark hair on the pillow. She was quite still. Jake closed the door gently and turned the handle so it didn't click shut and wake her.

'What are you doing?'

'Jesus!' Jake jumped at the sound of Aubrey's voice right behind him. He'd forgotten that Aubrey had the codes to gain entry to all the apartments. Jake put a finger to his lips in a shushing gesture and beckoned Aubrey to move away from the door.

Aubrey followed.

'How do you do that?' Jake whispered. Aubrey had been

making Jake jump out of his skin like that since Jake was a little kid. He had told Jake that it was his SAS training in Britain that had given him such stealth. But he had told Marcus a different story; he had lived on an Indian reservation for a time and had learnt the tracking skills of an ancient Indian chief. Needless to say, Jake and Marcus swapped stories and were not sure what to believe. What they were sure of was that Aubrey was mysterious, great fun, and William's best friend.

'I was just checking on Ellie. She's had a bit of an emotional day.' Jake raised his glass. 'Now, how about that drink?'

'Tea,' said Aubrey.

'Tea it is.' Jake smiled and walked into the kitchen. Aubrey didn't drink. Jake remembered asking him once why he never touched alcohol. *Because to be intoxicated is to be at the mercy of others, and you don't want that, I can assure you*, Aubrey had answered. Jake could see his point. He put the kettle on and poured himself his third double scotch.

They sat down on the large L-shaped cream sofa that dominated the centre of the room. Jake talked. 'So, I came home early,' Jake took a swig of scotch, 'expecting the same, you know, result; nada, because it's not like she's exactly whooping it up, jumping for joy or anything. And you know what?' Jake stared into his glass.

Aubrey shook his head. 'What is it, Jake?'

Jake gently moved his wrist in circular movements, watching the dark liquid swirl around the glass. 'I'm not sure if she wants this baby.' He couldn't remember exactly what she had said; maybe it wasn't even something she'd said – it was just a feeling Jake had that he couldn't put his finger on. He looked up, watching for Aubrey's reaction, but as usual he gave nothing away; his old, craggy face was expressionless.

Aubrey got up and walked over to Jake. He took Jake's glass out of his hand. 'That's the alcohol talking, not Jake.'

Jake watched him walk into the kitchen with his half-empty glass and guessed he was going to pour it down the sink.

He was right.

Aubrey returned with two mugs. He walked over to Jake. 'Let's talk.' He held out a steaming mug of tea.

Jake's lip curled in a semi-smile as he took it. 'I'm a bit old for this,' said Jake.

Aubrey sat in the corner seat of the sofa, kicked off his shoes and put his feet up. 'What – tea?'

'No, not tea. I'm talking about this.' Jake was referring to their man-to-man talks.

When Jake was young and William was busy with work, which he often was, Jake had always been able to call on Aubrey for advice and guidance. Aubrey stepped into the void when William wasn't around, just as William had stepped into the permanent void left by Jake's father. But, busy with work himself now, Jake had little time to call on Aubrey, even when there were times he felt like he needed to have a chat with him. 'I do miss them on occasion,' Jake admitted. 'But I'm …'

'Mr Campbell-Ross now,' Aubrey interjected, puffing out his chest and acting all self-important. 'Big cheese, married to the bosses daughter. And next in line for the head of the corporation.'

'No, I think that'll be Marcus,' Jake said seriously.

'And why do you think that?' Aubrey sipped his tea.

'Well, it's obvious.'

'How so?'

Jake sighed. 'Marcus is, you know, the son.'

'And what are you?' Aubrey said wryly.

'That's different.'

'Is it really?' Aubrey sat up and planted his feet on the floor. 'I'll tell you something. You're just as much a son to William as Marcus is – perhaps more so.'

Jake held up his hand. 'I don't want to hear this.'

'Why not?' said Aubrey, setting his empty mug on the coffee table.

Jake didn't answer. He knew Aubrey wanted to see him make it to the top. Aubrey had no children and had never married. Jake was also aware that out of the three of them – Eleanor, Marcus and himself – he had always been Aubrey's favourite. He had always sensed it.

'You know, you two are like chalk and cheese,' said Aubrey. 'You and Marcus remind me of myself and William – always at each other's throats. Yet the best of friends. I see it.' He pointed at Jake.

'So you know why I don't want to hear it, why I'm not going to the top of this company? It's not my place. It's Marcus's place. I could never take that away from him.'

'What about meritocracy? God knows, you must put in twice the hours he does.'

'So what?' Jake shrugged. 'When Marcus puts his mind to it, he comes up with the goods. He's a natural. Me? I have to work my socks off to achieve the same results.'

'All the more reason why you should be up there when he retires.' Aubrey glanced up, indicating William's massive apartment on the very top floor.

Jake shook his head and finished his tea in silence. He had noticed recently that every time he ran into Aubrey, the conversation always veered on to the subject of William's successor. Although William was now in his sixties and approaching official retirement age, he was still going strong and had no plans to retire in the near future; not as far as Jake was aware. And it wasn't as if he had a boss who could tell him when to call it a day. Jake couldn't envisage William ever letting go of the reins completely. But if and when that day came, Jake really didn't have any aspirations to move upstairs. Besides, he wanted some time to spend with his children.

Jake set his empty mug down on the coffee table and leaned back into the plump feather cushions. He stared at the ceiling, his thoughts turning to that massive apartment directly above, which took up the entire floor. Jake rubbed his face with two hands and thought about how most of the time he found his work as a lawyer, overseeing the acquisition of land for the Ross Corporation to build its shopping malls and skyscrapers, such hard work and so deadly dull.

'You know what, Aubrey?' Jake rolled his head on the sofa to look at Aubrey. 'Sometimes I think I'm in the wrong life altogether.'

'You think you would have been better off if William had never known your parents?' Aubrey said incredulously. 'What do you think would have happened to you, an orphan, no family? Boy, you were heading into the care system fast. You could have waited years for a suitable family to come along to foster or adopt you; they want cute babies, not troubled little boys.'

Jake stared at Aubrey, wishing he hadn't spoken his mind. He knew he was sounding ungrateful, and Aubrey was the last person he should say a bad word to against William. Besides, Aubrey was right: Jake knew that he owed a lot to the Rosses – his upbringing, his education, his work; in fact, his life as it had turned out was completely moulded by his involvement with the family.

Of course, he had the utmost love and gratitude towards William. But after all the huge advantages he'd been given in life, there was always something niggling away at the back of his mind, forcing him to consider just what his life might have been if William had never come along. He just had no idea why that was.

Aubrey stretched, resting his right arm along the back of the sofa. 'You shouldn't work so hard, Jake. I think the things you're saying about work, about Eleanor …' He paused. 'You push yourself too hard.'

Eleanor and the baby had gone completely out of Jake's mind.

Aubrey lowered his voice. 'Maybe as far as the baby is concerned, it's not Eleanor you're worried about.'

Jake sat up and turned towards Aubrey. 'What are you saying?'

'Now don't take this the wrong way, Jake …'

Jake pursed his lips, guessing that Aubrey was about to say something that he didn't want to hear.

Aubrey continued, 'Have you considered that perhaps ...' He glanced furtively towards the bedroom door and moved along the sofa towards Jake. 'Perhaps …'

'Are you saying I don't want this baby?' Jake raised his voice, forgetting that Eleanor was just in the next room.

Aubrey waved his hand for Jake to be quiet.

Jake slapped his hand over his mouth.

'Not exactly. I'm just wondering if you've thought about your reasons for wanting a child.'

Jake furrowed his brow. 'Couples get married. Couples have kids, and I want a family of my own.'

'I know that, Jake. But is this for you, or is it for William? You don't owe him anything more than your love and respect.' Aubrey glanced towards the bedroom door. 'And your honesty.' He looked back at Jake.

Jake stood up, enraged at what he thought Aubrey was implying. 'If you think for one second I married her because, because …'

'What's going on?'

Jake turned around, shocked into silence by the sound of Eleanor's voice behind him. She was standing in the bedroom doorway in her crumpled dungarees, rubbing the sleep out of her eyes. 'I thought I heard voices.' She looked from Aubrey to Jake. 'You woke me up.'

Jake stared open-mouthed at Eleanor, wondering how long she had been standing there and how much she had heard.

She smiled at Aubrey. 'It's nice to see you. What brings you to the apartment building?' Her smile faded and her head darted to Jake.

He immediately guessed what she was thinking – that he'd phoned Aubrey, told him the news, and invited him over.

She'd see right through him if he lied and said he hadn't told Aubrey the news, even though doing so hadn't been intentional. But if he told her the truth, he'd have to tell her what Aubrey had been doing in the apartment below. He didn't want to bother her with that news because she'd be upset to hear an employee was being evicted so close to Christmas. The corporation prided itself on its employees feeling like family. Eleanor would realise, as Jake had, that something serious must have happened to warrant it. He didn't want to bother her with that sort of news either.

Aubrey slowly got to his feet and placed a hand on Jake's shoulder, clearly noticing he was tongue-tied. 'We were just having a heated debate concerning ...' He paused and glanced around the room until his eyes alighted on the coffee table. 'Tea!'

Jake turned his head and focused on Aubrey, giving him a look that said, *couldn't you have thought of something a bit more plausible, like football?* Although in truth, Aubrey was known to be quite the tea connoisseur, and would, given half a chance, quite happily list the qualities he perceived to be found in Darjeeling compared to other teas.

'You and your tea, Aubrey,' Eleanor sighed. 'Just keep it down, will you?' She went back into the bedroom and shut the door behind her.

'Do you think she heard what I said?' Jake whispered, not wanting to risk any more verbal damage.

Aubrey studied him intently before answering. 'Do you want to tell me what's going on with you? Because lately I've noticed—'

'There's nothing going on,' said Jake curtly, brushing Aubrey's hand away from his shoulder. 'I'm just tired – that's all. I think I'll feel better when it's Christmas and I can get out of the city.' Jake held Aubrey's gaze.

'Alright, Jake,' Aubrey said flatly. 'But you've got my number if you decide you want to talk about it.' Aubrey walked out of the lounge.

Jake followed him outside the apartment. 'Will you be joining us at The Lake House for Christmas?' he asked while they waited for the lift.

'Not this year.'

Jake sighed. It was the same answer every year. But it didn't make sense; Aubrey practically lived with the Rosses, so why not spend Christmas with them? *Maybe he doesn't like Christmas*, Eleanor had once speculated, *or maybe he has some friends or relatives he likes to see over the vacation.* But as far as Jake was aware, Aubrey had no family, and his friends revolved around his work for the Ross Corporation.

There had been that one year when Marcus had been too ill to travel – chicken pox, as Jake recalled – and they had spent Christmas at their London home. That was the only year Aubrey had joined them.

The lift doors opened. The porter waited.

Aubrey walked inside the lift and turned around to face Jake, putting his hand to his ear, as the lift doors slowly closed, to remind Jake to pick up the phone and call him.

Jake turned to go then whirled on his heel. 'Wait!'

The porter frantically pressed the *hold* button.

'Aubrey.' Jake glanced at the porter. 'About the news …'

'My lips are sealed.' Aubrey ran two fingers along his thin lips.

The porter looked at Aubrey, then back at Jake.

'Can't you make it for Christmas, Aubrey? We were going to give the family the news on Christmas Day.'

'I'm not family, Jake.'

'I know that.' Jake laughed. 'But neither am I.'

Aubrey frowned.

The porter stared at Jake.

'Oh, come on. It would mean a lot to me. Besides, that's rubbish – you're as good as family, and you know it.'

The young porter looked at Aubrey.

'You accompany us on every other holiday, Aubrey. Why not Christmas?'

'I just can't, Jake. I have my reasons.'

Jake wished he knew what they were. He was used to the familiar excuse. He knew better than to ask; all he'd be met with was a stony silence. He had thought it was because something had happened in Aubrey's past at Christmas. It wouldn't be unheard of for a person not to celebrate that time of year if there were bad associations. But he *had* celebrated when they were in London for Christmas years earlier. Unless it had something to do with Scotland, and for some reason Aubrey did not want to venture to that part of the world. He couldn't imagine, after all these years of keeping his past close to his chest, that Aubrey would tell him his reasons now.

Jake glanced at the young porter, who was fidgeting in the corner of the lift. 'I'd better let you go. I suppose you've still got things to do downstairs.'

'Not at all. Surprisingly, this one went quietly.'

Jake nodded at the porter, who took his finger off the *hold* button.

The lift doors closed.

He stood for a moment, listening to the chime of the lift as it made the descent. Then he walked away from the lift and stopped outside his apartment door. He stood there for some considerable time, staring at the door, a series of insane *what if* scenarios running through his head like a locomotive: *what if I got in the lift? What if I went down to the ground floor, got out of the lift, and walked outside? What if I kept walking?*

What if I walked out of this life?

It wasn't as though he didn't love his wife. It wasn't as though he didn't want their child. For five years, he'd waited to hear this news; to hear that his little family would be complete. So why was he thinking of turning tail and bolting in the opposite direction?

5

Eleanor was sitting at her dressing room table when she heard the door to the apartment close. She cocked her head to one side, listening to Jake's footsteps as he crossed the marble hall. She didn't want him to come into the bedroom just then. She needed time to absorb the conversation she had overheard between him and Aubrey.

Eleanor sat forward in her chair and listened. The tinkling of glasses suggested Jake was pouring himself a drink in the lounge.

She crept to the bedroom door and opened it a crack. The back of Jake's head was visible on the sofa, and every now and then he raised his elbow and tipped his head back. The crystal glass momentarily twinkled in the artificial light.

With one hand flat on the door and the other turning the handle, Eleanor eased the bedroom door shut. She winced as the catch clicked. She listened again but couldn't discern any movement on the other side of the door.

Eleanor returned to the dresser and sat down in front of the mirror, staring at her reflection – staring at a young woman she wished was beautiful, smart and witty, just like the women she had met who worked for the company.

Only the previous week, she had been at the company's Christmas bash in London. As the wife of one of the two top executives, and the daughter of the boss, Eleanor was in the unenviable position of having to attend two Christmas events; she'd attended the first one in Chicago. Invariably, the conversation revolved around work. Those who did not know who she was often asked what position she held within the company. She'd reply that she was one of the wives. What else could she say? To which they'd reply, *oh, you're a homemaker* – the American turn of phrase for housewife. *How sweet*, they'd say, but she could see, written on their faces, *and how very boring*. Then they'd move swiftly on to conversations with others; conversations of a more interesting, more work-related nature.

Eleanor saw how the smart, sophisticated women flocked around Jake. That often meant that Eleanor spent the evening with other 'homemakers', discussing such things like baking and babies. And now, as if to prove her credentials as a certified homemaker, she was pregnant. Her homemaker 'friends' were never going to leave her out of the loop now. She really was one of them. And whilst it looked like a worthwhile existence, she somehow didn't feel it suited her any more than working for the company would.

'God help me,' she whispered. Eleanor was not looking forward to returning to Chicago.

She stared miserably at her reflection in the mirror, her thoughts returning to that abrupt wake-up call earlier when she'd heard voices and realised there was somebody in the apartment with Jake. She had listened intently until she had discerned it was only Aubrey – probably there to chuck out some other unfortunate who had failed to live up to Daddy's standards. She hoped that wasn't the case, though – not so close to Christmas.

It occurred to her that if Jake was going to tell anybody she was pregnant, it would be Aubrey. They'd always been close. A bond, Eleanor guessed, grown out of their common indebtedness to Daddy for all he had given them.

She didn't care if it was only Aubrey; she still didn't want anybody to know – not until Christmas at The Lake House. As Eleanor had approached the door, she'd heard Aubrey talking about how hard Jake worked and how much he deserved to take over once William retired. She'd nodded in agreement and had then got angry as Jake defended her brother, belittling his own efforts.

At that moment, Eleanor had been standing with her hand on the doorknob, about to open the door and tell Jake that he had every right to that top position. Then the conversation had abruptly changed direction, confusing Eleanor. Had he been talking about their marriage? She'd wanted him to stop. So she had flung open the door and announced her presence, stopping Jake in his tracks and putting an end to the possibility of him actually voicing her worst fear.

'Your worst fear …' she said to her reflection, wishing she could stop thinking about what she'd overheard.

Her worst fear was that her husband had not married her out of love. Her worst fear was that Jake had married her out of pity; the ugly duckling, the plain Jane who never turned heads at social gatherings like her taller, blonder, skinnier counterparts from other wealthy, well-to-do families.

Jake, like her brother, had no shortage of female admirers. Sometimes she watched him sleeping and wondered what he was doing married to her. At least she knew it wasn't the old scenario that he'd married her for her money. Jake would always have been part of the family, and the family money, whether he'd married her or not.

Eleanor reached up and undid her ponytail, letting her mass of dark brown hair fall to her shoulders. She pinched a plump cheek and smoothed a bushy eyebrow. To her father, she was an angel. To her mother, she was a disappointment. But what was she to Jake? Had he married her to please her father? Eleanor needed to know. It wasn't just her own future in the balance, but that of her child.

For all her mother's faults – and in Eleanor's eyes, she had a multitude – Eleanor and her brother, Marcus, had not grown up in the midst of a loveless marriage. Her father loved her mother dearly; of that there was no doubt. And that was what Eleanor wanted for her own child. She couldn't believe, after five years of marriage, that she was questioning Jake's motives for marrying her. But she was.

Eleanor took one final look at her reflection in the mirror, then stood up and walked to the door. She flung it open and stared at the back of Jake's head.

'Jake.' She walked towards the sofa.

He didn't turn around to acknowledge her presence.

'I overheard what you said to Aubrey.' She continued before she lost her nerve. 'I need to know, Jake …' She paused, staring at the top of Jake's head, wondering if she could face him while she spoke. She decided she could not, so she stopped just behind the sofa.

'I need to know if what Aubrey said is true,' she hesitated, 'about the reasons you married me.'

Eleanor stood stock-still, holding her breath, waiting for a response. When he didn't answer, she stormed around the front of the sofa. 'Well?' she said, folding her arms and walking right up to stand in front of him.

Jake's eyes were closed, his mouth half-open. He was breathing heavily. One hand lay limply on his chest. He was still holding a crystal glass in the other hand, which was resting on the seat next to him. The glass had tipped and spread a dark stain across the cream sofa cushion.

Eleanor knelt down in front of Jake, took the empty glass out of his hand and placed it on the coffee table. Then she looked Jake over. A dark shadow encased both his eyes. Eleanor couldn't remember the last time he hadn't looked exhausted. She reached out a tentative hand, running her fingers along his forehead and down his cheek. He stirred but did not wake.

Who would have thought the shy, gangly kid she had once known would turn into such a good-looking guy? She wondered whether that was the real problem in their relationship; that he was the looker and she was not. She didn't like these uncharacteristic feelings of jealousy that engulfed her when another woman looked his way.

Eleanor sat on the sofa next to him. It was late, but she was wide awake. She was never going to get to sleep now.

❖

'Eleanor.' Jake shook her arm gently and stroked her hair. She was out like a light. Jake's arm felt numb, but he couldn't prise himself from beneath her weight. He had woken up to find he was lying flat on his back on the sofa with Eleanor beside him. Her head was on his shoulder, her arm lay casually across his chest, and his arm was wedged between her and the sofa back. He wanted to look at his wristwatch. The winter sun was streaming through the blinds. He guessed it was late – well past 6.30 am – and he really needed to be in the office early to get his work completed before the Christmas break. He kissed the top of Eleanor's head. He didn't want to wake her, but had no choice. 'Eleanor,' he said softly in her ear.

She stirred. 'What is it?' her muffled voice spoke into his neck.

'Darling, I need you to get up.' Jake kept trying to lift his hand, attempting to get a look at his watch to see how late he was running.

Eleanor rubbed her eyes.

Jake smiled at her. 'Morning.'

'Morning.'

He felt her body move against his as she lifted her head, taking in the sofa and Jake lying beneath her.

'I don't know what we got up to last night,' said Jake, registering her surprise at their novel sleeping arrangements, 'but this was cosy. Almost like old times.'

He'd noticed the distance between them recently. Perhaps it was his busy work schedule, or the toll that unsuccessfully trying for a baby had taken on them. But that was all behind them now. Perhaps this was the start of things going back to the way they had been when they first married – that young couple, deeply in love, spending good times together.

'Darling, my arm,' Jake waved his hand behind her back.

Eleanor moved, resting more of her weight on Jake while he looked at his watch. 'Thank god.'

'What is it?'

'It's only 6 am. I'm not late.' Instead of plopping her head back on his shoulder as he expected, she sat up abruptly and climbed over Jake without a word.

'I don't have to be in the office until seven,' he said, hoping she would come back. She didn't. The bathroom door clicked shut and that was the last Jake saw of her before leaving for his final day at work before the holidays. The next day would be Christmas Eve.

6

'Jake! It's about time.' William answered the door, an apron tied around his waist. 'I was just about to send out a search party,' he joked.

'I had some things to finish at the office,' Jake said apologetically. The intended half day had been anything but.

'Nobody spends Christmas working, Jake.' William looked over Jake's shoulder. 'You drove? You could have caught a flight to Scotland from London City Airport. There should be a law against driving while looking as tired as you.'

Jake stood on the front step, looking at his shoes, feeling like he was all of five years old again. 'I know, but I preferred to drive myself this time. It helped me to unwind.'

'It's Christmas Eve. You normally travel here together the night before by sleeper train. I was surprised when I got a text from Eleanor to collect her from the train station and she mentioned she'd travelled alone.'

'Typically, something cropped up at work. Nothing to worry about, but I didn't make the train, obviously. How was her journey?'

'Sounded okay. She got off the sleeper this morning in Aberdeen. I was there to collect her. We were back at The Lake

House for a morning coffee and a lovely fruit scone. Shame you didn't make it.'

Jake sighed, thinking, *don't remind me.* By the time he'd arrived home to the apartment the night before, he'd missed Eleanor, and the Caledonian sleeper train they always took together from London to Edinburgh. She'd taken the sleeper on her own. He was pleased to hear she'd got straight on the connecting train and William had picked her up from the station.

William grasped his shoulder. 'Well, don't just stand there. Get yourself inside, son.'

Jake walked into the hall. The first thing he noted was that Eleanor was not there to greet him. 'Ellie around?' Jake glanced at the doors leading off from the hall, expecting her to make an appearance.

'I must say, I was surprised she took the train overnight on her own and didn't wait for you to travel up together, even if it wasn't your usual arrangement, coming by car. Got tired of waiting for you, did she?'

'Something like that.' Jake had kept meaning to speak to her. It had been like a game of phone ping-pong. She rang and he was in a meeting, he rang and it was just the answer phone. Eventually, after leaving a dozen or more messages, apologising that he wasn't going to make it home until late, and saying that they might have to rearrange their travel plans and go to Scotland the next day, he'd started to wonder if she was not answering the phone on purpose. If he wasn't going to be there to take her call, then she wasn't going to hang on the end of the phone for his. Tit for tat. She could be so stubborn sometimes.

After work he had found himself in the apartment – alone. She had packed his bag but had clearly got tired of waiting. He'd looked at the time and thought *who can blame her?* She had left a message to say she'd meet him on the sleeper train.

'She's still out,' said William.

'Out where?' They didn't have any friends in the area, so where could she have gone at this late hour?

William shrugged. 'Last-minute Christmas shopping, I imagine. Here, let me take that.'

Despite Jake's protestations, William bent down and wrestled Jake's overnight bag out of his hand, getting his long apron entangled in the straps.

'Grace!' He called for his wife as he tried to disentangle his apron from the bag while simultaneously lugging it down the hallway. The bag brushed the seven-foot Christmas tree, which had pride of place in the middle of the hall. It began to topple as William strode by.

Jake darted forward and made a successful grab for the tree, pushing it back to an upright position. He shook his head. Sometimes it was hard to believe that his father-in-law headed a multi-million-dollar corporation. William was loud, brash, clumsy and forgetful; not exactly the image one conjured up of a CEO. But Jake loved the big bear of a man with his deep Scottish burr.

'Ah, there you are.' William poked his head around the lounge door, unaware of the near-calamity behind him. 'Is Ellie back yet? Jake has arrived.'

Jake walked into the lounge, plucking a pine needle from the palm of his hand.

Grace was sitting on a chaise longue, her long slender legs reaching almost to the end. An old black-and-white movie was playing on the widescreen – the actors instantly recognisable, although Jake couldn't have named them if his life had depended on it. But Grace could; every actor, actress and movie from that golden era.

She turned her head and smiled at Jake. Her ash-blonde hair had given way to grey long ago, but no one would have guessed, for it still shone unnaturally blonde, thick and straight, curling out just above the shoulders in a perfect kink.

'Jake, darling.' She moved her legs smoothly off the chaise longue and stood up.

Jake was, as always, taken aback that in all the years he had known her – he was taller than her now, but only just – she never seemed to lose any of her stature.

'Finishing school, my dear,' she had said to Jake when he had complimented her on it one day. 'Deportment keeps the head high and the back straight.'

It was complete rubbish, Jake knew. 'Finishing school, my ass,' William had scoffed. 'She didn't even finish school.' He had winked at Jake. It wasn't said in a mocking, malicious way, though; instead, it was said with a fondness that surprised Jake.

On paper, they should have been a match made in hell; William, a no-nonsense, down-to-earth Scot was so different to Grace, who purported to have come from a wealthy, privileged background. Of course, it wasn't true; it was a fantasy created to hide the humble background she had come from, probably because she felt her origins would spoil her carefully cultivated public persona. That was what Jake knew Eleanor thought.

Some people, like William, never forgot their past and the hardships suffered, especially when they became successful in later life. Grace was the opposite, never wanting to acknowledge her true roots. Despite her privilege and wealth, and all the potential she had to work for charities – something that Jake knew Eleanor spent most of her free time engaged in – Grace was quite content to live out her little fantasies. It was something Jake would never understand. His eyes flickered to the television. He liked living in the real world.

And so did Eleanor.

He loved the character traits she had inherited from her father, her earthiness, her compassion. If she had been anything like her mother, then the world would have lost a beautiful soul, and Jake a wife; he would never have married someone whose fundamental concerns revolved around her next manicure or pedicure or whatever the hell it was. He had never wanted a trophy wife.

Jake watched Grace glide towards him. Her dress, gold satin, was sleek and slim-fitting on a slender body that was – Jake didn't doubt – the envy of women half her age. She had always been a stunner.

She rested her hands lightly on Jake's shoulders and leaned forward, air-kissing next to both his cheeks.

Jake rolled his eyes. At least he was used to it now. When he was a kid, familiar with his mother's great big bear hugs and huge sloppy kisses, Eleanor's mother had seemed quite strange.

She drew back to look at Jake. 'You look tired.' She glanced over Jake's shoulder. 'Are you working him too hard?' she demanded in a raised voice.

There was no answer from William; just muffled sounds coming from the kitchen at the back of the house.

'I'm fine, really,' said Jake, staring at her wide, mesmerising blue eyes. She looked like an ageing movie star from the silver screen. She could have been the Lauren Bacall of her generation if she hadn't met and married William, which she was wont to remind people. Still, her marriage had its compensations; she had wanted to be a film star all her life, and in a peculiar way, that was exactly what she had become – dressing up, living a luxury lifestyle, playing the parts she adored on screen for real.

Jake couldn't help wondering whether, if she hadn't married William, she would indeed have become that movie star. He wondered if she had any regrets. For some reason, Eleanor came to mind. Was she having regrets? Was that what this was all about? Had this pregnancy ignited Eleanor's worst fears – that her life was turning into a carbon copy of her mother's, revolving around the company, her husband, and the children?

But that was absurd. Where Grace spent all her spare time shopping, Eleanor spent hers working for charitable organisations. So much so that Jake was convinced she was putting in almost the same hours he was. He wondered where on earth Eleanor would find the time to fit in a baby.

Jake suddenly felt the urge to talk to Eleanor, to reassure her that she wasn't turning into her mother. Maybe she should have used her college education and pursued what Jake had always believed to be her first love – interior design. Maybe if he hadn't been so selfish, putting his own career in the company first, she could have had a chance to pursue her career – that is, if they'd stayed in the UK permanently. At the back of his mind was the life she might have had planned; the life she might have led if he hadn't proposed to her before she started college.

But he knew why he had done it – he had been afraid of losing her. He had been afraid that she would grow and change in her years away, meet somebody else and leave him behind to start a new life. And Jake had played on her fears, knowing she harboured the thought that if she didn't get engaged, one of those society beauties just like her mother would step in to replace her in her absence. When he thought back, Eleanor had spent her college years flying back and forth to wherever in the world he was working, at every opportunity, leaving her little time to build college friendships or even have a traditional college life. In hindsight, he felt guilty about that, although at the time he'd been selfishly pleased that she had little opportunity to meet somebody else and break off their engagement. He understood her insecurities, but she didn't realise he had some of his own too.

She'd said it often enough when they'd started dating – *why me?* Nothing Jake had said or done had seemed to wholly convince her that she was deeply loved until he had proposed. She'd accepted his offer, but her college life – it was all she'd talked about growing up, getting away and pursuing her career – had taken a hit. How could she have a career herself when her husband moved with his work so much? And it wasn't just that. The company always came first, and although he imagined she'd find it hard to acknowledge, it was expected of her that once she married him, she'd become a company wife, putting the needs of her husband and his career in the Ross Corporation first. Her career, if she'd had one, would not have been on an equal footing with her husband's in the way he imagined it would be for most other couples who both had careers.

Jake was starting to think it was time they put down roots in one city in the world. Now, with the baby on the way, it was something that Jake was intending to broach with William. He'd had time to think it through on the way in the car. That thinking time had been invaluable. Eleanor in those dungarees came to mind – the ones she wore to paint the apartment. Perhaps they could get a nanny, and she could finally do more than her charity work, and start that interior design business she'd been longing for. Perhaps the thought that she'd not yet had the chance to pursue it was the reason she wasn't exactly jumping for joy over the baby news. Maybe being a working mum would be the making of her.

Jake was beginning to wonder whether, if he didn't stop putting the Ross Corporation first, rather than his wife, it would eventually cost him his marriage.

'What's it to be, darling?'

Grace held a decanter, about to pour them both a drink.

'I don't mind, Grace. Whatever comes.'

She flicked her hair as she handed Jake a glass of bourbon.

He watched her sashay to the sofa and sit as though she was on a movie set and the whole world was watching her performance.

Jake resolved to talk to Eleanor. If she still wanted to pursue a career, then this time Jake was going to sort out his work life so she could have it all – a family *and* a career.

Jake walked around the sofa, but he was too hyped-up to sit. 'William said Ellie was out shopping. Any idea when she'll be back?'

Grace turned her wrist and looked at her delicate gold watch. 'Soon, I expect.'

Jake frowned. 'I can't believe she's out shopping.' It was an activity that Eleanor disliked.

'Yes, neither can I. She's not really one for shopping, I know, but even Eleanor has to shop for presents at Christmas.' Grace patted the sofa. 'Come sit down.'

Jake sat. He downed his bourbon in three large gulps.

'You know she didn't even invite her mother?'

Jake wasn't surprised. They didn't see eye to eye on anything as far as he could make out. Ellie had said that her shopping trips with her mother were about as much fun as visiting the dentist. But at least the dentist didn't criticise, she'd said.

Grace continued, 'When she said she was going shopping, I

got so excited, because I thought we might actually be going shopping *together*, just like my friends go with their daughters. They even spend entire days shopping. Imagine that.'

And that was all she could do – imagine. Jake thought he detected a hint of sadness, perhaps even regret, which made a real change from the usual derisory comments and criticisms that normally followed in the course of conversations with or about her daughter.

Grace got up and poured herself another drink.

'I'll have another.' Jake held out his glass.

By the time William made an appearance, the bottle of bourbon was almost empty, and Jake was fighting to keep himself awake.

7

'Started the celebrations without your drinking pal, I see,' said Marcus, pointing at the empty bottle of bourbon.

Jake rubbed his tired eyes and then his chin, feeling two days' worth of stubble. The room smelled like a brewery. He followed Marcus's gaze to the empty bottle of bourbon on the coffee table and decided it was himself that smelled like a brewery. He eyed Marcus, who sat, fresh-faced and in pressed casual clothes, on the chaise longue.

'What time is it?' said Jake, struggling to sit up under the weight of his hangover. He was all too aware that he had a busy morning ahead of him. William insisted on maintaining Christmas as a simple family affair, which sounded cosy, but which in reality meant no hired help of any kind. A simple family affair, much to Grace's chagrin, meant they all mucked in and did their bit towards the big day so that just once a year they were reminded of what was truly important – not the business, not the money, but family.

'A little after nine,' answered Marcus, looking alert and ready for Christmas Day. Jake knew he'd flown into Aberdeen that morning by private jet, chartered from a company that flew VIPs. The trip would have included a private chauffer to drive him to

The Lake House. In hindsight, Jake wished he had joined Marcus instead of doing the long, drawn-out journey by road the previous day. Then he probably wouldn't have ended up drinking way too much bourbon and falling asleep, exhausted, on the couch.

'Did you and Ellie have an argument last night?'

The mention of Eleanor prompted Jake to ask, 'Where is she?' as he threw off a blanket that someone had draped over him.

Marcus fell silent. He leaned forward. 'Everything alright between you two?' he said, lowering his voice.

'Of course, why wouldn't it be?' said Jake, annoyed by the question but avoiding eye contact. He wondered why Eleanor hadn't woken him up on her return. He was thinking that for someone who didn't like shopping, she had been out an awful long time the previous night. 'What time do shops stay open in Aviemore on Christmas Eve, anyway?' he said, thinking aloud.

'Pretty late, I guess.'

'I'm going to take a shower.' Jake swung his legs off the sofa, but a sharp pain ripping through his forehead stopped him in his tracks. He sat very still, massaging his temples with his fingertips.

'Bad one, is it?'

Jake nodded slowly.

'Well, you'd better get over it by this afternoon.'

Jake looked up. 'Why, what's happening this afternoon?'

'Are we suffering from memory loss with our hangover this morning?'

'Oh right.' How could he forget? Easily, with Eleanor and the baby and work …

'Don't tell me you're not coming either?' Marcus fell back in his chair. 'It's bad enough that I've got to think up something to get Ellie to change her mind.'

Jake stopped massaging his temples. 'Ellie said she's not going?'

'Yeah.'

Jake was relieved to hear it. 'Look, if she's said she's not going, then let's leave it, shall we?'

'What?' said Marcus, clearly taken aback. 'It's practically tradition: she says she's not coming. We harangue her for most of Christmas lunch. And then she relents. Touché!'

Jake looked at Marcus quizzically, thinking that someone really ought to tell him nobody used the word *touché* anymore.

'I'm going to think up something rather good this year,' Marcus mused, 'because she seems to have really made up her mind this time. So I could do with your …'

'She's not going skiing after Christmas dinner this year, and that's all there is to it,' said Jake with an edge to his voice and finality in his tone that he had little doubt would take Marcus by surprise. He certainly looked surprised when Jake glanced up at him.

'We'll see about that,' said Marcus, rubbing his hands.

There was no mistaking that look on his face; Jake knew him too well. The self-satisfied smirk said he'd already thought of something that he believed would change Eleanor's mind.

'I'd like to see you try,' said Jake, 'because I know for a fact she'll not go this year.'

'How do you know that?' Marcus folded his arms and stared fixedly at Jake.

'Because she's—' Jake slapped a hand over his mouth. *My god! I nearly said it, in passing, just sitting here with Marcus having a conversation.*

'She's *what?*' Marcus unfolded his arms and leaned forward.

'She's … she's made up her mind, that's all,' said Jake, trying to sound casual, trying to make it sound as though it was no big deal.

'And since when did Ellie develop this iron will?' Marcus stared knowingly at Jake.

His sister had always folded, given in, as a child; adulthood had done little to change this. Whenever yet another charitable organisation called on her time, she couldn't turn them down, even though she knew there were only so many hours in the day. She never stood up for herself. It seemed to Jake that there wasn't a single thing about her life that she could call her own – certainly not her time.

They sat in silence for a moment, Jake somewhat surprised that Marcus had let the matter drop.

'Come on, Jake. It won't be the same if the three of us don't go.'

Jake sighed heavily.

'Besides, why does this year have to be any different?'

'Because we're not kids anymore, Marcus. If you're going to try and persuade her, you can count me out. You're wasting your time.' There was no way she'd go skiing in her condition; she wasn't the strongest skier in the world anyway, and she knew it. That was why there was always fun and games at the dinner table as they tried to cajole her into joining them. But unbeknown to Marcus, this year things were different.

Jake leaned down and picked up his shoes. He really needed a shower and he really needed to open a window.

'There's something going on between you two,' Marcus probed, 'isn't there?'

Jake put his shoes on and kept his face expressionless; he didn't want to give the game away. Marcus – his best mate, his best man, his brother-in-law. There were no secrets between them, never had been. Until now.

Jake walked out of the room, smiling. He couldn't wait to tell Marcus their secret. It would make him an uncle. He would be thrilled. At least Jake hoped he would.

'How long have you been sleeping on the couch?' Marcus called after him.

Jake's smile dropped. Why hadn't she woken him on her return? Was she mad at him for working so late on Christmas Eve and missing the train? Was she still mad at him for refusing to change their holiday plans and stay in London like she wanted?

Or was it something else?

It was the *something else* scenario that bothered Jake. It was so unlike Eleanor, so out of character for her to stay mad for long, and especially at this time of year. Oh, how she loved Christmas at the old house in Scotland.

And what the hell had she been shopping for?

She didn't do much shopping at Christmas, at least not for family gifts. That was what she so loved about Christmas; it gave her a reason to use her creative side. Eleanor always made the most creative and imaginative presents. Jake knew he was biased, but he thought it was true, nonetheless. It certainly made Christmas interesting, because whatever they got, it couldn't be found in a shop. It couldn't be bought, which made each gift priceless.

The thought of this cheered Jake up somewhat as he trudged up the stairs towards the family bathroom.

'Ah, Jake. Marcus did wake you up – good, good.' William was walking down the stairs towards him.

They both stopped halfway.

'You look a little worse for wear this morning,' observed

William, looking him over.

'Bit too much bourbon last night, I'm afraid.'

'That and a combination of too much work. You, my son, are taking a vacation.' He poked Jake playfully in the ribs.

'That's what I'm here for.'

William shook his head. 'Nope. I don't mean here. Straight after Christmas you're taking my daughter, just the two of you, on a holiday. Understood?'

'Yessir,' Jake wasn't about to argue with that, although he'd much rather just spend it there in Scotland. However, although The Lake House was a large property, spacious enough to find a spare room and sit undisturbed for hours, it still wasn't the same as taking a holiday, just him and his wife, together.

That guilty feeling crept up on him again, that he hadn't bowed to Eleanor's wishes and spent Christmas together with her, just the two of them.

'Good, because I think the company is seeing more of you than she is, from what I hear.'

Jake blushed at the thought of Eleanor discussing him with her father, of all people – a man he admired, a man whose expectations he continually strived to live up to. He stared at William, trying to discern from his bright blue eyes whether she had told him the good news.

'Besides, I think you're not the only one who could do with a holiday,' said William. 'She's been looking a little peaky. Must be the weather.'

Jake watched William walk down the stairs and decided that she hadn't told him yet.

At the bottom of the stairs, William turned abruptly. 'Well, don't dawdle. Have you forgotten we've got a dinner to prepare?'

Jake turned on his heel and took the stairs two at a time, despite his headache. The thought of actually spending some time in the kitchen cooking was just as enticing as the thought of a holiday. He showered in double-quick time, feeling a pang of excitement that he had rarely felt since childhood; it certainly seemed to be a rarity for him nowadays. That was why he always loved the Christmas holidays spent in Scotland. It was his escape, albeit briefly, back to his childhood – just the small family unit gathering together and celebrating like every other ordinary family in the country; and like it had on many other occasions too, before William got seriously rich and the company monolithic.

Jake sighed. It was times like these that he contemplated how his life might have turned out if he hadn't grown up in this house. He towelled himself dry, thinking how insane he was to even question his good fortune. He had a loving family, a terrific wife, more money than he could spend in several lifetimes – what more could he possibly want?

Two days earlier, he had been able to answer that question in a heartbeat – he wanted a child, he wanted to be a father. But now he was even going to have that. So why was he still asking himself that same question that had plagued him for some time – *what if? What if, when his parents died, and he'd been left a young orphan, William Ross hadn't taken him under their wing?*

Jake opened the medicine chest on the wall and popped a couple of paracetamol tablets to ease the headache – and hopefully improve his mood as well. He felt so ungrateful; a perception not helped by his refusal to spend the holiday in London. It was little wonder Eleanor had avoided him since his arrival. He hoped that today, Christmas Day, would see a huge improvement on both scores.

Jake stepped out of the bathroom, and saw their bedroom door ajar across the hall. He stood in the doorway, slowly pushing the door wide, and looked into the room at the king-size comfy bed with the Egyptian cotton sheets. He should have been sleeping here with his wife last night, under the cosy duvet, and enjoying breakfast in bed together, if that's what she wanted.

He had thought he might find her still in bed, having a lie-in. Instead the bed was made up, scatter cushions depicting snowy winter scenes, neatly arranged on top of the duvet, along with a carefully folded throw in Christmas red, green and gold which Jake remembered he and Eleanor had received as a Christmas gift a year or so ago.

As he stared into the room, he still felt a sense of unease about his wife's behaviour since finding out she was pregnant. Was it all because he had not agreed to spend Christmas together in London, just the two of them?

He stepped foot into the room, and walked over to the frosted window, gazing out at the rugged peaks of the snow-covered Cairngorm mountain range in the distance. Soft snowflakes drifted down to the garden below. He opened the window and put his hand outside to catch the flakes, mesmerised for a moment by the beauty and stillness of the garden, and the vast silent landscape beyond.

Jolted out of his reverie by his name being called, he shut the window and hurried down the stairs to join William in the kitchen.

8

'There you are.' William plucked an apron from a row of pegs behind the kitchen door and flung it at Jake. With his sleeves rolled up, William resumed stuffing the turkey.

Jake put the apron over his head and in one deft movement tied the apron behind his waist, then in front. He clapped his hands together. 'Right, where shall I start?' He rubbed his hands in anticipation of the task ahead.

'Open the oven door, will you?' said William, breathing hard as he hoisted the roasting tray, containing a huge turkey, surrounded by potatoes, off the work top and aimed for the oven.

Jake did just that. He waited until William had positioned the roasting tray in the oven and then closed the oven door.

William adjusted the oven temperature and then reached for a packet of flour, dropping some on his black patent shoes as he passed it to Jake.

Jake smiled.

'What?' William followed Jake's gaze down to his shoes. 'Well, you know how I hate slippers. They make me feel old.' William wagged a playful finger at Jake, warning him against a smart retort. 'I don't need anybody reminding me I *am* old, thank *you* very much.'

Jake shook his head. 'No, it's not that – it's your shoes. They're covered in flour. It brought back a memory.' Jake elaborated, 'When I was a kid, you used to come home from work, walk in the kitchen and bake something.'

'You remember,' William commented. He momentarily disappeared into the larder and appeared a few moments later with an armful of vegetables.

'I used to sit there,' Jake pointed a floury finger towards the patch of floor directly beneath the table, 'and watch for you. I always knew it was you because of your black patent shoes.'

William laughed heartily. 'I recall that the tablecloth came down to your shoulders. You could hardly see me, apart from my shoes, that is, so you thought that you were doing a pretty good job of hiding.'

Jake laughed. 'I was pathetic, wasn't I?'

'No.' His tone became noticeably more serious. 'You were unhappy – don't you remember?'

'I remember sitting under the table, following your shoes and trying to work out by the splatter on them what you were baking. What I could never figure out was why, when you left the kitchen, there was never anything there to eat.'

'Ah! After all these years, I've been rumbled.' He winked at Jake and reached for the sharp knife and a carrot.

'What do you mean?' Jake got the butter out of the fridge.

'I wasn't going into the kitchen to cook.' William diced the carrot.

Jake momentarily stopped kneading the butter and flour. 'What were you doing – exactly?'

'I was looking for you.' William selected another plump carrot and diced.

'For me?'

'Yes.' He scooped the vegetables into a pan of boiling water. 'I always found you in the exact same spot, under the kitchen table.' William opened a bag of potatoes and began to peel.

'I don't understand ...'

'It started not soon after your mother passed away. We noticed you'd be quite happily playing or eating or reading, and then ...' William stopped what he was doing, momentarily lost in thought. 'It was the darndest thing.' He stared across the room at Jake. 'You would go and sit under this table, quite motionless, looking, waiting ... watching, I suspected, for your mother's familiar feet to walk right through that door and start preparing a meal, just as you had watched her all your young life, in this house.'

William sighed heavily. 'You were just too young to fully comprehend what it meant – death. You couldn't understand that gone is gone, and no amount of sitting under that kitchen table wishing was going to bring her back. But that's exactly where I'd find you, almost every night, waiting in your pyjamas. Waiting for the impossible.'

William reached for a potato. 'Of course, back then I couldn't cook a bean, you know.' He smiled at Jake ruefully.

'So what on earth were you doing?' Jake watched William peeling the spud.

'Trying to reach you.' There was a fondness in his eyes that warmed Jake's heart.

'What happened?' Jake absently kneaded the butter and flour as he struggled to find the memories. All he could remember were those floury black patent shoes.

'I'd go in the kitchen, take out random ingredients from the cupboard and look as though I were cooking in the hope that I could break the spell and get you out from under that table.'

'You did that, after a long day in the office?'

'Whenever I was home and we found you under that table – yes, of course.' William stopped what he was doing and focused all his attention on Jake. 'We'd consulted bereavement counsellors, the so-called experts, and all they could offer were reassurances that you were dealing with it in your own way – that it was a normal and natural part of the bereavement process. It was your unique way of coping and every child was just that – unique, as well as strong and resilient. Give it time, they said. So I did. I gave you as much of my time as I could with little clue as to what I was doing, but with the best of intentions that perhaps by just being there for you I was at least doing something.'

Jake stared at this man, who could show such love and devotion to a child who wasn't his own.

'Then one day, one special day – it must have been very late when I came in to make myself a coffee after a long day at work – there you were, sitting cross-legged as usual under that table. So I put my apron on and started fluffing about with ingredients. But this time I decided to actually try and make something for a change.' He chortled. 'I was absolutely useless. Tried to make myself a pie and all I succeeded in doing was making a mess. I distinctly remember cursing at the blasted cookbook. I had completely forgotten about you under the table when a little voice piped up: *you're doing it all wrong*. And there you were, standing right beside me, a look of annoyance on your little face.' William stood there, staring into space, smiling at the memory.

'Then what happened?' Jake prompted him, all cooking in the kitchen now temporarily suspended while they reminisced.

William looked at Jake. 'I froze. After all that time trying to coax you from under the table, and there I was, feeling like a complete fool, mentally going over the rather colourful language I had just let rip. So I just stood there like a lemon and watched you drag a chair from the table over to where I was standing, climb up and take stock of my ingredients – discarding some and adding others until you were satisfied. Then, together we cooked the pie. Actually, you provided a running commentary on how to cook the pie, and I followed instructions.' William guffawed.

Jake smiled.

'And that's how it began.' William smiled ruefully. 'Whenever I found you in the kitchen under the table I would put on an apron, open a page in your mother's cookery book and start to get out some ingredients – and by that time, you would be dragging a chair over and I would get that *tut-tut* expression of yours that said I was doing it all wrong. And so we would cook, recipe after recipe, until one day I came in after work and Ellie and Marcus said that immediately on hearing my car you had raced into the kitchen. I remember opening the kitchen door and there you were, standing on a chair, cookbook open, ingredients laid out, apron on, and a smile on your face that I hadn't seen in a long, long time.'

Jake stared at him. 'I don't remember that at all.'

William didn't appear surprised. 'You know, sometimes the mind can play strange tricks on us, making us believe things that just aren't true, making us do things that to the casual observer may seem quite irrational, insane even. But for that person, for you,' he lowered his voice, 'how you behaved … for that short time, I think your survival from the depths of grief depended on that peculiar routine of ours.'

Jake was quite blown away by the significance of it all. 'I know we've always cooked together, ever since I can remember. I figured it was because you liked to cook. I guess I just kind of accepted that some boys went fishing with their fathers, and others, well … baked.'

'Believe me,' said William, 'in the beginning, fishing would have been a heck of a lot more appealing. I mean, honestly, do I look like the natural choice for this sort of thing?'

Jake stood back and surveyed this ruddy-faced, big-built broad-shouldered Scot, who was wearing a bright red pinny tied around his ample waist. Jake's brow furrowed. Why hadn't he noticed it before? William actually looked quite funny.

William caught the smile on Jake's lips. 'There, you see? That's why nobody – and I mean *nobody*, knows – I'd be a laughing stock. I've got a reputation to consider, you know.' William waved the wooden spoon at Jake.

Jake laughed harder.

'But damn and blast it all, now I love cooking, and it's all your fault.' William gave Jake's arm an affectionate squeeze. 'And it's a damn good way to relax and unwind to boot.'

Those were Jake's sentiments exactly.

'How's that pastry coming along?' said William, indicating that it was time for them to stop reminiscing and return to the task at hand.

'It's coming,' said Jake, unable to shake off the smile creasing his lips. William always had been a sucker for good old-fashioned, home-made mince pies.

They spent the remainder of the morning, and half the afternoon, preparing the meal with no interruptions, which didn't surprise either of them; Grace, Eleanor and Marcus always did their best to avoid the kitchen at all costs. Everybody was quite happy to leave them to it which, as far as Jake and William were concerned, was just fine; this was their time and territory, just the two of them working quietly and efficiently like a well-oiled cooking machine.

'Shall I set the table?' Eleanor's unexpected voice broke their concentration. She poked her head around the kitchen door, not venturing completely in.

'Ellie!' exclaimed Jake, delighted to see her. He stopped what he was doing immediately and wiped his hands on his apron. 'How was the shopping trip?'

She studied him guardedly. 'Oh, right. The shopping trip. It was … great.' Her eyes darted to William. 'Shall I set the table, Dad?'

Jake stared at her. She never said that about shopping. She detested shopping.

'Thank you, Ellie – that would be helpful. Oh, and can you extract Marcus from his hiding place and tell him I need him to come and help out?'

She smiled at that and let the door swing shut behind her.

Jake stared at the door. *It was great? What is she up to?* He wondered. When he finally realised he wouldn't get any answers, no matter how long he stood staring at the kitchen door, Jake turned away to find William looking at him quizzically. William said nothing, which made Jake feel even more uncomfortable. Something wasn't right between Jake and Ellie, and it was becoming apparent to those around them – first Marcus, now William.

Jake tried to brush it aside, reasoning that it was just the anticipation of telling everyone the news. But this explanation didn't fit easily with Eleanor's recent behaviour. Jake had the distinct impression that she was hiding something from him.

'What do you want me to do?' Marcus's bored voice sounded out from behind the closed kitchen door. He didn't exactly sound thrilled to be summoned to the kitchen.

'If he wasn't such a whizz in the boardroom,' William remarked, 'I'd give Marcus a boot up his lazy …'

'I heard that.' Marcus swung the door wide. The look on his face said he didn't give a fig.

'Ellie's setting the table, but she's going to need a hand placing the presents under the tree.'

'Oh, no!' Jake stared at Marcus.

'Tut-tut.' Marcus shook his head at Jake. 'I think someone has forgotten their presents. Or maybe we were just too *lazy* to bother.' He gave a satisfied grin and let the door swing shut.

'Jake, it's not important,' said William, waving it away with his hand. 'I know you've been working hard lately and …'

'Yes, but that's not the point, is it?' Jake said crossly. William knew Marcus worked every hour god sent too.

'Jake, what's important is that you brought yourself, that's all. No gift can replace that.'

Jake looked at him, taking in his words and realising he *had* brought a gift. And not only that, it fulfilled all the criteria; he had made it – with a little help from Ellie, of course – and you couldn't buy it. They had made a baby – their gift was a grandchild.

Jake grinned insanely at William.

'Whatever you're on,' said William sternly, noting Jake's joyful expression, 'I want you to hand it over *right now*!' His face cracked into a smile. But Jake knew that William could still sense the distinct atmosphere in the room that had arisen when Ellie had appeared.

Jake caught William's gaze drifting to the door. He wondered what William was thinking; whether he had found it troubling, seeing Ellie standing at the door a moment earlier, avoiding eye contact with her husband. William had once said to him that he always felt secure in the knowledge that they were all settled and happy. That was all he had ever wished for at Christmas for his family, and each Christmas he had got his wish.

Jake's gaze shifted to the door. He hoped, god willing, that for his own sake, and for William's, this Christmas would be no different.

9

'Dinner is served,' William announced. It sounded like he was practising for a new career in service at a posh stately home. He walked into the dining room and proudly presented the enormous platter carrying the turkey and roast potatoes, setting it down in the centre of the table. Jake followed with a large hot plate of assorted vegetables.

Everyone took their seats. Jake sat opposite Marcus and Eleanor, and William took his usual place at the head of the table. Grace walked in from the lounge across the hall to take the seat opposite her husband, her back to the long Georgian window that looked out over the front lawn. A light dusting of snow covered the garden. With the flowers and evergreen shrubs delicately frosted, the winter scene outside added a quiet magic and resembled the Christmas cards adorning the fireplace.

William took a moment to savour the presence of his family, looking around the table and smiling fondly at each one in turn. Then he set to work carving the turkey. Plates with succulent turkey slices were passed around, and everyone helped themselves to the vegetable platter, cranberry sauce and rich gravy. With that done, a glass of wine was poured for each of them. They waited.

'To family,' William raised his glass. 'Past,' he nodded in Jake's direction. 'And present.' He nodded at each one of them in turn, then raised the glass to his lips.

'And future,' Jake added, staring intently at his wife. There had been no chance beforehand to discuss when she wanted to announce the news. Wasn't now as good a time as any? Apparently not. Eleanor shot Jake a look which said so in no uncertain terms.

There followed an awkward silence; everyone at the table was aware of the problems they'd been having conceiving a child and knew that because of that, the subject was normally avoided.

'And future,' William echoed, not all that convincingly.

Throughout dinner, Jake tried to make eye contact with Eleanor. Several times, she glanced his way, but too briefly for him to have time to try some sort of covert signal.

Yes, Jake decided, she was definitely avoiding him. How long was this going to go on? Jake shifted his attention to Marcus, who was whispering in Eleanor's ear, his dark eyes settling on Jake. Jake wondered what he was up to and scowled across the table at him. Marcus flashed his pearly white teeth back in a sly grin.

Jake guessed that Marcus was on the subject of the after-dinner ski trip, but he couldn't hear what he was saying because the ancient black-and-white portable television in the corner of the room was drowning them out with an old 1940s film that Grace had insisted on finishing over dinner. In the end, they were all concentrating avidly on the movie while eating their dinner, and despite their missing the first half, it really was quite good.

Music came on as the credits rolled.

'Anyone for pudding?' said William, slapping his ample stomach.

'No, I'm full,' said Eleanor.

'Later,' said Marcus.

Jake agreed.

'Looks like it's just you and me then, Gracie.' William looked across the table at his wife, who was dreamily staring at the television set, watching the credits roll, lost in her own little make-believe world.

'Mummy, do you want pudding or not?' Eleanor said in a patronising tone of voice.

'What did you say, darling?' Grace replied, slowly turning her head in Eleanor's direction.

William got up from the table and went into the kitchen to fetch the pudding.

Eleanor got up to dim the lights. Even if they weren't staying for pudding, it was tradition for William to heat up some rum on the Aga in the kitchen and reappear with a flaming, rum-soaked Christmas pudding.

And, as was also tradition, everyone clapped when he entered the room, carefully carrying the pudding to the table.

While they sat at the table, waiting for the flames to go out, William fetched two dishes from the kitchen. He set one in front of his wife after serving her a generous slice of Christmas pudding. She picked up the dish and spoon, got up from the table, pecked her husband on the cheek and said, 'The meal was divine, darling – simply divine.' She left the room.

William switched off the portable television. Everyone knew he didn't want it on during family get-togethers, most especially the Christmas meal, but unfortunately over the years it had become a tradition created by Grace, albeit one that William, and everyone else, just about tolerated. The unmistakable sound of another film drifted through from the lounge.

William sat down. 'So, are you guys off on your afternoon ski?' He plunged a spoon into the steaming Christmas pudding.

Marcus said yes and Eleanor said no simultaneously.

Jake looked at Marcus and smiled a big *I told you so* grin as William said, 'It's up to you, Jake – are you going to swing the vote?'

'No voting this year. It'll just be Marcus and me … if he says please nicely. Otherwise I won't go either.'

Marcus grimaced.

Eleanor turned to her father. 'Do you want some help with the clearing up, Daddy?'

'No – why don't you go and join your mother in the lounge. You look tired, Ellie.'

Eleanor got up from the table.

Jake rose from his chair, 'Ellie, when …?'

She shook her head furiously at Jake and left the room.

Jake sighed. She was probably right. Now wasn't the time; Grace had left the room and all Marcus had on his mind at this moment was the damn skiing.

'Do you want us to give you a hand?' asked Jake, glancing at Marcus, knowing he wouldn't appreciate being drafted in to help.

'No – you two kids go and have some fun.'

Marcus had bounced up from the table almost immediately the word *no* came out of his father's mouth. 'I'll get the gear,' he said excitedly and left the room.

Jake lingered behind, looking at the food-stained tablecloth and the piles of dirty crockery, aware that Grace wouldn't touch a dish cloth with a ten-foot pole. 'Are you quite sure you don't want some help?' If they'd had a dishwasher, it would have taken no time at all, but William wouldn't have the old, dated eighties kitchen replaced.

'Jake,' William's hand rested on his forearm. 'Just go,' he said patiently.

Jake got up slowly, still eyeing the mess on the table. He glanced at William, who was flicking his hand at Jake, telling him to get a move on. Admittedly, Jake wasn't sorry to leave, as he was aware that the sooner he got going, the sooner he would be back. Then they could share their gift. He could feel the anticipation building in the pit of his stomach at the thought of everyone – especially William – receiving such unexpected news.

Jake left the room and stood in the hallway. The basement door was open, the light was on, and he could hear noises filtering up the stairwell. He headed over to the basement door and listened. Marcus's voice could be heard, loud and clear. He was swearing profusely. He was obviously having trouble extracting the skis from their storage place amid the clutter of assorted family debris that had found its way down there over the years.

They only ever skied up there once a year, and that was weather-permitting. Jake loved Scotland. It was where he had been born, and where he had grown up, and where he had first learnt to ski with the Ross children. But the weather in the Cairngorms was unpredictable, the queues for the ski lifts could be maddeningly long, and poor snowfall would mean a wasted trip to Aviemore if the resort was closed.

He'd hoped that would be the case this year; Jake would have preferred to spend the afternoon with Eleanor. But they'd had some good snowfall in recent years, and it appeared that this year would be just as good. He'd seen the mountains covered in snow on his way to The Lake House. The ski trip was a family tradition and he wasn't going to get out of it – not if Marcus had anything to do with it.

Jake sighed heavily and backed away from the basement door. If Marcus wanted to go that badly, he could extract the skis by himself. Jake had something else more pressing to do – speak to his wife. He went into the lounge to look for her. William was right; Eleanor had appeared quite pale and tired. He was immensely relieved that she wasn't going skiing. She needed to rest, but unsurprisingly she had not joined Grace in the lounge. Grace was too engrossed in the afternoon movie for Jake to bother asking her where Eleanor was.

Walking back into the hall, Jake glanced at the tree. It was Grace's contribution to the do-it-yourself holiday; she had decorated the tree herself. Every decoration was silver, from the large baubles down to the little fairy lights. It looked stunning, and it also looked completely at odds with the simple Christmas they were meant to be having. But it was obvious that she'd decided that if her job was to decorate the tree, she was going to have it the way she wanted it. And you couldn't get a tree looking like it had just stepped out of a movie using only handmade decorations.

Jake stopped in front of it and bent down to pick up a piece of silver tinsel that had fallen among the presents. Each gift was similarly wrapped in old newspaper or simple brown paper with string – apart from Grace's, of course, which were wrapped in bright *Vogue* magazine covers. On one of the presents, he caught sight of his name. He picked it up and turned it over. It was from Eleanor. He stood up to examine the little package, turning it over in his hands.

'You're not meant to touch those until teatime.' Eleanor's stern voice caught Jake unawares.

'Sorry.' Jake quickly knelt down and carefully placed the small package back where he had found it. 'I was just on my way up to …' he paused while he got off his knees, 'see you.' He turned around to look at Eleanor. 'You've got your coat on,' he said in surprise.

'I need my coat if I'm going out,' she said, the edge to her voice unmistakable.

Jake walked towards her. 'I really don't think it's a good idea.' He tried to remain calm.

'What isn't a good idea?' Eleanor stared at him and then inexplicably started to laugh. 'Oh, I get it,' she pointed at Jake. 'I'm not going skiing, if that's what you think. Honestly, the lengths a girl has to go to, to get out of the Christmas ski.' She patted her stomach.

Was she having a little joke with him? Was Eleanor back to her normal self? Jake visibly relaxed. 'Then where are you off to? You should be resting.' He touched her arm.

She flinched. 'I'm not an invalid!' Her light-hearted tone evaporated. 'You've been watching too many of those stupid old movies.'

'I'm sorry,' Jake said, trying to placate her. 'I'm just new at this, that's all.'

'Me too,' she said, staring straight ahead into Jake's chest.

They both stood in awkward silence.

'So, what's with the coat?' Jake fingered her lapels, running his thumb and forefinger up and down the smooth suede leather.

'I'm going into town.' She stepped backwards.

Jake dropped his hands from her coat. 'What are you doing in town?' He tried to sound casual. He tried to sound as though he didn't want to know her every move. Which wasn't true; he did. It crossed his mind, not for the first time, that she was up to something.

'Oh, just some last-minute shopping. You know the sort of thing.' She backed away towards the front door.

Now she was the one trying to sound casual. And no, Jake didn't know what sort of thing. And where was she going shopping? He didn't think any shops were open on Christmas Day. Jake refrained from asking. Instead he said, 'Want some company?'

She stopped and eyed Jake. She didn't say no immediately, which Jake took as a good sign. 'I'll just go get my coat.' He headed for the stairs before she changed her mind.

'Wait!'

Jake stopped with his hand on the banister rail and his foot on the first stair.

'You go skiing. I don't want to spoil your fun just because I can't go.'

'No, no – you're not spoiling anything,' Jake couldn't get the words out quick enough. 'I'd much rather spend time with you.' Was this another test to see who he would choose? Because if it was, then this time, he was going to get it right – oh boy, was he going to give the right answer.

She cocked her head to one side. 'I must have been mistaken, because I thought you wanted to spend Christmas with my family – especially Marcus. That's why we're here, isn't it? So you two can spend some buddy time together?'

Not this again. Jake opened his mouth then discovered he had nothing to say. They were there – and that said it all.

She stared at him a moment longer, waiting for a response. When she realised none would be forthcoming, she turned her back on him and walked to the front door.

Jake watched her take a woolly hat and scarf from the clogged coat rack. She stepped in front of the long mirror by the door and put the hat on, trying it first this way, then that, as though she couldn't decide what looked best.

She buttoned up her coat.

Jake desperately tried to think of something to say – anything to break the ice before she left. But he couldn't think of a single word. His mind was blank. If he called her name, what would he say next? He was afraid of making it worse. Maybe when she came back, and she'd had a chance to cool off and get things in perspective, then they would talk.

Eleanor took one last look in the mirror before she opened the front door and stepped outside.

To Jake's surprise, she turned back to look at him. Her lips parted as though she had something to say.

Jake stepped forward in anticipation. He wanted this awkwardness to end right here, right now. He didn't want her to leave like this, didn't want them to part in this way, even if she was just going shopping. But it was not to be. Eleanor closed her mouth, shook her head and abruptly shut the door.

Go after her, said a voice in his head. He could picture himself running to the front door, pulling her into his arms and exclaiming, *Darling, I love you!* And Eleanor responding in mocking tones, *Darling, you've been watching too many old movies with my mother.* The spell was broken, the urge was gone.

Jake slumped down and sat on a stair, his hand still holding on to the banister. He couldn't believe it was Christmas Day, they had the best news to give the family, and they'd had their first major row after five years of marriage. They'd not once parted on a cross word – until now.

He could hear the television set coming from the lounge, the sound of William washing up crockery and cutlery in the kitchen, and Marcus's thudding footfalls growing louder as he climbed the basement steps.

'You must have heard me down there,' Marcus said impatiently.

Jake looked through the spindles at him. He was awkwardly carrying one ski. Jake turned his attention back to the front door.

'You could give me a hand instead of just sitting there!'

'I'm not coming.'

'Oh, for god's sake, what is with everyone this year?' Marcus stood in front of Jake tapping the ski impatiently on the hardwood floor.

What indeed? thought Jake, staring past Marcus at the front door. He was trying to figure out what was really going on. There had to be more to Eleanor's bad mood than his refusal to spend Christmas in London.

Marcus headed back into the basement. He returned with another ski.

'I knew there was something going on with you two.'

'Just leave me alone, will you?' Jake said.

For a moment, Marcus didn't move. When he did, he didn't go away but put the skis to one side and sat beside Jake on the stairs. 'What's going on, Jake?'

Jake turned his head slowly to look into Marcus's dark eyes. 'We had an argument.' He didn't want to go into the details. He knew she was still angry with him for insisting they joined the family for Christmas, but if he'd known she was going to carry on like this, he wouldn't have insisted on them going.

'Oh, is that all? So you've had a marital tiff. It's not the end of the world. You'll get over it. She'll get over it. When she comes back, she'll have forgotten all about it. You'll see,' he said cheerfully.

Jake looked at him doubtfully.

'Where did she go, anyway?' Marcus looked at the front door.

'Out,' Jake said sulkily. 'Shopping.'

'Shopping? On Christmas Day?' Marcus looked towards the door. 'That's weird.'

'That's what I thought.'

'On the other hand …'

Jake turned to Marcus. 'What are you thinking?'

'Perhaps she's organised a surprise for you – like a making-up present.'

Jake studied Marcus and felt that his words made some sense. In fact, they made a lot of sense. Eleanor was out shopping for the baby – he was sure of it. She was buying something with which to surprise him and she was keeping him in suspense by pretending she was still mad at him. Jake wanted to believe it. He let a tentative smile flicker across his lips.

'There. You see? You know it makes sense.' Marcus patted him on the back. 'Now, what say you and me go skiing? By the time we arrive home, she'll be back.'

Jake narrowed his eyes. 'You're not just saying that to make me go skiing, are you?'

'Hey!' Marcus feigned surprise. 'I'm hurt that you could even suggest that.' But the twitch at the corner of his mouth said otherwise.

Jake reached out and grasped Marcus's shoulder. 'You're a selfish bastard, do you know that?' Jake shook his shoulder. 'Get my damn skis before I change my mind.'

'Great!' He bounced off the stair and headed for the basement.

Jake looked back at the front door. He told himself Marcus was right; Eleanor had a surprise in store, and he couldn't wait to find out what it was.

10

Closed for the Holiday, the sign read.

Eleanor tapped softly on one of the small panes of glass in the front door and took a step back to look down the deserted street. She had been taken by surprise that Jake had actually believed her. This wasn't exactly London. There wouldn't be a single shop open on Christmas Day in the small town of Aviemore. *Trust a man not to know that*, she thought. All the shop fronts along the thoroughfare were dark and devoid of life, apart from this one. A soft glow emanated from within, filtering through the slats of the wooden blind that hung in the front window. It illuminated the large Roman lettering, etched in black on the window in an arc, which read *Wilbur's Bookstore.*

Eleanor stepped up to the door and tapped again, urgently this time. She couldn't shake the feeling that someone was watching her. Eleanor looked up and down the street once more and spotted a car parked a little further up the street. It had its lights on, so she couldn't see who was inside the car.

Eleanor shivered, and not because of the cold. Ever since she'd arrived in the Cairngorms the previous day, she'd felt like she was being followed. Clearly, the feeling had no basis in reality. It was true that she hadn't felt that way in London, but she was still putting her heightened sense of anxiety and paranoia down to the pregnancy. She started to think about the morning sickness and cravings she had to look forward to. And those things would just be the beginning.

Eleanor was raising her hand to the door for the third time when she heard the sound of a key in the lock. She was so relieved when the door opened.

'I decided to pay you a visit,' said Eleanor as she stepped into the dimly lit shop. She could smell freshly brewed coffee.

She took a seat in the cosy café corner by the window. When the blinds were open, it had a view of Aviemore's little train station across the road. The station was popular with tourists because it wasn't just an ordinary station. On Platform 3 was the Strathspey Steam Railway, which offered a step back in time to a bygone era with nostalgic train journeys through the stunning scenery of the Cairngorms.

Eleanor took a peek through the slatted blinds at the station across the road, promising herself that, one day, she would make that trip. But at that moment she was back in the same seat where she had sat just the previous day, Christmas Eve, when she'd nipped out before Jake had arrived at The Lake House.

She looked about her at the bookshelves lining the walls of the small second-hand bookshop while she listened to the sound of cups and saucers being arranged on a tray, and the coffee machine brewing the coffee.

Her mind wandered back to the events leading up to her visit there the day before. She'd known that if Jake missed the train, he would want them to drive up to Scotland together on Christmas Eve. That was why he had been on the phone, leaving her a dozen or more messages. But she hadn't answered the phone on purpose; she had been angry and hadn't wanted to give him the satisfaction of having his own way. She had agreed to spend Christmas in Scotland, which was just what he wanted, so she had expected him to make the effort to catch the train, just like they normally did. Rather than hanging back at the apartment, waiting for him, Eleanor had decided she was getting the sleeper train – with or without him.

Once she'd arrived, she'd decided she wasn't going to make it easy for him. He had spoiled her Christmas, so she was going to make his as unpleasant as possible.

Well, that had been her line of reasoning at the time. Sitting in the back of the chauffer-driven car on her way to London Euston Station to catch the sleeper train, her temper had cooled off considerably; so much so that she felt quite embarrassed by her behaviour in not answering his calls. She'd wished Jake was with her or that she'd held on in the apartment and travelled with him by car instead of insisting that Edward take her to the station alone.

She recalled turning around and looking out of the back window, as if by some miracle Jake would be in his car, travelling right behind them, flashing for the Jag to pull over so that she could resume the journey with him. Eleanor had turned back in her seat to resume her solitary sulk while staring out of the front window.

She had slid down further in her seat to avoid Edward's judgemental glances, which said, *I told you to wait for him*, and had stared miserably out of the car window. It was two-thirty in the afternoon, and the mass exodus from the city had already begun. 'The traffic gets worse every year,' Edward had commented.

'That's why we get the train,' Eleanor had shot back. At least, that was what she and Jake had been doing for the past few years.

When they had been kids, it had all been part of the fun; the anticipation of the Christmas holidays spent in that most magical of places – Aviemore in Scotland. The ridiculously long drive from London – an entire day spent bored in the back of the car – had been worth it. But back then, the family hadn't been able to afford to fly or take the overnight Caledonian sleeper.

At first, after they had got married, Eleanor and Jake had continued that tradition. But Edward was right; every year the traffic got heavier, the going got slower and the urge to drop the absurdly long car journey and just fly grew stronger. Of course, it wouldn't be the same – but then, Eleanor knew that over time, nothing ever was.

Eleanor had enjoyed the long car journeys with Jake, and she knew he'd felt the same. However, as Jake's career in the company took off, doing that long journey and arriving exhausted just spoiled Christmas Day. That was why they'd compromised and started to get the sleeper train.

She'd caught Jake fast asleep on the sofa that morning and had been surprised to find out he'd driven up rather than catching a flight from London with Marcus when he'd missed the train. It was little wonder he'd fallen asleep on the sofa and was too exhausted to wake even when she'd gently lifted his head to position a pillow and had draped a blanket over him.

'You look sad, Ellie. What's the matter?'

Eleanor snapped back from her reverie and looked down at the cup of coffee that had just been placed in front of her. 'Won't you join me?' she said, looking up at her companion.

'Yeah – just like old times.'

That made Eleanor smile. 'Yes, just like old times.' That was a joke. They'd met only the day before, right there in the bookshop – two strangers joining one another with a cup of coffee on Christmas Eve, sharing their troubles.

'Let me get rid of this first.'

Eleanor watched Robyn put her fingers in her mouth and pull out a thick wad of bright pink bubble gum.

'Not very lady-like, I know,' said Robyn, holding the sticky goo between her thumb and forefinger, 'but a girl's got to have some vices.' Robyn stood and walked to the far end of the shop, her bangles clanging, her short black skirt flapping above quite spectacular red and green striped wool tights, her oversize black army boots clumping on the wooden floor. She returned empty-handed.

Eleanor couldn't help but watch her and smile. Robyn was the antithesis of her old school friends or any friends she had ever known, and yet when they had met just the previous day, they had inexplicably hit it off.

There were no old times, as Robyn had put it, but Eleanor wished there had been. She would have loved to have taken Robyn home to see the look on her mother's face. She would have loved to have had a friendship from school that had survived into adulthood and not dropped away as quickly as you could say, *university-educated with a career*, or *tall, tanned and stunning, seen at all the right parties, often linking arms with a celebrity*. Eleanor believed the latter called themselves It Girls – whatever that was meant to mean.

Of course, she knew all too well the real reason her so-called friends had dropped her like a stone, and it had nothing to do with the fact that she didn't have a career or long legs. It was jealousy. She possessed the one thing most of them wanted desperately but did not have – a husband. And it couldn't be just any man; it had to be someone handsome, clever and powerful in order to cement their social standing and elevate them to the glossy pages of *HELLO!* magazine.

The so-called friends who *had* stuck around, Eleanor had later realised, were only after one thing – her brother. So it probably hadn't helped that Marcus had rejected them all in favour of an American. It was a long-distance relationship that, to begin with, they'd all said wouldn't last. But to everybody's surprise, it had. She was a bright, beautiful, sassy, Harvard-educated East Coast lawyer from a distinguished line of East Coast lawyers, and she was blessed with beauty *and* brains. But what set Marcus's fiancée, Lydia, apart from her contemporaries was that she and Eleanor had something in common – they both supported charitable organisations, and, like Eleanor, she took her commitments very seriously.

Eleanor had been disappointed to discover that she wouldn't be joining the family for Christmas that year, but she supposed it was understandable that she would spend Christmas with her own family. Once she and Marcus were married, they would spend the Christmas holiday together. The only question on everybody's lips was: when were they going to set a date? Eleanor hoped it would be soon, because the plan was that Lydia would move to London to live with Marcus permanently. At present, Eleanor's only girlfriends – if you could call them that – were the older women sitting on the charity boards and the circle of company wives who, with their tales of baking and babies, made Eleanor want to run to the hills.

Robyn was just so refreshing. Eleanor smiled affectionately at her new friend.

'You'd think I'd be glad that the bookshop is shut for

Christmas Day, but business has been so slow that sometimes I think I'll go mad without someone else to talk to.' Robyn sat down opposite Eleanor, her bangles clicking on the wooden table. Her dark hair, which was piled high on her head, looked messier than Eleanor's, and her eyes were lined with thick black make-up, contrasting with Eleanor's natural, make-up-free complexion.

Eleanor glanced at the bookshop door with the *Closed* sign in the window. There would be no trickle of customers today. She turned to Robyn. 'You've always got Wilbur to talk to.'

Robyn looked at her. 'Are you serious?'

Eleanor nodded solemnly, although she couldn't imagine a single thing that Wilbur, the bookshop owner, and Robyn could have in common.

Robyn confirmed this. 'You know, I think I'd go insane if I had to talk to him all day. In fact, there'd be nothing for it – I'd have to do him in, or myself – one of us would have to go.' Robyn offered Eleanor a wicked grin.

Eleanor empathised. She'd bumped into Wilbur, literally, on her way into the bookshop just as he was leaving for the Christmas holiday. He visited family in England for Christmas and he wouldn't be back until the New Year, when Robyn's job there would finish. He'd left Robyn in charge on Christmas Eve. Wilbur was stuck in a fifties time-warp, with his thick bottle-bottom glasses, hand-knitted, patterned jumpers and a permanent look of surprise on his face, like a startled rabbit caught in the headlights of the modern world. He was about as uncool as Robyn was cool.

Eleanor glanced furtively at Robyn's low-cut black top, which revealed bare, porcelain-white shoulders, and felt very prim all of a sudden. She undid the top button of her blouse. 'It was getting late,' Eleanor began, 'and I guessed you weren't going to take up my invitation.' She remembered watching the clock on the wall and half-listening for the doorbell during Christmas lunch.

Robyn put her coffee cup down. A white, frothy moustache covered her upper lip. 'Christmas is for family, Ellie, and I wasn't about to intrude on yours.'

'Family *and* friends,' Eleanor corrected her. Although they had only met the previous day when she was browsing in the bookshop, she had invited Robyn over for Christmas dinner. She had been very disappointed when her new friend hadn't turned up.

Robyn licked her upper lip.

'Besides, who wants to spend Christmas on their own?' said Eleanor. It was that very thought had motivated her to go back and find out why Robyn hadn't turned up.

'I do,' Robyn said, surprising her. 'The little flat isn't bad,' she continued, glancing at the ceiling to indicate the living quarters above the shop. 'And it's been a pretty good holiday job so far.'

Eleanor looked around the bookshop; there were rows and rows of books that appeared to be in no discernible order; it was more like a crusty old public library than a bookshop. It wouldn't have surprised Eleanor if Wilbur didn't exactly do a roaring trade. Presumably his one concession to modernity had been the coffee corner, and that had all been down to his wife's insistence, apparently.

'When do you go back to college?' Eleanor asked, secretly hoping Robyn would be around until she returned to London with Jake.

'To tell you the truth,' Robyn confided, 'I'm not sure I want to go back.'

'You're dropping out?' Eleanor said, putting her coffee cup down. 'But why?' She felt that if she had been in Robyn's position, she'd definitely be going back; St Andrews University, art history – studying on the same course as a member of the Royal Family had a few years earlier, no less. It was all so exciting.

Robyn was uncharacteristically silent. She singled out a bright red bangle on her wrist and studied it intently.

'What will your parents think?' Eleanor persisted. And come to think of it, exactly where were Robyn's parents on Christmas Day? Nobody spent Christmas alone; not someone Robyn's age, anyway.

Robyn looked up. 'How was the book?'

'The book?' Eleanor repeated.

'Yes, you know – that book on babies you bought yesterday.'

Eleanor understood; the subject was now closed. Whatever problems she was having at college, be it academic or otherwise – and Eleanor strongly suspected the latter – Robyn didn't want to confide in her. She had no choice but to accept that – for now.

'Not exactly my chosen reading material.' Eleanor sighed.

'Me neither.' Robyn grimaced.

Eleanor found it strangely comforting that she wasn't the only young woman on the face of the planet to find the whole business of babies and motherhood rather, well, disturbing. 'I'm just surprised you managed to find the book so fast.'

Eleanor's brief perusal of the bookshelves yesterday had revealed a chaotic mix of fiction and non-fiction. There was little chance she would have found anything remotely resembling what she was after from those crammed bookshelves. But Robyn had produced the book almost immediately, as though she knew instantly what Eleanor was after the moment she had walked into the shop. Either that, or Robyn had been reading the book herself.

'Don't you feel …?' Robyn hesitated. 'Don't you feel a little young to be having a baby just yet? I mean, all that responsibility, and it's, like, a lifetime thing. Don't you feel you haven't lived a little first?'

'I *am* twenty-six.' Eleanor wondered why she had said that. Then she realised. In her mother's day, twenty-six had been a perfectly acceptable age to be married with a child, and her mother hadn't hesitated to tell her so on the one occasion she had voiced her doubts. But she wasn't living in her mother's day, and no self-respecting career woman started thinking about babies until her biological clock was making loud gonging noises – at least ten years on from where Eleanor was now. But as her mother was wont to remind her, despite her charitable work, she was no career woman. Eleanor stared forlornly into her empty coffee cup.

'Look, that was really thoughtless of me.' Robyn reached across the table and clasped her hand.

'No, it's alright. Really.' Eleanor looked up. 'It's nice to have someone I can really talk to for a change. My mother and I don't exactly see eye to eye.'

'Oh, don't worry. I know exactly how that feels.'

'You do?'

Robyn patted her hand affectionately. 'Let's just say I think you and I have a lot in common.'

'We do?' Eleanor resisted the urge to ask Robyn exactly what she meant by that. Of course, she was intrigued. She wanted to know more about her new friend. What had happened at college to make her consider not going back? Why wasn't she spending Christmas with her family? Had they had a falling-out? But for now, Eleanor was content just to hope they could stay friends; maybe in time, Robyn would open up to her the way she had already opened up to Robyn. Had that really happened only the day before? Yet again, her thoughts wandered back to Christmas Eve ...

❖

The previous day, Eleanor had decided not to hang around The Lake House waiting for Jake's arrival. She hadn't expected him to reach the house until late that day, and hadn't been able to bear the thought of a whole day filled with her mother's disapproving asides when she found out Eleanor had not waited behind in London for her husband to finish work.

So Eleanor had taken herself into town – alone. Shopping was the only option, even though the thought filled her with dread; almost as much as getting into a car and driving. That was why she loved London; it was the perfect place to live if you hated driving, and she always had Edward on hand if she desperately needed a car.

She'd walked up and down the long parade of shops. Aviemore, nestled in the valley of the Cairngorm mountains, consisted of one long shopping street. Many of the shops sold souvenirs, with others selling walking and skiing clothes and equipment.

The small town was the last stop before the long country road, which wound through forests of pines and picturesque lakeshore scenery, led you past the Cairngorm Visitor Centre. It also passed the Cairngorm Reindeer Centre, which offered guided walks to see free-roaming reindeer up on the mountains. Not far past the centre, the road climbed to a dead end at the car parks below the ski lifts up to the Cairngorm Mountain ski resort.

Eleanor had felt relieved that she had got out of the ski trip, although as she had walked through the town, she hadn't enjoyed being jostled by last-minute Christmas shoppers and tourists who had descended on the small town for the start of the ski season.

Eleanor hadn't been able to think of a single thing she needed to buy. Then she had found herself standing outside a decrepit little shop across the road from Aviemore railway station.

At first glance, the shop had looked closed, even though the sign hanging haphazardly on the front door had said *Open*. Unlike the other shops, there had been no last-minute Christmas shoppers there. The lacklustre Christmas decorations didn't exactly entice people inside, and nor did the dimly lit, poky shop that she could just about see through the grimy window. But Eleanor had stepped inside just to get away from the shopping frenzy just about everywhere else.

As she had absently scanned the cluttered bookshelves, it had occurred to her that it was probably the time to start finding out more about this business of babies. She had a strong feeling she wasn't going to be one of those women to whom motherhood would be second nature. She didn't want to turn to her mother for advice – she wasn't exactly Eleanor's picture of the ideal parent. Her mother spent far too much time in la-la land, as far as she was concerned. She'd never been a hands-on mum. Eleanor recalled criticising her mother once, on that score, and her response had been, *Darling, that's what nannies are for.* Unlike her mum, Eleanor wasn't even going to entertain the idea of a nanny, so she had to find out about motherhood elsewhere.

The young woman dressed all in black who was working in the bookshop had handed her a book with the front cover bearing a picture of a woman, her face smiling adoringly down at the baby in her arms.

Then, something unexpected had happened. Eleanor had taken one look at that picture and had just disintegrated into a shaking, snivelling wreck.

The tears wouldn't stop.

The humiliation wouldn't stop.

This had never happened to her before. She was just thankful the shop was deserted.

The young woman had disappeared in a fit of embarrassment, or so Eleanor had thought. But then she had reappeared carrying two empty cups and saucers and with a box of tissues tucked under her arm. She'd guided Eleanor to a seat at the table near a wood-burning stove, placing the cups and saucers on the table in front of her. She'd opened the box of tissues and offered Eleanor one. Eleanor had taken one and blown her nose.

'Wait here.' The young woman had pulled down the blind at the window, flipped the sign on the door to *Closed*, and disappeared again.

Eleanor had taken another tissue from the box and had looked towards the back of the shop, where she could see a large picture window that overlooked a small but pleasant garden and the snow-capped mountain peaks rearing up beyond the town.

The young woman had returned a few moments later, carrying a tray with two mugs of black coffee along with sugar and cream. 'Do you want to talk about it?' she'd asked, passing Eleanor a cup of coffee.

And, quite bizarrely, Eleanor had done just that, pouring out her heart to a complete stranger.

'Everything will turn out ok,' Robyn had said to her, and for some reason, Eleanor had found the words of a stranger comforting.

'Will you come and spend Christmas Day with us?' she had said on impulse.

Robyn had clearly been taken by surprise, 'I'm not sure I …'

'Of course. How stupid of me,' Eleanor had realised she was forgetting her manners. 'We've only just met, and you don't even know me.'

'What's there to know?' Robyn had shrugged her shoulders. 'All I know is that I like you. We could be friends, at least for the Christmas holiday. I don't know a soul in town yet, apart from Wilbur.'

Eleanor had been surprised to hear this. She'd assumed Robyn was home from university for the holidays and was working in a shop local to where her parents lived. She'd said this to Robyn, asking what she was doing in Aviemore, but Robyn had just shrugged in response, and had said cryptically, 'I have my reasons.'

Eleanor had found herself hoping they would be friends long enough for her to find out those reasons – certainly longer than just the Christmas holidays. 'Will you come then, and spend Christmas with me and my family?'

'Maybe.'

Eleanor had got up to go and had nearly left without the book. When Robyn had handed it to her, the cloud had resurfaced. It was blacker than ever.

❖

'Ellie?'

Eleanor looked up from her coffee cup. 'I was just thinking about yesterday – how silly I must have looked, sitting here crying my eyes out.'

'Yeah, you've cost Wilbur a fortune in tissues.'

Eleanor smiled.

Robyn scooted over to the seat next to the window and

opened the blind. She breathed on the window pane and drew something on the window, making a squeaky noise on the glass pane.

'What are you doing?'

'X marks the spot,' said Robyn putting her face close to the window. She looked back at Eleanor. 'The mountain up there.' Robyn pointed out of the window. 'I came for the skiing, but all I've seen so far is the inside of this bookshop.'

'How come?' Eleanor hadn't known she could ski. But then, how much could you really learn about a person in one afternoon?

'My fault, really. I forgot my skis.'

'How did you manage that?' Eleanor could imagine forgetting to pack your ski gloves or something incidental that you could easily overlook, but forgetting your skis for a skiing holiday was pretty, well, funny.

'Are you laughing at me?'

'Uh-uh.' Eleanor shook her head, casually resting her elbow on the table and her hand over her mouth.

'You are, aren't you?' Robyn pointed an accusing finger at her.

Eleanor shook her head furiously.

Robyn reached over and grabbed Eleanor's hand away from her mouth to reveal a wide grin.

'Well, it is rather funny, isn't it?' said Eleanor in between fits of giggling.

Robyn's lips parted into a toothy grin. 'I guess it's not the sort of thing you forget to bring on a skiing holiday.'

They both stared out of the window at the snow-covered peaks.

'I've got an idea,' said Eleanor suddenly. 'I've got skis, the whole shebang. You can borrow them.'

Robyn turned away from the window to look at her.

'Oh hell, you can have them. Think of it as a Christmas present. And you don't have to worry about giving me anything in return,' she added hastily, 'because you already have – your friendship.' She knew she had been sorely in need of a kind word and a sympathetic ear. 'I doubt I'll be going skiing again in the foreseeable future. Anyway, I've always hated skiing.' Eleanor had expected Robyn to jump at the chance, but instead she sat there, calmly considering it.

'It won't be the same,' Robyn said finally.

'I know that,' said Eleanor, 'but we're near enough the same height and build. I'm sure you could get used to …'

'No, that's not what I meant.' She turned back to the window and scrubbed out the X in a couple of squeaks.

'What is it, then?'

Robyn stared out of the window. 'We used to come here for holidays when I was a child.'

'Really?' Eleanor was pleased to discover that they really did have something in common. Perhaps Robyn had had her first experience of skiing there; perhaps she had joined one of the kiddie clubs to learn to ski, just as Eleanor had. Perhaps they had even met already in one of these clubs years earlier. But something in Robyn's voice stopped Eleanor from asking for the details of happy childhood memories. She wondered if the memories had become sad ones, maybe because of recent events.

'Your parents don't come anymore?' Eleanor said softly.

Robyn shook her head, 'One can't and the other won't,' she said cryptically.

'Why?'

'You don't want to hear my pathetic sob story.'

'Tell me.' Eleanor leaned over and touched Robyn's shoulder. Robyn turned away from the window, her face streaked with black where her thick mascara had run with her tears.

11

Carrying a ski in each hand, Jake reluctantly followed Marcus outside. It was very cold and wintry, the fresh flurry of snow covering the rooftop and grounds of the old house. Jake made fresh footprints in the snow as he trudged to the car. He had seen the recent snowfall on the way there in the car yesterday. Fortunately, the roads into the Cairngorms had been passable, but the heavy snowfall on the mountains suggested the weather was just about as good as it got for skiing. But Jake felt very tired; the emotional rollercoaster of the last couple of days concerning Eleanor and the pregnancy had finally caught up with him. The long drive to Scotland had also taken its toll. He felt as though he could go back inside and crawl into bed for a week.

'Come on, Jake – get it together, will you?' Marcus said impatiently as the ski slid out of Jake's hand for the second time before he could get it secured onto the roof of the car. 'Here, I'll do it.' Marcus shoved him out of the way and gave him an exasperated look. 'You just – just stand over there.'

Jake stepped out of the way and left him to it. He loaded some of their equipment into the boot instead and then sat in the car and waited. Marcus opened the driver's door and got in. He didn't start the car. They both sat in silence. Jake waited for the inevitable question.

'Look,' Marcus turned to him, 'if you really don't want to do this …'

Jake rubbed his eyes. He was sorely tempted to call it off, but he had upset Eleanor already and he wasn't about to spoil Christmas for Marcus on top of everything else, so despite the fatigue, he forced a smile. 'Just start the car, Marcus. I'm tired, that's all. I'm sure the mountain air will perk me up.' He hoped so. 'But if you don't get me there soon,' he warned, 'I am liable to fall asleep.' He yawned. He wasn't fooling.

As Marcus drove through Aviemore and took the turn-off at the small roundabout just outside town, Jake was looking forward to the drive through the Caledonian pine forest and catching glimpses of the picturesque scenery surrounding Loch Morlich and the Cairngorms rising up in the distance. The drive was always one of the highlights of the trip.

However, the closer they got to the cold white peaks, the more inviting the thought of his bed became. He glanced at Marcus, who was smiling from ear to ear, obviously looking forward to arriving. Jake was not. He rubbed his eyes again and frowned as they passed the Cairngorm Reindeer Centre. A few hundred yards up the road was the ski resort. They had arrived far too quickly for Jake's liking, and his mood didn't improve when he saw the queue for the funicular railway; the unexpectedly good snowfall seemed to have brought out the whole community.

Marcus swung the car into the car park.

'Why aren't these people at home, unwrapping their presents or stuffing themselves like turkeys?' Marcus complained.

'What - like normal people?' Jake sighed.

'Exactly,' said Marcus, completely missing the point.

Marcus hated waiting for anything, but Jake's spirits were bizarrely raised by the sight of the queue – it was maddeningly long, which meant there was still a strong possibility Marcus would change his mind.

Marcus looked at his watch. 'We'll give it ten, maybe fifteen minutes, and then we're out of here.'

Jake smiled, 'I'll second that.'

Twelve minutes later, they were squeezing into the Cairngorm Mountain Railway carriage that ascended the northern slopes of the ski resort. Jake was no longer smiling.

Jake shuffled in behind Marcus, both moving further to the back of the funicular as the queue behind them shortened and the numbers in the carriage swelled.

Jake stared out of the window at the people on the platform in their brightly coloured ski suits. The door to the carriage closed on the disappointed crowd. He wished he was one of them. He wished he was heading back so he could talk to Eleanor and put things right. Then he snapped to attention; he thought he'd seen some familiar ski wear.

He pushed passed Marcus.

'Where are you going?'

Jake ignored him. 'Excuse me. Excuse me.' Jake fought his way through the people crammed in the carriage to the door, ignoring complaints from the other passengers, who recognised that he was one of the first on and mistakenly believed he now wanted to get to the front to be the first off.

He reached the door just as the train lurched forward to begin the ascent.

Then he saw her.

'Ellie!' Jake banged on the window, trying to get her attention. Her ski wear was unmistakable; the purple ski suit, the familiar hat and glasses, the wisps of dark hair escaping the scarf wrapped around her face.

Jake banged on the window again. She saw him. Jake waved. She waved back. What the hell was she doing there? This was one surprise he could do without.

'We'll wait up top,' Jake shouted and signalled to her upwards.

Jake watched her until she was out of sight. Then he turned towards Marcus, his face like thunder.

'Excuse me, coming through,' he announced before pitching himself into the throng of bodies. 'Excuse me, yes, I'm coming back,' he said to some, who were purposely making it difficult for him to get through. He reached Marcus, who said, 'I saw her.' His face was positively beaming.

Jake grabbed him by the shoulders in fury. 'What the hell did you say to her?'

A child started to cry. He looked around and noticed that despite the cramped conditions, the other passengers were giving him a wide berth. They were also looking anywhere else but in his direction. His behaviour was frightening people.

Jake dropped his hands from Marcus and turned his back on the spectators to look out of the train window.

'What is the big deal?' Marcus whispered in his ear.

Jake planted his hands on the metal rail in front of him as a necessary precaution against the instinctive urge to hit Marcus. 'I just want to know what you said that made her come,' said Jake through gritted teeth.

'Oh, you mean at the dinner table.' Marcus paused. 'It was nothing – really.'

Jake turned to look at him. 'If it was nothing, how come she's here?'

'OK, I probably said something I shouldn't have. To be honest, I thought it would have put her off. It seems to have had the opposite effect.' Marcus shrugged and smiled weakly.

Jake gripped the rail tightly, his knuckles turning white with the strain. 'What did you tell her?'

'That I was thinking of skiing off-piste, and she wouldn't know what she was missing.'

'What the hell, Marcus? We never going skiing off-piste.'

'Well, there's a first time for everything. Besides, just because she's here, doesn't mean she'll do it. You know my sister – she won't take risks, especially skiing.'

Jake sighed heavily. It wasn't Marcus who needed a good going over, Jake realised. It was himself for being a complete idiot and not listening to his wife. She had been right; they should have spent Christmas in London. He had been wrong not to put Eleanor first.

Perhaps the time had come to ditch this family tradition of spending Christmas in Scotland. It was, after all, for his own benefit. He didn't need to do this any longer. He wasn't a kid anymore. It was time to move on.

'Come on, come on.' Jake silently willed the cable car to make faster progress to the top. He had a plan, and it was simple; he and Eleanor were taking the funicular back down, returning to The Lake House, collecting their bags, and driving straight back to London. They might just make it before Christmas Day was over.

It was insane – yes. But Jake's mind was made up. It was to be his Christmas present to his wife, his proof that he loved her. Nothing and no one – Jake glanced at Marcus – was going to stop it from happening.

12

‘Robyn Parker?’

She let her eyes drop from the TV set suspended high in the corner of the room to the young woman in the white coat standing at the end of her bed. She was holding a clipboard, waiting for a response. She wasn’t going to get one.

‘I’m Dr Jamieson,’ the woman in the white coat continued. ‘I want to speak to you about—’

‘Robyn.’ A man’s voice interrupted.

She turned her head away from the doctor and looked at the young man standing in the doorway.

‘David.’ She smiled and held out her hand as he entered the room, a couple of magazines tucked under his arm and a bouquet of flowers behind his back. She could see them but pretended she couldn’t.

‘How are you today?’ He clasped her hand. ‘I got you these.’ He put the magazines on her bed, and then, with a flourish, withdrew his hand from behind his back.

She did her best to act surprised.

‘Shall I put them in a vase?’ he asked. He glanced around the room and then caught sight of the doctor standing with her arms folded at the end of the bed.

'Oh.' He stopped when he saw the doctor. 'Excuse me.' He looked back at Robyn. 'Is everything OK?' he asked anxiously.

'I need to speak with Robyn.' The doctor unfolded her arms. 'So, if you don't mind …' She indicated the door.

'No – he can stay,' Robyn said abruptly, giving the doctor a look of defiance. 'Why am I still here? The nurse said I had to stay in for observation.'

David walked around the bed, taking a seat by the window. Robyn smiled at him.

Dr Jamieson glanced at David. 'You were at the scene of the accident, weren't you?'

He nodded. 'Yep. Piece of luck, being in the right place at the right time like that.' David smiled.

'Yes, it was,' Dr Jamieson said flatly. She continued to look at him. His smile faded in the awkward silence.

'Maybe I should leave.' He got up.

'No.' Robyn shook her head. 'Please don't go.'

The doctor spoke to David again. 'Do you mind if I ask you how long you and Robyn have been seeing each other?'

'Seeing each other?' David repeated. 'You mean like dating?' He looked at Robyn. They both laughed.

Dr Jamieson frowned.

'I've been seeing Robyn since yesterday. We aren't dating. Although,' he looked at Robyn, 'I suppose if you call visiting a very pretty lady in hospital on Boxing Day *dating*, then …'

Robyn leaned over and slapped him playfully on the arm.

'So you two didn't know each other before the accident yesterday?'

'Never seen her before in my life.' David winked at Robyn

playfully. 'Although I wish I had.'

'In that case, Robyn and I will need to speak privately.'

They both looked at her, then exchanged glances. David got up. 'I'll go and get myself a coffee.'

Dr Jamieson nodded.

He squeezed Robyn's hand, then left.

Dr Jamieson pulled up a chair and sat down by the side of Robyn's bed. She tapped the clipboard.

Robyn's stomach churned. She touched the bandage on her forehead. 'It's a brain tumour, isn't it?'

'No it isn't, Robyn – nothing like that. It's a bump on the head.'

'Then why—?'

'The memory loss?' Dr Jamieson finished.

Robyn nodded.

'The head trauma has, in your case, led to temporary amnesia. The CAT scan is back, and I can assure you it isn't a tumour.'

Robyn sank back on the pillows, relieved. 'But why can I remember everything since the accident, but nothing before it?'

Dr Jamieson didn't answer.

'And why can I remember how to eat, how to dress, all those things?'

Dr Jamieson sighed and leaned forward in her seat. 'Despite all the advances in medical science, we are only beginning to understand the workings of the human mind. Sometimes people do lose their memories to such an extent that they have to be taught everything from scratch; reading, writing, even walking in some cases, usually as a result of some severe trauma to the head.'

Robyn ran her fingers along her bandage. 'But mine wasn't that bad?'

'No.' Dr Jamieson shook her head. 'Some suffer from selective amnesia, which is probably the end of the spectrum that you fit into, where you can remember how to use a knife and fork, dress yourself, things like that, but for some reason memories of your past, people you knew, experiences you've had, are temporarily closed off to you.'

'Selective?' Robyn repeated.

'Yes. In such circumstances, the theory is that the mind is choosing not to remember. It might not be physical.'

'How do you mean?' Robyn wasn't sure she liked where this is leading.

'Children who suffer a trauma in their childhood – maybe they were abused – often shut a door on that memory; bury it so deep in their subconscious that as adults they genuinely cannot remember the events that happened to them. It's a psychological rather than a physical trauma that has caused their memory loss, and it is usually selective, involving those events that they can't cope with and they need to forget – for now. It is possible that as adults we have the ability to protect ourselves, in the way a child's mind can, from some traumatic event.'

Robyn was quiet for a moment, taking the information in. She fiddled with her bedsheet, smoothing it out on her lap. Without looking up, she said, 'Are you saying that my memory loss is not to do with me hitting my head in the car accident?'

'It's a possibility, Robyn. Only you will be able to answer that. Give it time.'

Robyn looked up. 'But how much time? I couldn't even remember my own name.'

'I can't quantify that, Robyn. But something will trigger your memory; a familiar face, a place, your belongings even. There were letters in the car from your mother, some unopened. Perhaps you could read those. It might help. You know, you are a lot luckier than some. At least you had identification – of sorts.'

'Of sorts?'

'The police on the scene couldn't find a handbag or purse, or your driving licence, but they did run a background check on the car, and your name came up as the owner.'

'That's lucky,' said Robyn, although she wasn't feeling particularly lucky. 'What happened to my purse?'

'I would imagine that some of your belongings got thrown from the car during the accident. The woodland is quite dense along that stretch of road. Although the police couldn't find it, perhaps some hikers or dog walkers will come across a purse or handbag eventually.'

Robyn swallowed. She hoped her driving licence was in her purse. She'd be in trouble for driving with no licence if she couldn't find it to show them if they wanted to see it.

'Some people wake up with nothing – no clue as to who they are, and it can take them years to put all the pieces back into place.'

'Years!' said Robyn alarmed. 'Are you saying …?'

'That's a worst-case scenario when there aren't any familiar triggers. But take heart, Robyn – I'm sure yours will return soon. Just give it time. Try not to get anxious about it, and it will come.'

Robyn didn't like her predicament, but then Dr Jamieson was right: she supposed she was luckier than some under the circumstances.

'Robyn.'

She looked at the doctor.

'There's something else, isn't there?' Her stomach churned again.

'This is difficult.' The doctor paused.

Robyn stared at her intently.

'Robyn, before the accident you may have been aware that—' She halted. 'It's incidental now,' she said, more to herself than to Robyn. She took a deep breath before she continued. 'The memory loss complicates this.'

'Complicates what?' Robyn watched the doctor walk over and sit down in the chair by her bed.

She said softly, 'You were pregnant, Robyn.'

'I'm pregnant?' Robyn said in alarm, involuntarily pushing herself up in the bed.

'No.' Dr Jamieson rested a hand on her shoulder. 'I'm so sorry, but you lost the baby in the accident.'

Robyn stared straight ahead, unable to take it in.

Dr Jamieson continued. 'I know this must be hard for you. You may have known you were pregnant, but it was in the very early stages.'

'So I might have lost it anyway.' Robyn turned to the doctor with pleading eyes.

'According to David, it sounds as though you weren't wearing a seatbelt and were nearly thrown from the car, so—'

Robyn held her hand up. The doctor didn't have to say any more.

'But yes, it was in the very early stages, so if it hadn't been for the accident, you might not have carried it to full term anyway.'

Robyn knew the doctor was just being kind. She hadn't worn her seatbelt, and she couldn't even remember if she'd known she was pregnant.

'The father?' Robyn said in a quiet voice.

'I can't help you with that. But you see now why I had to ask David to leave the room.'

'Yes, of course.'

Robyn watched Dr Jamieson get to her feet and pause by her bed. 'Shall I send David in now?'

'No.' Robyn looked up at the young doctor. 'Can you tell him I feel tired and that I'm resting?'

'Alright, Robyn.'

'Thank you.'

'But that he can come back tomorrow if he likes,' she added quickly. She couldn't bear the thought of losing her only visitor.

'Oh, I'm sure he'll come back tomorrow. He knows how crummy being laid up in a hospital bed is.'

'He does?'

'He's quite the local celebrity.'

'How come?'

'He's our most famous sports star from this small town.'

'Sport?'

'Ice hockey.'

Robyn shook her head. She didn't know anything about ice hockey. David had not talked about it.

'Until he ended up back here with a shattered knee and a shattered career.'

'I had no idea.'

'It's probably not the easiest thing in the world for him to talk about, having lost so much.'

'You know David, then?'

'We went to high school together, and we both got out of this small town – he did it on a scholarship, and I went to medical school in London. But we've both ended up back here. Mine's a happier story, though. I chose to come back. After all those years of working hard to leave Scotland, once I'd left, I missed this part of the world. The Cairngorms, and the people, are just so lovely. So I came back.'

'What about David? How does he feel about being back here?'

'I don't know. You'd have to ask him.' There was a slight, almost undetectable edge to her voice, and Robyn wondered if the young doctor and David had a past.

For a moment, all Robyn's worries seem to dissipate in the knowledge that hers wasn't the only sad story. At least she could try to pick up the pieces of her life, even if she had lost part of her memory. It didn't sound as though David would be so fortunate. She wanted to know more, but at that moment, the doctor's bleeper went off. Robyn watched her lift the little black box from her trouser waistband and read the message.

'Just a few more days, Robyn – then you'll be free to go.'

Free to go where? thought Robyn as she watched the doctor walk to the door. All she knew was her name. But where had she come from, and where had she been going yesterday – Christmas Day?

Dr Jamieson stopped at the door. 'I know it's no fun at all spending Christmas in hospital. But merry Christmas anyway.'

'But when can I leave the hospital?' She watched the doctor flick through a file. 'Can't you be a bit more specific than *a few more days*?'

Dr Jamieson looked up. 'It's Boxing Day. I will discharge you before New Year. All being well, in three days' time – the day before New Year's Eve.'

Robyn felt better on hearing a firm date for being able to leave the hospital. 'Dr Jamieson?' she called as the door was closing.

The door flew open. 'What is it, Robyn?'

'I would rather nobody knew about …' The door was wide open and Robyn didn't want to spell it out.

'No one will know unless you choose to tell them.' Dr Jamieson smiled reassuringly.

'And my memory … I'd rather keep that to myself for the moment too.'

'All right, Robyn. We don't discuss patients' medical histories unless it's with another health professional. Although if the police have any questions, do I have your permission to tell them about your memory loss, if necessary?'

Robyn nodded, realising that if she was questioned, at least a medical professional would corroborate her story.

'But if you're asking whether I'll tell David, of course nothing we've talked about leaves this room, unless you want it to.'

Robyn sighed in relief and sank back into her pillow. The doctor understood. She wanted to be reassured that the conversation would remain private, especially after the doctor had told her that she knew David.

The doctor didn't leave the room. She pulled the door to behind her, keeping her hand on the doorknob, and lowered her voice. 'You might find it easier if you tell people about your memory loss, otherwise you might find yourself making things up – you know, to cover for what you can't remember. And you know where little white lies lead to.'

'Even bigger white lies.' Robyn nodded. 'I know. It's just that, this may sound silly, but I feel kind of …' She was searching for the word to describe how she was feeling.

'Vulnerable?'

'Yes, that's it. I guess it's like how you feel when you meet people for the first time and you don't know anything about them. But do you know what it feels like to meet strangers who might know more about you than you know yourself?'

'Scary, I imagine.'

'Yes. This is going to sound stupid, but until I know me, I'd rather—'

'Not let your barriers down.'

Robyn nodded. She frowned. 'Besides, if I tell people I've got this selective amnesia thing, they're liable to think I'm a bit crazy – or lying.'

'Well, I one for one know you're not crazy – or lying. I'm afraid the look on your face when I told you that you had been pregnant said it all.'

'I wish I could just remember.'

'I know,' Dr Jamieson said empathetically. 'Look, I think you should do what you feel is best under the circumstances, Robyn. Go with your instincts, because that's just about all you've got to go on at the moment.' The doctor smiled at her for the first time. Her bleeper went off again. She rolled her eyes. 'Sorry, but I have to go.' She quietly shut the door.

Robyn stared up at the TV in the corner of the room as a newsreader appeared on the screen. She watched the blonde woman's expression theatrically turn serious as the word *Accident* flashed up on a bulletin board behind her and her bright red lips moved as she started to speak.

Robyn could hear her voice, but only faintly. She wanted to hear this. It could be about her accident. She kept her eyes glued to the television set as she reached for the controls on the side table next to her bed. Her hand brushed them and there was a loud clatter as they slid off the table onto the floor.

'Damn!' she exclaimed loudly as she peered over the side of her bed. The controls were on the floor just beneath her, within easy reach, but the battery lid had come off. She could see one battery over by the door and the other had disappeared under her bed. Robyn threw off the bedcover and swung her legs over the side of the bed. She knew she wasn't meant to get out of bed.

13

'Are you alright in there, or shall I call for someone?' A woman's voice came from behind the door as it opened a crack.

Robyn sat back in bed and hastily pulled the covers back over her. 'I'm fine!'

The door opened further and a middle-aged woman dressed in dark blue skinny jeans and a cosy but loud woollen Christmas jumper with a large Santa on the front stood in the doorway. Despite the sudden interruption, Robyn smiled at the stranger. She loved her braided afro hairstyle, especially with the beads she had added to the ends of her braids, which were in the Christmassy colours of red, green, and white, matching her jumper.

'Sorry to disturb you. I was next door and I thought I heard you call out.'

Robyn sighed and threw the covers off again. For a moment, before the lady opened the door wide, she'd thought it was a nurse come to check on her. 'I dropped the television controls,' she said as she flung her legs off the bed again.

'You stay there – I'll get these.' She bent over to look under the bed.

Robyn winced. She anticipated that any second, the lady's

jeans were going to give way with an enormous ripping sound. It wasn't that the woman was carrying a lot of weight – on the contrary, she had a very slim, almost athletic figure – but her trousers were so tight that it looked as though they had been stitched up with her in them.

'There,' she panted when she stood up with the single battery in her hand. 'Now for the television controls.'

Robyn watched in amusement as she tried kneeling. Her knee wouldn't reach the floor. So, with one arm on the bed, she lowered herself down and picked the controls up. 'Gotcha,' she said as she hoisted herself up. She put the battery in the compartment.

'Oh, where's the other one?' she grimaced.

Robyn didn't think she could go through one more bending session. She wondered how the lady ever sat down in her jeans.

'Don't worry.' Robyn held up her hand, deciding to put the poor woman out of her misery. 'I'll get the other battery.'

A look of relief crossed the woman's face as she handed Robyn the controls. 'Wasn't much help then – was I?'

'Thanks all the same.' Robyn was about to get out of bed when she looked at the silent TV screen and sighed. The TV was positioned too high on the wall to reach the sound controls. And now the accident bulletin had given way to the weather.

'Dammit!' Robyn swore. She looked wide-eyed at her visitor, and clamped her hand over her mouth. 'Sorry,' she said through her hand.

'Whatever for?'

'You must have heard me swear earlier when you were next door.' Robyn indicated the room next door. Guessing at the age of her visitor, who was in her early forties, it had just occurred to Robyn that there may be a child next door.

'Oh, not to worry – it's just my father next door, and he's too far gone to be aware of anything.'

'I'm sorry.'

'Don't be, honey.' She flashed a wide grin, showing a perfect set of pearly whites. Her infectious chuckle made Robyn want to join in, as though they were children sniggering in the playground. Robyn smiled. 'I must have sworn awfully loud.'

'Oh, yes. I wasn't sure what nasty ogre was sitting behind the door.' She pointed at Robyn's door. 'And who would have thought language like that would come out of a pretty little thing like you.' She chuckled again, and that made Robyn's smile broader.

'I bet I looked pretty cross when you opened the door.'

'Hmm, I'll say. A bit like a pouting princess whose prince had run off with someone else. Say, talking of princes, or should I say knights in shining armour, where's yours?'

'My what?'

'Knight in shining armour. You know the guy who saved you from going over that cliff like that.'

'David.' Robyn smiled. She added. 'You know about him and the accident?'

'I've seen him in and out of your room, fetching you this and that. Sorry, I know I sound so nosy, but there's not a lot to do, hanging around the hospital over Christmas, and you're new, so it kind of piqued my interest.'

Robyn understood. She expected there weren't many head traumas brought in on Christmas Day, unless someone had drunk far too much and slipped over and banged their head. But normal people should be sitting around the table eating Christmas dinner, unwrapping presents, and watching old Christmas movies, or the King's speech – enjoying spending time with their families, not going out in a car on a snowy afternoon and having an accident.

As she thought about that, she remembered they were in the Cairngorms. She only knew because David had chatted about the weather in that part of Scotland and had mentioned how good the skiing was that year. She guessed it was possible that there could be more head traumas or broken bones – the Christmas break wasn't over yet.

'Don't tell me he's missed a visiting session,' the lady said in mock surprise, interrupting Robyn's thoughts.

'No. I felt tired.'

'You had a headache?'

'No, I just—' Robyn looked up and caught the lady pointing at her bandage and chuckling.

'Oh. Right.' Robyn realised her new visitor was having some fun with her. She laughed at the joke too.

'Did you say your visitor is called David?'

Robyn nodded.

The woman repeated. 'Not David Gillespie?'

Robyn gave a noncommittal nod, as she didn't actually know his last name.

'I thought I recognised him,' she said, snapping her fingers.

Robyn didn't find that surprising after her chat with the doctor. It sounded as though everyone in town would know of the once-famous ice hockey player.

'You wait right here.'

Robyn found the instruction quite funny, as she obviously wasn't going anywhere. She watched the lady walk out in her high-heeled sandals and wondered how she didn't get frostbite, wearing such shoes in the middle of winter.

A moment later she reappeared, flapping a newspaper. 'You

made the local newspaper – today's edition!'

'I did?' Robyn said excitedly, reaching out for the paper. She didn't think newspapers were printed on Boxing Day, but she was glad they were. She thought the publicity would be good because perhaps someone who knew her, family or friends, would come and visit her when they saw her name and picture in print.

'You're the girl that this David fellow saved from going over a cliff like that!' She flapped the paper under Robyn's nose.

Robyn took the local paper, the *Strathspey and Badenoch Herald*. She read the news article, and saw a photo of one of the cars, a badly damaged sports car that had been recovered from the scene, the bonnet crumpled. The car looked beyond repair.

'See. You made the front page.'

Robyn stared at the photo. Beside the picture of the car was a small picture inset of a young man wearing a black gown and a college mortarboard – a photo obviously taken a few years earlier. There was a caption reading, *Local Hero David Gillespie.*

'Well, I'll leave you to read it in peace.'

Robyn mumbled a thank you, not taking her eyes off the picture.

'Oh, and here.'

Robyn looked up as the woman handed her a set of TV controls. 'My father doesn't need these. Just in case.'

Robyn took them. 'My name's Robyn, by the way.'

'I know.'

Robyn eyes were wide. 'You do?' She caught the woman's bemused expression, and glanced at the newspaper.

'You're in the paper, remember?'

Robyn frowned, wishing she hadn't used that word – *remember.*

'I know there's no picture of you,' she continued, 'but I

recognised your boyfriend, and I'm pretty good at putting two and two together.' She tapped her temple.

Robyn didn't bother correcting her when she said the word *boyfriend.*

'Hey, buck up. It may never happen.'

Robyn looked down at the paper on her lap, thinking that it already had.

'I'm Gayle, by the way.' She held out her hand.

Robyn shook hands, but Gayle didn't let go. 'Will you do me a favour?'

Robyn couldn't imagine what she could do for Gayle, but she nodded all the same. 'What is it?'

'When I visit my father, can I sneak in here from time to time, just for a bit of light relief? It's so dismal in hospital. I just sit watching my father, and he doesn't say much – well, nothing coherent, anyway. So then I just watch TV, but I feel guilty if I don't come – especially over Christmas. This afternoon has been the most fun I've had in this place.' Gayle gave an infectious chuckle, which made Robyn laugh.

'Yes, please do come and see me again,' she replied enthusiastically.

'Great.' Gayle patted her hand before releasing her grasp. Then she pointed at Robyn and her tone turned serious. 'Just don't ask me to bend down again. I think I nearly split my skinny jeans.'

They both laughed, and Robyn was still giggling as Gayle left the room. She wiped a tear away from her eyes and listened to the click of Gayle's sandals as she entered the room next door.

Then she looked down at the newspaper in her lap and her face fell. She looked at the black-and-white picture of the two cars again. She hadn't realised the accident had been so serious. She wondered whose fault it had been. Then she had a terrible thought. Perhaps David was just being nice to her to find out whatever he could before suing her for wrecking what looked to have once been a very nice sports car.

However, she realised that David hadn't asked her a single question about herself. That was why she appreciated his company, under the circumstances. He hadn't made her feel uncomfortable because he hadn't asked her about her past. But then, come to think about it, he had not talked about his either.

Robyn started to read the article. She was anticipating finding out some information about herself, imagining that the journalist who had written this article had been interested in uncovering the facts.

After she finished reading the article, she threw the newspaper across the room in frustration. She knew no more about herself than when she had started.

She should have known that the article would be about David Gillespie. After all, the headline did read, *Local hero saves young woman.* The article more or less repeated what Dr Jamieson had said about David being a famous sports star until an injury had ended his career. But the article also touched on his family background. His mother had left when he was a child, leaving him and his younger brother to be brought up by their father. There was no mention of a wife, or a girlfriend.

Robyn cast the newspaper to one side and sat staring at the flickering images on the silent TV screen. The familiar face of the newsreader she had seen earlier appeared. Robyn resigned herself to trying to lip read when she remembered she had the TV controls. Robyn hoped they would work, as the word *Accident* had just flashed up behind the newsreader. Robyn hoped they had more to say about her than the single line afforded her in the local paper. She turned up the volume.

'This is an update. In what police are describing as a tragic incident, the daughter of William Ross, the philanthropist and owner and CEO of the Ross Corporation, who went missing on Christmas Day, is now believed to have suffered a tragic skiing accident in the Cairngorm mountains. The family are not available for comment, and will not be making a press release at this time.'

Robyn leaned forward, listening intently. 'There but for the grace of god go I,' she said under her breath as she saw a photo of three people flash up on the screen. It looked to Robyn like a pose from a TV series that she couldn't remember. The three were linking arms. The two tall, handsome guys were wearing tuxedoes. One of the young men was dark-haired with black eyes and pale skin – he was quite striking in appearance, and his eyes were partially covered by a flop of hair. He was looking across at the other guy, who was blond, with faintly tanned skin. They looked like male models who had just stepped out of a magazine.

The blond guy was looking down at the woman in between them. Her lack of height contrasted with the tallness of her brother and husband. She wore a gorgeous, flowing, black silk evening gown that Robyn imagined had cost a small fortune. Her head was thrown back in what looked to be a laugh-out-loud moment, so her features were obscured by the camera angle. But then, who wouldn't be laughing, leading a glamorous lifestyle like that? Robyn frowned at herself for enviously thinking such a mean thought after what had happened to the young lady.

Robyn listened as the newscaster continued.

'Although the Rosses live in London, and travel abroad frequently, sources say they always spend Christmas in the Cairngorms. But this year

their trip has ended in tragedy. It is believed she was skiing with her husband and brother. She leaves behind her husband of five years, Jake Campbell-Ross.'

Robyn shook her head. How sad. It didn't sound as though they had any children. Perhaps that was just as well.

'This isn't the first time her husband has suffered a loss. He was taken in and raised by the Rosses after his parents tragically passed away when he was a child. The family are asking for privacy at this time as they come to terms with the tragedy.' She paused. *'And now for the weather …'*

The camera panned to a young man standing by a map of the Cairngorms, looking subdued. *'Thank you, Jane. What a tragic end to Christmas Day.'* He turned to face the camera. '*Now, let's look at the weather map …'*

Robyn clicked the TV set off. She leaned back on her pillow and stared up at the ceiling, thinking that she wasn't the only one who'd had a Christmas Day from hell. She thought how lucky she was that she'd crossed paths with David and that he'd been there to save her. If he hadn't, things could have been a whole lot worse.

14

Robyn felt in high spirits. After two more mind-numbingly boring days, punctuated by visits from David and Gayle, who had done their best to relieve the tedium of Robyn being stuck in a hospital bed under observation, Dr Jamieson had stuck to her word and had told her that she would be kept in for just one more day. Robyn would be discharged on the 30th of December, as promised. As far as Robyn was concerned, it couldn't come soon enough.

She still had no money, not in terms of cash in her purse, although she was hoping there was some money in her bank account. That wasn't the only thing worrying her; she had no idea where she was going to go. But she was doing her best to look on the bright side; at least she'd be walking out of there and not being carried out in a box. If that thought didn't lift her spirits, nothing would.

Robyn plucked another tissue from the large box sitting on her lap and extended her arm. 'Here,' she said softly to Gayle as she passed her the tissue.

Gayle looked up through tearful eyes, sniffled a thank you and took the tissue. She dropped the sodden tissue in her hand into the wastepaper basket, which was by now overflowing.

'Look at me. Aren't I just the big fool?' she sniffed.

Gayle's father had passed away peacefully in the night. It had not been a surprise to anyone; he had been well into his eighties and suffering with a plethora of health issues. Although Gayle acknowledged that it was a relief, she was understandably still heartbroken. There was never a right time to lose a member of your family, Robyn thought as she slowly started to pull out another tissue in readiness.

Then she had a terrible thought; she had no idea who her own parents were or whether they were alive or dead. She was beginning to feel a lot less enthusiastic about leaving the hospital. She had no idea what she was going to find out once she left. Suddenly she didn't feel ready – not at all.

Robyn handed Gayle another tissue.

'I really shouldn't be bothering you like this,' said Gayle, blowing her nose. The flow of tears was ebbing and the passing of tissues was slowing.

Robyn tutted. 'Don't be silly. What are friends for?'

Gayle wiped her eyes. 'That's a lovely thing to say, us being friends, because I don't know another soul in town. Well, apart from Mother, and she's, you know …'

Robyn had seen Gayle's mother wandering past the door, a dreamy smile on her face, singing while her husband was dying. She was oblivious to his passing. It was very sad that Gayle couldn't share her grief with her mother, but she said she was glad of it; her mother and father hadn't been apart for fifty years, and Gayle hoped she remained unaware that he had gone.

'Oh, I assumed you were from around here.' Robyn realised she'd made an assumption, especially as Gayle seemed to know of David Gillespie's past as an ice hockey star.

Gayle wiped her nose and shook her head. 'I am. I grew up here, but I wanted to move way to see the world. Familiar story.'

'And did you?' Robyn leaned forward.

'Move away? Yes. See the world?' She chuckled. 'Not exactly.' I got as far as London, then I met someone. And my dreams were put on hold. You know how it is.'

No, Robyn didn't – at least she didn't think so. Robyn was just about to ask Gayle a bit more about her life in London, and the *someone* she'd met there, when she saw the nurse appear at the door.

'Well, aren't you popular today?' said the nurse. 'You've got more visitors.'

'I have?' Robyn said excitedly, looking at Gayle. 'Do you mean that David has come today too?' So far, Gayle and David seemed to have visited her in shifts. It hadn't been intentional; it was just the way the days had turned out. David visiting in the evenings, and Gayle visited during the day.

The nurse shook her head. 'No, it isn't David.'

Robyn sat up straighter in bed, staring at the open door, waiting to see who it was. She couldn't wait to find out who had come to see her. Her parents, perhaps, or her siblings. Robyn glanced at the newspaper that still lay forlornly in the corner of the room by the door where she had thrown it the previous evening. Someone must have recognised her name after all.

Gayle said, 'Robyn, is it your family, do you think? Would you like me to leave now?'

Robyn was just shaking her head at her new friend, about to tell her she wanted her to stay, when she heard someone call her name.'

'Miss Parker?'

'Yes?' She looked over at a portly older gentleman who was

standing in the doorway. She recognised his uniform immediately: black t-shirt, dark trousers, and a high-viz yellow and silver tabard that she knew would have the word *Police* written on the back. He was holding a police cap in his hands.

Her chin dropped to her chest. She had thought it might be her family. Was she in trouble? Robyn didn't dare ask.

'I'm sorry to bother you, ma'am.' He lingered in the doorway. 'The doctor said you were well enough for us to see you now.' Robyn looked up. She'd had no idea that the police were going to pay her a visit, although she imagined it was routine after a car accident – at least she hoped it was.

Robyn caught the officer looking Gayle's way.

'My friend stays,' Roby said, then looked at Gayle. 'If that's alright with you?'

Gayle nodded and reached for her hand. 'Of course it is, sweetheart.'

Robyn felt like she was a fugitive from the law. But she had no reason to feel that way. She had done nothing wrong. At least she hoped she hadn't, because she wasn't sure of anything. That was the problem with the blasted memory issue. At least Gayle's presence made her feel reassured that she had friends in her corner.

'This won't take long,' said the officer as he entered the room and closed the door behind him. 'The doctor has informed me of your condition.'

'Oh.' Robyn looked at Gayle. She couldn't very well tell her to leave now she had invited her to stay. Besides, maybe Dr Jamieson was right: it would be far easier in the long run to tell her friends the truth about her selective amnesia.

The officer stood at the end of her bed. 'I understand you have amnesia. Can you tell me if there's anything you *can* remember about the accident?'

Robyn opened her mouth to speak, but the officer held up his hand. 'Could you hold on for a minute? I nearly forgot something.' He placed his hat on the end of her bed and started tapping his trouser pockets. 'Ah here we are.' He produced a small notepad and flipped it open. 'Now, where were we?'

'I think you were asking me what I remember.'

'That's right, that's right. Thank you.'

'Well all I do remem—' she stopped when he held up his hand. 'You wouldn't have a pencil handy?'

Robyn shrugged and cast a glance at Gayle, who was already opening her handbag. She brought out a diary. She picked at the spine with her fingernail and a small thin pencil popped up. She got up and handed it to the officer. When she turned back to Robyn, she rolled her eyes before taking her seat. Robyn smiled at her, although she wasn't really amused. This was going to take all afternoon.

The tiny pencil disappeared in the officer's chubby fingers. 'Right, where were we?' He licked the pencil tip, for what reason Robyn couldn't fathom. 'Oh yes.' He answered before anyone else could respond. 'You were going to tell me what you remember of the accident.'

Robyn stared at him. His hand hovered over the notepad as though he were a scribe waiting for divine inspiration. She thought that a toga wouldn't have been out of place either. Robyn caught Gayle's expression and wished she hadn't. She had the impulse to laugh. Instead, she reached over for the beaker of water on the side table and took one large gulp. It would not do to laugh at the police officer.

'I remember the aftermath of the accident.' Robyn wished she could remember what had led up to it, or even driving the car. But there was nothing – no recall, no memories before waking up after the accident.

Recalling how she had come to be there, who she was, and why she'd been out on the road on the afternoon of Christmas Day, when most other people were at home with their families, was still a mystery. She had thought that by now, someone who knew her would have come forward.

She looked at the officer hopefully. It occurred to her that perhaps someone had contacted the police, reporting a missing person. Maybe he would tell her after she'd answered his questions.

She told the officer, 'I remember David, Mr Gillespie, talking to me, asking my name over and over.' That wasn't all she remembered in the aftermath of the accident. She had woken up and had lifted her head from the steering wheel. Her forehead had felt wet. She'd realised afterwards that it was blood. When she'd turned her head to look out of the driver's side window, there had been a man, soaking from the sleet and snow, with blood on his face, banging on her window.

She had been frightened. She'd attempted to start the engine, pumping the gas in desperation for the car to start; to be able to get away. She'd stolen a glance at the lunatic outside the car. He had been even more frantic than before, waving his arms like a mad man, and this had made Robyn even more determined to get the car going. But as the engine had started sputtering to life, she'd got the shock of her life. The mad man had been running towards her at full pelt with something in his hand, held high above his head. As he had come closer, Robyn had thrown herself across the passenger seat. Something had been hurled at her side window, and the shattered glass had sprayed over her.

The door had opened, and she had been dragged, kicking and screaming, back over the driver's seat and out of the car. She was sure she had got some good right hooks into his ribs. Then she had realised he was lying next to her, very still. Only then had she stopped and looked back at her car to see the front wheels dangling over a precipice. The last thing she remembered was a huge crashing sound and then a smell of smoke.

'He saved me, and that's all I can remember.' Robyn looked away, embarrassed. She was not going to tell the officer what a fool she'd been, mistaking David's intentions when all he had been trying to do was save her from going over the cliff in her car. She was very surprised that David came to see her so religiously after the way she had treated her rescuer. But he had never made fun of her for behaving like a fool and, much to her relief, they had never spoken of the accident – not once.

The officer stopped writing. The one sentence didn't take him long. Robyn expected a barrage of further questions about why she had been travelling in such awful conditions – the road conditions had been very poor with the snowfall. But to her surprise, he just flipped his notebook shut. 'There. I told you it wouldn't take long.' He handed Gayle her pencil.

'What happens now?' said Gayle as she took the pencil.

'That's a good question. Now, let me see.' He took a moment to think about it while Robyn and Gayle stared at him. 'I'll go back to the station and write up a report from what you've told me.'

'What's it going to say, this report?' Robyn asked.

'It was an accident. I imagine that not being from around these parts, you got lost as the weather closed in.' He paused. 'You know, you were one lucky lady. If it wasn't for David, you'd most likely be at the bottom of that quarry, and I'd be seeing the coroner. And between you and me,' said the officer, pointing his little notepad at her, 'I'd rather see your pretty face than his any day of the week.'

Robyn could feel the colour rising in her cheeks. It had only just occurred to her that the officer must already have spoken with David about what had happened. She really hoped he'd left out the part where she'd attacked him, although she'd clearly been confused and concussed at the time.

He tucked the notepad back into the jacket pocket and picked up his hat from the bed.

'This is why I joined the force.'

'To get to the bottom of difficult cases such as this one?' Gayle said innocently.

Robyn turned wide eyes on Gayle. Was she seriously taking the mickey right now? She marvelled at her audacity.

'Well, kind of,' he said seriously. 'But really I like the uniform; especially my hat. I think I look good in it – don't you?' He looked from Robyn to Gayle for approval.

They nodded, both lost for words.

'Thought so.' He said with satisfaction.

'Is he for real?' Gayle whispered as he busied himself putting the notebook back in his trouser pocket.

Robyn sighed. She hoped he was. Although it occurred to her that perhaps he was the one taking the mickey. All the same, she was relieved that she was leaving the hospital the next day just in case he wasn't a real officer and was just some kind of reporter, and the real cops would come to grill her even further.

He looked up, but he didn't appear to have heard Gayle's comment. 'This is my second career. I've just got through my probationary period. I wanted to do something with the rest of my life that makes me feel I'm making a difference, at least until I have to retire from this job in a few years.'

Robyn looked at him sheepishly, wondering if he *had* overheard.

He left the room.

'Have you really got amnesia?'

Robyn sighed. Gayle finally asked what Robyn had been expecting.

'Uh-huh.' Robyn really didn't want to talk about it.

'Can't you remember *anything*?'

Robyn shook her head and held back the tears. 'Nothing before the accident.'

'But you remembered your name?'

Robyn shook her head. 'Not exactly. There were some letters addressed to me in the car.'

'Oh.'

'So, those letters. Who are they from?'

'My mum. From the letters, I gather she's abroad.'

'Oh dear. It's times like these you could do with your mum. You could get in touch. I'm sure she'll fly back.'

'That would be a good idea if I had her mobile number, or I even knew where she was.'

'But the letters …?'

'They were dated a while ago. She could be anywhere now.'

'Oh dear.'

They sat looking at one another until Gayle broke the silence. 'What happens tomorrow, when you leave hospital?'

Robyn sighed. 'I don't know.'

'Where will you go?'

'I said I don't know!' Robyn said, then hastily retreated from her outburst. 'I'm sorry, Gayle. I didn't mean to be rude. I just don't know anything except these four walls.' She turned to Gayle. 'I feel scared.'

Gayle got up and sat on the side of her bed. She patted Robyn's hand. 'I've got a wild idea.' She chuckled, and Robyn couldn't help but smile.

15

Robyn was awake before it was light, waiting for the trundle of the breakfast trolley coming down the corridor. After breakfast, it wasn't Gayle who appeared at the door as she'd expected, but David.

'You're dressed.' He leaned on the doorframe and folded his arms. 'Well, I guess I had to see you fully clothed one of these days.'

Robyn threw a pillow at him.

He caught the pillow. 'What was that for?'

She glanced at him sideways.

'I know my jokes are pretty awful.' He walked in and placed the pillow back on the bed before joining her at the window. 'Looking forward to getting out?'

'In a way.' Robyn said, staring out of the window at the hospital car park below. 'But I guess you know how that feels.'

'Pardon?'

'I saw the newspaper article about my accident.' Robyn pointed her thumb over her shoulder at the newspaper lying on the side table.

'What article?'

Robyn looked at him. 'You haven't seen it?'

He shook his head and walked over to the side table. He picked up the newspaper. It was already folded at the article. He started to read, then grimaced and slowly sat down on the bed. 'I told him not to speak to reporters,' he said, not looking up.

Robyn didn't ask who David was referring to. His demeanour spoke volumes – he wasn't pleased.

She turned to look out of the window once more while he finished the article in silence. She heard the creak of the bed and looked around as David got up, his eyes still fixed on the newspaper in his hand.

'I hadn't realised it had been so serious.' She'd assumed he'd spoken to reporters and got his name into print as the local hero. 'The article *is* mostly about you.'

'I can see that,' he said sulkily. 'My father must have spoken to a reporter. He still wants everyone to know I was a famous ice hockey player.' He tossed the paper on the bed. Robyn guessed that David didn't want his life history in print for everyone to see. She could empathise with that.

'Why didn't you tell me that you were—'

'Famous?'

'An ice hockey player?' She nervously shifted her weight from one foot to the other. David's mood had changed since reading the article. She wished that she had never mentioned it.

He joined her at the window. 'It has been really refreshing to meet someone who doesn't know about my past – the fame, the money.' He glanced at Robyn. 'But I don't suppose you'd know how that feels.'

Robyn shook her head, which to David meant *no*, she wasn't famous, but to Robyn meant she didn't actually know either way.

She imagined that if she were famous, then people would have been beating a path to her door and she wouldn't have been sitting there, all alone except for her two visitors.

David stared silently out of the window. He turned to Robyn. 'That's what I like about you. You haven't given me your history, and so I felt I didn't have to give mine back.'

'I'm sorry. I know it's none of my business.'

He smiled. 'It's not your fault that my life history was printed in that article. I told my father that I didn't want him to speak to reporters about it. But, as usual, what I think is not important to him.' His smile faded. He turned back to the window. So did Robyn.

She wasn't sure what to say next. It was difficult at times to hold a conversation with David. Before Gayle had given her the article to read, she'd already got a feeling that just as she wouldn't talk about her past, he steered clear of his past too.

She decided to avoid the subject of his past. She didn't want to lose his friendship. David and Gayle were the only people she knew right now. If her own family appeared, she wouldn't even recognise them.

David broke the silence, pointing out of the window. 'See that old van?' He pointed to a grey, weather-beaten, rusty van parked below her window. 'She's a beauty – isn't she?' David grinned. He was being sarcastic. 'I can't believe my father still does deliveries in that thing. It should be in a museum. I'm afraid that's all the wheels I've got at the moment.'

Before Robyn could apologise for his wrecked car, he added, 'But I'd rather have you standing here today than have a fancy sports car.'

Robyn managed a weak smile.

Besides,' he paused, 'that sports car doesn't really fit my new image.'

'What are you talking about?' asked Robyn.

'Delivery boy extraordinaire.' He bowed. 'My father was always complaining he couldn't find someone responsible who he could rely on to make the grocery deliveries.'

'And you're that person?' said Robyn, quite surprised by his relaxed attitude to going from the dizzy heights of being a sports star with a sports car to delivering groceries in his father's rusty van.

'Not exactly. I think he may be a little put out when he finds out his delivery boy has been spending most of his time delivering flowers and magazines here.'

Robyn blushed.

'Anyway, I know it's a piece of junk, but it will get us from A to B. So where can I take you?'

Robyn caught sight of another old vehicle turning into the car park, although this was a car in mint condition. Robyn watched as the door opened. A woman seemed to be having difficulty getting out. When she did, the tight blue jeans and heeled sandals were unmistakable.

She grinned and turned to David. 'Actually, Gayle arranged to pick me up today. She's just arrived.'

'Right.' David looked disappointed as he glanced out of the window. 'Did you just say Gayle?'

'Gayle Belafonte – do you know her?' Robyn asked, wondering whether, in a small town such as Aviemore, everybody knew everybody else.

'No, I don't. Where's she from?'

'Here. Um, not the hospital, obviously, although the time she's been spending here, visiting her father, she might as well have been. Her father was next door. It's how I got to know her.' Robyn's eyes roved to the television set. 'Apparently, she lives on the other side of town. She returned to the area to look after her parents and apparently she's got a room to spare,' Robyn said excitedly.

'You're staying in town?' David said, surprised. 'How long for?'

Robyn shrugged her shoulders. 'I don't really know.'

'Don't you want to go home, to see your folks?'

Robyn looked at her shoes. She could see this was where things could get complicated if she didn't come clean about her condition. However, she recalled what Dr Jamieson had said; something would trigger her memory – a familiar face, a place, her belongings. She'd mentioned there had been some letters amongst her belongings that the police had found, along with her ID, in the car. Her memory could just click into place like Dr Jamieson had said. She looked sheepishly at David. Why did she have to tell him about her memory problems? Especially if there was some psychological rather than physical reason. She didn't want him to feel sorry for her, or think she was crazy.

'You never said where you were from,' David continued.

Robyn turned from the window and fussed around the bed, picking up magazines and putting them in a neat pile, trying to look busy while she waited for Gayle. How was she going to answer that question? She could just lie; say the first town that came into her head. But she didn't want to lie to David. Robyn frowned. She knew she wasn't exactly being truthful by not telling him she'd lost her memory.

Robyn tried to make light of the situation. 'Why the sudden interest? Is this the same David Gillespie who said that what you like about me is that I don't talk about my past, so you don't feel you have to talk about yours?'

David held up his hands, 'OK. You got me.' He smiled at Robyn. 'Can I ask where this Gayle lives just in case I may have a delivery?'

'I don't know. I'll have to ask her.' Robyn hunched her shoulders. 'I don't even know if Gayle has her groceries delivered or even shops at your father's shop. For all I know, she could shop at the local supermarket – if there is one.' Robyn knew that wasn't very helpful. She finished her sentence and wondered why David was staring at her.

David smiled. 'Actually, what I meant was that I might have a delivery for *you*.'

'For me? But I haven't even been to your father's shop. I wouldn't know what—'

David interrupted her. 'These women's magazines keep appearing in my van. Being a responsible employee, I have to deliver them to somebody. So I need your help because if I can't deliver them to you, then this delivery boy is going to get mighty depressed not being able to properly fulfil his job requirements.'

Robyn stood there, open-mouthed. She didn't realise the job meant that much to him. Then she saw the side of his mouth twitch and he started to laugh.

'Oh, very funny.' Robyn smiled too.

'So, how about that address?'

'What address?'

Robyn turned at the sound of Gayle's voice. She stood in the doorway, staring at David with a look on her face that said, *Is this guy bothering you?*

'Oh, Gayle. Meet David Gillespie.'

Gayle's face erupted into a massive smile. 'Hey, I thought I recognised you.' Her eyes flickered to the discarded newspaper on the bed. 'You're the knight in shining armour.' She pointed at David as she stepped into the room.

'I'm what?' David said, looking at Robyn in confusion.

Robyn whispered, 'It's nothing.' She did not want to broadcast the fact that Gayle had also read the article.

'I want to shake your hand.' Gayle reached out and took his hand, shaking it enthusiastically.

David smiled weakly at Gayle, then glanced at Robyn. He was still looking confused.

'That was a very brave thing to do, rescuing Robyn.' Gayle pumped his hand.

Robyn cast her eyes up, praying that Gayle wasn't going to mention the newspaper article.

He mumbled, 'It's nothing, really.'

'Nothing?' Gayle said indignantly, glancing at Robyn, who was staring back at her and trying to put across a telepathic message to let things be. She caught Robyn's expression and let go of David's hand without another word.

He looked relieved to get his hand back. Or was it the fact that Gayle had dropped the conversation?

'Are you ready to get out of here?' Gayle said to Robyn.

'Oh, yes.' Robyn nodded her head enthusiastically and walked to the door, dodging a wheelchair that had appeared in the doorway.

'What's this?' Robyn said to the nurse, watching her wheel it right into the room.

'This,' she said, tapping the handles, 'is hospital policy.' She held up an authoritative finger. 'And before you protest, I've heard it all before, so how about not wasting your breath, or my time, and just get in the chair.'

Robyn looked from David to Gayle. They both shrugged. Nobody was going to come to her rescue this time – not when they had a surly nurse to contend with. Robyn slowly sat in the chair without saying a word. 'Oh, my magazines!' She attempted to get up, but felt a firm hand on her shoulder pressing her back down into the seat.

"I'll get them,' Gayle offered.

David asked, 'Is it hospital policy for the nurse to push the chair?'

'No, but I don't see …'

'Good.' David crossed the room. 'I'm driving.'

Robyn twisted in the chair to see David standing beside the nurse, staring at her intently. The nurse lifted her hands off the handles.

'Thank you.' David grasped the opportunity, and the handles, and winked at Robyn.

Robyn turned back in her seat with a satisfied grin on her face. If she had to be wheeled out of the place, at least she didn't have to see that surly nurse anymore.

Gayle started placing the pile of magazines on Robyn's lap.

'I don't think you should put the magazines …' the nurse began but stopped when she caught the three of them staring at her.

'Have it your way,' she conceded.

'Yes we will,' said Gayle, placing the last of the magazines on Robyn's lap.

'Right. Are we ready to boogie?' David turned the wheelchair left and right very quickly before rearing it up like a horse, much to the nurse's frantic protests. 'And off we go.'

Robyn was spun out of her room and down the hallway at break-neck speed. Gayle was jogging alongside, falling back, then catching up, this time holding her high-heeled sandals in her hands. The nurse disappeared altogether.

Robyn twisted in her seat to see her standing in the middle of the wide corridor, her hands on her hips and a look of thunder on her face. By the time they reached the entrance – amazingly without any collisions – all three were laughing hysterically.

'I can't remember the last time I had so much fun!' exclaimed Robyn as she got out of the chair, her smile fading when she realised what she'd just said. She had only meant it as a figure of speech, but even so, it brought home her situation. Just for a brief moment, she'd quite happily forgotten all about it.

With the magazines balanced precariously in her arms, she walked to the double doors. She couldn't wait to get outside and breathe in the fresh air. The doors slid open, and she stepped out into the morning sunlight. A biting wind slapped her face and she shuddered. But even the warm hospital climate wouldn't entice her to step back inside. She looked back through the doors to where Gayle and David were still standing, catching their breath. Robyn felt cold. She hugged her magazines and motioned to them to get outside. She saw the surly nurse approaching, and waved more frantically.

David saw her too, and they were out within seconds. He took off his coat and gently placed it around Robyn's shoulders. Behind him, Robyn could see Gayle smiling approvingly at Robyn's knight in shining armour.

Robyn turned to David, who was trying to wrestle the magazines out of her hands. 'I am not an invalid,' she said crossly.

'Let me just take a few off the top then.'

Robyn lifted her hand from the top of the pile and David whisked away over half of them, making her load a lot lighter.

Gayle walked past them, leading the way to the parked cars.

'Look – you've parked right next to each other,' Robyn observed, looking from Gayle, who was grimacing at the rust-bucket, to David, who was admiring Gayle's fancy Bentley. Robyn smiled when she saw him stroking the bonnet.

Gayle slapped his hand away. 'Keep your paws off.'

'She's a beauty. How much?'

'What do you mean *how much?*' said Gayle as she opened the front passenger door. She waited for Robyn to climb in, then shut it.

'The car. How much would you sell her for?'

'For one thing,' Gayle opened the driver's door, 'this car has had one careful lady owner all its life.' She emphasised the word *lady*. 'And another thing …' she continued as she got into the seat next to Robyn and closed the door.

David's head appeared and he tapped on the window.

Gayle tutted and wound the window down.

'What is the other thing?' David rested his hand on the window ledge, and looked at Gayle.

Gayles raised her eyebrows.

David removed his hand.

'If she *were* for sale, which,' she lifted her finger, 'she isn't – you couldn't afford her.' She pointed at David's excuse for four wheels.

'Oh, I see.' He paused. 'You know, appearances can be deceptive.'

Robyn grimaced and thought of the photo of David's squashed-up sports car in the paper that she'd had the run-in with.

Unfortunately, his little sports car had rather taken the brunt of the accident. It was just a miracle he'd walked away virtually unscathed.

'You'll tell me if she is ever for sale?'

'Sure I'll tell you, but it still doesn't mean you'd be able to afford her.'

'Good.' David replied in a more serious tone.

Gayle started the engine.

'Wait, Gayle. David, your coat.' She struggled to take it off.

'It's all right. I'll come and collect it,' he said loudly so he could be heard over the roar of the old engine, 'on one of my deliveries.'

'His deliveries?' Gayle glanced at Robyn.

'The magazines.'

'Oh, I *see*.' Gayle said drawing out the last word. 'I assumed he'd just brought them as an excuse to visit you in hospital. I guess his visits are not going to stop any time soon.' She chuckled, and said under her breath, 'Young love!'

Robyn pretended that she hadn't heard. She waved to David as Gayle manoeuvred the car out of the parking space and headed for the exit. 'Oh, no!' Robyn exclaimed. 'Stop the car!'

'What is it?' Gayle said, alarmed. She slammed on the brakes.

'I forgot to give David your address.'

'Well, you know what that means, don't you?' Gayle said.

'No – what?' Robyn had twisted in her seat and was looking out of the small rear window, but she couldn't see the old grey van anywhere amid the sea of cars in the large car park.

'It means that David is going to think you forgot on purpose because you don't really want to see him.'

'Really?' Robyn turned back in her seat and looked miserably out of the window.

'No, I'm only joking. Now, don't you worry. He'll find you. And do you know why I know this for a fact?' Gayle said mysteriously.

'No – why?' Robyn asked, perching in her seat and staring intently at Gayle, anticipating her answer: *because he likes you.* She knew this, but she rather wanted to hear it all the same.

'Because you, my dear girl, are wearing his coat.'

'Oh, of course.' Robyn rolled her eyes and looked down at the coat as if it had magically appeared and had not been there the whole time.

'And he likes you,' Gayle added. 'But then I don't think you need me to tell you that.'

Robyn smiled at Gayle.

'I didn't think so.' Gayle smiled as she turned from Robyn and looked at the road ahead.

'Can we visit the town later so I can catch David at work?'

'You know, I was sure I recognised that old van,' Gayle mused. 'It used to deliver our groceries way back when.'

'Way back when?'

'When I was a kid, right up until leaving home. I'll have to ask Mother if she still gets her groceries delivered from Gillespie's. That's if she can remember – she barely recalls what day of the week it is now.'

'David works for his father now.'

'I used to see a little lad in the pickup with Mr Gillespie.'

'Maybe it was David, helping his father.' Robyn said, delighted at the thought that perhaps everybody did know almost everybody else in small towns. *But does anybody else know me?* she wondered.

16

They drove down a wide, tree-lined street. Robyn could see that ahead it was a no-through road, the street ending at a clearing in a forest of pines. They passed imposing detached houses that were clearly very old, all set back from the road. No two properties were alike; they had obviously been individually built by wealthy families who must have employed their own architects to build their grand homes – or perhaps second homes. She caught glimpses of them down their long drives.

'The houses here are amazing.'

Gayle nodded. 'It's a lovely leafy street, isn't it? These houses were all built in the Scottish Baronial style, apparently. At least that's what my parents told me. Hence the abundance of turrets and gables you can see.'

Robyn couldn't wait to arrive at Gayle's family home. She'd had no idea she would be invited to stay in such a wonderful street, with large, opulent houses that reminded her of historic mansions or country estates.

Robyn raised her eyebrows, wondering why these grand houses would remind her of mansions and country estates – after all, she doubted she was rich and had ever lived in one. Robyn guessed she'd probably seen the like in a glossy magazine.

They reached the end of the street and the car swerved unexpectedly to the left through an almost indiscernible gap in a high, overgrown hedge. Robyn looked at Gayle. She couldn't see a house from there – in fact, she'd thought they had passed all the houses in the street.

'Bet you wondered where I was headed,' Gayle said, winking at Robyn as she slowly made her way up the drive. Either side of the drive, which was overgrown with weeds, was the lawn, which was overgrown too with weeds and wildflowers.

Robyn gaped, speechless, at the house that came into view.

Gayle parked the car on the gravel driveway outside the house.

'It's beautiful!' Robyn cooed.

'What, this old wreck?' Gayle switched the engine off and turned to Robyn. 'You're just being kind.'

Robyn turned quickly to Gayle. 'No, I mean it. It's a lovely house.'

'Maybe once upon a time, but I think it's seen better days, don't you?' Gayle said, getting out of the car.

Robyn sat for a moment, admiring the house. Yes, it had seen better days. It was certainly in need of some updating. The gorgeous yellow stone brickwork had mellowed with age, making the striking house look distinguished, like a gentleman's residence from another era, but the peeling paint on the window frames, which were down to bare wood in places, really let it down. Shutters hung forlornly on broken hinges, and some of the windowpanes were so dirty that they looked like someone had forgotten to remove the blackout curtains from World War Two. She noticed that one of the windowpanes even had a large crack in the glass. But she could see through all that to the grand residence it must once have been.

Robyn quickly got out of the car. 'I love it, Gayle, truly.'

'You do?' said Gayle warily, raising her eyebrows.

When Robyn could tear her eyes away from the house, she reached into the car for her magazines and followed Gayle, who was waiting for her by the front door with a suitcase. That reminded Robyn of what she had to do. 'I need to go to the police station to collect my stuff.'

Gayle gave her a quizzical look. 'You aren't fooling, are you?'

Robyn didn't understand.

'You really have got amnesia.' Gayle said flatly, lifting up the old case.

Robyn looked at it. 'That's mine?'

Gayle nodded. 'I stopped off at the police station this morning, when I was on the way to collect you. Where do you think those clothes came from?'

Robyn looked down at the clothes she was wearing. 'I thought they were yours.'

'How did you figure that? Do I look like I'd wear those sorts of clothes?'

Robyn stared at Gayle in her jeans and colourful blouse, which were so unlike her own black jeans, t-shirt and sweatshirt. 'So, if you stopped off to collect my things on the way here, where did this outfit come from?'

Gayle shook her head. 'Oh, Robyn. I can see this is going to be rather tiresome. Not your fault, though – obviously. It's the blow to the head.'

Robyn gingerly touched the bandage at the mention of a blow to the head. 'What do you mean?'

'That was the outfit you were wearing when you had the

accident. I took the clothes home and laundered them. Fortunately, they weren't torn in the accident.'

'Oh, I see,' Robyn said, embarrassed. 'Look, I can stay in the bed-and-breakfast in town if this isn't going to work out.'

'No, absolutely not. You're staying here, and that's that.'

Robyn offered up a wisp of a smile. 'All right. As long as you're sure …'

'Of course I'm sure. Now, let's get you and your suitcase inside.'

Robyn eyed the suitcase in Gayle's hands suspiciously. Hadn't Dr Jamieson said that her memory would click into place at the sight of familiar things? Since it hadn't worked with her luggage, Robyn guessed it would take something more significant, like familiar surroundings, perhaps, or a familiar photo.

Gayle trudged up the steps leading to the front door. She stopped when she realised Robyn wasn't following. She turned around. 'Are you sure you still want to stay here? I know it must be a bit of a shock seeing the state of the place compared to the neighbouring properties.' Gayle pointed the old, tattered suitcase at the house. 'You're having second thoughts about staying here.'

'No, not at all. I want to stay,' Robyn said, enthusiastically striding up the steps with the heavy magazines as she caught up with Gayle.

'Didn't the doctor say you've got to take it easy for a while?' Gayle admonished. She put the case down by the door and took some magazines out of Robyn's arms as she said conversationally, 'This was the first house in the street to be built, you know.'

'Really?' Robyn said, turning slowly around on the spot to take a closer look at the house.

'And it used to be the grandest,' Gayle said, standing beside

Robyn, 'I guess it's a bit like those new houses they build, where they make the first just a bit larger and roomier and grander to encourage people to buy one of the others that will be built.'

'Like a show home,' Robyn said, watching Gayle put the key in the large wooden door.

'That's right.' She opened the door. She shook her head. 'They don't make them like this anymore. No two houses in this street are the same, you know.'

Robyn had noticed.

'They are all individually designed,' Gayle said with satisfaction as they stepped inside. 'Mother?' she called as she closed the front door.

Robyn watched Gayle walk up a wide spiral staircase as she called for her mother. The old stairs were fitted with a very worn patterned carpet that lay in a strip in the centre, leaving the rest of the wooden stair treads exposed.

'It looks like something out of *Gone with the Wind*,' Robyn exclaimed in delight. 'It's like stepping into an old movie set.'

Robyn deposited the rest of the magazines in her arms on the pile Gayle had left on a large mahogany sideboard. She ran over to the stairs, skipped up two, turned, and said passionately, *'Where shall I go? What shall I do?'*

Then she turned around and deepened her voice. *'Frankly, my dear, I don't give a damn.'* She giggled hysterically.

'You'd make a terrible actor,' Gayle chuckled over the landing banister.

Robyn skipped up the stairs towards her.

Gayle stood there with her mobile phone to hand. 'That's odd. Everyone remembers that iconic line from Rhett Butler in *Gone with the Wind*. But I bet very few people can quote what the character Scarlett O'Hara said to warrant that response. I had to Google it to check.' Gayle stared at Robyn. 'How on earth did you know that?'

Robyn said, 'Wait a minute. I couldn't remember anything since before the accident. But I remembered that old movie.' Her eyes went wide. 'You know what that means?'

Gayle grinned. 'I think so.'

'My memory must be coming back! It's weird. It was those stairs.' Robyn turned around and cast her gaze down the stairs. 'They must have triggered something …'

'Okay,' Gayle said slowly. 'Can you remember anything else?'

Robyn furrowed her brow, holding her breath, trying to concentrate really hard. Finally, she let out a deflated breath. Her shoulders sagged as she turned to look at Gayle. 'Nope, nothing.'

'Well, give it time.'

Robyn frowned. That was what the doctor had said.

She followed Gayle down the hallway. 'That's odd,' she said.

'What is?' said Gayle as she humped Robyn's case down the long, dark, wooden hallway.

Robyn followed after her. 'David was talking about some movie showing at the local cinema.'

'Trying to ask you for a date,' Gayle chirped knowingly over her shoulder.

Robyn stopped. That hadn't occurred to her. 'Anyway,' she continued, 'apparently it was a digitally re-mastered version that they were showing. He seemed a bit surprised that I couldn't recall having seen it before. In fact, I've never heard of it.'

'Well, we're not all into the same kinds of movies, are we?' Gayle said matter-of-factly. 'What was the name of the film, anyway?'

'I think he said it was *Star Wars*.' Robyn shook her head, unsure.

'Ah.' Gayle stopped abruptly, turning to face Robyn. 'Darth Vader, Obi-Wan Kenobi, R2-D2, C-3PO.' She gazed at Robyn. 'Ring any bells?'

'What are you on about?' Robyn didn't understand Gayle's strange litany of words. 'I take it,' she said, looking at Gayle's expression, 'that this *Star Wars* is quite a well-known movie.'

'You could say that.' Gayle smirked. 'But not any more well-known than the movie you remembered.' She opened a bedroom door and walked in.

'I remembered,' Robyn said slowly, standing in the doorway. 'I really remembered something!' she said excitedly.

Gayle put her suitcase on the bed.

'But why that old movie?' Robyn said, confused.

Gayle shrugged. 'I'm afraid I can't help you there.' She suddenly stopped, staring at Robyn, wide-eyed. 'Wait a minute. I forgot that there's something of yours I haven't given you.'

Robyn looked at the suitcase. 'There's something else?'

Gayle said, 'Wait here.'

Robyn watched her run out of the room. She walked over to the window. She looked down at the overgrown front garden and caught Gayle opening the car door and leaning inside. She couldn't see what her friend was collecting from the car. Gayle slammed the car door shut and disappeared back to the house before appearing in the bedroom doorway with a handful of letters.

'Here, this is your bag.'

Robyn looked at the rucksack that Gayle had brought in from the car. Unfortunately, she didn't recognise the bag either.

'And these are addressed to you. The desk sergeant at the police station handed them to me when I collected your luggage.

I didn't want to open your suitcase, so I put them in the glove compartment for safekeeping instead. Then I forgot about them. Sorry.'

Robyn recalled that the doctor had mentioned some letters from her mother that the police had found in the car. Some were unopened, so the police had obviously noted who they were from. Dr Jamieson had suggested they might jog her memory.

Robyn took the letters, her hand shaking as she quickly read a couple of the short notes. Her fears were not unfounded. Her mind remained a blank – she couldn't even picture her own mother, who had apparently written the letters.

'Are you okay?' Gayle asked.

Robyn looked up. 'According to these letters, my mum is travelling abroad.'

'On business?'

'I don't know.' She glanced at the unopened letters, wondering if they'd shed light on why she was out of the country.

'There was this too,' Gayle said, handing her a note. 'It's from the police.'

'Oh.' Robyn looked at her anxiously.

'It's nothing to worry about. They understand you've got some memory problems as a result of your injury, so they wrote down your address.'

'They did?' Robyn had wanted to ask the police officer when he'd visited the hospital, but the thought that she might be in some kind of trouble had held her back. Until her memory came back, she didn't want the police delving into her or her past.

Robyn took the note and frowned. 'Oh. I thought it would be my home address.'

'Well, at least you know one thing.'

'What's that?'

'You're a student at university.'

'A mature student,' said Robyn, wondering what she had been doing with her life after her A-Levels and before she'd started university. Most people graduated when they were twenty-one, but according to the police, who had identified her through the car registration, she was twenty-one, and by the sound of it still a student. Perhaps something had happened, and she'd dropped out for a bit or had taken a gap year. Was that something that deep down she knew, or was she just guessing?

Robyn sighed. She suddenly felt so tired. She agreed with Gayle's sentiments; this memory thing was getting really tiresome.

Gayle said, 'I hope the room is okay. It's a bit ... dated, I'm afraid.'

'Don't be silly. It's ... great.' Robyn smiled for Gayle's sake as she looked around the dark, musty room. *Beggars can't be choosers*, she thought. She obviously had student accommodation, but she didn't know if she paid all year round or was expected to vacate it over the holidays. The fact that she had a suitcase with her suggested she might have been on her way home. But the question was still there – why so late on Christmas Day? Surely, she would have left university days earlier, when the term finished.

She stared around the room, wishing she hadn't left her magazines downstairs and thinking that having them lying around would brighten up the room a little.

Gayle must have caught her expression. 'If you don't like the room, there are others down the hall. Just take your pick. But I'm afraid they're all pretty much like this one.'

Old-fashioned, dark and musty, Robyn thought. But the place was growing on Robyn. It had character. And it wasn't hospital.

'Robyn?'

Robyn was twirling around, taking in the room, the high ceiling with its ornate coving, the worn cream wallpaper with a delicate green flowered print, and the large cast iron fireplace in which she imagined servants had once lit the fire each evening for the master and mistress of the house, or their guests – if this had been a guest bedroom.

'It's great – really.' Robyn had a question. 'How many bedrooms are there in this house?'

'Oh, goodness. There are six bedrooms. Far too many for just me and Mum now.'

Robyn nodded.

Gayle pointed at the letters. 'So, nothing jogs your memory?'

Robyn slowly shook her head.

'David doesn't know about the memory thing, does he?'

Robyn turned to face Gayle. 'No, because I ... it's just that ...'

'He might not believe you?'

Robyn frowned. 'You must admit, it does sound a little wacko – like something out of a bad movie, where they can't think of a decent plot, so they resort to the tired memory loss thing.'

'Yes, it does,' Gayle agreed. 'What did the doctor have to say about it, if you don't mind me asking?'

Robyn glanced at the strange suitcase that Gayle had left on the bed. 'It could come back just like that,' Robyn clicked her fingers. 'That's why I'd rather not waste my time telling people today what could be all changed by tomorrow.'

'Okay, your secret is safe with me.' Gayle winked at Robyn. 'I won't tell a soul, I promise.' She paused. 'Except perhaps …' Gayle put her forefinger to her chin and looked up at the ceiling, '… my mother.' She chuckled.

Robyn relaxed.

'Where is the crazy old woman anyway?' Gayle said, smiling at Robyn as she walked out of the room, closing the door behind her.

17

Robyn stood in the bedroom, staring down at the suitcase, unsure as to whether she wanted to open it and find out what was inside. Or, more to the point, find out that she didn't recognise any of her own possessions. She had given a very abridged version to Gayle of what the doctor had said.

Now the doctor's words were ringing in her ears, sounding a warning bell. Perhaps if she opened it, and nothing clicked, then it would mean that her memory loss had a psychological rather than a physical cause. If that were true, she wondered if it had anything to do with the other news that Dr Jamieson had given her. She involuntarily put the palm of her hand on her tummy. At the time, she had been just so relieved not to be pregnant that the enormity of the situation hadn't hit her. But now it had.

She sank onto the edge of the bed, nearly sliding off the very soft, springy mattress. Who was the father? What had she been doing, travelling along that road on Christmas Day? Why, for that matter, was she here in this place at all, spending the Christmas holidays alone? Had it had anything to do with the pregnancy? She took her hand away and looked down at her stomach. Then she glanced sideways at the suitcase. She hoped it held some of the answers. She sat cross-legged on the bed in front of the old suitcase and ran her fingers along the creased brown leather, tracing its rough outline. She examined the old worn stickers with words partially obscured by time. She thought one said Tahiti, another Bombay. She wondered if she had visited these places, but the stickers looked far too old; the representation of flight attendants on one looked very dated. Besides, this case didn't look like something a woman in her early twenties would own. She glanced at the rucksack. Perhaps the suitcase wasn't hers. That would explain why she didn't recognise it, but then the rucksack hadn't jogged her memory either. Perhaps the old suitcase had belonged to someone in her family, and she'd kept it because it had a special significance.

When she had finished examining the case, she held her hands either side, with her thumbs on the old catches, ready to click them open. She took a deep breath, closed her eyes and pressed her thumbs hard. She heard two clicks, not quite in unison. The lid was unlocked. She opened her eyes and lifted the lid. It was heavier than she had expected. She looked inside the case.

She breathed out.

Clothes. Just a crumpled assortment of clothes. What had she been expecting – a suitcase full of money?

Robyn plunged her hand into the suitcase, picking out a particularly drab piece of clothing.

She held it up. *Do I really wear these?* There was an assortment of clothes, mostly grey and black, like the outfit she was wearing. They looked as though they had come from a charity shop or a vintage clothing store. She picked out a grey tartan skirt, long stripy socks that she imagined wouldn't have been out of place in the eighties, and a matching grey jumper that appeared too big for her but looked cosy and warm. She held them up. 'At least this makes a change from black.'

Robyn continued to rummage through the suitcase to see if there was anything of interest besides the clothes. Her hand glided through the sea of clothes, and she felt something hard. Thrusting the pile of clothes to one side, she revealed a plain brown shoebox, almost as weather-beaten as the suitcase.

'OK. I'm guessing there is the most grotesque pair of shoes in here.' She lifted the shoebox out of the case. She glanced at the oversized, thick-soled army-style boots she had been wearing before she'd slipped them off to sit on the bed. She did not like them at all.

She'd discovered she didn't much like her clothing style. *Perhaps because I'm a student, this is all I can afford.* Another thought occurred to her; maybe the bang on the head had changed her personality. It wasn't a possibility she had thought to ask the doctor about in respect of her memory loss. She looked at her case, and the old shoebox, and thought *how strange*. She felt as though she was going through someone else's things. It almost made her feel like an imposter; as though she had stolen someone else's identity and was masquerading as Robyn.

She shook her head as she lifted the shoebox, thinking it would be lovely if it was full of cash. Even though Gayle had so kindly let her stay at her house, she couldn't stay indefinitely, and even while she was there, she wanted to pay Gayle some money for room and board.

Robyn lifted the shoebox lid and was about to cast it to one side when something caught her attention. There was picture of a skull and crossbones drawn in thick black marker pen followed by the words, *Private – keep out!* written directly underneath the crossbones. Robyn held the lid closer to read a scribbled message underneath, this time in plain biro. *If you go any further, you should be ashamed of yourself. Only a real creep would read someone else's diary.*

'I kept a diary?' she squealed, both delighted and surprised. 'Oh my god!' she clapped her hands together. This was just what she needed to jog her memory.

As if that message might not be enough to deter an intruder, there was a further warning. Robyn read it out loud: *'This diary is in an exact reference order, so I will know if anyone has so much as breathed on it.'* A miniature skull and crossbones ended the message.

Robyn discarded the lid, but not without taking a second glance at the skull and crossbones, which bizarrely gave her a pang of guilt, despite it apparently being her own diary, in her own writing. She put the lid down and leaned forward to examine the contents of the box. There was an assortment of jewellery – bangles and necklaces which didn't look like real gold or silver. Robyn picked each one up, turning them over in her hands. She frowned. 'How would I know real gold or silver from fake?' She raised her eyebrows. 'Perhaps my memory is coming back and I just know they're pretty, but worthless.'

Robyn put a couple of the bangles on her wrist. She didn't like them much, and cast them to one side, along with the fake jewellery. She focused on the scrapbook at the bottom of the shoebox instead. She carefully lifted it out of the box.

Robyn felt a ridiculous twinge of guilt that she was about to read a stranger's diary. She toyed with the idea of putting it straight back and slapping the lid back on the box. She looked from the box to the lid and thought, *I could wait until tomorrow, until my memory returns, or perhaps the day after.* She knew that was silly. Why wait? In fact, wasn't she in a unique position? How many people had the opportunity to stand back and look at themselves, evaluate themselves as a stranger might on their first meeting? Granted, you wouldn't find out the most intimate details about a person from your first meeting, and they'd have to be an exceptional best friend to let you read their innermost thoughts. But what an experience it would be to find out about yourself. Perhaps she would discover things about herself that she did not much like. Her gaze drifted to the pile of clothes on the bed and the boots on the floor. But then, if so, what better time to start to change? To see her flaws just a stranger might without rolling out excuses for herself – perhaps a lousy childhood, or being bullied at school.

If she waited until the next day, and her memory came back, the opportunity might be lost forever.

Robyn's mood suddenly changed from euphoria over the discovery of the diary to being downright scared of what she might discover in its pages. She was afraid that she might not like the person who had lain bare her intimate self in this scrapbook that was lying in a tattered old shoe box. But she was just a young woman, she reminded herself, and she had committed no heinous crime – so what was she so afraid of? She wondered how far back this diary went. She imagined that when she'd written this diary, she had just been a typical teenager laying bare her teenage angst, just like millions of other teens across the globe.

Robyn liked that thought. There was something oddly comforting about finding her diary. That in itself said she was just as ordinary as any other person her age. It was just that she was going through an extraordinary experience.

But it certainly wasn't what Robyn had envisaged a diary to be. It wasn't a hardback book with fancy gold lettering, announcing that it was a diary; one of the ones that sometimes came with a little lock and a tiny key that you eventually lost. Robyn wondered if that was a memory – perhaps she'd originally had one of those conventional diaries, with embossed lettering on its fancy cover, but she'd lost the key and had resorted to this old scrapbook.

Robyn eyed the diary in her hand. Still, there were some things about a diary that were a given, whether it was a fancy book or not.

Sitting on the bed, she gingerly opened it to the first page. Unexpectedly, there was no *Dear diary*, no date – in fact, no reference of any kind; just drawings and sketches.

'So, I'm an artist.' Robyn frowned. 'I don't get it. Why call it a diary when there's nothing written inside?' She turned the next few pages, still looking for some entries about her everyday life: her parents, her friends, a special friend – girl or boy. Just the sorts of things people wrote in their diaries.

She was beginning to feel frustrated.

With her thumb holding back all the pages, she slowly let them flick by until she came across something. There was a sketch of a coffin, and a girl standing, head bowed, beside it, a church in the background. Robyn stared at the sketch. 'So, if that's me, then someone I knew died.' Robyn grimaced. 'Well, that's depressing.' What was also depressing was that despite seeing her own diary entries, she still couldn't remember a thing.

She continued absently flicking through the pages in case anything jogged a memory. She stopped at the last page, which had a pencil sketch of a bookshop. She knew it was a bookshop because it said *Wilbur's Bookstore* on a sign above the door, and there were books in the window along with the outlines of two women.

She furrowed her brow, closed her eyes, and concentrated hard, trying to remember. 'Is that me and a friend? Or just two random, or even imaginary, people I've drawn in? Perhaps the bookshop isn't even real.'

Robyn opened her eyes and exhaled. Nothing, absolutely nothing came to mind. It was useless. She tossed it aside in frustration. Sure, she could wait for her memory to return, but why wait when the answers should be here? She recalled Dr Jamieson's advice just to be more relaxed about it and her mind would do all the work for her.

She stared at the so-called diary and realised the contents were meaningless unless her memory returned. She was about to replace it in the box when something fell out of the diary onto the bed. Robyn picked up a small, thin booklet with a plastic cover. She turned it over in her hands. The words *Instant Saver* were written in bland white lettering.

Bemused, Robyn opened the first page. Her name and what appeared to be an account number were printed in light grey type on the inside cover along with the name and branch address of the bank.

'It's a savings account.' She breathed a sigh of relief. Hopefully, this meant she had some money.

She flicked through the pages in the passbook to find the last entry.

Robyn gasped and dropped the passbook. She scrambled off the bed, backing away until she was standing with her back right up against the bedroom door, her hand feeling for the doorknob as though she were about to bolt right out of the room.

She clamped both hands to her mouth. She started to giggle, then caught herself. She shook her head and walked back to the bed. She was acting like an idiot. She was sure she must have misread the figure in the passbook. The day had taken its toll. She was tired. She was disorientated. And she didn't trust anyone at the moment, least of all herself.

She plucked the passbook off the bed and slowly opened it, flicking the pages slowly until she came to the centre page, where the typewritten entries stopped abruptly halfway down the page. Robyn's eye settled on the last entry. This time she counted the zeros in the sum that had been deposited into her account.

Robyn closed the savings book, placed it back in the scrapbook, and put it back in the old shoebox, replacing the lid. The skull and crossbones now looked darker and even more menacing. She put the shoebox back in the suitcase and whipped the lid on quickly. It clunked shut. She flipped the catches and pressed hard until she heard them click. It was locked. She breathed out.

She walked to the easy chair at the far end of the room and sat staring into space.

The suitcase really was full of money, as it turned out.

But this time, the image of the old tatty suitcase full of bank notes, just like in the movies, no longer filled her with a sense of excitement and wonder. Instead, her newfound treasure filled her with dread.

She glanced at the rucksack and frowned. She didn't feel in the mood to open it and find more surprises. Although when Gayle had deposited it in the corner of the room, she'd spied an article of clothing peeping out from the top of the bag where it had been unfastened, presumably by the police, checking the contents. She guessed it was just full of more clothes that she would not like one bit.

Looking at her clothes and her poor excuse for a diary, she was the last person she would have expected to have that kind of money. Once again, the question came to mind: where had she been going in such a hurry on Christmas Day? She must have been in a hurry to crash her car like that. The police officer didn't mention she'd been speeding – but how would he know unless the speedometer had got stuck on the speed she'd been travelling when she crashed into David's car?

Or did he crash into me? she wondered. She furrowed her brow, wondering why she'd thought that. She was the one who'd caused the accident – she must have been, otherwise David would have owned up. She imagined that if she'd been speeding, he hadn't mentioned that fact to the police.

Robyn breathed a heavy sigh and sat back down on the bed. She picked up the pile of letters from her mother. From amongst the letters, a few cards fell out. She picked them up. They were postcards from far-flung countries. Looking at the postmarks on the letters, it appeared her mother had been travelling for the best part of a year, although whether she'd touched base in England during that time, Robyn had no clue.

She read the postcards and opened the remainder of the letters. Inside each of the unopened letters, along with a note about her mother's current destination, and how much she was enjoying her travels, was a cheque addressed to her, and an invitation to join her mother at that destination.

Robyn stared at one of the cheques. 'That's generous,' she remarked. She guessed it was enough to cover air fares, accommodation and spending money. The letters and postcards didn't mention her father. Perhaps they'd split up, or she'd grown up in a single-parent household. 'Oh, god – it's so frustrating. Why can't I remember?'

Robyn had a sudden thought. She reached for the suitcase and got out the old shoebox. She took out the savings book again and flicked through the pages. She picked up the letters that had already been opened and noted the date at the top of the letter, along with the address of a hotel or guesthouse, and the comment at the bottom of each letter saying that another cheque was enclosed.

She cross-referenced those dates – give or take a day or two – and noted that the cheques had been paid into her savings account, but there had been no withdrawals. That answered her question – she had not seen her mum, or had a holiday with her, in all the months her mum had been away. The question was: why hadn't she? It wasn't like she was at work and didn't have the time; most university courses had generous holidays. And it wasn't like she didn't have the money.

It looked as though she had never intended to go, otherwise she imagined she probably wouldn't have deposited the money into a savings account which might not be easily accessible. Surely she had a current account too.

It occurred to her that if she could visit the bank where she had a savings account, she might find that she had a bank account with them too – one with a bank card.

A shrill sound jolted Robyn out of her reverie, and out of her chair. She stood, her head darting around the room.

The single long, shrill sound came again. Robyn saw the phone and unclenched her hands. She stood up as the sound died and walked to the bedside table. She hovered over the phone. It rang again and she picked up the old-fashioned, matt-black receiver, which was heavier than she had expected. She looked at it before putting it to her ear.

Robyn coughed. Her throat felt dry. 'Hello,' she said meekly.

'Lunch is served.'

Robyn eyed the suitcase. She hesitated for some time before she replied, 'I'm sorry, Gayle, but I feel a bit tired. I'll skip lunch and just have a bite to eat this evening if that's alright.'

She waited for a response. When none was forthcoming, she realised Gayle must have already put the phone down. 'Damn!'

That meant she had to offer her apologies in person, which she didn't feel like doing. Perhaps if she didn't emerge from her room, Gayle would assume she was having a nap. Robyn doubted this. More than likely, Gayle would think there was something wrong. She would most certainly come and check on her. She imagined it was a condition of her discharge that she had someone to keep an eye on her after the head injury. For some unfathomable reason, Robyn didn't want Gayle to visit her room and see the suitcase again. She was afraid she might not be able to contain herself, and might blurt, 'I'm rich, and I have no idea why.'

Robyn walked to the bedroom door and reached for the doorknob, but then she decided there was something she wanted to do before leaving the room. Kneeling down, she slipped the suitcase under the bed. She returned to the door and opened it. As she was shutting it behind her, she glanced back into the room, her eyes darting to the bottom of the bed, to the valance that was barely concealing the hiding place of the old brown suitcase. Of course, she knew that if somebody wanted to find her suitcase, then once they had looked in the large double wardrobe, the next place would be under the bed. But it just made her feel more comfortable that it was out of sight, almost – although she couldn't imagine Gayle rifling through her stuff. She reasoned that if the suitcase wasn't on show, and someone had to drag it out from under the bed, it would take time, which would be a deterrent.

Closing the door, Robyn realised she was being paranoid. This memory loss business was obviously getting to her. She was still worried about that ridiculously large deposit in her savings account. *But the money is in a bank, so it must be bona fide – right?* She nodded to herself as she walked down the stairs, but she still didn't feel very hungry. Instead, she just felt scared. Try as she might, she couldn't shake the feeling that something had happened on Christmas Day; something *before* the car accident.

18

Gayle emerged from the kitchen with a dishcloth in her hand. 'Ah, there you are. I was about to run upstairs and check you were okay.'

Robyn stared at her knowingly. So, she *was* keeping an eye on her. The doctor must have had a quiet word when she found out Gayle was taking Robyn home with her.

'Please can you give me a lift into town, Gayle, after lunch? I'm not really very hungry at the moment, to be honest, but I can wait until you've had something to eat.'

Robyn wanted to find out if there was a bank where she could withdraw some money from her savings account to give Gayle some rent money. But she didn't want to tell Gayle this in case she objected, which she imagined she would. And the other reason she didn't want to mention it was in case she had a problem withdrawing funds. What if it was one of those high-interest accounts that had some sort of extended notice period before she could access the money? Or she'd forgotten how to sign her name?

Robyn frowned at that possibility, along with another thought; she had no other means of identification – no driving licence, passport or even a bank card. That would not be helpful at all if it turned out she did have an ordinary bank account with the same bank, and all she needed was her bank card, which she'd lost along with her purse in the accident. 'Damn!' she said under her breath.

As she followed Gayle into a large, old-fashioned kitchen, with an Aga and oak-fronted kitchen units that looked like a throwback to the eighties, she had a feeling it might turn out to be a wasted trip.

Gayle turned around, hand on hips, and said, 'I hope you're not thinking of leaving. That would be shame, honey. It's nice to have some company in this big old house.'

The house seemed to creak at every step, and the dark wooden doors and picture rails, beige swirly patterned carpet, and large-flowered print wallpaper harked back to another era. But the moment Robyn had stepped foot in the imposing detached house, which she'd barely explored yet – she wanted Gayle to give her a tour – she had loved the place.

Robyn replied, 'Not at all. It just feels like I've been cooped up in that hospital for an age. I just wanted to get out and about for a bit.' She wasn't lying. She did feel like popping into town to have a look around. Perhaps something would jog her memory.

'Was there anything in particular you wanted to do?'

Her diary, if she could call it that, suddenly came to mind. 'Actually, I was wondering if there was a bookshop?'

'Yes, there is.'

'It's not called Wilbur's Bookstore, by any chance?'

Gayle exclaimed, 'Oh, my goodness, girl! Your memory is coming back!'

Robyn rolled her eyes. 'Not exactly.'

'Then how did you know about the bookshop?'

'I found a diary in my things.'

'Oh, I bet that was interesting.'

'Not really. Turns out I'm a bit of an artist. It's just full of sketches. One is the bookshop.'

'Perhaps if you go there it will jog your memory?'

Robyn raised her eyebrows. 'Fingers crossed.'

'Let's hope the bookshop is open between Christmas and New Year,' commented Gayle. 'Sometimes places close down for the whole holiday. Which reminds me, while we're in town, I'll get a bottle of wine – or several – for New Year's Eve tomorrow.'

'I forgot it was New Year's Eve,' admitted Robyn. She wondered how she normally celebrated seeing in the New Year.

'Me too. Because my father was in hospital, this holiday season seems to have passed by in a blur …' she trailed off.

Robyn frowned. 'You don't have to buy some wine and feel you have to celebrate on my account. I quite understand if that's the last thing you feel like doing. You *have* just lost your dad.'

Gayle shook her head. 'Actually, I think some wine, and some company, would do me the world of good. In fact, I rather feel like a little celebration this evening, like a pre-New Year's Eve.'

Robyn grinned. 'Me too.'

'Why don't I get some popcorn too, and we can watch a movie?'

Robyn thought that sounded perfect.

'I'll just get my coat,' said Gayle, undoing the apron from around her waist.

'We don't have to go right now. I thought you were having lunch?'

'I'd rather pop into town first, in case the shops close early.'

Robyn wanted to go straight away too. 'Great.' She waited by the front door, watching Gayle nip upstairs to check on her mother before they left. A moment later, Gayle raced down the stairs.

'Right, she's having her afternoon nap, so she's not having lunch either. I've just texted my neighbour a couple of doors down who has a key. She's going to pop over and keep an eye on Mother while we're out.'

Gayle stepped out on to the porch and locked the front door.

They travelled into town in silence. Robyn stared out of the car window, glimpsing a beautifully serene loch through a forest of pines, with a backdrop of the snow-covered peaks of the Cairngorm mountains. 'I love this place,' commented Robyn. 'I much prefer it to the city.'

'Which city?' asked Gayle.

Robyn stopped and turned to Gayle. 'I don't know.'

'But you must have had a memory, or part of one. You did say you much prefer it here.'

'I did, didn't I? Perhaps Dr Jamieson is right, and if I just relax and don't even think about it, my memories will return. It's just so frustrating.'

Gayle glanced at her. 'I know. Which university are you studying at?'

'Oh, right. It's St Andrews.' That was what the note from the police had said regarding the address on her driving licence. It sounded as though her student accommodation was in halls of residence there. And it was where her mother had addressed her letters and cards over the past year. 'Perhaps when I said I preferred the Cairngorms to the city, it's because I don't like the city where the university is.'

'Oh, I doubt that very much. It's in a beautiful setting in a town called Fife.'

Robyn turned in her seat to look at Gayle. 'Have you been there?'

'Oh, yes. When I was a child, we went on holiday there several times. It has the most idyllic beaches in Scotland – at least, that's what my parents thought.' Gayle paused. I've got an idea. We'll look up when the spring term starts. You can stay with me until then, and I'll take you back to university, get you settled in for the start of the new term. How does that sound?'

Robyn wasn't sure what to say. Wouldn't it be better if she went home? But where was that, exactly? Did she even have a family home, or had her mum sold up – or given up a rental, if she hadn't owned her own home – and just gone travelling when Robyn had gone to university?

Right now, until she wrote to her mother and let her know what was going on, Robyn didn't have a clue. It was a shame that her phone must have been lost, along with her handbag, in the accident, otherwise she could have just phoned her mum. She'd have had her number in her phone.

Robyn looked at Gayle. She wasn't sure she wanted to go back to St Andrews, even if the town was lovely and the beaches idyllic. It was the memory thing – that was the problem. She wouldn't know what lectures she was meant to go to, who her friends were, or whether she could even cope with the course. But it was the pregnancy that bothered her most. The child she'd lost. Who was the father of the baby she'd been expecting? She imagined he was another student. But who? She just couldn't go back to her old life, and face him, until her memory returned.

But she couldn't stay on with Gayle in her lovely house forever.

She was resigned to the fact that she'd have to return to university. 'Thanks, Gayle. That sounds great,' she said.

'Does it?' Gayle glanced at her. 'Something tells me you're not keen on the idea of returning to uni.'

Robyn heaved a sigh, and admitted she wasn't, and the reasons why. 'And don't say that if I go back it might jog my memory.'

'Not at all. There's a bit of time until then yet, anyway. You've got time to decide what you want to do. Who knows – perhaps that's what you were doing here over the Christmas break; deciding on your future, and whether you wanted to go back.'

Robyn hadn't thought of that. She couldn't even remember what course she was studying. Perhaps she'd discovered the subject wasn't for her, and she'd come to Aviemore to get away and consider her options.

Gayle reached over and patted her hand. 'You are welcome to stay for as long as you like, all right?'

Robyn smiled in relief. 'Thank you, Gayle. That means a lot.'

'Fantastic – that's settled, then.'

Robyn continued to enjoy the scenery. As they approached the picturesque Highland town surrounded by snow-capped peaks, and frosty pine forests, Robyn wound her window down to feel the invigorating chill in the air. She caught a glimpse of the icy loch through the trees, which glistened under the pale winter sun, its frozen surface shimmering like glass.

They reached the town limits. Aviemore sparkled with festive lights, its bustling shops looked warm and inviting, enticing shoppers inside from the wintry weather. Gayle left the main road and started driving through Aviemore, looking for a parking space. 'Did you have a chance to open the rest of the letters? Perhaps your mum is coming home soon?'

Robyn frowned. *But where is home?*

As they drove through the town, Robyn looked for the bank.

'I would have thought she'd want to spend Christmas with you.'

Robyn recalled the cheque she'd received in the post, and the last letter she'd received, in November time, from Rhodes. 'I think her idea was that I went to her for Christmas – abroad.'

'Ah.'

'Obviously I preferred to stay in Scotland.'

Gayle nodded. 'Who wouldn't want to spend Christmas in this beautiful part of the world, eh?'

Gayle pulled up at the kerb in front of a parade of shops. 'We'll have to walk to the bookshop from here. I thought I'd get parked in the station car park opposite the bookshop, but it's only a small car park, and it looked full.'

Robyn knew they'd passed the railway station and had parked at the other end of the long street that was Aviemore's main shopping street. 'This is fine. I wouldn't mind the walk.' Robyn admitted, 'I wanted to pop into a bank as well, if there is one in Aviemore.' She realised she'd have to mention it as they walked through the town together.

'All right. Sorry to ask, but do you remember who you bank with?'

'I don't have to.' Robyn got out her savings book. 'I found this in my suitcase.'

'Oh, Robyn, that is good news. I wouldn't be surprised if you have a debit account with that bank too. Then you can stop your bank card.'

Robyn frowned. 'How do you mean?'

'They're lost – right? Your handbag, or purse, whichever you had on you at the time, hasn't been found, so at least if someone comes across them on a walk, and they're not, you know, honest, and they try and use your bank card, you can put a stop to that possibility.'

Robyn had been so surprised and relieved at the large sum of money that had been deposited into her savings account that she hadn't thought of informing them her bank card, if she had one, had been lost. She was glad she'd mentioned to Gayle that she wanted to go to a bank after all.

'The thing is, Gayle, I don't have the details of my bank card.'

'Well, you have your name and date of birth. And that savings account. I'm sure under the circumstances, they'll be able to locate a bank account, if you have one with them.' Gayle looked at the savings book. 'So, what's the name of the bank?'

Robyn told her.

'Ah, I'm not sure if there's a branch in Aviemore, or close by. To be honest, there have been so many branch closures, we're lucky to have even one bank.'

As they walked along the street together, Robyn said, 'Oh, Gayle, that's going to be a problem if I can't withdraw any money.'

'How come? You could phone your bank when we get back to the house, and explain what happened, and that you bank with them, and may have a bank account, and you lost your card. Then they can issue you with a new one, I'm sure.'

'But they might send my bank card to my address at university.'

'Or they might send it to your home address.'

Robyn frowned. She didn't know where that was, and she doubted the bank would give out those personal details over the phone. Besides, it would raise questions if she admitted she didn't know her home address.

'I wanted to withdraw some money now, otherwise I can't pay you any rent money – for the room.'

'Rent money?' Gayle laughed. 'Robyn, it would be a crime if I charged you rent. It's not exactly a des res with all mod cons, is it?

The plumbing always packs up just when you want to have a bath. Or the boiler decides to go on the blink so there's no hot water. I don't think I told you that. The place needs rewiring – power cuts are frequent, and it can be blooming cold because there isn't central heating, just night storage heaters. No matter what setting I put them on, they always, always lose all their heat by the time you want to sit in the warm in the evening. So, I couldn't possibly charge you rent to stay in my parents' creepy, rundown old place.'

Robyn didn't think it was creepy – although she hadn't slept there yet – but Gayle was right: it was rundown. 'But it's still a roof over my head, Gayle.'

'Yeah, so is a bench in Paddington Station, but you don't have to pay for that, do you? Besides, you're my friend, and my guest – and that's that. I don't want to hear another word about it.'

Robyn smiled. 'All right, Gayle. I'll stay on while I sort myself out, on one condition …'

'Which is?'

'You pay *me* rent to stay there.'

Gayle burst out laughing.

They were both still smiling at Robyn's little joke as they approached the railway station and started across the road to Wilbur's Bookstore.

19

'Well, this is it,' said Gayle. 'Wilbur's Bookstore.'

Robyn frowned. 'It's closed.'

'Yes, that's what the sign on the door says.' Gayle peered through the window. 'There are no lights on.'

Robyn tried the door anyway. She wasn't surprised that it didn't open.

Gayle stepped back from the window and looked at Robyn. 'So, there's a sketch of this bookshop in your diary?'

Robyn nodded. 'Yes.'

'Does the shop—?'

'No!' Robyn interrupted. 'It has not jogged my memory.'

'So, you obviously have no idea why you sketched this shop.'

Robyn turned her gaze on Gayle, throwing her an exasperated look.

'Ah, of course not.'

'Although the sketch did have two women sitting in the window.'

Gayle said, 'When I looked in the window, I saw a small table and two chairs.' She beckoned Robyn over. 'Look.'

Robyn cupped two hands above her forehead and peered

inside. 'Oh, yes. So there is.'

Perhaps it was you and a friend in the sketch?'

'So, why didn't they visit me in hospital? The accident, along with my name and David's, were in the local paper.'

Gayle shrugged.

'They couldn't have been a very good friend.'

'Or perhaps it wasn't you at all. Perhaps it was just two people you saw sitting in the window.'

'Yeah, I thought of that too.' She turned around and looked across the road at the train station. 'I always wanted to go on the steam train that leaves from Platform 3. Do you know they do afternoon tea, and at Christmas there's mulled wine and mince pies?'

Robyn turned around to find Gayle staring at her. 'What?'

'How do you know that?'

'Know what?'

'That there's a 'steam train that leaves from Platform 3, and that you've always wanted to take a journey on one?'

Robyn stared at Gayle, open-mouthed. 'Oh, my god! I think I've just had a memory. How else would I know it's something I've always wanted to do?'

'Exactly!' Gayle smiled. 'I think we should make a point of returning to the bookshop when it reopens to see if anything else comes back to you, or if the bookshop owner recognises you.'

'I think that's a brilliant idea.' Robyn turned to the door, wondering when it would reopen.

'In the meantime,' continued Gayle, 'I think this calls for a double celebration. Let's go to the supermarket and buy some wine, and whatever else takes your fancy tonight.'

❖

Arriving for the second time at the big old house, Robyn suddenly had the urge to see the house as it had been years earlier.

'Gayle?'

Gayle had one foot on the gravel and a hand on the steering wheel and was just about to lift herself out of the car. She turned awkwardly to look at Robyn. 'I was wondering if you had any photos of the house I could see. The way it was before …'

'We let it fall into disrepair like this?' Gayle nodded her head.

'Oh no, I didn't mean—'

'I know you didn't.' She smiled. 'You're a strange one. In town, I believe you had it in mind to leave here if you couldn't pay me some money for your stay, and now you want to see old family photos.'

Robyn shrugged.

Gayle winked at her. 'Sure, you can.' She got out of the car.

Robyn smiled to herself. She had the most bizarre idea. She opened the car door.

'Although you'll have to find them first,' commented Gayle.

'Huh?' Robyn looked at Gayle. She was getting the shopping bags from the back seat.

'The photos,' Gayle continued as she kneed the car door shut.

'What about them?' Robyn took one of the shopping bags.

They walked up the front steps.

Gayle said, 'I imagine the photos are gathering dust somewhere, perhaps the basement or attic. I haven't had a chance to sort through my parents' things.' Gayle closed the door behind them. 'If you can find them, you're more than welcome to have a look at our family albums.'

'You don't mind me exploring the house while I look for them?'

'Not at all. Go right ahead. I'll put the kettle on, and we can have some lunch. I'll see if Mother is up.' She picked up a note on the sideboard. 'Ah, from my neighbour. She checked on Mother, and left just before we arrived.'

Robyn heard the clink of wine bottles as Gayle took the shopping bags into the kitchen. 'Perhaps I'll have a glass of wine now,' she heard Gayle say.

'Thank you, Gayle,' Robyn called after her. She looked around the hallway, trying to envisage how it would have appeared when it was first built. She was keen to explore the rest of the house. She knew exactly how she was going to repay Gayle's kindness, but first she had to find those photo albums.

20

Robyn was getting used to Gayle's constant ruminations over her mysterious past. Robyn didn't think *mysterious* was the right word to describe her past. She was just an art student at college who'd had an unfortunate accident over the Christmas holidays and lost her memory – nothing more.

She tried not to think about that huge sum of money that had been deposited into her bank account.

Gayle thought it was rather exciting, losing your memory and discovering yourself again.

'In fact, the best bit about it would be if you had lost your memory for good.'

Robyn looked aghast.

'No, really.' Gayle continued. 'Just look at it this way. All the negative things that you learnt about yourself over the years would be forgotten.'

'But so would the good things,' Robyn intervened.

Gayle reached for the bottle of wine on the coffee table. She poured herself another large glass of wine and offered Robyn a refill.

Robyn shook her head. She was having trouble keeping her

eyes open as it was. She wanted to go to bed, but didn't want to disappoint Gayle, who wanted to stay up and chat.

It didn't help that the old-fashioned sofas, covered in green leaf-effect throws, were so squishy and comfortable. The heating was on full blast – Gayle had fiddled with the night storage heaters, and for the first time in a long time they were emitting more heat in the evening than during the day.

However, the downside was that this made Robyn feel even more sleepy. *Perhaps I should stop snuggling under the soft, cosy throw?* Robyn didn't want to move from her spot on the sofa in front of the open fire, the red-hot coals throwing out yet more heat. Despite the large TV in the corner of the room, Robyn's eyes kept being drawn back to the mesmerising warm yellow flames flickering in the hearth. She could feel her eyelids growing heavy.

Gayle was sitting in a matching armchair to one side of the sofa, under an old-fashioned standard lamp with a huge shade, her feet on a footstool. As if sensing that Robyn might fall asleep, she turned the sound on the television up. An old black-and-white movie was on, scheduled to end at midnight.

Robyn wasn't enjoying the movie, but she didn't like to mention it to Gayle, who seemed to be enjoying it. Despite having mentioned *Gone with the Wind*, Robyn had discovered something else about herself – she didn't care for old movies; not at all.

'Perhaps I will have another glass of wine, after all,' Robyn said, sitting up and planting her feet on the modern, Aztec-style rug. Apparently, Gayle had bought it to cover the old carpet in the lounge. It looked out of place in the room, with its old-fashioned furnishings, but Gayle seemed so pleased with the rug that Robyn didn't want to tell her what she really thought.

She poured herself another glass of wine – this time a rosé

from one of the three bottles on the table – and sat back down on the sofa to finish the movie. She helped herself to some nachos. There were also bowls of crisps, popcorn, and peanuts. She wasn't particularly hungry after the hotpot and dumplings that Gayle had served up for dinner, but she did like the little nibbles Gayle had put out.

Robyn stared at the TV, willing midnight to come round quickly. She didn't know how she'd get to the end of the movie without falling asleep. The television was rented, apparently, from a local electrical store. It was about the only modern thing in the lounge, other than the rug. The sofas, the antique furniture, the old prints in heavy wooden picture frames, the wallpaper and the carpet were just like the rest of the house – dated and dark.

Gayle commented, 'Can you imagine what it would be like to discover what you are good at and what you enjoy in life without any knowledge of what untrue things people have told you about yourself over the years?'

'Which self-help book did that come from?' Robyn said in mock humour.

To Robyn's surprise, Gayle reeled off the title of some book by a professor of psychology and even gave the chapter heading.

'I have the book, if you want to borrow it?'

'No, thank you.'

'Suit yourself. But it's in the library if you change your mind.'

'There's a library?'

'I thought you went exploring?'

'I did. I started in the attic, and was going to work my way down, but then I found the photo albums up there.'

They both glanced at the piles of photo albums littering the long coffee table. After dinner, they'd spent most of the evening, before putting on the late-night movie at ten, looking through them. Gayle had reminisced about her childhood there – her father had been a doctor, her mum a nurse – and the wonderful time she and her siblings had had growing up in the big old house.

'Ah, that's where you were when I called you for lunch and got no answer. I thought you'd gone for a lie-down and had a nap. I did knock softly on your door.'

'I was in the attic the whole time.'

'Blimey, you must have got cold up there. As my mum would say, you're lucky you didn't catch your death.'

They both paused for a moment to glance at Gayle's mother, who was sitting in an old-fashioned, high-backed chair, knitting as she watched the television. Apparently, she tended to wake up at night, and sleep during the day, which was difficult for Gayle.

Robyn felt ever so guilty for what she was going to say next. 'Gayle, I found an old electric heater up there, so I kind of used that. Sorry. Bet it cost a fortune.'

'Well, fortunately I'm not paying for it. The bills are still in my mother's name, and I know she's got direct debits set up for that sort of thing.'

'Still, I feel bad.'

'Please don't. I'm just so pleased you found the photo albums. I had no idea what my parents had done with them. And I haven't had a chance to look for them.'

'There's a lot of stuff in the attic. Hope you don't mind …' Robyn looked down at the Christmas jumper she'd found in a trunk of old clothes. She'd slipped it on up there before she found the heater, and had kept it on.

Gayle smiled approvingly. 'Actually, it suits you, and it makes a nice change from all the grungy black clothing you seem to wear.'

'I know. To be honest, Gayle, I don't much like my clothes.'

'There, you see. I told you there were some advantages to losing your memory and starting your life anew. You're taking stock and making changes already.'

Robyn still wanted her memories back. 'It's only a Christmas jumper.'

'Yes, but who knows where it will lead. This might be the start of the new you.'

Robyn would rather know the old her before she decided she needed to change.

'Why don't we make some New Year's resolutions?'

'Tonight? But it's not New Year's Eve until tomorrow.'

'I know, but who knows what you young-uns will be up to on New Year's Eve. You know New Year's Eve celebrations are a big deal in Scotland.'

Robyn nodded, although she couldn't imagine this young-un would be up to much of anything. She imagined she'd be sitting there with Gayle and her mum the next evening, seeing in the New Year together. And she didn't mind that – not at all. But she was happy to go along with making New Year's resolutions that night, if that was what Gayle wanted.

'Is that what you normally do, Gayle – make New Year's resolutions?'

'Not at all, but like you, I want to start over.'

Robyn already knew what her New Year's resolution would be, apart from getting her memories back. There was something she wanted to do – and she was starting first thing in the morning. She grinned at Gayle.

Gayle narrowed her eyes. 'I know that look. One of my sisters used to pull an expression like that when she was up to something.

What are *you* up to?'

Robyn's attention was drawn to the photo albums. 'You'll see.'

21

The following morning, Robyn stood outside the basement door. She'd explored the rest of the house, including the bedrooms upstairs, apart from Gayle's bedroom, and her mum's bedroom too – her mum was still sleeping. The house was double-fronted, which meant it had rooms off both sides of the central hallway downstairs. Robyn liked the layout. Across from the lounge were two rooms. One was the dining room, which was at the back of the house. She had discovered that it was a rather lovely room with a large dining table and a bookcase full of old novels next to another old standard lamp, like the one in the lounge, with a huge shade. There were old, framed photos, and potted plants in the deep recessed windows either side of the fireplace. Two leather chairs with cushions and throws were positioned either side of the fireplace. French doors led out on to the rear gardens, and through the French doors, Robyn could see the kitchen extension.

The door next to the dining room led into a smaller room which overlooked the front lawn. Robyn had realised it was the study; it had bookshelves lining one wall and a large oak desk by the long Georgian window, where faded heavy, red curtains hung. Robyn had tried to pull the curtains further open to let more light into the room, but they were too heavy.

Robyn had seen the various medical books, some still open on the oak desk, and had felt sad for Gayle that her father had passed away. Robyn knew Gayle's father had been a local doctor. They'd come to the UK from the Caribbean in the fifties, and although Gayle had been born in the UK, there was a gap between her and her three older siblings – two boys and a girl – who had not.

Gayle had mentioned that the previous night when they had been flicking through the photo albums. Gayle had told her about her family's background; it had made Robyn wonder whether Gayle, the baby of the family, was perhaps not as close to her three older siblings, who had a shared history; they had been born and had spent their early years in Trinidad before moving with their parents as part of the Windrush Generation.

There were two more rooms downstairs. One had a single bed, which Robyn imagined Gayle's father had perhaps used when he had become too frail to get upstairs. The other room, a snug, had small sofas, old bean bags, lots of boxed games, and old toys. It looked like a playroom. She imagined Gayle and her brothers and sister playing in that room years earlier. Gayle had mentioned she has grown-up nieces and nephews. Robyn imagined this had been their playroom too when they'd come as young children to visit their grandparents.

The basement was the last place Robyn planned to see that morning. Then she would have finished exploring the entire house. She imagined it would be dark, dusty and cobwebby, so she'd slipped on an old pair of denim dungarees she'd found in the trunk full of old clothes in the attic the previous day. Gayle had said she could have whatever she wanted out of that trunk. Robyn had thanked her. She really didn't like the clothes in her suitcase. She wanted to buy some new clothes or pop into a charity shop for some second-hand ones, but there was a problem – she'd need some money. She couldn't access her savings just yet, but she remembered that she still had a cheque to cash. She'd forgotten about the cheque the previous day when they'd popped into Aviemore to buy some wine and nibbles. Perhaps the bank there would let her cash a cheque – then she'd be able to give Gayle some money and buy some new clothes.

Robyn smiled as she looked down at the cosy blue jumper she'd also found. The dungarees were a bit big, so she'd worn them over the jumper. 'At least I'll be warm when I venture down here.'

She could just imagine the chaos and clutter that was going to confront her at the bottom of those basement stairs, if the attic was anything to go by. But if she could find any more photos then it would be worth it. This was all part and parcel of her plan to repay Gayle for letting her stay there.

Gayle, her hair wrapped in a towel, passed her in the hallway and wished her luck going down into the basement.

'Thanks,' Robyn replied. She could tell that Gayle didn't envy her task. Gayle paused. 'Why you are taking such an interest in my old family photos is anyone's guess,' she muttered.

Robyn heard her. 'Like I said, I'm interested in what the house used to look like in its heyday, when your parents first moved here.'

Gayle just nodded. 'I'm surprised you were up with the lark this morning after the late night last night. I heard you wandering around.'

'Oh, sorry about that.' Robyn silently cursed the creaky floorboards. 'Did I wake you?'

'Only for a moment. I thought it might be my mother, so I went to check on her. Then I drifted off to sleep again. Did you enjoy having a look around the house?'

'Oh, yes. I love it. All those nooks and crannies. The house is fascinating.'

'In an old way.'

'In a good way. It just needs some TLC, that's all.'

'Yeah, right,' Gayle scoffed. 'And some redecorating, refurnishing …' she trailed off as she wandered down the hall towards the kitchen.

Robyn smiled after her. It was true. She watched Gayle step into the kitchen.

Robyn was about to head down into the basement when Gayle called out, 'I'm making some eggs on toast. Why don't you join me?'

Robyn turned around. Gayle was standing in the kitchen doorway. 'That's really kind of you, Gayle, but I already helped myself to a bowl of cereal this morning.' She winced, and added sheepishly, 'Hope you don't mind.'

'Oh, goodness, Robyn – why would I mind? Although as I said before, you're my guest, so I should have made you breakfast.'

Robyn shook her head. On the contrary, she wanted to do something for Gayle, which is exactly what she'd be doing very soon. She smiled.

Gayle caught her smiling to herself. She did a double-take, and wagged a finger at Robyn. 'I still think you're up to something.'

Robyn grinned as she opened the basement door.

Gayle said, 'At least let me make you a cup of tea.'

'All right.' Robyn peered down the gloomy basement stairs, having second thoughts about exploring that part of the house.

Gayle said, 'I'll pop your cuppa down to you.'

'You don't have to do that.'

'No, it's fine.'

Robyn imagined she was interested to see what was down there herself, after all.

She heard Gayle in the kitchen, putting on the kettle. She flailed her hand around for a light switch. Her hand brushed a thin chord. She caught it and pulled hard. The top of the stairs was now bathed in a harsh, bright light.

'Found any more photos yet?' Gayle called out from the kitchen.

Robyn rolled her eyes at Gayle's humorous tone. Of course she hadn't. She'd barely had time to venture down the stairs. Adjusting to the bright glare of the naked bulb swinging only inches from her face, Robyn descended the stairs to the darkness below. She guessed there must be another light switch. She cursed herself silently for not asking Gayle for a torch. What if the bulb needed replacing?

Standing at the bottom of the stairs, she couldn't make out anything in the darkness. She brushed her hand against the right-hand wall, praying she didn't disturb any leggy, hairy creature. She hated spiders; the thought of them sent her spine tingling. Her fingers caught a switch. She flicked the switch and found herself utterly surprised. The basement was massive, and it was empty, save for some neatly stacked packing boxes in the centre of the room. It was not how she had pictured it at all.

Robyn took a few hesitant steps, hoping there weren't rats or mice down there. But the floor was swept, with not a cobweb in sight, and nothing untoward scampered past. She tutted at her own silliness and walked over to the boxes, then stood with her hands on her hips, wondering if Gayle had been having some fun with her.

The way Gayle had described the basement, and her insistence on at least lending Robyn some old clothes, had made it sound as though she'd be climbing over old furniture, bric-a-brac, and a lot of clutter that had been collected over the years and then left forgotten and untouched in the basement of the house.

Robyn lifted a box off the pile. There was no indication of what was inside, which Robyn thought a little odd. If someone had gone to the trouble of sorting out the mess that Gayle had intimated was down there the last time she'd looked, which sounded like it must have been years earlier, then surely they'd also have gone to the trouble of labelling the box with its contents. The box felt too light to contain photos. This box was labelled with a name – Xavier.

There were several more boxes labelled *Xavier* and several with the name *Jerome* in thick black marker pen. The writing wasn't faded. And the packing boxes looked new, as though they had been bought in the recent past, packed and labelled. Robyn thought of Gayle's two brothers. She imagined the boxes contained all the embarrassing childhood mementos that parents insist on keeping. The boxes suggested that they had packed up their own stuff. She couldn't imagine Gayle's father had done it, nor her mum; neither would have been capable. Perhaps Gayle wasn't aware that the basement had been sorted out at some point; maybe her siblings had visited before she'd arrived to take care of her parents.

Staring at the boxes, Robyn wondered if somewhere in some attic, or perhaps even in a basement just like this one, there were mementos of her childhood just waiting to be discovered again.

The next tier of boxes had another name – *Dinah*. That was Gayle's older sister. These boxes were larger, and one was open. Robyn couldn't resist lifting the cardboard flaps to have a peek inside. She pulled out the protruding object from between the flaps, grabbing on with the other hand, as it was heavier than she had expected. Taking it out of the box, she carefully lowered it to the floor and stood back, pressing the palms of her hands into her lower back. 'Wow – that was heavy.'

It was an antique. Robyn didn't know why she was so sure; perhaps she'd seen one in a museum somewhere, or a magazine. All she knew for sure was that such a vase was not from a second-grade pottery class. Robyn chewed her fingernail. Now she was worried that she wouldn't be able to get it back it the box. If she called for Gayle's help, then she would know she had been opening boxes that clearly were not full of photos.

22

‘Robyn – you alright down there? You’re awfully quiet.’

Robyn looked up. She could hear Gayle coming down the stairs.

‘Everything’s just fine – really it is.’

‘You know I feel rather mean, leaving you down here to get on with it.’ Gayle continued her descent down the stairs. ‘So I thought I might as well come and give you a hand.’

Robyn’s glance shot from the stairs, where Gayle’s legs had come into view, to the vase standing right in front of her. There was nothing she could do about it now. ‘You don’t have to give me a hand.’

‘Well, I have your cup of tea here, and I’m bringing myself a mug down too.’

Robyn rolled her eyes. She’d forgotten about the tea.

‘Otherwise, you’ll be down here looking for those wretched photos all … day.’ She stopped abruptly in mid-sentence on the last stair. ‘What in heaven …?’

Robyn looked from the vase to Gayle, who was still standing on the last stair, holding two mugs of tea.

‘I can explain,’ Robyn began, looking back at the vase, ‘really I can. I didn't mean to pry. I just thought it was some embarrassing, you know, childhood art project or something, from your sister's school days. I did not expect that such a beautiful vase would be in this box. I was going to put it straight back, but then I was afraid I might drop it if I lifted it again.'

Gayle stepped down into the basement, looking all around her, just as Robyn had done.

'There's no rats or mice down here, if that's what you're afraid of.' She caught Gayle's wide-eyed expression, much like her own when she'd seen how big the basement was, and how empty. Robyn commented, 'Anyone would think you hadn't been down in your parents' basement before.' Robyn knew this wasn't the case because Gayle had warned her about venturing down there.

'I haven't.'

'Huh?'

'Not like this.' Gayle moved cautiously around the boxes. She couldn't hide her surprise.

'When I first stepped down here, I thought you were winding me up, saying it would be full of stuff, when in actual fact it wasn't.'

Gayle turned to Robyn. 'It *was* full of stuff – loads of discarded furniture, and bric-a-brac my parents hadn't bothered to get rid of over the years. You could say they were hoarders. I think they wouldn't throw anything out in case they needed it. They would never replace anything if they didn't have to.'

Robyn had seen the house. She could vouch for that. She had a question. 'So, who do you think cleared it all up?' she asked, although, given that the packing boxes were labelled with Gayle's siblings' names, she had a good idea.

Gayle shrugged. 'Beats me.' She pointed at the vase instead. 'What's this?'

'Well, that's what I was saying a moment ago.' Robyn continued where she had left off by way of explanation. 'Your sister's box was open, you see, and I know I shouldn't pry, but I couldn't help myself. Well, I did help myself . . .' Robyn faltered.

'My sister?'

Robyn looked quizzically at Gayle; hadn't they just had this same exchange not two minutes earlier?

Robyn was getting a little frustrated. 'The box.' She stabbed her finger at the thick black lettering.

Gayle's gaze followed Robyn's outstretched hand until her eyes settled on the box. She tentatively opened a flap to look inside. Then something piqued her interest. She reached inside and lifted another item out of the box. Robyn felt a little relieved that she wasn't the only one prying into Dinah's box.

Gayle brought out an ornate jug and set it down next to the vase. They matched. Gayle looked at Robyn. Robyn shrugged. Gayle dived in the box for another item. As she got it out, Robyn took her cue and picked out another item. Together, they took out the entire contents, and put them carefully on the floor surrounding the vase.

Robyn knelt. 'Stunning,' was all she could say, taking in the intricately painted fine bone china tea set. 'They should be in a museum.' She turned to look at Gayle. 'I'm so glad I didn't try and put the vase back in the box. Imagine if I had dropped it or put it on one of these pieces of china. I would have ruined this beautiful set.' Robyn glanced at Gayle, waiting for her to agree, but Gayle seemed preoccupied as she turned one of the smaller items over in her hands, tracing the delicate patterns.

'Why does your sister store her stuff here? Is she away travelling?'

Gayle shook her head. 'These don't belong to her. They are my parents' things.'

'They are?' Robyn glanced at the other labelled boxes with Gayle's brothers' names on the boxes.

'I'd wondered what had happened to my mother's bone china tea set and crockery,' commented Gayle.

'Must be worth a bit,' said Robyn.

'Yes, I'm sure.' Gayle placed the china plate in her hand carefully on the floor. 'Let's look in another box, shall we?'

'All the other boxes are sealed,' Robyn observed.

'Are they, now?' Gayle got up off her knees, and selected another box. 'And what have we here? Ah, my brother, Jerome. Of course.'

Robyn watched in anticipation as Gayle picked at the end of the tape and then peeled the long strip off the top. It was like watching someone unwrapping their Christmas presents, excited to see what they had got. Robyn moved closer as Gayle undid one flap, then the other.

Gayle took out a very nice piece of silverware that most definitely was not some embarrassing schoolwork that their parents had kept and boxed up.

'I bet this …' Gayle waved the silverware at Robyn before she placed it back in the box, 'was my sister's idea.'

Robyn was quiet.

'It certainly explains why they didn't want me to *meddle* in Mother's affairs.'

'What does that mean?' Robyn looked at her askance.

'They didn't want me to come and look after Mum and Dad. The last time I heard from one of my nieces, I found out that my siblings had discussed it between themselves and had decided that if she needed to be cared for, the house would have to be sold so she could go into a home. As usual, I'm not included in any conversations when it comes to our parents. It's like there's only the three of them. It's always been like that.'

'Well, that's just not right.'

'I know, but I suppose I've just got used to it, over the years. I expect that's why they came here, unbeknown to me, before I turned up, and cleared out all the stuff that was down here for when the house has to go on the market.'

'Yeah – and helped themselves to stuff they wanted too.' Robyn shut her mouth. She whispered, 'Sorry, I shouldn't have said that.'

'No need to apologise. That's exactly what I was thinking.' Gayle cast her gaze around the packing boxes.

'They shouldn't have done that, though,' Robyn added. 'It's a bit mean, picking and choosing what they fancy when your parents, well, your mum, hasn't even … gone.'

'Yeah, I agree.'

'And what about you?' Robyn asked.

'What do you mean?'

'Well, there has to be something you would have liked, a keepsake to remember your parents by.'

'This house,' Gayle blurted. She quickly backtracked. 'But that's not possible. My siblings are right: the house will probably have to be sold to pay for care home fees.'

'Can't you stay here, looking after your mum? Then you wouldn't have to sell the house to pay for a care home.'

'It's not up to me.'

'Why?'

Gayle stared at her.

'You're the one here, aren't you? Taking care of your mum. Surely, you're the one who gets to say whether she goes into a home or not. Besides, I bet she'd rather stay put, and it is sad, having to sell the family home.'

'It will have to be sold one day.'

'How come?'

'Well, there's four of us, so the house will have to be sold to divide the proceeds equally between us.'

'Do you want the house to be sold?'

'Of course not, but there's no way around it, I'm afraid. I haven't got the money to buy them out.'

'Buy them out?' Robyn looked at her quizzically.

'Oh, you know, buy their shares of the house from them.' Gayle frowned as she waved her hand at the boxes. She changed the subject. 'I obviously interrupted their, their …'

'Sort-out?' Robyn offered.

'Dinah always was the organised one.' Gayle's voice was full of disdain. 'Talk about count your chickens before they're hatched. Mum's still alive, for goodness' sake.'

'Perhaps …' Robyn hesitated, feeling uncomfortable even mentioning it. 'Perhaps they thought that as you were looking after your mother, that you might, um … well … inherit the house.'

'Inherit this house? Just me?'

'Yes.'

Gayle shook her head. 'Robyn, you have met my mother. No lawyer in their right mind would let her amend her will.'

'Well maybe it was in there already, before she … got sick …' Robyn trailed off.

Gayle put an arm around Robyn's shoulders and squeezed her affectionately. 'If you're trying to make me feel better, you'll have to think up something else. My brothers and sister all know what's in the will, and the house and contents are to be shared equally between us.'

'Oh. So if everything is meant to be shared equally, how come there aren't some boxes with your name on? I think they should have included you in their sort-out.'

'Perhaps it was the only time they could make it.'

'But they didn't tell you they were coming …'

Gayle shook her head. 'No, they did not. But I expect they were quite busy. Did I tell you that my brother, Xavier, followed Dad into the medical profession? He's a surgeon. And my other brother, Jerome, is a lawyer. And Dinah's done very well for herself with her own estate agency, selling expensive property.'

Robyn frowned at her friend. She was making excuses for them. Her gaze shifted to the boxes. Gayle was very generous and kind-hearted – unlike her brothers and sister, by the looks of things. They had done this behind her back. Robyn felt like warning Gayle that she'd better stand her ground when the time came. It looked likely that her siblings were going to walk all over her otherwise.

'What is it?' Gayle said. 'You suddenly look all serious. Did you remember something?'

'No, no.' Robyn said, staring at the boxes. 'Hey, there is a box here without a name on. Perhaps it's for you?'

'Or perhaps the contents are just not worth having,' Gayle said glumly, eyeing the box Robyn had come across. She sighed. 'Oh, go on then. Open it.'

Robyn set the large box on top of the others and started to open it.

Gayle turned for the stairs.

'Aren't you going to wait and see what it is?'

'Well, if they didn't want the contents, then it's probably not worth keeping.' Gayle shrugged.

Robyn turned back to the box. The fact that they hadn't just chucked the contents had to count for something. She tore off the wide strip of tape securing the flaps and opened the box.

Gayle paused on the stairs. 'What's inside?'

'Some more family photos.' These ones weren't in photo albums; there were just lots of photos, some in their original paper envelopes from the shop that had developed the film, others just lying in piles on top.

Gayle walked up behind her and peered into the box.

'I'm sorry there's nothing of value in this box.'

'Oh, on the contrary. You know, I'd much rather have my memories, and the family photos, than expensive bone china or silverware any day.'

Robyn grinned. 'Me too.' Her smile faltered. She felt a hand on her shoulder.

'Perhaps you should write to your mum, explain what happened. She could come stay here too, while you recuperate. There's plenty of room. And then she can tell you all about … well, you.'

Robyn smiled. It was an idea, and very generous of Gayle to offer. 'That's so kind of you, Gayle, but I just need a bit of time, that's all. I don't think I really want my mum fussing around me.'

'I understand.'

Robyn wasn't sure she did. She wasn't sure she understood herself. Why would she rather stay with a stranger than be with family – with her mum? It didn't really make any sense, but Robyn just had a feeling, a gut instinct, that contacting her mum wasn't the right thing to do. Not now, at any rate. She just had to trust her instincts – they were all she had to go on. Just then, she was happy staying with Gayle and her mum. She was also hoping David would visit.

She had thought he might ask her the previous day before she left the hospital or might call her later in the day and ask if she was doing anything special for New Year's Eve. Well, New Year's Eve had arrived, and she was still waiting to see if he would get in touch. She knew it was still early, so she wasn't expecting a call until later. She just hoped he hadn't forgotten about her.

'You're thinking about him,' said Gayle as she reached inside the box.

Robyn had been crouching in front of the box, lost in thought. She looked at Gayle. 'Him – who?'

Gayle cocked her head to one side. 'David, of course.'

Robyn nodded. She didn't really want to talk about it.

'You miss him.'

'Yeah, but it's not like he's been gone for long. I only saw him yesterday.'

'One day is an eternity if it's true love,' said Gayle, picking a photo at random out of the box.

'True love?' Robyn scoffed. 'What makes you say that? I've only known him for a week!'

Gayle shrugged. 'Trust me – I've seen the way he looks at you. And you at him.'

Robyn looked away, embarrassed. 'But what if …' She quickly shook her head. 'Oh, never mind.'

Gayle shifted her gaze from the photo. 'I know what you're thinking – what if there's someone else, and you just can't remember?'

Robyn nodded and sighed. 'Exactly. I could be in love with someone else.'

'Maybe.'

Robyn shot her a look. 'What does that mean?'

'Well, if you've got feelings for David, and I suspect quite strong feelings that have taken you by surprise after just one week, then perhaps if there was someone else, you weren't really in love.'

Robyn stared at Gayle. It was a big leap to offer up that conclusion when she didn't even know if there was someone else, let alone whether she was really in love with them.

Robyn really didn't want to talk about it. What if they turned up at the hospital, looking for her, and found her at Gayle's, and she didn't even know them? That would be just awful, for her and the person she was meant to be in a relationship with. Robyn hoped she was single, even if that meant one less person looking for her.

Robyn looked at the photo in Gayle's hand. 'Hey, is that you with your siblings?'

'Yeah.' She frowned at the photo, and put it back. 'You can seal that box back up when you've finished having a look through.'

'Oh, okay.' Robyn watched Gayle pick up the two cold mugs of tea and head for the stairs. She guessed Gayle wasn't in the mood to go through any more family photos after all.

'All right. We could bring the box upstairs,' Robyn suggested, wondering if Gayle would like to take a look later.

Gayle shook her head. 'It's heavy, and the last thing I want is for you to have another accident. These stairs are steep.'

Robyn looked at the large box. Gayle had a point.

'Don't be too long, Robyn. It's cold down here.'

'I won't, I promise.'

'Good. I'll put the kettle on and make us another cuppa. Our tea got cold.'

Robyn nodded before turning her attention to the box. She took out the photo that Gayle had her hand. There were four children in the photo. She turned the picture over to see the names of Gayle and her brothers and sister carefully printed on the back along with their ages in brackets. She flipped the photo back to take another look, armed with more information.

Gayle's brothers were twins, non-identical, ten years old and looking very smart and handsome in their suits and dickie bow ties. Dinah was eight, wearing a pretty floral dress. She wasn't looking at the camera but at a very bonny, bouncy toddler sitting next to her with arms outstretched, chubby cheeks, and an endearing grin. Gayle was looking straight at the camera. Her sister was leaning away from Gayle, giving her a sideways glance. Gayle was nine months old, and she was the new baby of the family – obviously not to the delight of her elder sister.

Robyn smiled at Gayle as a toddler. She was very cute. Then her smile faded as she looked at Dinah once more.

What a shame that sibling rivalries had to carry on into adulthood. Why couldn't people just grow up?

Last night, when Gayle had drunk too much wine, she'd opened up about her upbringing and had mentioned that it had been very different to that of her brothers and sisters. The age gap between her and her siblings meant that she had still been a child living with her parents, with this big house all to herself, when her siblings had been off at university and making their way out in the world.

By the sound of things, Gayle's parents had changed by the time they'd had her; they had no longer been so hot on education as they had been with their older children. They had been more relaxed and content in themselves, less pushy, with a different perspective on life. Gayle believed it was because they had finally been content with their life in England.

So, when Gayle had left high school, instead of going straight to university as her siblings had done, she had intended to go travelling. She'd left home for London and had worked in odd jobs to support herself, eventually falling into hairdressing because that was what a friend was doing. The friend had persuaded her to take up a vacancy as an apprentice hairdresser.

Later, when she was in her late twenties, she had met a guy who she'd thought was the love of her life, and had imagined they were going to settle down. She didn't talk much about that relationship. Robyn guessed she'd been let down. But the upside was that after it had ended, she had chosen to go into the medical profession and had trained as a midwife.

Gayle told Robyn all this, along with the fact that she couldn't have children of her own, but that each and every baby she'd delivered had become, in a way, part of her family – and some she had continued to keep in touch with over the years.

Robyn sighed and put the picture back in the box. These were not the kind of photos she was after. She just wanted ones of the house. Which was just as well, because she was finding the photos of Gayle and her siblings rather unsettling. She closed the flaps of the box, wondering why she felt that way – was it something to do with her own family? Were there hidden rivalries in her own past? She frowned. If only she could remember.

Robyn left the box where it was, sealing it up with the tape as best she could. She walked up the basement stairs and switched off the light, closing the door behind her.

She turned towards the kitchen and walked straight into Gayle. 'Ah! I was just coming to get you. I've made the tea, and some toast.'

Robyn said, 'Let me just check I've shut the basement door properly.'

'I'm sure it's fine. I'll lock it later. Come on. The tea will get cold. Hurry up!' Gayle's fingers closed around Robyn's arm.

Robyn flinched. 'Don't touch me!'

Gayle let go of her arm immediately, and looked at her in surprise. 'What's the matter, Robyn? Are you okay? All the colour has drained out of your cheeks all of a sudden.'

Robyn winced, feeling embarrassed. 'Sorry – I … I don't know what came over me.' She looked at her arm, expecting to see red finger marks, where fingers, much stronger than Gayle's, had closed around her upper arm, tight. Far too tight. She felt a shiver run through her even though there were no finger marks; Gayle had only taken hold of her arm gently, and besides, Robyn had a thick jumper on.

But this was how it always started – the hand tightening around her arm. She raised an eyebrow, realising she'd just had a memory. But what had happened in her past that made her feel so afraid?

23

'You and me are going to get out of this house for a little while.'

'We are?' Robyn said, sitting at the kitchen table, feeling the warmth from the Aga as she finished her lovely cup of tea and her toast, which was slathered with butter and marmalade. She cast a disappointed look towards the lounge, where the boxes of Gayle's family photos rescued from the attic were still waiting for her to have another leaf through. That had been the plan for after her second breakfast of the day; at least it had been before Gayle suggested going out.

Robyn supposed a walk on New Year's Eve wouldn't do any harm. A few minutes later, she joined Gayle at the front door, wearing a lovely warm bright pink parka with a cosy faux fur lining. 'Do you mind?' Robyn asked, doing a twirl in the coat in front of Gayle. 'It's from the trunk in the attic.'

Gayle shook her head. 'Of course not. It suits you.'

'I know.' Robyn still didn't fancy wearing any of the mostly black clothes from her own suitcase.

Gayle opened the front door.

Robyn glanced at the stairs. 'Wait! What about your mum? Is she up yet? Should we take her with us?'

Gayle smiled. 'Oh, Robyn! You're always thinking of others. While you were down in the basement, the minibus arrived to take her to the community hall in Aviemore, where they hold a coffee morning and activities.'

'She's okay going on her own?'

'Oh, it's all supervised; there will be others there with my mother's condition too. It's the only way she still gets to meet up with old friends.'

Robyn smiled. 'What a lovely idea.'

'One of my brothers pays for the sessions. I couldn't afford it.'

Robyn nodded as she followed Gayle out of the door.

'Talking about going out,' said Gayle, locking the door behind them. 'Don't you want to know where we're going?'

Robyn shrugged. 'I don't mind.' She was trying to be diplomatic. She wasn't really interested in where they were going; she was more interested in spending time looking at the other photos of the house that she'd found in the basement. But she didn't want to upset Gayle by not accompanying her. Besides, Gayle could probably use the company.

'We'll be back by the time Mother arrives home this afternoon. Then she takes her afternoon nap. Has done ever since I could remember. Says it rejuvenates the body. Me, I couldn't sleep in the day.'

'Me neither.'

'Still, nap time has its uses.'

'Like what?'

'I can go out for a couple of hours.'

'What if she wakes up while you're gone?' Robyn didn't like to think about the possibility that Gayle's mum might wake up and, because of her dementia, be unable to remember where she was, and feel frightened, alone in the big old house.

'Won't happen.' Gayle said, sounding very sure of herself. 'Remember, we have a neighbour whose known us for years and years. Although she's quite elderly now, she doesn't mind popping in and keeping an eye on Mum while I'm out shopping, or when I have one or two clients who have booked appointments.'

'Clients?' Robyn paused before she got in the car, and looked at Gayle.

'Remember I said I trained as a hairdresser years ago before I went into nursing?'

Robyn nodded as she joined Gayle in the car. Gayle switched on the car engine and set off. 'I took early retirement from nursing to look after my parents, so I've fallen back on hairdressing to earn money to top up my pension. I would have been much better off financially staying in nursing, but this works well because I can fit in appointments around caring for Mother.'

Robyn looked out of the car window as Gayle drove down the street. 'So, is that where we're going – to one of your appointments?'

'You sound disappointed.' Gayle eyed Robyn.

'Oh no, not at all.' Now she was out, in the car, enjoying the scenery as Gayle drove, and feeling the warmth of the winter sun, which was streaming through the car window, Robyn felt differently. 'It's nice to get out of the house for a break and a change of scene.'

'Ah, I thought you'd come around.'

Robyn blushed when she realised Gayle had sensed her reticence to go out. She wasn't quite sure what she was going to do with herself during the appointment, though. She'd probably sit and listen to Gayle catch up with her client. And there would be plenty of magazines she could sit and leaf through. Hairdressers always had piles of old magazines. Robyn began to smile. *What woman wouldn't want to while away an afternoon in the company of some hot celebrity gossip in a magazine?* she thought.

''There, you see? The change is doing you good already,' Gayle said, catching her smiling.

'It's very good of you to work on New Year's Eve,' commented Robyn.

'Oh, not at all. I don't mind. Besides, like I told you, New Year's Eve is quite the occasion in Scotland, so hairdressers tend to work so that women can get their hair done before they go out.'

As they headed for town, passing the loch, the expanse of water glistening in the morning sunshine, Robyn asked, 'What's it called?'

'What is what called?'

'Your hairdressing business.' Robyn was wondering whether, if Gayle told her the name of her hairdressing salon, she would remember it. She knew that she must have visited Aviemore before the trip she had made with Gayle the previous day to buy some wine and nibbles, because of the sketch of Wilbur's Bookstore in her diary or sketchbook – whatever it was. How could she think of it as a diary when there was no writing in it? *I'm weird*, she thought.

'Ah, it's just Gayle's Hairdressing.'

Robyn frowned. She didn't recognise the name.

'Hope you don't mind that we're going to be making a couple of visits this afternoon. Sorry, I suppose I should have warned you before you came along.'

Robyn turned to look at Gayle. 'A couple of visits?'

'Yes, that's normally the case. I'm going to Rose's, and time permitting, because I did tell Mrs Henshaw that I must be home by 3pm sharp,' – she wagged her finger at an imaginary Mrs Henshaw – 'all going well we might make it to her house too.'

'You don't work at a hairdresser's in town?' Robyn couldn't hide her disappointment. The vision of piles of juicy gossipy magazines evaporated.

'Well, whatever gave you that idea?'

Robyn shrugged. 'Sorry, I thought you had a hairdressing salon.'

'I haven't got a premises where I run a salon. I visit clients in their homes. I work freelance. I'm a mobile hairdresser.'

'Where's your stuff?' Robyn glanced at the back seat, which was empty. She hadn't seen Gayle take a bag out of the house with her.

'I keep all my equipment, scissors, combs and hairbrushes, hairdryer, straighteners, curling tongs, hair products, and towels and gowns in a carry case.'

'I didn't realise you needed to take so much stuff with you.'

'Oh, yes. All the equipment and products you see a hairdresser in a salon use, I have to provide.'

'It all sounds very professional.'

'Absolutely. I'm properly set up; I pay my taxes. I haven't the time to do it any other way. I can't take on a job in a hairdresser as they most likely will need me to work fixed hours, which I can't guarantee. As I said, I need the flexibility. And renting a chair in a salon to see my clients there just eats into my profits.' Gayle sighed, 'I don't know how long I'll be hanging around these parts.'

'Oh, don't say that, Gayle.' Robyn knew what she was getting at; how long she stayed on living in her parents' house all depended on her mother's health, and how much time she had left. She thought of Gayle's mother's possessions – the ones worth anything financially, her silverware and fine bone china, already distributed and boxed ready in her basement to be taken once she passed away. How sad. Robyn was suddenly glad that Gayle's mother had no clue what had been going on when her three other children had visited.

Gayle said, 'Things change, Robyn. That's just a fact of life.'

'But wouldn't you like to stay here – perhaps open a salon of your own?' Robyn ventured. She could see Gayle smile at the thought. 'And then all your mobile clients would know about you and hopefully would come to your salon.'

Gayle's head bobbed up and down.

'And you could call it …'

'Gayle's Salon.' Gayle dreamily intoned.

Robyn stared at her. 'You *have* been thinking about it.' she said wryly. 'Why didn't you say anything?'

'Oh, I don't know, because people might think it's silly. Some people dream of travelling the world or saving endangered species or having children. And I dream of …' she cocked her head to Robyn and said in a silly voice, 'Gayle's Salon.'

'What's so silly about that?' Robyn replied. 'It's not silly at all. And you know how I know for sure?'

'How?'

'Because it's what *you* want, Gayle, and nobody else. It's what's in here.' Robyn pointed at her chest. 'Your heart's desire. And no parents or siblings or friends can tell you what you should or shouldn't do. That's how I know.'

They travelled along in silence for a moment. Robyn could tell Gayle was still savouring the vision of her little salon with its sign above the door. Robyn turned away from Gayle to stare out of the window, wishing she knew what her dream had been before the accident. She knew she'd been at college, but what was it that she really wanted to go on and do afterwards?

'You've gone awfully quiet, Robyn. Is something the matter?'

Robyn stared out of the car window. They'd left Aviemore behind, 'I wish … I wish I knew what my dream had been.'

Gayle glanced at her. 'Oh, right. The memory thing.' Gayle pursed her lips. 'I was going to ask you what your dream in life is. What about your diary? Isn't there a clue in there?'

'That's useless. Just a load of meaningless sketches.'

'So, start over. Make a new one.'

'A new diary?'

'No, a new dream in life. What did you say about it being right if it comes from the heart? Well, your heart is still the same, even if your memory isn't.'

Robyn stared at Gayle. She felt envious of Gayle – she knew exactly what she wanted out of life, which Robyn felt was one of the great mysteries that each person had to solve for themselves. And Robyn guessed the trick was to discover it pretty early on. That way, a person could start figuring out they were going to do about it and how they were going to get there.

Robyn felt she was starting with a massive disadvantage – not knowing who she was. She didn't want to share this thought with Gayle, who was only trying to be helpful and upbeat. But as Gayle had said before, she couldn't really put herself in someone's shoes who had lost their memory.

They drove the rest of the way in silence. Robyn was worried that she was not being good company and that Gayle would wish she hadn't brought her along, but every time Robyn stole a glance over at Gayle, she still had a whisper of a smile on her face. She imagined that her friend was preoccupied with thoughts of Gayle's Salon. Robyn smiled too. She was pleased for Gayle. Her smile faded when her thoughts turned to her own predicament. She didn't want to start over. What she wanted, more than anything, was for her memory to come back.

24

'Well, here we are,' Gayle said as she turned the nose of the car sharp left off the main road on to a deep-rutted dirt track that had been worn away by very thick tyre treads. In the corner of her vision, Robyn caught sight of an old tractor that looked as though it had been abandoned in the middle of a field.

'Is this a farm?' Robyn asked, expecting the farm buildings to come into sight any moment.

'Might have been once, I guess.'

'Once?'

'Look.' Gayle pointed straight ahead.

Robyn could see two large banners on massive poles standing on either side of the unmade track. They flapped in the wind, but Robyn could still make out the wording. '*Pine Ridge*,' she read aloud.

'Yes, that's what it's called. A development of new and exclusive residences. Aren't we just the lucky ones.' Gayle screwed up her nose in disgust as Robyn shuddered.

'It's going to be a sprawling estate when it's finished. God knows how many houses are planned.'

'How awful,' Robyn said as the first architectural monstrosity came into view. She wondered at how the developers had got planning permission.

'Aren't they just?' Gayle agreed. 'Just don't let on to the Gordons. They're nice folks and you can't blame them.'

Blame them for what, Robyn was about to ask, but Gayle was already waving as she pulled the car to a halt. Robyn guessed Gayle was referring to the fact that the Gordons had bought one of these new-build properties that were blighting the beautiful landscape.

Gayle opened the car door. 'I'm just going to get my bag of hairdressing equipment out of the boot.'

Robyn asked, 'Do you need a hand?'

Gayle glanced back at Robyn and shook her head. 'No, it's fine. I still think you need to take it easy.'

Robyn saw Gayle's eyes drift upwards to the bandage on her forehead. She had become so used to it herself that she'd almost forgotten about it.

Gayle asked, 'Do you want me to take a look at that for you when we get back?'

Robyn touched the bandage. 'Would you? The doctor gave me some bandages, and explained how to self-care at home, as she called it, showing me how to change the bandage. She said they wouldn't send a community nurse. I get the gist that you have to be housebound for care in the community, and I'm clearly not housebound.'

'Don't worry. I'll have a look at it for you.'

Robyn breathed a sigh of relief. 'Good, because I don't fancy another trip to the hospital if it's not healing.'

'Is it uncomfortable? Does it feel sore, or painful?'

'A little sore still. But not too painful.'

'Sounds as though you're on the mend. Have you got stitches that will need taking out?'

'No, the doctor said that as the cut was shallow, they used steri-strips.' Robyn hadn't removed the bandage yet, so she wasn't sure what that meant.

'Ah, they can be used for shallow wounds with straight edges, instead of regular stitches, pulling each edge of the skin together and sealing the wound. But the best part is they are just thin adhesive strips and are easily removed.'

'Does that mean you can remove them?'

'Of course. But first we'll see how it's healing. I'll take a look this evening.'

Robyn smiled at Gayle. She thought again about how she wanted to repay her friend's kindness by putting her plan for Gayle's parents' house in motion.

Gayle got out of the car and was about to shut the car door when she paused. 'We should get you signed on with a GP practice here,' she said.

'That's what Dr Jamieson at the hospital said. They looked up my records, and I'm signed on with one at the university I attended. Do you think it's really necessary?'

Gayle pointed at her bandage. 'In case you need to have it checked out by a GP, it is necessary. And even if you don't, if you are unwell, and not registered, then it might mean another trip to A&E.'

Robyn shuddered at the thought. 'In that case, I'll sign up with one, for sure.'

Gayle smiled. 'Good girl. If it wasn't a bank holiday today, I'd take you along to mine to see if you could register.'

'Another time, then.'

Gayle smiled. 'Yes, of course.'

Robyn turned in her seat to watch Gayle as she walked around to the back of the car. She heard her pop the boot, and a grunt as she lifted her bag, which Robyn imagined was quite heavy, out of the boot.

Robyn turned back and stared out of the car window at the house. A grey-haired woman waved from the front window of the new-build semi-detached house with a pathway leading up to the front door. Either side of the path was an immaculate lawn with newly planted flower borders.

It looked like a show home, which wasn't surprising; the adjoining semi *was* the show home, and had an identical manicured front lawn and flower borders. The only difference was that it had a *Show Home* sign outside, a small additional parking area, and an office in the attached garage, which Robyn imagined would be converted back into a proper garage once the development was completed.

Robyn saw a lady, dressed in a suit, sitting behind a large desk with a pile of site brochures. She imagined they detailed the other properties that could be bought off-plan and that would soon spring up.

It was probably the strangest thing Robyn had ever seen – as far as her memory would allow, anyway. All around the oasis of newness and perfection of the two semis she could see mud and clay and diggers and workmen. It was like someone had taken the two semis and plonked them slap bang in the centre of a massive muddy field. And to cap it all, the resident of the house looked like a very sweet elderly lady who ought surely to be in quieter, more sedate surroundings. Poor woman.

'Robyn!'

Robyn was jolted out of her reverie by Gayle tapping on the car window. She heard her muffled name called again. She opened the door to the deafening roar of mechanical machinery.

'Now close your mouth – it really isn't all that bad,' Gayle insisted as they walked up the pathway together.

'And for goodness' sake, smile!'

Robyn felt like putting her hands to her ears instead. But she stood beside Gayle at the front door and did her best to ignore the noise and to smile for the sake of Gayle's client.

They both stood at the front door. Gayle rang the doorbell.

Robyn was about to tell Gayle that ringing it wasn't necessary because Mrs Gordon had seen them in the window, but she thought better of it in case Gayle then thought that Mrs Gordon had seen Robyn's miserable face.

'Just keep smiling,' Gayle added, 'at least for an hour.'

Robyn had a question. 'What did you mean when you said, *you can't blame them*?'

'Shhh! Not now.'

The door opened.

'Gayle, dear! How good of you to come.' She spoke as if Gayle was a dear old friend who had taken time out of her busy schedule to pop in and see her for a social visit, rather than for a pre-booked hair appointment.

'Not at all, Rose. It's good to see you.' Gayle stepped in.

Rose touched her arm. 'We are so sorry for your loss, Gayle,' she said solemnly. 'We heard your father passed away. He was such a wonderful man, and such a devoted GP to our small community in Aviemore.'

'Thank you, Rose. That's very kind.'

Rose turned her attention to Robyn. 'And who's this?'

Robyn opened her mouth, but Gayle got there first.

'This is Robyn Parker.'

'Robyn,' Rose said slowly, 'Parker.' Something in the way she said the name made Robyn feel that Rose didn't believe her. She seemed to be looking her over, deciding whether to invite her in.

Robyn really didn't feel in the mood to explain the circumstances surrounding how she came to be with Gayle.

Gayle added, 'She's a friend who's staying with me for the time being. I hope you don't mind her tagging along.'

'No, no. The more the merrier, as they say.' She waved her hand at Robyn to come in. They gathered in Rose's lounge. 'Now, you two take a seat while I put the kettle on and go to find that husband of mine. I did tell him what time you'd arrive. Men,' she sighed. 'Never around when you need them, and always around when you don't.'

She left the room.

'What did that mean?' Robyn said.

'That they're always under your feet, dear.' Rose's voice carried from the hallway as she went in search of her husband.

Robyn put her hand over her mouth, and looked at Gayle with an apologetic look.

'She may be old, Robyn but she's got hearing like a hawk, I'll tell you. Either that, or she's got this place wired.'

'You mean like those cop shows?' Rose asked, her voice sounding further away this time.

Robyn sniggered into her hand.

Gayle shook her head, and put her finger to her lips.

Robyn got the message; she stared at Gayle, and held her lips together tightly, resolving not to say another word until Rose was in the room.

Rose came back carrying a tea tray neatly arranged with delicate teacups and a large teapot hidden under a woollen tea cosy which looked hand-knitted. There was also a plate of assorted biscuits.

Gayle and Robyn bounced up together, intending to help Rose with the tea tray. 'Oh, do sit down you two. Honestly, I may be old, but I'm not an invalid.'

'Sorry,' they said in unison. They looked at each other, then sat down.

Rose passed a plate to each of them and offered the biscuits. 'Now I know how Gayle likes her tea, but how does …' she stuck her chin out at Robyn.

'Robyn,' Robyn said, although she was sure Rose hadn't forgotten her name. She took a biscuit from the plate.

'That's right, silly me. How does Robyn like her tea?'

'Black with one sugar, please.'

'No milk? Why, a growing girl like you needs to keep up with the calcium, surely.'

She poured the tea and leaned forward with Robyn's cup. 'Say, how old are you?'

Caught off-guard Robyn hesitated. 'Um … twenty-one.'

'Really?'

Robyn took her teacup and looked at Gayle, who sat expressionless, drinking her tea. Robyn wondered what she was getting at. It sounded as though Rose didn't believe her.

'Still, I guess it's your height. You are a small little thing, aren't you?'

Robyn was starting to feel embarrassed under Rose's penetrating gaze. If she'd known she was going to face the Spanish Inquisition from Gayle's client, who had appeared to be a sweet old lady, then she would never have come.

'The hair doesn't help.'

Robyn involuntarily flicked her ponytail.

'Makes you look like a schoolgirl.'

Robyn turned to Gayle, wide-eyed, guessing that it wasn't a compliment.

Gayle just smiled as if to say, *that's Rose for you – says it like it is.* 'Well, I can do something about that. I can cut your hair, give you a new style, if you'd like, Robyn.'

'Can you make me blonde too?' Robyn blurted.

'You want to change your hair colour?' Gayle said in surprise.

Robyn felt just as surprised at her own words as Gayle looked. She chose not to share why she had suddenly felt the urge to change her appearance. Somehow, it was to protect herself. It was a bizarre thought. And that thought led to another thought that was just as disturbing – if she wanted to change her appearance, and it wasn't just to look older, but to protect herself, the question was – from whom?

The one thing Robyn hadn't considered when she had tried to remember the reason she'd been on the road on Christmas Day, as opposed to being at home with her family and friends – whoever, and wherever they were – was that rather than being on her way somewhere, on her way home, maybe she wasn't going anywhere; at least not anywhere in particular. Had she in fact been running away from something – or someone?

25

'So, where's that husband of yours?' Gayle said, diverting Rose's attention – much to Robyn's relief.

'I'm coming!' A man's voice rang out from somewhere in the house.

'I must say, you and your husband have the most amazing hearing,' Robyn blurted.

'Not at all – it's the walls.' Rose set her teacup down, and with her knuckle tapped the wall beside her chair. 'There, you see? Paper-thin. Not solid, like my old house. They just use plaster board, you know. I pity anyone who buys one of the apartments on the estate. Still, it's good for me and George; we can speak to each other no matter where we are in the house. No more hollering when dinner is ready. Isn't that right, George?'

'Why, yes dear.' George walked into the lounge. He appeared older than Rose, and a bit doddery. 'The only place it doesn't work is in the garden.'

Gayle nodded. 'And we know how much you love your gardening, Mr Gordon.'

Rose said, 'He never used to. Strangely, his interest in the garden only started when we moved here, which is rather odd, especially as there's nothing that needs doing out there. It's been laid to lawn, and landscaped, which I'm at pains to remind him.' Rose rolled her eyes at her husband.

'But dearest, we want to keep that way – don't we?'

'Yes, but I didn't think you'd be out there with a litter-picker the moment a leaf dropped on the lawn!'

Robyn gave Rose a sideways glance when she remembered what she'd just said about the paper-thin walls. Wherever her husband was in the house, he was in hearing distance of his dear wife. But he wasn't when he was in the garden. Robyn cheekily asked, 'I bet it's peaceful in your garden.' Of course, she wasn't referring to the diggers and the workmen.

'Oh, by heck – isn't it just!' And clearly neither was George.

Rose shot him a look.

Gayle got up, walked over to George, and linked her arm in his. 'Right, are you ready for that haircut, Mr Gordon?'

'Oh yes. But on one condition.'

'Okay,' Gayle said slowly. 'There have never been any conditions before.'

'Well, there's one now.'

Robyn stole a glance at Rose, who was looking at her husband quizzically, her eyebrows raised. This was obviously news to her too.

'My condition is this, Gayle. You must call me George.'

Gayle said, 'Oh, um … okay. George.'

Robyn caught the relief in her voice. She understood. Gayle had a round of clients on her books, and this wasn't a social visit. She needed the money. Robyn resolved to pay Gayle for cutting and colouring her hair.

Robyn took another sip of her tea and looked around the

room, taking in the new modern sofa suite and coffee table, and the old ornaments and collectibles that the couple must have brought with them when they had moved house. Her eyes eventually settled on Rose, who was sitting across from her, staring at her intently.

'So, Robyn. Tell me about yourself.'

Robyn sighed. She got the feeling that this was going to be a long appointment. She couldn't wait for Gayle to cut George's hair so that it would be Rose's turn.

'Can I have another cup of tea, do you think?' She was stalling. Perhaps by the time Rose had made the tea, she would have forgotten her question.

'A top-up?' Rose pulled the cosy off the teapot, holding it in mid-air. 'Of course.'

Robyn frowned at the teapot. She'd forgotten about that. She watched Rose pour the tea.

'Milk and sugar?'

'Yes please. I don't think I've had my share of calcium for today.' Robyn winced. Now she was being sarcastic. *That's not like me*, she thought. She raised her eyebrows, realising she'd remembered something about herself. Surely, that was a sign her memory was slowly resurfacing.

'Milk and sugar.' Rose spooned some sugar into Robyn's tea and added a splash of milk from the jug.

Robyn realised that her sarcasm had fortunately been lost on Rose, who busied herself with the teapot and its cosy while Robyn searched for something to say. 'I'm at university.'

'That's nice. What are you studying?'

Robyn had no idea, but she said, 'Art.' That was what she was assuming, going by the rather good sketches in her so-called diary.

She could phone the university and explain the situation. But she couldn't imagine they'd give out any information over the phone, especially considering what she'd have to say: *I've lost my memory – can you tell me everything you know about me, along with my home address, and my parents' or relations' contact phone number?*

Robyn winced at the thought of that embarrassing phone call. She knew she would be told it was not university policy to give out students' personal details, even if she claimed to be one of them.

She looked at Rose.

'So, you're here on holiday?'

Robyn stared at Rose, thinking, *Hurry up, Gayle!*

Rose asked, 'How did you meet Gayle?'

Finally, a question she could answer – except she didn't want to. Robyn sighed. 'I had a car accident on Christmas Eve.'

'Oh, Robyn. I'm so sorry to hear that.'

'That's how I met Gayle.'

'Oh, she didn't say anything about being involved in an accident.'

'No, she wasn't *in* the accident too. I met her in hospital while I was a patient, and she was next door visiting her dad.'

'I see. That explains it.'

'Explains what?'

Rose pointed at her own forehead. 'I didn't like to ask what had happened.'

Why not? You asked me everything else, said a voice in Robyn's head. She touched her bandage and thought, *Now I'm just being mean*. Rose wasn't to know she'd lost her memory. 'Gayle is going to look at it when we get back.'

'Is she good at first aid?'

'First aid? I should think so. She was a—' Robyn was

interrupted by the sound of laughter. It sounded as though Gayle and George were sharing a joke while she was trimming his hair. She turned in her seat. Rose was right: the walls were paper-thin.

'She was a …?' prompted Rose.

Robyn raised her voice. 'She was a nurse for years, before she returned to hairdressing.'

'Really? I had no idea.'

'Oh.' Robyn bit her lip, wondering if there was a reason Gayle hadn't told them. She had thought that hairdressers chatted to their clients.

'Was that back in London?'

Robyn nodded. So Gayle had told them she lived in London.

Rose said, 'I got the feeling she doesn't like talking about her life. I guess that's what you've both got in common.'

Robyn pursed her lips.

'I suppose you've got your reasons.'

Robyn knew what her reasons were. Gayle hadn't talked too much about her past in London, and she had a feeling it had to do with the breakup of her relationship.

They both finished their tea in silence. Then Rose busied herself with putting the used cups and saucers back on the tea tray, while Robyn searched again for something to say.

She looked out of the front window. 'So, when did you move in?' Robyn raised her voice above the sound of a digger rolling past the bay window. A saucer rattled suddenly, and Robyn turned back to Rose. A cup was on its side and cold tea was running over the coffee table and down the table leg.

Robyn jumped up. 'Oh, let me get a cloth – your tea is going to soil your carpet.' Then she noticed Rose. Her head was buried in her hands, and her head was shaking from side to side. 'Never mind the stupid carpet,' she mumbled into her hands. 'I never did like the colour anyway.'

Robyn looked from the dripping table leg to Rose and back again. A sob escaped from Rose as she slumped back down on the sofa. Robyn forgot the cloth and sat down next to Rose. Desperately, she searched her pockets for a tissue. She looked around and there on the mantel shelf was an open box, with a clean tissue waiting to be plucked. She bounced up and took out a tissue. After a glance at Rose, she grabbed the box instead.

'Here.'

Rose looked sideways at Robyn, her nose running and her eyes streaming. She took the tissue and blew her nose, then reached for the box and placed it in her lap.

Robyn sat next to her, not quite sure what to do next.

Several tissues later, Rose's tears had abated. She looked at Robyn and gave her a little smile. She patted Robyn's hand. 'I'm being such a silly old woman.'

'What is it?' Robyn asked softly.

'This house,' she said, blowing her nose again. 'I mean it's not as if anyone's died or anything. I just don't know what I'm making a big fuss about, do you?' she sniffed. 'Silly me, of course you wouldn't.' She suddenly got up from the sofa. Robyn watched her walk over to the bay window carrying her box of tissues. She pulled another one out when she arrived at the window, and Robyn was afraid she was going to burst into tears again. But she didn't. She just had the tissue on standby.

This house. Robyn raised her eyebrows, her attention drawn to the window as another digger rolled by. Of course, Rose wasn't unaware of what was going on outside.

'I mean, it's not as if I didn't know it was going to be like this.'

Her back was to Robyn.

Robyn got up, walked over to the window and stood beside Rose. 'It's not always going to be like this.'

'I know.' Rose snuffled. 'We got such a good deal, selling our old house to the developer in exchange for this one. It was practically falling down; it needed so much work to put things right, and that would have cost us so much money. The estate agent next door said we got such a good deal because we were the first ones to buy, and as the development went on the houses would just come up for sale for more money.' Rose turned from the window to look at Robyn. 'Do you think that's true?'

Robyn didn't know what to think, although she did nod in agreement, for Rose's sake. She stared out of the window and thought of Gayle's parents' house, in its quiet, tree-lined cul de sac surrounded by gardens, with privacy from next-door neighbours. She thought how awful it must be to wake up to this wasteland every day. But she could imagine something worse – waking up to tightly packed-in, carbon copies of houses just like your own as far as the eye could see.

'Close your eyes.' Robyn said.

'Pardon?' Rose snuffled.

Robyn turned to her. 'Just close your eyes.'

She did.

'Now you're standing looking out of your window and there's a beautiful house right opposite you, with a lovely green lawn and spring flowers.' Robyn checked Rose still had her eyes shut. She was moving her head about as if she was looking at the image, so Robyn continued. 'It's very quiet, except you can hear the twittering of birds around a bird table, and the sound of children's voices.'

'The estate's for over-fifties,' Rose interrupted.

'Oh, right.' Robyn smiled. She hadn't seen the plans for the new development, but perhaps it wouldn't be as bad as she imagined. There would be bungalows, and detached houses for the comfortably retired. There might be neighbours who were Rose's age. 'Are your eyes still shut?'

'Yes, yes – go on.'

'Well, you can hear voices. It's your neighbours across the way, waving and saying good morning. They are watering their plants. And now you see yourself walking down your path and across to visit your new neighbours opposite. You're carrying a pie.'

'A pie?'

'Yes, you're welcoming and introducing yourself to your new neighbours. After all, they're going to be your new friends.'

'I'm not a very good cook.'

Robyn sighed. 'It's the thought that counts.'

She finished and stood watching Rose. After a minute, Rose opened her eyes. She turned to Robyn and took her hand. 'Thank you.'

'Don't thank me,' Robyn said. 'I only described to you the picture on the massive billboard as you turn into the estate.'

'I know, but sometimes you need somebody to give you a boot up the backside to stop you feeling sorry for yourself. Goodness knows, I've been driving George mad these last few weeks, wondering whether we'd done the right thing moving from our old, draughty house. No wonder he's been spending so much time in the garden. I know why – to get away from me!'

Robyn shook her head, trying to come up with some little white lie and pretend that was not what she believed.

'Don't shake your head. I know it's true because he'll find any excuse to be out there, even though there isn't a single thing to be done in that garden.' She laughed and wiped her tearful face; this time they were tears of laughter.

Then Robyn remembered. 'Your carpet! Where's your kitchen? We must get that stain out.'

'What stain?' asked Gayle, appearing at the doorway.

'Silly me – I spilt some tea,' said Rose.

'Oh dear,' said George, appearing behind Gayle, his grey hair neatly trimmed. He reappeared a moment later with a dishcloth.

'Here, let me do that,' offered Robyn.

'No, no. You sit down. You've been such a help already,' said Rose.

Robyn caught Gayle raising her eyebrows, obviously wondering what Rose meant.

You know, George. I think we're going to love it here after all.'

'Really?'

'Oh, yes. I promise I won't say another bad word against this house.'

Gayle sidled up to Robyn while Rose was busy mopping up the tea from the carpet. George was busy staring at his wife in surprise.

Gayle whispered, 'I don't know what you did, but I think it's the first time I've seen Rose look truly happy since she moved to this house.'

26

'I thought of bringing along my curtains from home – I mean my old house. Honestly, just listen to me. I lived there for so many years that I still call it home.'

After her haircut, Rose insisted on giving Robyn a tour of the house while Gayle packed away her hairdressing equipment. They hadn't got very far on their tour. They were still in the lounge. George was sitting in an armchair, reading a newspaper.

'What's wrong with these ones?' Robyn asked.

'Well, just look at them – no colour.'

Robyn agreed. 'Bland.'

'Yes, not like my old curtains, all velvety with rich colours.'

'Why didn't you bring your old curtains when you moved? You obviously liked them very much.'

'Too old, like me.' Rose smiled. 'Besides they would have been far too long and heavy; you know the ceiling heights of old houses.'

'Not intimately,' Robyn said flatly.

'And just imagine the dust we would have dislodged after forty-five years.'

That got Robyn's attention. 'Forty-five years?' she said. 'You lived in your last house all that time?'

'Oh yes,' Rose said proudly, as though she had achieved some incredible feat.

Robyn was impressed. It was little wonder that Rose was having a hard time settling into their new home, and the noise and disruption outside made it all worse. Robyn had the urge to help in some way.

'You know, the front room in my old house was enormous, with bay windows to the front nine feet high, and a ceiling rose to die for,' Rose said. 'And the kitchen …' Rose beckoned Robyn to follow her down the short hallway to the kitchen at the end. 'It was twice – no, I tell a lie – three times the size of this one.'

Robyn followed Rose into the kitchen with its wood-effect flooring and its bland white kitchen units.

'My old kitchen had proper floor tiles, you know. And an Aga.' Rose suddenly moved closer to Robyn and said in a low voice, 'Although between you and me, it never worked properly. I do hope the new owners don't get rid of it, because it was a dear little thing – when it worked.'

They both stood and stared at the integrated cooker under the integrated hob.

'Not the same, is it?' remarked Rose.

'No,' said Robyn, imagining Rose's beautiful old kitchen. 'But hey – this cooker works, at least,' she added, trying to brighten the mood, 'and you said yourself you weren't much into cooking.'

'What a good memory you have,' said Rose.

Robyn tried not to laugh aloud at that comment.

'Don't you believe it.' Gayle's voice piped up from close by.

Rose left the kitchen and led Robyn into the next room. 'This is the dining room – or the hairdresser's today.'

Robyn stood in the doorway, smiling at Rose's little joke as she watched Gayle packing her equipment away. There was a vacuum cleaner plugged into the wall.

Gayle said, 'I won't be a minute, Rose. Then I'll just hoover the room.'

'No need to rush, Gayle. I'm giving Robyn a tour of the house. Not that it's going to take long – not like my old house. Now that would have been a *very* long tour.'

Robyn followed Rose back down the hallway towards the stairs.

'Downstairs cloakroom.' Rose pointed at a door on the left before they started up the stairs.

'Did I tell you that the kitchen hasn't got a pantry?' Rose sounded aghast and obviously expected a similar reaction from Robyn. On the landing, she stopped to glance over her shoulder.

Robyn sucked in a breath, eyes wide in mock surprise.

Satisfied, Rose continued the tour upstairs. 'Guest bedroom one.' Rose opened each door in turn, and Robyn poked her head in.

'Guest bedroom two. Main bedroom.'

Robyn noted how bland the rooms were, painted in magnolia.

'Nursery.'

Robyn glanced in the small box room. She turned around to look at Rose. 'But I thought there were no children on the estate.'

'I said that exact same thing to the estate agent when I viewed the show home next door. I did wonder if something had changed and that maybe the estate wasn't earmarked for over-fifties anymore, but they said it's a standard build and they just refer to the room as a nursery.'

'I suppose it's useful if you have young grandchildren to stay.'

'Can you imagine one of my teenage grandchildren staying in this room? It's so small. I can see why they call it a nursery. It would fit a crib and chest of drawers or changing table.'

Rose shook her head and closed the door.

'It would make a useful study. There's room for a desk and bookshelves.'

Rose turned to look at Robyn. 'I say, you're full of good ideas. I would say you're quite a creative person.'

'Thank you.' Robyn smiled. 'Or it would make a lovely craft room, overlooking the garden.'

'Craft room?' Rose blinked.

'Yes, you know – some people enjoying knitting and crochet, or scrapbooking.' Robyn's sketchbook diary came to mind. The look on Rose's face said she wasn't into arts and crafts.

'Or if your husband has any hobbies, like stamp-collecting or—'

'Trains,' said Rose.

'Ah, I don't think that room would be big enough for a train set.' Robyn imagined he'd probably need one of the larger guest bedrooms, or even the garage to accommodate that sort of hobby.

'No, not model trains. He enjoys trainspotting. Do you know how many times he's been on the steam railway from Aviemore?'

Of course Robyn had no idea, but she did reply, 'I'd love to go on the steam train from Aviemore.'

'Well, I'm sure George would love to accompany you. Any excuse to go again. He's very knowledgeable. He'd give you lots of information. He'd be like your very own personal tour guide.'

"I'd love to go with him. And why doesn't he volunteer there? He could share his knowledge with visitors.'

Rose stopped to look at her. 'You know, that's not a bad idea. Not bad at all. I'll tell you one thing – it would save us so much money if he could ride the trains for free.'

'I bet he could help out at the station too.' Of course, it was only an idea. Robyn had never visited Platform 3, where the steam trains ran from – at least if she had, she couldn't remember. So she had no idea what George could do there, although she imagined they would appreciate enthusiastic volunteers.

'It would get him out of the house, and he wouldn't be under my feet all day,' commented Rose.

Robyn kept her expression neutral, wondering if George would spend a lot less time hiding in the garden if he had something to go out and do, to have a break from his wife. They seemed a lovely couple, but their old house sounded quite large, with room enough for them each to have their own space when they needed it.

'And finally, this is the bathroom.' Rose opened the door on a plain white suite. 'Not very inspiring, is it?'

Robyn wasn't sure if she was referring to the bathroom, or the house as a whole. She asked, 'Would you prefer your new home if it was more like your old house?'

'Goodness gracious, what a thought! With ceiling roses and velvety curtains and carpets with enormous patterns? No, that wouldn't do at all.'

Robyn couldn't hide her confusion. 'But you said you missed your old house. I just assumed—'

'I did want a change, and we were ready to downsize.'

Robyn nodded.

'It's just all this was the developer's choice, from the décor to the carpets, curtains, and the choice of kitchen, bathroom, wall tiles, and flooring. You see, both properties had been set up as show homes, then they sold one to us. I guess they thought it would look better if one of the properties had sold, and we moved in. They even left the furniture. The place came with a furniture package.'

Robyn thought about it. 'Changing your kitchen and bathroom would be expensive, but if you really can't live with the carpets, curtains, and soft furnishings – why don't you just change them for something you do like? Just go along to a big shopping outlet or something.'

'Well, where would you suggest?' Rose said, not without a hint of exasperation.

Robyn inwardly sighed. She had no clue.

Rose continued, 'There's nowhere local, and we don't feel like travelling for miles to the nearest city. And we just wouldn't have the energy to walk around the place; you know how big those superstores are. And not very friendly, I'm sure.'

Robyn followed Rose back down the stairs. 'Do you have any magazines?' Robyn asked as they passed the dining room, where Gayle and George appeared to be discussing the merits of employing a gardener for Gayle's mother's house.

'Magazines?'

'Yes, you know – anything, really.' Robyn stood in the doorway to the front room.

'I don't buy women's magazines. The only things I still have lying around are the weekend newspaper supplements.'

'Oh, they'll do just fine.'

'Let me go and see if George didn't put them out for the rubbish.' Robyn watched her walk towards the dining room. 'George!'

'Yes, dear?'

Robyn glanced out of the window. For once, there was blessed peace and silence. She looked at her watch as she resumed her seat on the sofa, aware that Gayle had to get back for her mum, and that she'd wanted to get to another client if possible first.

Rose came in carrying a bundle of glossy newspaper supplements and put them on the coffee table in front of Robyn.

'There – that will keep you occupied. I expect Gayle won't be too long now.' She turned to leave the room.

'Rose,' Robyn called. 'The magazines are for you, not me.' She beckoned for Rose to join her on the sofa.

'For me? But I've already read those.'

'Oh, we're not going to read them.' Robyn smiled knowingly.

Rose moved into the room, staring at the magazines, obviously intrigued. 'What are we going to do with them?'

'We're going to look for ideas.' Robyn said, still patting the sofa seat beside her.

Rose came and sat next to Robyn.

Robyn picked up the magazine on the top of the pile. 'Suppose we don't read the magazines, but we just look at the pictures instead. You can usually find lots of interior shots of houses and rooms.'

Robyn opened the first page of the magazine on her lap, and discovered something about herself – she loved flicking through magazines, looking at house interiors. 'There – you see? On the very first page, we have a study. It's an advert for home office furniture.'

Rose looked at the magazine sceptically. 'Yes, I can see that. But I don't need home office furniture.'

'I know.' Robyn moved her finger up the page and tapped it, pointing at the curtains in the corner of the photo. 'Do you like those?'

'Not really – they're a bit flowery for my taste.'

'Mine too.' Robyn flicked past a couple more pages of writing until she came to another picture.

'Ah! Now I quite like those.' Rose peered at the magazine, and Robyn moved it on to her lap for her to take a closer look. 'And the carpets are quite nice too,' added Rose. 'What colour would you say that is?'

'Burgundy.' Robyn was a little surprised that she could reel off the colour without a second thought. She asked, 'Rose, have you got a pair of scissors?'

'Scissors? Yes, of course.' She got up and left the room, reappearing a moment later with a pair of scissors from the kitchen.

Robyn cut out the curtains and the carpet from the picture. She put the cuttings on the coffee table while Rose continued to leaf through the supplements. Sometimes she just shook her head; other times she seemed to consider for a moment before deciding on something she liked. Each time she did, Robyn cut it out.

Halfway through the pile of magazines, she pointed at a photo of a room. 'Now this, I like.' She beamed. 'What do you think?'

Robyn took the magazine. 'This room?'

Rose nodded.

Robyn held the picture up, casting her gaze around the lounge. 'This might just work.'

'You think so?'

'Oh, yes.' Robyn nodded. Now they were getting somewhere.

Rose winced. 'I'm not convinced about the carpet.'

'No, neither am I.' Robyn studied the picture some more and looked around the room. 'I think a lighter shade to offset the curtains.'

'Yes, that's it!' Rose sounded excited. 'I'm going to make a pot of tea. This is thirsty work.'

While Rose was out of the room, Robyn furiously flicked through the remainder of the magazines to try and find a more suitable carpet. She was having fun – even more than when she was sitting reading celebrity gossip, which she had found she enjoyed.

'How about these?' Robyn had folded several magazines at the appropriate pages while Rose was busy making tea. Gayle had finished hoovering. She could hear her chatting to George in the dining room next door.

Rose reappeared with a tea tray. Robyn passed Rose the magazines. 'Here, let me pour the tea.' She poured them both a tea from the pot and added milk and sugar. 'Shall I make George and Gayle a cuppa too?' Robyn offered.

'How thoughtful of you. I had clear forgotten about them.' she chuckled. 'You'll have to fetch two more cups from the kitchen.'

Robyn knocked on the dining room door and opened it. 'Anyone for tea?'

'Yes, please.' George said straight away.

Robyn looked at Gayle. 'Have you got time for another cup of tea before we leave? I'm just having a chat with Rose.'

Gayle looked at her watch. 'Yes, I'll have another tea.'

Robyn fetched two more cups from the kitchen, nipped into the lounge to pour the tea, and took them to George and Gayle. The noise outside had resumed. As Robyn closed the dining room door, she thought she heard the front doorbell. She stood still, listening. There was another faint chime. Robyn looked toward the lounge, but Rose didn't appear; she was obviously too engrossed in the magazines.

Robyn decided not to disturb her. She walked over to the front door. Through the small bubble-glass window in the door, she could make out somebody wearing dark clothes. They had an enormous yellow head. Robyn squinted at the strange figure. She opened the door, 'Yes?'

'Oh, excuse me. I must have the wrong house.' The man laughed at his own joke. He caught his breath. 'Sorry – I just couldn't resist.'

Robyn looked at him askance. It wasn't funny. He obviously didn't have a clue what the first inhabitants on the estate were going through, moving into a building site. Either that or he just didn't care. 'Sorry,' he said again. 'I couldn't resist.'

She folded her arms and leaned on the door frame, studying the young man. She guessed he couldn't have been much older than herself. He took out a white handkerchief from the top breast pocket of his smart beige suit, gave it a brief shake and then dabbed his eyes, which were just visible under a yellow plastic hard hat. It swamped his head, sitting so low on his brow that it was a wonder he had even made his way to the house.

'Can you tell your grandmother that we're finishing up early today? She'll have some blessed peace and quiet again until Monday.'

Robyn unfolded her arms. She didn't bother correcting his assumption that Rose was her grandmother. 'Hold on, I'll just get her.'

'No need to disturb her. I'm sure we do quite enough of that – aren't you?' He gestured to the building site all around.

'Yes, I am.' Robyn was quick to reply.

'Why are you finishing early today? Will it be a regular occurrence?' Robyn felt chattier, as Mr Yellow Hard Hat was a bit more sympathetic than she had first thought. The joke had not made a good first impression with Robyn. Perhaps he'd like to stay there a week and see what he thought of living with all the noise.

'I'm afraid not.' He sounded apologetic. 'I'm the site manager. I'm leaving early, so I thought it only fair to let the crew off early too. Besides, I like to be on site while the building work is carried out. But they're a pretty good bunch of guys. They're working their butts off. Um, what I mean to say is—'

Robyn nodded. 'I understand. And I imagine Rose knows some colourful language.'

'Oh, I've seen her standing at the window, arms folded, saying something. I can just imagine too.' He shook his head. 'Anyway, it's going to be nice and quiet while I go and look for some lodgings. Not that I expect to have any luck finding somewhere.'

'You just arrived here today?'

'Oh, no – I've been here since the beginning, when they first started clearing the land. It's just that the landlord of the bed-and-breakfast in Aviemore told me he had a ski party booked for the New Year, and of course, what with one thing and another, I clean forgot that I had to vacate the place so soon. I rang a couple of other B&Bs, and some hotels in the area, but they said they're all fully booked.' He sighed. 'Who would have thought it would get so busy around here at this time of year?' I'm not into skiing myself, so I had no idea.' He sighed. 'How about you? Do you ski?'

Robyn opened her mouth and scratched her head.

'Ah, I see you're not a skier. Like me, it's not the sort of question you get asked, is it?'

Robyn just shook her head, leaving him to make his own assumption.

'So here I am with my suitcases in the car and nowhere to go.'

He breathed a heavy sigh.

Robyn had a thought. She stepped out under the porch and pulled the front door to. She said in a whisper, 'I know where there are vacancies.' Robyn glanced over her shoulder, thinking of Gayle inside. She was going to throw a fit when she found out Robyn had invited someone to stay at her house, but then Robyn knew that she was not in the habit of turning people away who had nowhere else to go.

It was agreed then. After work, he was going to turn up and yes, Robyn could guarantee they'd still be a vacancy on New Year's Eve, and no, it wasn't expensive and yes, she could highly recommend it.

'I'm staying there myself. Gayle, the lady who lives there is a good friend.' At least Robyn hoped they would still be friends after this. She gave him the address.

'What about your grandmother? I thought that you were staying with her?'

Robyn assumed that Rose must have a lot of family, especially her grandchildren, to stay. Rose had shown her the guest bedrooms. 'I think you've mistaken me for one of her grandchildren who've visited.'

'You're not one of her grandchildren?'

Robyn shook her head. 'Nope.' She had a question. 'Why did you assume I was?'

'Oh, Mrs Gordon, Rose, always offers me a cup of tea.' He stepped closer and lowered his voice. 'Actually, I'm glad she didn't answer her door today. It was only a courtesy call, and she always invites me in, then I feel bad when I have to try and find excuses to leave.' He paused. 'I think they're quite lonely, you know. And to answer your question, she talks about her grandchildren, and that she's invited them to stay. I just assumed that one of them had finally come.' He peered at Robyn. 'Guess I was wrong. What a shame for Rose and George.'

Robyn thought so too. She looked at the young man and thought that perhaps he could stay there, with Rose and George. Although she couldn't imagine that the company would allow an employee to move in with a couple who'd bought a house on the estate while he worked there. So she didn't even suggest it.

'I'm Nicolas Addison, by the way. But please call me Nick.'

Robyn shook his hand. 'I'm Robyn.'

'I'm glad to see Rose finally has someone visiting. Thank you, by the way, for the guesthouse information. I'll look forward to seeing you later, at the house.' He looked at his watch. 'Well, I guess I'd better go and tell the guys the good news that the early finish is cancelled.'

'Won't they be disappointed?'

'I think not. They get paid by the hour, so I'm sure they weren't all keen on losing money today.'

That was what Robyn had been thinking about – money for Gayle – when she'd offered Mr Yellow Hard Hat a room in Gayle's mum's house.

Gayle's mum! Robyn realised she hadn't thought the idea through at all. Even if it had been Gayle's house, it wasn't Robyn's place to offer a guy a room there – she didn't even know his name. And worse still, she had made it seem like it was a guesthouse.

27

Back in the lounge, Robyn winced from the noise as the work resumed outside.

Rose looked up from the magazine on her lap. 'Everything all right? You were gone a long time, handing George and Gayle a cup of tea.'

'Well … I …' Robyn didn't want to lie.

'I thought I heard the doorbell.'

Robyn nodded. 'Yes, it was the site manager.'

'Oh, he's such a nice young man.'

Robyn was pleased to hear it, seeing as she'd invited him to stay at Gayle's mum's house.

'Always stops for a cup of tea.'

'Was he calling about anything in particular?'

'Just that the workers were going to be leaving early today, but … um … there's been a change of plan.'

'No matter,' said Rose, dismissing that conversation with a flick of her hand. 'Now, what do you think of this?' she said holding up the picture in the magazine for Robyn's inspection.

'I would love to see your old house, Rose. Those long velvety curtains you described. I can't quite picture them. Do you have any photos?' Robyn thought that seeing Rose's old house might give her more of a feel for what Rose liked.

Rose shook her head adamantly. She put the magazine down on her lap and turned to face Robyn. 'You know, I feel in such high spirits just now; better than I've felt in a long time. Well, since moving here … and I don't want to go and spoil it by dragging up the past. This is much better, don't you think?' Rose picked up the magazine from her lap and flapped it at Robyn. 'Don't look so disappointed, pet. I'll show you some photos later, I promise.'

Robyn perked up, although she did wonder whether Rose meant later, in a few minutes, or later, during another visit. Perhaps when she had finished looking through the magazines, thought Robyn hopefully.

'George – is that you?' Rose leaned sideways on the sofa, looking past Robyn.

Robyn turned in her seat at the sound of footsteps in the hall.

'Who else would it be?'

'Well come into the room and let's have a proper look at your haircut. I wasn't really paying attention when you came in earlier.'

'Yes, dear.'

Robyn watched George shuffle dutifully into the room and give a doddery twirl for Rose's benefit. Robyn realised that Rose had been so busy showing her round the house after her own haircut, and had then been so preoccupied with leafing through the magazines, that she hadn't taken notice of George's perfectly coiffed hair.

Rose said, 'A bit short this time, don't you think?'

It sounded like a criticism. Robyn got the impression that Rose wasn't easily pleased. Robyn hoped Gayle hadn't heard.

'I thought I needed a good cut and …' George looked at the

floor. 'Gayle thought so too.'

Rose didn't offer any further comment, which was just as well because at that point Gayle walked into the room carrying her bag and coat.

'All finished.' Gayle piped up, 'and I must say George looks very handsome. Most men half his age don't have a head of hair like that.'

George's face creased in a smile.

Rose looked sideways at him with a hint of displeasure. 'Oh, do sit down, George,' she said irritably. 'You're making us feel uncomfortable.'

He was making Robyn feel no such thing – just a little sad for him. She really hoped they had new neighbours soon, to give Rose something better to do than nag poor George.

'Robyn,' Gayle prompted as she put on her coat.

Robyn looked apologetically at Rose. 'I've got to go now,' she said. But did she really need to?

❖

Robyn closed the front door. She heard a car start outside, and hoped she wasn't making a big mistake by deciding not to accompany Gayle on her next appointment. Gayle was going to swing by Rose and George's afterwards and pick her up. Robyn hadn't yet mentioned to Gayle her new guest. She thought she'd save that conversation for on the way home in the car.

'I'm so glad you could stay longer,' Rose said, her voice carrying from upstairs.

Robyn retraced her steps down the hall. 'Well, I just couldn't wait to see what you'd choose for the other rooms in the house.'

Robyn had a feeling that Rose just wanted the company.

In the main bedroom, Rose was having trouble with her colour scheme. In fact, she appeared to Robyn to be a lot less enthusiastic about it all than before.

Robyn hoped she decided to take a break from sorting out the colour schemes for the bedrooms so they could look at her photo albums instead. She suggested this to Rose.

Surely, Rose wasn't really considering redecorating the entire house? Robyn had thought it was just going to be the lounge. What had started as a way to pass the time, with Robyn showing Rose the various possibilities to transform their bland lounge, had only served to highlight Rose's dissatisfaction with her entire new-build home.

'What's upsetting is that the developer didn't take the time to find out what I liked in the first place.'

Robyn didn't have the heart to tell her that all they wanted was her money.

'Goodness knows what the others will think.' She looked out of her bedroom window.

'Others?' Robyn said as she came over to stand by the window and followed Rose's gaze down to the foundations of the house opposite, which would belong to her neighbours-to-be. 'Oh, you mean the people who will be moving in.'

'They'll probably be just like us, you know. From a big old house that they'd lovingly done up and stayed in for years.'

Robyn nodded.

'You know what I would most love.' She turned to face Robyn. 'This.' She looked down at the magazine she was holding, with a photo of rooms full of colour, some wallpapered, and with matching curtains and cushions with delicate flowered prints, making the lounges and bedrooms warm and inviting, not bland.

Now Robyn was worried that what had started out a harmless bit of time-wasting had turned into something else; she had a feeling she was going to land herself right back where she'd started, with Rose tearful about what she had lost when she moved. She looked around for a box of tissues.

'Do you think they'd do this for me?' asked Rose, staring at the magazine in her hands.

'Who?'

'The developer?'

'You mean redecorate your place?'

Rose nodded.

Robyn looked at Rose. In that instant, Robyn saw a sad old lady longing for times past and realising that she had made a big mistake moving there. She couldn't go back. It was all gone.

Robyn didn't want to answer, but she didn't have a choice. 'I don't think so, Rose.'

'But why ever not?' she said crossly. The terse, objectionable Rose was back. Robyn liked that much better.

'I've got a ten-year guarantee if something goes wrong. Well, something has gone wrong – the horribly bland décor.'

Robyn pursed her lips. 'I'm pretty sure the ten-year guarantee would not cover that sort of thing.'

Rose wasn't stupid. The look on her face said she knew that too.

Robyn added, 'Besides, for one thing, it would cost quite a bit of money to do all this.' Robyn gestured at the magazine in Rose's hand.

'Oh, money's not an issue.' Rose waved that problem away with a characteristic flick of her hand.

Robyn guessed not; after all, she must have downsized from a large house. Her new home had four bedrooms, so Robyn guessed Rose and George were pretty comfortable, financially.

'And the other thing?' prompted Rose.

'That's obvious,' Robyn continued. 'Look around you. Why do you think it's decorated like this in the first place, and there's limited kitchen and bathroom choices too?'

Rose looked around as though she had never seen the place before. Her eyes darting from ceiling to floor, from curtain to door. 'If they'd only asked me what I wanted, I would have paid more, you know, much more.'

'Okay, but that's not it.' Robyn shook her head. 'The issue is time.'

'Time?' Rose didn't understand.

Robyn pointed at the magazine. 'Can you imagine how long it would take for you to make a decision if you had all the choice in the world? How long would it take them to find the perfect materials, colours – things like that?'

Rose considered. 'Quite a long time.'

Robyn continued. 'Exactly. So you see, they limit your choices, and the time they spend completing each property, and as we all know, time is …' she pointed at Rose.

'Money.' Rose nodded.

'Hole in one.'

Rose shook her head slowly. 'You know, Robyn, you're one smart lady.'

'I am?' Robyn was taken aback. She had a very strong feeling that no one had ever called her that before. Me, smart? Robyn blushed. 'Thank you.'

'You're welcome.'

'Doesn't solve my problem, though. I want to make the place

more like *my* home.' She paused, staring at Robyn. 'Actually, I've just had a grand idea.' Rose sidled up to Robyn, grinning as she linked her arm in Robyn's.

Robyn looked at her nervously, wondering what had brought about this sudden display of affection.

Rose patted her hand. 'There's no reason why a smart young lady like yourself shouldn't be able to do all this.' Rose pointed to the magazine she'd left on the bed.

'You mean—?' The words caught at the back of Robyn's throat.

'Oh, don't be so surprised, young lady.'

When Robyn had recovered her composure, she turned to Rose, who was beaming with expectation. 'I am surprised. I've got no credentials to speak of. No references from other clients – nothing.'

'Oh, come now,' said Rose, shaking her head as though Robyn was being merely modest instead of genuinely honest. 'Besides, did I get credentials or references from the girls in that office over there?' She flung her arm at the window, pointing in the direction of the sales office. She added, 'I would trust a friend to do a nice job, wouldn't you?'

'I guess.' Robyn replied. 'And I have got some time on my hands at the moment,' she thought aloud. 'But I'd have to find out the cost of the materials—'

Rose held up her hand. 'Don't you worry. I know how these things work,' she assured her. 'An expense account will be arranged, of course.'

'An expense account?' Robyn repeated.

'Of course.' Rose sounded pleased with herself. 'As you said, for materials and things.' Rose left the window and headed for the door. 'Oh, and your rate.'

Robyn turned and stood with her back to the window. 'My rate?'

'You know, what do they call it nowadays? That posh sounding word. I know, your *commission*. Silly me, now we wouldn't want to forget that – would we?'

Robyn shook her head, 'I'm doing this as your friend. I couldn't possibly take your money other than for materials.'

'You can, and you will.'

A car horn sounded outside, then trailed off as though something had died.

'I think that will be your ride.' Rose said from the door.

Robyn was surprised that Gayle was back so soon. She glanced out of the window. Perhaps her other client had changed her mind about the haircut, or hadn't been in when she'd turned up.

Rose said, 'Don't go yet!' She disappeared down the hallway and returned with a black handbag. She got out her purse.

For an awkward moment, Robyn just stood there, staring at Rose. What was she getting out her purse for? She still couldn't take in what had just happened. What had started out as a way of filling in time and occupying Rose had now turned into a job.

Rose had found an envelope from somewhere. She handed the sealed envelope to Robyn. It had her name scrawled on the front. 'There's more where that came from.'

Robyn felt the sealed envelope with her fingers and guessed there was a wad of bank notes insides. She was about to protest that she hadn't done anything yet, when Rose said, 'Come on then, what are you waiting for? No time to dawdle.' She added. 'And you'll need these.' Rose thrust a pile of magazines, along with the cutouts she'd made, into Robyn's hands.

'Oh, and this!' Rose said, getting a plastic card out of her purse.

'I can't take your bank card!' Robyn shook her head.

'Robyn, it's fine. It's not my bank card. It's a credit card. I want you to use the card to make any purchases for the house.'

Robyn reluctantly took the card, although she'd already decided she would not use it.

Robyn could feel fingers in her back prodding her out of the door. 'Now, you can come any time with samples like wallpaper, carpet samples, that sort of thing,' Rose said.

Robyn turned and mumbled, 'Okay,' over her shoulder as Rose marched her to the front door.

George appeared at the lounge door. 'Bye, Robyn. Hope to see you again.'

'Oh, you most definitely will,' said Rose as she closed the door.

Robyn walked down the path towards Gayle's waiting car, carrying the pile of magazine supplements and still wondering what had just happened. Now she had two things to tell Gayle on the way home. She wasn't looking forward to telling her about her new guest – Nick. Even though he would be paying for his room and board – and she imagined rather generously, as it would be coming out of the developer's pocket and not his own – what if Gayle just refused to have him to stay?

But she *was* looking forward to telling Gayle about her new job. She just hoped Gayle didn't think she was taking advantage of her hairdressing clients. She wasn't. Not at all. In fact, Rose had rather railroaded her into it. Robyn hoped she was up to the job. She assumed she didn't have any interior design qualifications or experience. She looked at the magazines and guessed she was about to find out.

28

Gayle stared at Robyn. 'What on earth happened to you?'

Robyn looked at Gayle. 'Why?'

'It makes a big difference, Robyn.'

'What does?' She had no clue what Gayle was getting at.

Gayle flipped the visor down in front of Robyn. In the little mirror, Robyn was smiling broadly back at herself.

Gayle started the engine. 'You know, I've never seen you look so happy. I don't find it particularly easy visiting Rose because she's not very happy in her new home, so I'm quite surprised you've walked out of that house in such high spirits.'

Gayle carefully manoeuvred the car down the drive to avoid the builders' trucks.

'I know it sounds mean to say it, but Rose is probably the last person I'd expect to put a smile on someone's face; on the contrary, I'd expect her to put a dampener on your mood. That's happened to me enough times in the past.' Gayle glanced at her. 'Well, don't keep me in suspense. What happened while I was gone?'

Robyn was about to tell her when she got sidetracked. 'Talking of being gone, that reminds me – you weren't gone long at all. Was your client out or something?'

'Or something. Turns out she wasn't feeling well. She was trying to get in touch but of course I wasn't home, and I had my mobile switched off. I must remember to switch the thing on, especially when I'm out and about, in case someone calls about Mum – like the community centre, or my neighbour.'

Robyn nodded. 'Is it switched on now?'

'Oh, yes. Plenty of messages from my client that I missed, but none about Mum – thank goodness. So, what about you and that great big grin on your face?'

It was true: Robyn couldn't stop smiling. 'Well, turns out I've got a little job.'

Gayle glanced at her. 'You have?'

Robyn nodded.

'Here – on the building site? Are you working in the sales office?' Gayle glanced at her again.

'Nope. I'm working for Rose. She told me how unhappy she was with her new house, so I suggested making some changes to the décor and soft furnishings – make her feel more at home. We had a lovely time looking through some supplements, magazines from the weekend newspapers. Thing is, I didn't expect her to ask me to do it.' Robyn quickly added, 'I wanted to help out as a friend, not get paid. I only asked for the money to buy paint, wallpaper, flooring – that sort of thing. But she insisted on paying me a commission.' Robyn paused, wondering what Gayle's reaction would be. She added, 'I wouldn't want you to think I was taking advantage of them.'

'You, take advantage of someone?' Gayle shook her head. 'I would never think that. In fact, what I do think is that you're such a kind soul, Robyn, that the shoe might be on the other foot, if you're not careful.'

'Huh?'

'Honey, I just get the feeling, with your sweet nature, people might take advantage of you.'

Robyn frowned. Had that happened to her in the past? She wished she knew. She stared at Gayle. It occurred to her that perhaps Gayle would have liked the money to do the job. 'Sorry, Gayle.'

'What on earth are you apologising for?'

Robyn winced. 'I guess maybe you might have liked the job yourself. I think the money will be good. I get the impression that Rose and George are well off.'

'Yes, I believe they must be. They sold quite a large house in the street where I grew up. It sold for more than they expected, even though they'd lived there for years and it needed a lot of updating.'

'Oh, is that how you know them?'

'Oh, yes. It was strange because when Rose first answered the door, she appeared to recognise you.'

'Really?' Robyn said, surprised.

'Yes, but then she did say her memory obviously wasn't what it once was, and you weren't who she thought you were.'

'And who was that?'

'She didn't say.'

Robyn decided that the next time she visited Rose, she'd ask her who she reminded her of.

She stared out of the window at the beautiful scenery – the forests of pines, the shimmering green loch, and the snow-peaked Cairngorm Mountain rising up majestically in the distance. It was the same scenery she'd seen that morning; the same route on the return journey to Aviemore, but for Robyn the scenery would never, ever get old, no matter how many times she travelled this route.

'So, when do you start?'

Robyn looked at the magazines on her lap. 'I guess I already have. I did say to her that I haven't got any professional qualifications in interior design, or references, or anything like that, but she didn't seem bothered. She just said she trusted me to do the job.'

Robyn turned in her seat when she heard Gayle gasp.

'She trusts you?'

'Yes, like a friend. That's what she said.'

'Well, you've clearly made an impression. Rose does not suffer fools gladly, or make friends easily, I can tell you.'

Robyn felt quite chuffed hearing that. She caught Gayle glancing at the magazines in her lap. She said, 'I imagine you made some suggestions for her décor?'

'Oh, yes. It was such fun.'

Gayle smiled. It sounds to me as though it's something you're going to really enjoy doing. Perhaps it was something you were studying at university – something arty like interior design.'

Robyn thought that was a possibility.

'I'd trust you to do up my mum's place too, you know.'

Robyn smiled at that comment as they drove through Aviemore and approached the small roundabout on the outskirts. A left turn took them along the forest road that ran along the loch. They were well on their way back to Gayle's mum's house.

Robyn was still smiling to herself. Little did Gayle know that this was exactly her plan. That was why she had wanted to look at all the old photos of the house back in its heyday, before it fell into disrepair. Of course, she wouldn't want a commission. She'd insist

Gayle accepted it as payment for staying rent-free in the house. She wasn't sure where the money would come from yet to do up the house, or whether Gayle would even agree to it. But Robyn had been enjoying a rather lovely daydream of turning Gayle's big old family home into the best house on the street.

'And you know what they say …' Gayle gave Robyn a knowing glance and raised her eyebrows.

Robyn felt one of Gayle's self-help quotes coming on.

'Whether you think you can, or you think you can't …' Gayle nodded at Robyn, 'you're right.'

'Hey, that's a quote from Henry Ford. I like that one,' Robyn said, turning in her seat.

'I thought you might. It's rather apt, don't you think?'

'I do,' said Robyn, smiling approvingly. 'But I still feel like a fraud.' She folded her arms, her smile fading.

'Hey, how did you know that was a quote from Henry Ford?'

Robyn shrugged. 'Doesn't everyone? I mean he was a world-class businessman.'

'Yes, I suppose he was. But that's not my point. You actually remembered something.'

'Huh?'

'You remembered it was a quote from Henry Ford.'

Robyn looked at Gayle. 'How strange. I wonder why I'd remember that?'

Gayle shrugged. 'Perhaps it was something you studied on your university course.'

'Perhaps …' mused Robyn, although for some reason she had a feeling that this was not the case.

'Hey, with your commission, I think I should charge you rent,' Gayle joked.

Robyn said, 'I wish you would.'

Gayle kept her eyes on the road as she replied, 'You're my guest, and my friend, so I don't want to hear anything more about that.'

Robyn did. She felt guilty earning money and not paying her way. Thinking of charging rent … Robyn bit her lower lip. She knew she had to bring it up sooner or later – Gayle's new guest. She was relieved he hadn't left work early, which would have meant he would arrive before them.

'I just don't see how I can charge anyone to stay in this dump,' Gayle mused as she pulled the car up in front of her mother's house.

'It is not a dump,' Robyn protested. She'd have to get Gayle to change her mind on that score, otherwise poor Nick would have to find somewhere else.

Gayle switched the engine off and turned to Robyn. 'What's that in your hand?' she asked.

'The magazines.'

'No, the other hand.'

Robyn showed her the bank card, and the envelope full of cash, and told her what Rose had done.

'Well,' Gayle said, 'the suspense is killing me. How much has she given you to do the job?' Gayle paused. 'You don't want to look – do you?'

Robyn shook her head. She didn't want to know how much Rose had given her, although she'd have to look sooner or later. 'I still feel bad for taking her money.' Worse still, whatever was in that envelope, she guessed was only part of the commission. She bet that Rose gave her another wodge of cash when the work was complete.

Looking at the envelope, Robyn said, 'Please let me pay you some rent money.'

'I told you before, you'll do no such thing. I don't care how much money is in that envelope, it would be a crime to charge anyone to stay here.'

Nick leapt to Robyn's mind – yet again.

'Here, I'll open the envelope if you won't.'

Robyn shrugged and passed it to her, wondering how she was going to explain to Gayle that she now had a paying guest. She was going to be really upset.

'Oh, my god!' Gayle exclaimed.

'What is it?' Robyn sat bolt upright in her seat and looked out of the car window at the house, expecting to see something untoward had happened while they were gone, like some roof tiles blown off, or a windowpane broken.

But there was nothing wrong with the house as far as Robyn could see.

'What is it?' she said to Gayle.

Gayle was staring wide-eyed at her. 'Hmm, you know, I may have to consider charging some rent after all,' Gayle mused. 'In fact, quite a lot, if I'm going to be introducing you to fat commissions like that.'

'What?' Robyn looked at the wodge of cash, all twenty-pound notes, in Gayle's hand.

'Oh, dear.' It was more than she'd thought. 'I couldn't possibly …'

'You've got to take what's offered in this life, honey,' said Gayle. 'If you don't, there's a queue of people lining up right behind you to take what's rightfully yours.' She nodded her head slowly, as if to say, *I know what I'm talking about.*

Robyn smiled. 'Well, in light of that reasoning, you'll accept some rent money from me after all. Say one hundred pounds a week?' For some reason, Robyn didn't know whether that was an acceptable amount or not. 'Remember, you've got to take what's offered in life,' she said smugly.

Gayle laughed. 'Certainly.' She got out of the car. Not!' She said emphatically.

Robyn got out of the car too. She had an idea how she was going to approach Gayle about her paying guest. It was simple. Gayle had introduced her to a bit of business, by way of meeting Rose, so she had done the same for Gayle. That was exactly what she intended to tell Gayle.

29

'Putting a bit of business my way?' Gayle slammed the boot shut and looked at Robyn as though she was mad. 'Is that what you call it, inviting someone—'

'Nicolas Addison. But he likes to be called Nick.'

Gayle looked at her wide-eyed, and finished her sentence '—to stay here without discussing it with me first?'

Robyn pursed her lips. She'd known this was coming.

'Robyn, honey, I'm not running a bed-and-breakfast business.' Gayle shook her head and strode toward the house.

'But it could be,' Robyn called after her. Gayle didn't stop, or comment, on her way to the house.

Robyn stood for a moment by the car, deflated. What on earth was she going to tell poor Nick when he arrived?

Robyn ran after Gayle to catch up, which was heavy-going on the gravel. She felt like she was running in slow motion, expending a lot of energy going nowhere. Gayle was just putting her bag down outside the front door.

Robyn caught up with Gayle at the front door. She was getting the key out of her purse.

'But he had nowhere else to go. And you took me in. So I thought …'

'You thought I'd just agree to take in anyone?' Gayle snorted, glancing at Robyn over her shoulder. 'Do you think I'm running a charity?'

'No, of course not. He knows what the daily rate is.'

'Daily rate?'

'For a bed-and-breakfast in the area,' Robyn clarified.

Gayle paused before putting the key in the lock and turned with a bemused look on her face. 'Robyn, I told you that I'm not running a bed-and-breakfast.'

'Why not?' Robyn paused. 'You said yourself you didn't know how you were going to keep this place going.'

Gayle nodded her head.

Robyn took this as a cue to keep talking as Gayle put the key in the lock, 'and besides, I know you wouldn't have the heart to …'

'I know, I know.' She turned around and stared at Robyn for a long moment.

'Does that mean?'

'It means a house full of strays.' She looked heavenwards then turned back to the door. 'Now what an earth is wrong with this lock?'

Robyn leaned forward and turned the handle. To her surprise, it opened.

They exchanged glances. Robyn pushed the door. They stood and watched the door swing open.

'Ah, I saw you arrive from the lounge window. Sorry, thought you knew there was someone home.' David stood a few feet away from them in the hall, a teacup and saucer in hand. He noted the look of surprise on their faces. 'Oh, this?' He held up his teacup.

'Your mother kindly made me a cup of tea while I was waiting.'

Robyn and Gayle exchanged glances again. Then, as if they were reading each other's minds, they turned to look back down the drive. There, only a few feet away, stood David's beaten-up old van. They had been so busy bickering that they had missed it completely.

'You see, a house full of strays.' Gayle swung her arms in the air, then walked in. 'Mother, what have you been up to?'

Robyn heard a clatter of cutlery in the kitchen and guessed that it was where Gayle would find her.

'Gayle.' David nodded at her as she strode past him. 'Yes, yes, make yourself at home, everyone and their mother seems to be, lately.' She eyed Robyn as she turned toward the kitchen. She turned back to David and asked, 'When did the community bus drop my mum home? I thought I'd have plenty of time to get home before she did.'

'Ah, the driver said there was some issue with the heating in the community centre, so they had to cut the session short. I'd turned up and no one was home. I was about to leave when the bus turned up.'

'How did you get in?'

'Your mother had a key in her purse.'

'She did?'

Robyn heard this exchange, and Gayle thanking David for hanging around and keeping an eye on her mum. 'Obviously one of my mother's better days,' Gayle commented. 'She found her door key, and made a cuppa.'

David said, 'They tried to get in touch with you.'

Gayle rolled her eyes. 'Oh, damn. My phone was switched off.'

'Never mind,' David said cheerfully as he finished his tea.

'I'm going to see what she's up to.'

Robyn watched Gayle disappear down the hall to the kitchen.

David followed her gaze too. He turned to look at Robyn. 'Everything all right?'

Robyn called after her. 'What about Nick?'

Gayle didn't answer.

Robyn frowned. She hoped she hadn't changed her mind about letting him stay.

Robyn walked up to David. 'What are you doing here?'

'Having a cup of tea – what does it look like?' he replied good-humouredly.

Robyn shook her head, then turned abruptly and plodded into the lounge. She guessed that it was a stupid question – he'd come to see her, obviously. She slumped down on the nearest sofa, landing with a plop on the sofa cushions.

She felt a bit down, and wished she hadn't stupidly taken it upon herself to invite Nick to stay. Now, she wasn't looking forward to him turning up.

A teacup tinkled from the hall.

She turned her head to look through the doorway at David standing there awkwardly. He walked towards her, the cup still rattling on the saucer. He stood in the open doorway. 'Who's Nick?'

Robyn frowned. 'I don't want to talk about it.'

David's smile dissipated. 'Is he … like, a friend?'

'No. I only met him today.'

'You only met me the other day.'

Robyn rolled her eyes. 'What are you getting at?'

'We're friends. At least I hope we are.'

Robyn stared at David. 'Yes, of course we are. Good friends.'

David's smile returned. 'Great! Can I come in?'

Robyn patted the sofa beside her. 'Of course.'

'Do you mind putting that down,' she gestured at the cup and saucer. The little tinkling noise was getting on her nerves.

He swung around, obviously unsure where to put it.

'Here, let me take that.' Robyn bounced off her seat, took it and unceremoniously dumped it on the nearest piece of furniture, which was probably an antique.

'So, what's with Gayle? She seems a bit, you know, out of sorts.'

'Never mind.' Robyn was curt.

David looked around the room. 'Nice room.'

'It's ok,' Robyn wasn't feeling in a talkative mood. It wasn't just because of Nick. She was feeling a little put out that David hadn't stopped by the previous day. She knew that she wasn't really being fair. They'd only just met. Perhaps he'd been working. Besides, he was visiting now.

'I brought you something.' David swung the backpack he was carrying to the floor and opened it as he took a seat on the sofa next to her.

Robyn leaned forward.

'Here.' He handed her a magazine.

She'd had just about enough of magazines for one day. 'You came here today to deliver that?'

'They keep appearing in my van, and I have to deliver them to somebody.'

Robyn offered a weak smile at the joke, recalling what he'd said at the hospital, intimating that the magazines would be an excuse to visit her at Gayle's. She smiled, happy that he hadn't forgotten her, although she would have been quite happy at that moment to never set eyes on another magazine. She knew she would enjoy working on Rose and George's house, but she still felt guilty about taking their money. And Nick was still on her mind. She wished she'd never answered their front door.

Robyn looked up to see David walking out of the room. She'd been so preoccupied with her thoughts that she hadn't noticed he was leaving. 'David?'

He looked back, 'Yes?'

'Are you leaving already?'

'It looks to me as though you've got things on your mind. I thought perhaps I should go. I just came to deliver the magazine.'

'Thank you.' She held up the magazine. 'I really appreciate it.' She actually did, on reflection. It would come in handy for her new job.

He leaned one shoulder on the doorframe. 'Robyn …' He studied his shoes as though he had come over all shy. 'That wasn't strictly true when I said I'd just come to deliver the magazine.'

Robyn stared at him.

'It's Hogmanay. That's Scottish for the last day of the year. There are some fantastic celebrations around Aviemore. Hogmanay in the square in Grantown-on-Spey is quite the event. It's one of the largest gatherings for Hogmanay in the Highlands. I love the atmosphere, the music, the streets around the town just come alive. The whole town comes together. It really is something special.'

Robyn wondered why he was telling her all this. 'It sounds fantastic. I don't think I've ever been to one.'

'Oh, you'd remember it if you had.'

There was an awkward silence. David took a deep breath, and said, 'I was hoping you'd come.'

Robyn felt apprehensive. Was he asking her out on a date? And should she be going when she had no memory of her past? It had been one thing, enjoying his visits in the hospital, but now he was visiting her at Gayle's, even though she had desperately wanted to see him again, it felt different. This would be going out together.

Robyn really wished she could remember. Did she have a boyfriend, a fiancé, someone special already in her life? But if that were the case, surely she wouldn't have been on her own in that car on Christmas Day.

She looked at David, and shrugged. 'Sure – why not?' Although she was wondering where this Grantown-on-Spey was, and how she'd get there. 'I'll have to ask Gayle if she's going.'

'Why?'

'How am I going to get into town?' With that thought, she also wondered how she was going to get to Rose's house to do her job. It wasn't like Gayle could give her a lift each time. She had other things to do, like looking after her mum, and running her hairdressing business. And running a guesthouse.

Robyn frowned at that last thought. She was still feeling nervous about Nick turning up and Gayle turning him away.

David laughed and shook his head. 'Actually, the idea was that you came with me, Robyn.'

'Oh, right. I see.'

'I'll pick you up. It's no trouble.'

'Will there be many people there?'

'Oh, it's going to be huge.'

Although she'd agreed to go, Robyn was now undecided. If there were going to be a lot of people there, what if someone from her past recognised her? But that would be a good thing, wouldn't it? It would, but perhaps not if she was out, on a potential date, with David. Robyn decided she should scrutinise her diary to see if there were any clues about whether she was in a relationship.

Robyn looked at David. She wished she hadn't been so quick to accept. She was seriously thinking of backing out already.

'We'll take Gayle too, then.'

'Really?'

'Hell, let's take Gayle *and* her mother.'

'Take my mother where?' Gayle walked past David, who was still standing in the doorway, and carried two steaming mugs of tea into the lounge.' 'Here.' Robyn took the mug that was offered. 'Thanks' she said sheepishly.

'Don't think you're forgiven.' Gayle said, adding, 'And don't look at the mug like that – it's tea, not arsenic. Although it did cross my mind that I could always poison the stray if I didn't like him.' Gayle smiled wickedly.

'I didn't see a cat.' David looked around him.

Robyn looked at Gayle and they both laughed.

'What?' David looked at them bemused.

'Nothing.' They both said in unison. 'Now what's this about my mother?' Gayle asked, looking at David as he sidled back into the room, and took a seat opposite them.

Gayle said, 'I think you've been getting her into enough trouble for one day.'

'Trouble?' David looked concerned.

'Dementia,' Robyn chipped in, then turned apologetically to Gayle, wondering if she shouldn't have said anything. But she waved the comment away.

'Sorry – I hadn't realised,' David said. He looked toward the kitchen. 'Ah, that might explain why my tea was lukewarm.'

Gayle nodded. 'You weren't to know. We have some new house rules, due to her condition. I've written them down on post-it notes and stuck them in various places around the house. One of the notes has a picture of a kettle with a cross through it. I stuck it to the kettle, and the cupboard where the cups and saucers are …'

David glanced at the cup and saucer that Robyn had taken from him.

Gayle continued. 'And I even put a sticker on the fridge, so she knows not to go in there either. If she dropped a carton of milk all over the floor, she might slip over.' Gayle frowned. 'She knows not to boil water in case she scalds herself.'

'I'm so sorry,' David apologised.

'Don't be. My prompts usually make her stop and think, that is, until we have visitors. Then she slips into being a host and offering drinks and food like she used to do. But no harm done – this time.' Gayle paused. 'So what were you saying, something about bringing my mother too …?'

'Ah, I was talking about Hogmanay.' David said, 'I can pick you all up later – around seven?'

'You've invited us all to go along with you to a Hogmanay celebration?' Gayle leaned forward and put her empty mug on the coffee table in front of Robyn.

'Yes.' David started to repeat what he'd told Robyn until Gayle held up her hand. 'I know what they are, David.'

'Well, I've asked Robyn, and I'd like you and your mother to come along too.'

'I'll bet.'

Robyn looked at Gayle. Was she being sarcastic?

'Anyway, sorry to disappoint you, David, but Mother obviously can't go. So that's one down and me to go.'

Robyn shot her a look. She was definitely being sarcastic. 'Gayle, please come. It would do you good to get out and do something different,' Robyn urged.

'If I wanted to do something different, it would not be a street party.'

'But it sounds like it's going to be fun.'

David chipped in, 'It most definitely is.'

Robyn started to protest, but Gayle insisted she wasn't going. 'Believe me, wild horses couldn't drag me out to stand in the freezing cold to watch fireworks and listen to music, when I can do all that in the comfort of my own home with the heating on, wrapped in a cosy duvet, with my feet up on the sofa.'

Robyn smiled. That was what they'd done the previous night, with a bottle of wine too, watching TV and chatting. Her smile slipped when she realised that if she went out with David that evening, Gayle would have to see in the New Year on her own.

Gayle must have noticed Robyn's expression. 'Do not worry about me. Perhaps if I was twenty years younger, I'd feel like braving the cold. But you, girl, should have a night out. And you'll love the Hogmanay celebrations. As for me …' She pulled a face. 'Thanks for the invite, but sorry, David, it will just be Robyn going with you.'

Gayle didn't look very sorry.

And neither did David.

30

'Honestly Robyn, what on earth made you invite me and my mother to the Hogmanay party that David is taking you to?'

Robyn sighed. That wasn't exactly how the invitation had come about. It had been David's idea. She suspected it had been to make sure she went. Robyn got up from the sofa. She stood at the lounge window and watched David walking to his van on the gravel drive.

'Anyone with half a brain would realise he was asking you out on a date.'

'A date?' Robyn turned around, trying to act surprised.

Gayle rolled her eyes. 'I know what your game is.'

Robyn shrugged. 'Whatever do you mean?'

'You know very well.'

'Oh, all right.' Robyn admitted, 'Yes, I kind of thought it was a date. At first I didn't mind the idea, but then I started to get cold feet because …

'Because …?' Gayle prompted.

'Well, I don't even know whether I should be going out with someone. What if there's somebody else – and I'm not even aware?'

Gayle breathed a sigh. 'I see. Yes, that is a bit of a conundrum.'

'Just a bit!' Robyn said, immediately regretting that sarcastic remark. It wasn't Gayle's fault that her memory wasn't coming back.

'Look, Robyn, rather than thinking of it as a date, just have a night out and enjoy yourself. It will do you good, being around young people for a change.'

'But I love being here with you and your mum, in this big old house.'

Gayle smiled. 'And I love having you here. But still, that doesn't stop you having a night out. Besides, I'm not going to be on my own.'

'You've got your mum.'

'And Nick what's-his-name.'

Robyn pursed her lips, and said in a small voice, 'Addison. Nick Addison.' Robyn turned to the window, half-expecting to see him turn up, but it was still too early if he worked nine to five. As expected, she didn't see him arriving outside the house. But her attention was drawn to David. 'Oh dear.' Robyn put a hand to her mouth.

'What is it?' said Gayle rising from her armchair.

Robyn had just seen David slip over on the gravel on his way to the van.

'Has my new guest arrived?'

'No.'

Robyn watched David get up slowly, as though he was having trouble. He turned to look at the house and check if anyone was watching. Robyn moved out of sight of the window. She sensed that he wouldn't want to have been seen. She stole another glanced out of the window and saw David bent over, rubbing his knee.

She had the impulse to run out and check he was okay, but somehow she didn't feel it would be the right thing to do.

'Everything all right?'

'Er, yes – fine.' Robyn decided not to mention what she'd just witnessed. She had a feeling that the last thing David would want was anyone making a big deal of it – especially Gayle, a former nurse. Robyn pictured her running out of the house with a first aid kit.

'I'll go and wash the mugs.'

Robyn nodded. Once Gayle had left the room, she stole another glance out of the window. She watched David limp back to his van. She was surprised he'd caused himself an injury from slipping on the gravel. He reached the back of his van, opened the door, and was just reaching in for something when he stopped and looked back at the house again.

Robyn moved quickly away from the window, wondering why she was behaving so childishly. Then again, why did he seem to be checking that no one was watching?

She stole a glanced out of the window again as David closed the door on the back of the van. He was leaning heavily on a walking stick. She watched him as he climbed into the van, using the walking stick as a lever.

As the van engine rattled into life, Robyn moved away from the window in case David caught her in his rear-view mirror.

'Gayle,' Robyn called out as she ambled down the hall to the kitchen. Gayle was busy washing up the mugs, together with the breakfast dishes which had been left from that morning.

'Oh, here – let me help.' Robyn darted to the tea towel and picked up a spoon from the draining board to dry the crockery and cutlery.

Robyn glanced at Gayle. 'What do you know about David, and his career?'

'What, the ice hockey thing?' Gayle put a soapy mug on the draining board, and Robyn picked it up.

'He had some sort of injury, didn't he?' Robyn recalled reading about David in the newspaper article about her car accident.

Gayle put another mug on the draining board. 'I don't know much about it; only that an injury ended his career. That was what the papers said, anyhow. You read the paper, honey; you know as much as I do.'

Robyn looked disappointed.

'You're seeing him later. Why don't you ask him?'

Robyn didn't think that would be a good idea. Back in the hospital, during his visits, they'd had an understanding – they didn't talk about the past. That suited Robyn – for obvious reasons.

Now she'd seen David with a walking stick, which he'd never mentioned, and had witnessed the way he'd kept glancing at the house, checking no one had seen him slipping on the gravel, she understood why he didn't want to talk about his past. The injury that had ended his ice hockey career was still causing him problems. She did wonder what had happened, but she wasn't going to ask.

Robyn continued to wipe up, her head swimming with thoughts.

'If you go any faster, you'll be wiping the dishes before I've had a chance to wash them,' Gayle quipped.

Robyn saw herself reaching for the mug that was in still in Gayle's hand. She snatched her hand back. 'Sorry.'

'I think someone's had quite a long, eventful day, don't you?' Gayle smiled at Robyn.

Robyn agreed, 'I know it's only the middle of the afternoon, but would it be daft if I had a nap?' She yawned. She was tired.

'I think that's a good idea. Remember, you're still recovering from that accident. Go have a rest. You don't want to be tired for the Hogmanay celebrations this evening.'

Robyn folded the tea towel, placing it on the rack.

'The celebrations go on well into the early hours.' Gayle finished the dishes and dried her hands. 'And there will be dancing, plenty of dancing to the ceilidh band.'

'The *what* band?'

'Ceilidh – it's Scottish Gaelic for a gathering or, in the case of Hogmanay, a party, obviously. There's always a band, playing traditional Scottish folk music. These bands are very popular at all sorts of celebrations, including weddings. That's why dancing is one of the highlights of the evening.'

Robyn wished she knew if she liked dancing. She wondered why David hadn't mentioned it, especially as it appeared to be one of the highlights of the New Year's Eve celebrations.

Gayle folded the tea towel and hung it on a rack above the Aga. 'Didn't David mention it?'

Robyn shook her head.

'Hmm.'

'What's *hmm*?' Robyn was always irritated by an answer like that, which wasn't an answer but an unsaid thought. She preferred it if people just spoke what was on their minds.

'Oh, nothing.'

'Come on, Gayle, I know it's not *nothing*.' Robyn persisted.

Gayle studied her for a moment. 'I think your David—'

'He is not *my* David.'

'All right, but it's obvious he is fond of you. Now maybe there has already been someone special in your past …'

Maybe, thought Robyn. That was what she found disturbing. She didn't know, and she guessed Gayle understood this. What if she still loved another and didn't know it? What would happen if she started to fall in love, and then found out she still loved someone else? Worse still, what if she'd made a commitment? What if she was engaged?

Robyn didn't want to think about that. Surely, if they were that special, she'd remember them?

Gayle eyed her. 'Let me just say that if you were with someone else, and your relationship was that important, then why were you alone in that car at Christmas?'

Robyn took this in. Of course, she'd considered this. But there was something more; something that she hadn't confided in Gayle. She hadn't told her that she'd been pregnant at the time of the accident.

'There – you see? It does make sense, doesn't it?'

Robyn nodded, even though she knew things were a lot more complicated.

'So, there's no reason why you shouldn't give David a chance – is there?'

Robyn sighed, wishing she'd confided in Gayle. But she hadn't, and she really didn't want to bring it up now. She felt quite tired, and just wanted to crawl into bed for a couple of hours. Before she went upstairs, she had a question. 'How come you're so keen to get me and David together?'

'Oh, let's just say I like to play matchmaker.'

'Matchmaker.' Robyn thought that was an absurd answer.

'Oh, all right. I like you and I like David. and I think you would make a lovely couple. I'm a romantic at heart. I'd like to see my two new friends together. That's all. Besides,' Gayle smirked, 'it's kinda cute, a love story in the making, and I like to think I had some hand in making it happen.'

Robyn didn't quite see how. It wasn't like Gayle had introduced them.

Gayle raised her eyebrows. 'You're here – aren't you? In this house, where David can still visit you?'

'Ah.' Robyn smiled. 'I see what you're up to. Like a modern-day fairy godmother?'

'Hey, now we're talking – and you're Cinderella who lost her memory and …'

'Slipper,' Robyn corrected.

'I know that.' Gayle playfully slapped her arm. 'And David's your Prince Charming.'

'David – my Prince Charming?' Robyn raised her eyebrows at Gayle. 'He's not really a Prince Charming, is he?'

Gayle shook her head. 'More like Prince Miserable, sometimes.'

'That's not fair. He *has* been through a lot, losing his career and—' Robyn halted before she mentioned the slip on the gravel outside, and the walking stick she'd seen him using.

'Ok – I'm only joking with you.' Gayle put her hands on her hips, 'Aren't we the protective one?'

'Of course not,' Robyn said in a don't-be-absurd tone of voice.

'Hmm.'

Robyn turned around and headed for the hallway. She paused in the kitchen doorway. 'How did we get on to this, anyway?'

'Don't ask me,' Gayle threw back. 'Ah, hold on. It started with you wanting a nap, then it got on to the dancing at Hogmanay. You were asking me why I thought David hadn't mentioned it.'

'And …?'

'I guess he didn't want to scare you off in case you thought it sounded like …'

'Like what?'

'A date, which it is. Obviously.'

Robyn thought they'd already established that it was a date. That didn't explain why he hadn't mentioned the dancing, though. Perhaps it *was* simply the case that he was worried it would put her off if she didn't like to dance.

Gayle added, 'And where there's dancing, there's almost always a slow dance, at some point, to wind things down.' Gayle grinned. 'However, when it comes to the ceilidh band, they often have the slow dance at the beginning.'

Robyn rolled her eyes. She decided it was probably that prospect that had put him off mentioning dancing or the band; he was probably worried that she might not be interested in a slow dance with him. In fact, the idea appealed to her very much. She avoided Gayle's gaze, feeling embarrassed at the thought.

Robyn looked at the time by the clock on the kitchen wall. There was something she wanted to do before her evening out with David.

'Gayle, after I've had a little nap, would there be time for you to drive me into town?' she asked.

'You don't have to take anything with you to Hogmanay.'

'Oh, I wasn't thinking of that.' Robyn felt guilty that it hadn't even occurred to her. 'I just wanted to visit the library.'

'The public library?' Gayle said in surprise. 'What's wrong with the library here?'

'You know very well,' Robyn folded her arms. 'It's ok if self-help books are your thing.'

'Well, they are,' said Gayle.

'I know that.' There were also a lot of medical books, which Robyn wasn't interested in either, although the thought did suddenly occur to her that there might be something worth reading about her memory loss.

'So, what are you looking for in the public library?'

Robyn shrugged nonchalantly. 'Just some news articles.'

'About your accident?'

'No, not mine – David's.'

'Why?'

'I just wanted to look at old newspapers, to find out more about David's past.'

'But honey,' Gayle threw her arms up in the air, in exasperation, 'why don't you just ask him? Date night is the perfect time to get to know one another better.'

Robyn still felt uncomfortable, Gayle using the word *date*, even though there was no escaping the fact that a date was what it was.

'Well?'

Robyn looked at her shoes. 'I get the feeling he doesn't like to talk about his past.'

Gayle shook her head. 'Well, don't you two make a pair.'

Robyn looked up. 'How do you mean?'

'David won't talk about his past and you can't.' Gayle let out a deep breath. 'What *do* you guys talk about?'

It wasn't what they talked about, but what they didn't talk about that was bothering Robyn as she wandered up the stairs, Gayle's words ringing in her ears. Although she could quite understand David not wanting to talk about his injury, which she now suspected was worse than he was letting on, she sensed that there was something else he was keeping from her.

31

David's hand clasped hers as he led the way. They walked past a swirl of dancing bodies, heading in the direction of a long trestle table covered by various tartan tablecloths that didn't match. She could see cakes, and nibbles, and a mobile café serving hot drinks.

Robyn wanted to dance. Watching the couples, she was sure she could get the hang of the steps, but she wondered how David, with his bad knee, would fare. She hadn't seen him limping, but then she wondered if the pain and stiffness, if that was what he suffered from, came and went, hence the need for a walking stick at times. Maybe dancing was not a good idea. Before the music began, someone in the ceilidh band had announced the dance; it was called *Strip the Willow*. The first dance of the evening hadn't turned out to be a slow dance at all. It was a very lively dance, with people forming two lines, turning to face each other, and then weaving in and out to the fast-paced music.

Robyn loved it. It appeared really fun. People were laughing, having a great time. She looked at David, who was still holding her hand and leading her through the crowd of people in the centre of the village. She wouldn't blame him if he'd just come up with an excuse to avoid the dance; he had said there was something important he wanted to do first. It all sounded rather mysterious, so Robyn went along with it.

They stopped just before the table, behind a small group of people huddled together in the cold with their backs to them. David gave Robyn a nervous smile before he tapped a tall, greying man on the shoulder.

The man turned, his smile fading when he saw the couple. Robyn watched him looked her up and down as though appraising her, without even so much as a *hello*. Then he looked at David.

David said, 'This is Ro … Rob …' He swallowed. 'Robyn.' He breathed out.

Robyn glanced up at David in surprise. Had she just heard him stutter?

She looked back at the stranger, waiting for introductions. None were forthcoming. *Who was he?* Whoever he was, David clearly wanted to introduce her. She held out her hand, and said, 'Hi.'

He took her hand; reluctantly, it seemed. His large square hand enveloped hers, and inexplicably, Robyn suddenly felt trapped. She wanted him to let go right away and had the impulse to pull away. What suddenly came to mind was the notion of someone holding her hand – not like David did, gently, but instead squeezing her hand, making it hurt.

She hoped to goodness that it wasn't a memory, because if it was, then she'd rather her memories didn't come back.

The handshake was perfunctory. She drew her hand back, relieved. Then the man turned his back on them, barely acknowledging her presence.

Robyn frowned at his back. He hadn't shown her the courtesy of introducing himself.

She looked at David, who was also staring at the guy's back, frowning. He was trying to speak, moving his lips, but he couldn't seem to get the words out.

'David,' Robyn pleaded in a whisper. She was feeling embarrassed. 'David!' She hissed. That got his attention. 'Let's go.' She took his hand and pulled him away from that horrible man. Through the crowd, she spotted another area with wooden trestle tables, and a pop-up café in a little caravan on the other side of the village square.

They stopped in the queue for the mobile café.

'Who was that?' Robyn asked as she turned her attention to blackboard propped up beside the trestle table, with a list of drinks and snacks available.

'What can I get you?'

Robyn turned to find that the queue had disappeared. With three people serving inside the tiny caravan, the service was quick. She looked up at the rosy-cheeked young woman behind the counter, who didn't look old enough to be serving drinks.

'I'll have a hot chocolate.'

She turned to ask David what he wanted, but he appeared preoccupied. 'David, the lady wants to know what you want. Would you like a hot chocolate too?'

He shook his head, still looking preoccupied.

The young woman leaned across the counter, staring at David. 'Something stronger for the cute guy, then?'

Robyn frowned at her. She looked sixteen – if that. The two people serving, a middle-aged couple, whom she resembled, were obviously her parents.

'Just something alcoholic,' said David.

Robyn raised her eyebrows. 'Oh, okay.' She turned to look at the young girl and discovered the middle-aged woman had stepped in, pointing at the girl to serve someone else. The lady smiled at Robyn. 'My daughter can't serve alcohol – she's only fifteen. So, what'll it be?'

David wasn't being very communicative, so Robyn shrugged. 'A draught beer, or a cheap shot, please,' she said, without thinking, raising her eyebrows, wondering where that had come from.

The lady shook her head. 'Um, sounds like something you'd buy in a sleazy bar.' She smiled. 'No offence.'

Robyn felt the colour rising in her cheeks.

'Now, what we've got are cans of cider, bottles of beer – not a cheap one, I might add – or wine by the glass.'

Robyn glanced at David. He still looked preoccupied. 'David?'

'Hmm?'

'What do you want to drink?'

'Oh, right. Just a beer.' He paid for the drinks.

Robyn watched the lady take the cap off the beer and pour a hot chocolate into a takeaway mug.

Robyn thanked the lady for her hot chocolate, warming her hands on the takeaway cup as she took a sip. It tasted delicious. She picked up the beer to hand to David. She carefully turned so as not to bump into anyone in the queue behind her and spill the drinks.

'So, who was the guy we met over there – was that your dad?' She looked up, expecting David to be right behind her, but instead she looked straight into the face of a stranger.

'Sorry, I thought you were someone else.' Robyn gave the young man a wisp of a smile before scanning the crowd, looking for David. She couldn't see him anywhere.

'Where did he go?' she said under her breath. Her forehead

creased into a frown. Not only had David introduced her to someone who had virtually insulted her, but now he had left her standing on her own with the drinks.

'I see we've both lost our partners.' Robyn turned back to the young man, who was trying to strike up a conversation again. She hoped he was not trying to chat her up. He held up his two drinks. Robyn looked down at hers. 'Oh, I see.' She smiled more genuinely this time.

'Is he a local?' the guy asked.

'Huh?'

'The guy you're with.'

She stared at him, thinking that it was a strange question.

'Oh, excuse me – I'm a police officer. I'm not on duty this evening, but I do know pretty much everyone in town.'

'You do?' Robyn began to relax. 'The guy I'm with is David,' she said, raising her voice.

'David what?'

'Gillespie.' Robyn shouted back. She thought it was kind of the off-duty policeman to help find him, although looking at the huge crowd of people, she didn't know how. 'I doubt you could find anyone in this crowd.'

He moved closer, so neither of them had to shout above the music. He was big-built and broad-shouldered. If you had to have someone to protect you, then this would be your guy, Robyn thought. But protect you from what? Robyn had no idea where these strange thoughts were coming from. She looked into his soft, pale eyes, and his kind, concerned expression.

He raised an eyebrow. 'Are you Robyn?'

Robyn looked at him nervously. 'How do you know my name?' She thought it must be the bandage that had given her away. He was a police officer, and she imagined he was aware of the car accident on Christmas Day, and those involved.

There was something she'd been avoiding, putting it to the back of her mind. That morning, when she'd been searching through her things to find something else suitable to wear for the Hogmanay party, she'd been stunned to discover an awful lot of cash in the bottom of her rucksack. She wished she hadn't found it. She'd been so shocked at what she'd discovered that she'd tried to forget about it; to pretend it wasn't there. Now she wondered what she'd done, and what or whom she might have been fleeing from on Christmas Day.

Was it stolen? That possibility had occurred to her. It was a wonder the police hadn't discovered it among her things when they'd retrieved them from the car. But they would have, if only they'd taken out *all* the clothes, for there at the bottom of the bag were some wads of cash carefully wrapped in cellophane to keep the notes in neat little piles. Of course, she'd attempted to innocently explain it away to herself, but the last thing she needed was some small-town police officer looking into her past, and discovering something she'd rather the law didn't know about her – let alone something she didn't want to discover about herself.

The other thing that had been bothering her was that she might not turn out to be at all what she appeared to be – kind, helpful, sincere. Was it possible to go through a complete personality change on top of losing your memory after a head injury?

She had wanted to visit the public library in town earlier on to find out more about David and the accident that had ended his career. She had also wanted to do something else – to look at old newspapers and see if there was mention of a theft from a house or a shop over Christmas. A large theft, judging by the wads of notes in the bag. Local law enforcement was bound to be on the lookout for anyone who had stolen that amount of cash – if it had been reported. But in the event, she had been unable to go. Gayle's neighbour had been out, so there had been no one to keep an eye on her mum while they drove into town. And now she was standing in front of a police officer, wondering what he was going to say next.

What a fool I am to think I could just turn up at a big social do like this and think I wouldn't run into the law, she thought. And that was the other thing – what if she ran into someone who recognised her – not the kind, empathetic Robyn, but one who might have stolen all that cash, and quite possibly was involved with some shady people.

Robyn frowned, wishing she could stop thinking such thoughts. If only she hadn't found that money …

Robyn looked at the hot chocolate in one hand, and David's cold beer in the other, and lifted the bottle to take a swig. It was frothy, making her throat tickle as she swallowed the cold liquid. She lowered the bottle and coughed.

'I'm Joe.' She watched him put one of the drinks he was carrying down on the nearby table and hold out his hand.

'Oh.' Robyn hastily put the hot chocolate down on the table. She was keeping hold of the bottle of beer. They shook hands. Robyn wondered what was going on with all the formal introductions tonight. Didn't anyone just say *hi* around there?

He smiled as he spoke. 'You don't have a clue who I am, do you?'

'Yes, I do. You just said you're a police officer.' *And you're about to arrest me*, she thought.

She picked up the bottle and took several gulps of David's drink. Within seconds, the bottle was empty. 'Just one moment …' Robyn held up a finger in front of Joe. She turned around, and stepped back up to the mobile café. The queue had disappeared. They were the only ones standing there. 'I'll have another of whatever this was.' She put the bottle down in front of the middle-aged lady.

'All right.'

Robyn watched the lady reach over to a tall glass cabinet, presumably a fridge of some sort, and get out a bottle of beer. She undid the top and placed it in front of Robyn.

Robyn took it.

'Um excuse me … sorry, but we're not running a free bar.'

Robyn had just put the bottle to her lips. 'Oh, of course.' She'd forgotten that without David around, she'd actually have to pay for it herself. She stole a glance at Joe as she lowered the bottle. Well, this was beyond awkward. If he hadn't intended to arrest her for stealing, he would now.

'Cash or card?' the lady asked.

A nervous laugh escaped her. She wasn't exactly short of cash. Would the lady believe her if she said she had wads of cash, just not on her. Oh, and she had a passbook full of money, and a nice fat cheque, but she couldn't find a bank yet where she could withdraw the cash.

She was staring at the bottle, wondering what to say, when Joe said, 'Here, let me get that. And another one for me, too.'

'Thank you,' said the lady, and got out another beer.

Joe picked it up. 'Now, where were we?' he said, turning to Robyn.

She said in a small voice, 'You were about to arrest me for not paying for the beer.'

He threw his head back and laughed. 'I told you, I'm off duty,' he said, swigging from his bottle. 'Honestly, where is that brother of mine? I can't believe he ditched his pretty date.'

Robyn looked at him, wide-eyed. Did he just say he was David's brother? She couldn't see the resemblance, but there was something familiar about his voice. She cocked her head. 'You're David's brother?'

'One and only.' He looked at her. 'I'm guessing you didn't know he had a brother – much less one who's an officer of the law.'

'You're guessing right.' Robyn took a sip of beer, aware that she really should save it for David. But he wasn't there. As his brother had said, he'd ditched his date.

She looked at the bottle, looked at David's brother, and thought *what the heck*. She might as well keep the bottle and spend the evening in his brother's company instead. At least she had someone to talk to.

32

After downing a bottle of beer, she was feeling suddenly rather more relaxed. She was unsure whether it was the effects of the drink or that the fact that she wasn't going to be arrested after all.

It had never occurred to her that she would meet any of David's family that night. It had never occurred to her that he even had any. Of course, she knew he had a father who ran the general store in town, but other than that, she had assumed he was all alone, like her. She suddenly realised that she knew a lot less about her date than was probably wise. Finding out his brother was a police officer should have been a comforting thought, but in her current predicament it was not – far from it.

'David told me he was bringing a girl called Robyn to the Hogmanay celebrations, but what I want to know is the reason he has never mentioned how you met.' Joe studied her intently.

Robyn looked away from his penetrating gaze, unwilling to answer that question. So, it turned out that Joe wasn't aware of the accident on Christmas Day after all. For some reason, David had kept what had happened to himself. She thought that was rather odd. Joe had obviously not been at work that day, and hadn't read the local paper or spoken to their father, who knew all about it. It was him who'd spoken to a news reporter about it – or rather, about his once-famous son, David.

Thinking of that, she looked at Joe and wondered if maybe the two brothers weren't especially close because of David's fame. She could just imagine sibling rivalry; how one of them making it big and the other living a small-town existence might cause jealousies, bitterness. But looking at Joe's friendly, easy-going, relaxed demeanour, she couldn't imagine that being the case. Besides, the life David had enjoyed once, the fame and the money, was all gone now. Well, she didn't know about the money, but the fame, along with his career in sport, certainly was.

David was a good few inches taller than Joe, who was broader, and heavy-built, with nothing like the athletic slim build and dark good looks of his older brother. She guessed they must take after different sides of the family. She wondered which side David took after – his mum's or his dad's.

Joe looked in the direction of the crowd. Some people were dancing in the street, and others were sitting at trestle tables that had been laid out in a u-shape in the centre of the square, chatting amiably and eating burgers and hotdogs.

Robyn looked too. She spotted him first. 'There.' She pointed. 'He's with that man. Do you see him?' Robyn looked at Joe, who nodded.

David and the man appeared to be arguing.

'Who *is* that guy?' Robyn said, more to herself, although she spoke out loud. 'He was so rude when I met him. I don't know why David even introduced us. He didn't even have the decency to give me his name.' Robyn gave the rude man a hard stare.

'Ah, I see you've had the pleasure of meeting the old man then,' Joe said cheerfully, raising his beer in the direction of David and the rude man before swigging a mouthful.

Robyn's eyes shot to Joe. His grey eyes and solid build were familiar; now she knew why. Joe took after the man she'd shaken hands with – his father. Robyn cringed. 'Sorry.'

'Don't be. He *can* be rude. That's just the way he is, I'm afraid, but I'm not excusing his behaviour. I'd like to apologise, on my father's behalf,' Joe said sincerely. 'I guess David didn't give you any advance warning about who you were about to meet when—' Joe stopped abruptly. 'Excuse me.'

Robyn watched him put his beer down. He strode off quickly in David's direction.

'Well, how rude!' exclaimed Robyn, surprised that amiable Joe had just walked off like that, mid-conversation. *Like father, like son*, she thought. But then she looked over and caught sight of David being pushed hard by his father. Joe must have seen it coming; that was why he was heading in their direction at pace.

She couldn't see what happened next, as Joe's broad shoulders blocked her view.

Robyn put her drink – which she'd hardly started – down on the table too, and then waded through the crowd. She could see Joe standing in between his father and brother, a hand on his father's chest, keeping him at arm's length, and a hand on David's shoulder. He was looking at his father and saying something. David had his hand to his mouth.

No one around them seemed to have noticed the brief fracas. The music was still in full pelt and people were dancing and drinking as frantically as ever.

As she neared them, she saw their father backing away from David, shaking his head. Joe turned his attention to his brother. She could see Joe, still with his arm on David's shoulder, lifting

David's chin. Only then did she see that David was bleeding.

'Oh god, what happened?' she said in dismay.

David brushed Joe's hand away, 'It's alright. Really.'

'I can charge him with assault,' said Joe.

Good idea, thought Robyn, eyeing their father as he turned his back on them. She'd be a witness, gladly, even though she hadn't actually seen the punch being thrown. Robyn looked at David, hoping for a positive response to this suggestion.

'No.'

Robyn was about to object when David said, 'It was my fault, Joe. I started it.'

'So what!' Robyn persisted. 'He threw a punch.'

'Yep, I agree,' said Joe.

'Still my fault,' said David.

'No, actually – it was *my* fault, wasn't it?' said Robyn. She'd guessed what had happened; why David had suddenly disappeared. He'd gone to have words with his father about being rude to his date when he'd introduced her.

David and Joe looked at her.

'How so?' asked Joe.

'If David hadn't introduced me …' Robyn trailed off, not bothering to finish what was obvious.

Holding a handkerchief to his bloody nose, David shook his head. 'No, it's not your fault, Robyn. I shouldn't have bothered introducing you to my father. When will I ever learn?' He rolled his eyes at Joe.

She saw the brothers exchange a knowing glance.

She looked at David and noticed he didn't just have a bloody nose. There was a trickle of blood coming from his forehead too. 'You're bleeding,' she said, pointing at his forehead.

Joe peered at David. 'How did that happen?'

'I think his ring caught the side of my face.'

Robyn couldn't believe David's dad had just walked off and left him like that. *What a mean, horrible man*, she thought, hoping she never had to meet him again.

'You two are going to end up with matching bandages.'

David frowned at his brother. 'That's not funny, Joe.'

'No, it's not, is it?' Joe turned his gaze on Robyn. 'Sorry.'

Robyn smiled at Joe. 'It's okay.' She could tell he wanted to ask what had happened to cause her injury, but thankfully he didn't. Instead, he said, 'Why don't you two call it an evening?'

Robyn thought that this was a good idea. Although she'd heard there were going to be fireworks, and she would have loved to stay for them, and perhaps dance a slow dance with David, she didn't want to risk running into his father again.

David caught Robyn smiling at his brother and took her hand. 'Yep, time to go.'

David used the handkerchief to dab his forehead. He looked at the handkerchief. 'I think it's stopping.'

Joe nodded at his brother and sighed. 'Like old times – eh?'

David grimaced.

Joe said, 'I think you should get that checked out.'

'I'd rather not have to make another trip to A&E.'

'What did you go to A&E for?' Joe asked, concern in his voice. 'Was your knee playing up again?'

David frowned at his brother. 'No!' He stole a glance at Robyn.

Robyn really didn't want to get into the reason that David had been at the hospital. There was an awkward silence. David stood dabbing his forehead, avoiding Joe's question. Robyn looked at David. Their eyes met. Neither of them wanted to talk about the accident on Christmas Day. She imagined Joe would find out sooner or later, either through his dad, when he spoke with him, or when he returned to work.

'You ok to drive?' Joe asked David.

'Oh sure.' He gingerly lifted the bloodstained handkerchief. A trickle of blood seeped down the right side of his face. 'Damn,' he muttered.

'Didn't think so,' Joe replied.

Robyn didn't feel like a ride home in a police car, even if it was David's friendly brother. Then she remembered that Joe had said he was off duty. Even so, she didn't want to get on to the subject of David's trips to the hospital to visit her.

'I think you need that looked at,' said Joe, pointing at David's head. 'I'll drive you to the hospital, get you checked over.'

'I said I'm fine.'

'I can drive,' Robyn blurted. David didn't want to go to A&E, and the last thing Robyn wanted was to see in the New Year at the hospital. She had an idea. If they went back to Gayle's together, then Gayle could fix David up and give him stitches if he needed them.

'Yes, Robyn will drive.' David turned to face Joe. 'I'll be fine, really.' He headed off in the direction of the van, leaving Robyn standing there awkwardly with Joe.

'I'd better get going.' She was about to follow David when she stopped and did an about-turn. Joe was still standing there, his hands on his hips. She asked, 'Why doesn't your father like me?'

Joe dropped his hands to his sides. 'Robyn, I think you will be good for my brother, and that's all that matters. Drive carefully.' He turned toward the crowd. 'Now, where's that wife of mine?'

Robyn stared after him. She barely knew David, although what she did know was that she liked him – a lot. She didn't want them to stop seeing each other. And she didn't want his father getting in the way of their budding friendship.

She turned towards the car park in the village, where David had parked the van. As she made her way through the crowd, she recalled the times he'd visited her in the hospital. He hadn't asked her a single question – where she came from, where she was going in such a hurry, or how she'd come to be on that country road alone on Christmas Day.

The questions would come, sooner or later. It was inevitable that he'd want to get to know all about her, as she wanted to know about him. *But will David even like the real me when he finds out who I am?* she wondered. She frowned, wishing she could answer that question. *I don't even know who the real me is.*

But what was really playing on her mind as she made her way over to David, who was waiting for her in the van, was the possibility that if something did get in the way of their relationship, it would not be his father, but something, or someone in her past.

33

Robyn opened the van door. David wasn't sitting in the passenger seat. 'What are you doing? I thought I was driving?'

'Robyn, you haven't driven this thing before and you don't know how temperamental it can be.'

'Oh, you think I'm going to drive us both off a cliff?'

David eyed her without answering.

Robyn looked away, embarrassed. She had meant it as a joke, but she realised as soon as it was out of her mouth that, considering the car accident, it was in very poor taste.

'And you've been drinking,' David added.

Robyn looked at him, wondering how he knew that. She'd left the two bottles of beer behind, but had only drunk one of them anyway.

He guessed what she was thinking. 'I can smell it on your breath.'

'Well, I needed a drink this evening after I met—' she caught herself from saying something rude about his father.

David held the handkerchief to his forehead.

'Oh, for goodness' sake, you can't drive like that!'

David moved along the seat to the passenger side as Robyn

climbed in. She caught him giving her a sideways glance, his expression giving away what he was still thinking – that she shouldn't drive.

'I'm fine, honestly. I only had a beer.'

'Beer?'

She shouldn't have told him that. She felt her face flush. 'It was only a small bottle.'

Robyn turned the key in the ignition. The engine shuddered into life, but to Robyn's annoyance David was acting like a back-seat driver as she manoeuvred the van out of the car park.

'Mind that car!'

'I'm not going to hit that car!' Robyn said, then nearly did.

'The gear shift is a bit tricky,' David commented.

'I do know how to operate a gear shift, you know.'

'Not this gear shift.'

Unfortunately, Robyn crunched the gears as she changed up.

'There – see, I told you!'

Robyn sighed; it was going to be a long drive home.

When David had finally been persuaded that she could drive the hunk of metal, he calmed down.

Robyn concentrated on the road ahead. Everything was silent and eery, like something out of a scary movie. She expected some dark ominous figure to jump out from the shadows in front of her. Large pine trees lined the straight road ahead, bending inwards to create a tunnel effect. It was spooky.

Robyn discovered that she enjoyed driving in the dark; the roads were quiet. She imagined that everyone was either at home, to see in the New Year, or at one of the Hogmanay parties, waiting to toast the New Year and then carry on the celebrating into the early hours.

She'd driven as a passenger with Gayle that way several times before, but never in the dark. She felt as though she had entered another world, another dimension. There had been snowfall earlier in the evening, which only added to the atmosphere; the tall pine trees were dusted with snow, their white branches illuminated in the headlights as they drove through the night.

Robyn took her eyes off the road for a second, glancing upwards to the night sky. It was a clear night, with so many twinkly stars that she couldn't imagine she'd seen anything quite like it before in her life.

David broke the silence. 'Scotland and the Cairngorms National Park are world-renowned for their dark skies.'

Robyn glanced at David. 'Dark skies?'

'Yes, like that.' He pointed up. 'Scotland is, like, *the* best place for stargazing.'

'It is?'

'Oh, yes. There's even a place called the Cairngorms Dark Sky Park.'

'For stargazing?'

'Yes. In a village called Tomintoul on The Glenlivet Estate. The village has had the title bestowed on it, *The Highest Village in the Highlands*.'

'I would like to see that village,' commented Robyn.

'But it's the Snow Roads on the way there – that's where the spectacular scenery is.'

'Snow Roads?'

'Oh, you haven't heard of them?'

'I don't think so.' She might have, but it had already been quite an eventful evening, for all the wrong reasons – she glanced at the bloody handkerchief in his hands – so she didn't want to get into her own problems. Just then, she was just enjoying the drive, and seeing the spectacular dark skies, as David called them.

'Tourists come here to do the Snow Roads Scenic Route.

'But why are they called Snow Roads?'

'They are the highest roads in the UK, where you can travel among snow-covered plains high in the Cairngorms. Of course you can travel them in the summer when there is no snow, but you have to travel a Snow Road at least once in your lifetime in the winter. The scenery really is … well I can't put into words how amazing the scenery is, driving along those roads.'

'Where does it start – the Snow Road?'

'Actually you can take one of the roads from the village we've just come from – Grantown-on-Spey.'

Robyn took her foot off the accelerator and crunched the gears, slowing the big van down. She pulled over on the verge.

'What are you doing?'

She turned to David. 'I want to travel along the Snow Road to the highest village in the Cairngorms, Tomintoul, and see the dark skies.'

'What – now?'

'It's a beautiful evening. The sky is clear. I can't think of a better way to see in the New Year than in the highest village in the Cairngorms, looking up at those amazing dark skies, stargazing – can you?'

When she didn't get an answer, she dropped her gaze from the night sky and looked at David.

He stared at her and said, 'I don't care where I see in the New Year, as long as it's with you.'

Robyn had to stop herself bursting into tears at that comment. It was the most romantic thing anyone had ever said to her. She immediately wondered how she knew that.

❖

They were travelling along the Snow Road, having doubled back to Grantown-on-Spey and taken a road that started to climb up and away from the village.

It soon flattened out, quicker than Robyn expected, with a further gentle climb and some twisty turns until eventually there was a flat straight road ahead of them for as far as the eye could see – which wasn't that far in the pitch darkness. But Robyn didn't care about that. She was on the mountain plains, and it was exhilarating.

Robyn could see, from the headlights lighting the road, and the verges either side, that there was snow on the plains, just as David had described. They were heading for the highest village in the Cairngorms, which was along this Snow Road, where – if David's timing was correct – they might just make it to wish each other a Happy New Year.

Robyn was still driving. They were both silent, travelling along the not-so-deserted road in hushed silence. Cars passed from time to time, obviously heading down to the village from whence they'd come to see in the New Year. They lit up the road and the beautiful scenery surrounding them. But it was the sky that kept grabbing Robyn's attention, drawing her from the road ahead. It was velvety black, and just so full of stars, like glitter lighting up the night sky.

'David?' She glanced at him. His elbow rested on the window ledge, holding the handkerchief to his forehead. His eyes were closed.

They opened.

'Has the bleeding stopped?'

'Yeah.'

She exhaled in relief. She'd been so intent on having this adventure that she hadn't thought about what they would do if the bleeding didn't stop and they need to go to A&E for some stitches. She had been aiming to return to Gayle's for her to look at the gash above his eye, but she'd forgotten about that the instant David had mentioned the Snow Roads and the highest village in the Cairngorms.

Robyn dropped her gaze and looked at the road ahead. The headlights caught something crossing the road. It stopped. Robyn instinctively braked, jolting them both forward. Luckily, although they were surrounded by snow on the plains, the roads were black asphalt, completely clear of snow. David had warned her, though, to brake carefully in case she hit black ice.

'Sorry,' Robyn apologised, wondering if David was going to insist he took over the driving now.

'Don't be,' David replied. 'I would have done exactly the same.'

'What was that?' Robyn asked.

Whatever was standing in the middle of the road suddenly took flight, bolting from the headlights into the blackness of the snowy plains.

'Wow, I think that was a stag!' David exclaimed, pressing his nose up against the window in the direction the stag had fled.

Whatever it was, it was big, thought Robyn.

'That's not the only wildlife you'll see up here. When we return to do the Snow Roads in daylight, you might be lucky and spot a golden eagle.'

Robyn grinned at David. It wasn't the comment about the other wildlife she might see, but the fact that he was already thinking ahead about meeting up again.

'Look – up ahead!' David pointed.

Robyn could see lights twinkling in the distance – civilisation. She glanced at David. 'It's the village, isn't it?'

'Oh, yes!'

Robyn glanced at him and smiled. He hadn't been that enthusiastic when they'd backtracked to the village to embark on their journey along the Snow Road at this time of night. It wasn't taking the van that was on his mind. Apparently, he'd done this journey many a time in the van, making deliveries to this village. It was the thought that they wouldn't make it in time to celebrate the clock striking midnight on New Year's Eve in the highest village in the Cairngorms.

Robyn wouldn't have minded if that had turned out to be the case – she wanted to experience the journey on the Snow Road and see the dark skies. However, she too wanted to arrive in the village before the clock struck midnight. It would make their trip even more memorable.

'Are we going to make it?' she asked David.

He looked at his phone. 'Two minutes!'

'Just two minutes?' She put her foot down. With the main beam on, and a clear, straight road ahead of them, as long as they didn't meet any more stags standing in the middle of the road, she was determined they'd make it.

'Look – we're coming into the village!' David pointed.

As they entered the village and drove down the long main street, they saw a crowd of people up ahead. Robyn could hear folk music.

'We'd better park here.'

Robyn pulled the van up to the kerb. They both jumped out of the van, slamming the doors in unison.

David took her hand. 'If we hurry, we might make it for the fireworks.'

'There's fireworks too?' Robyn shouted above the sound of the band, which was getting ever louder as they ran towards the crowd of people.

'Quick!'

Robyn looked at David. She wasn't sure why they were running towards the crowd. They'd made it to the village, hadn't they?

Then she heard a church bell start to toll. It was counting down to midnight.

The band had fallen silent, and the revellers in the town square up ahead were forming a circle.

'What's going on?' Robyn asked breathlessly.

'They're preparing,' replied David.

'Preparing for what?'

As they neared the crowd, David kept hold of Robyn's hand. She was surprised when he walked up to a line of people, strangers, and he took one of their hands. The stranger nodded, and smiled. Robyn felt someone take her hand. A young woman next to her also smiled.

Robyn didn't know what to make of it, but she kept hold of the young woman's hand. She saw others all holding hands, a large circle of people forming in the small village square.

David whispered, 'It's a tradition in Scotland. At the stroke of midnight we all hold hands and sing.'

Robyn nodded. 'Okay.'

They all stood in hushed silence listening to the tolling of a single church bell.

Then they started to chant: *ten, nine, eight, seven, six, five, four, three, two* … and on the stroke of midnight, the singing began – *Auld Lang Syne.*

Robyn looked at David. He only had eyes for her as he sang the song.

Robyn's smile faltered at the lyrics: *Should old acquaintance be forgot. And never brought to mind* …

A moment later, the song was over, and a collective cheer of 'Happy New Year!' went up from the crowd. And then couples and families turned to one another, hugging and kissing.

Robyn stood there, still holding David's hand, looking at the crowd of people rejoicing in the New Year, and wondered what the New Year would bring for her; what she would find when – *if* – her memory returned.

Robyn felt David's hand on her cheek, gently turning her head to look at him. He leaned in, and an inch from her lips, he paused to ask, 'May I kiss you?'

Whatever lay ahead, good or bad, and whatever she was running from – because she had the strongest sensation that that was the reason she'd been on the road on Christmas Day – in that moment she didn't care about the past or the future. All she wanted was for David to kiss her.

'Oh, yes,' she said.

As they kissed, a loud boom sounded, making Robyn jump out of her skin. 'Oh, my god.' She shivered in David's arms, even though she wasn't cold.

'Hey, are you okay?'

'What was that?'

'It was just a firework – look up!'

Holding hands tightly, they both turned so that they stood shoulder-to-shoulder, looking up at the dark sky lit up by fireworks.

'I didn't know there would be a firework display here.'

David smiled. 'This is Hogmanay. Wherever you are in Scotland right now, this is what you will be doing.'

Unless you're Gayle, sitting at home with her mum, who has dementia. Robyn suddenly felt terribly guilty that she'd decided to go out. She could have been at Gayle's, and they could have all celebrated the New Year together.

She had a sudden thought. It had only just turned midnight. It wasn't too late to get back to Gayle's and have a little glass of wine with her to celebrate the New Year.

'What's wrong?' David asked.

'Do you think we can leave now?'

'Of course. Are you tired?'

'Yeah, but it's not that. I'd really like to go back to Gayle's and wish her a Happy New Year.'

'Let's go. I'd like to wish Gayle a Happy New Year too.'

Robyn smiled to herself as he led the way back to the van. She cast a glance behind her at the large group of people wrapped up in coats, hats, scarfs and gloves, standing around to watch the fireworks and warming themselves with hot chocolate.

This place, the Cairngorms, was somewhere she knew in her heart she'd been yearning for. It was a place to put down roots, where she could stop moving around and settle down. No specific memory had come to mind; just a strong sensation that that had been her life, before – constantly on the move, but not out of choice, always yearning for a place to call home. It wasn't just the place, though – it was the people.

She climbed into the van next to David. He caught her staring at him and asked, 'What is it?'

She shook her head and forced a smile. 'Oh, nothing.'

But it wasn't nothing. It felt like her new life was just beginning. But there was the spectre of her past hanging over her, like a ghostly presence that wouldn't go away. When would it come back to haunt her?

34

She'd been tempted to stay for the rest of the firework display and a warming hot chocolate before returning to the van, but she'd resisted the urge, thinking of Gayle and her mum alone on Hogmanay. This time, David drove. It was now in the early hours, and although he was tired, like Robyn, he knew the road. She couldn't wait to get back to see them.

Robyn glanced at him. 'What did Joe mean when he said it was like old times?'

'I could drive this road with my eyes closed.'

'I'd rather you didn't,' Robyn joked. He was avoiding her question – she was sure of it.

They travelled some distance in silence.

Robyn's eyes had been growing heavy as the movement of the van lulled her to sleep. She'd just been drifting off when David's voice startled her awake.

'It was his idea,' David said.

Her eyes shot open. 'Huh – what did you say?'

'I said it was his idea, me going into ice hockey.'

'Whose idea?'

'My father's. He said I was talented, had a gift for the sport.'

He glanced at Robyn. 'You don't know anything about the ice hockey league in Scotland, do you?'

Robyn shook her head, feeling frustrated that she couldn't distinguish between what she didn't know because she'd lost her memory, and what she genuinely had no idea about.

'There are eight teams that compete in the Scottish National League. I'd just transferred to one of the teams that compete in the EIHL when it happened.' He slapped his knee. 'And that was the end of my career.'

She didn't want to ask him about his accident. Robyn glanced at his knee and asked, 'What's the EIHL?'

'Oh, sorry – that the Elite Ice Hockey League, the top tier, if you like, of ice hockey in the UK. Two Scottish teams compete in that league, and I was going to be in one of them until …' he trailed off.

She had the urge to reach out and place her hand over his, but then he lifted his hand from his bad knee and put it on the steering wheel. She made do with throwing him an empathetic smile instead. She wanted to reassure him it was alright if he wanted to talk to her, about anything. She would listen. But she didn't know how.

'When did you start playing ice hockey?' she ventured.

'I picked up a hockey stick – well, no, that's not strictly true; actually, my father put one in my hand as soon as I could walk. He tried Joe out as well, but he was less agile and didn't take to ice-skating the way I did. He's heavier-set, broad-shouldered. I imagine he might have been good at rugby, but he didn't have the build for ice hockey. Joe would always be too slow to compete in the game.'

Robyn thought of Joe's big, broad shoulders. 'He might have

made a good football goalie too.'

'Yeah, he might have.' David stared out of the front window. 'But my father wasn't interested in football or rugby. It had to be ice hockey. He wanted a son who would be an ice hockey legend.'

'Why?' Robyn couldn't quite understand. 'Did your father never make it beyond little league, or something?' *How awful*, she thought, *to impose your own dreams on your kids*. She'd never do something like that.

David laughed. 'He never played a game of ice hockey in his life! Just loves the game, I guess.' He sighed. 'He put me on the ice, and a stick in my hand, and I took to it like a duck to water.' David didn't sound happy about it. 'I wish I hadn't, because it turned into my whole life, until recently. But there you are. No one can change the past.'

'So, your father was right – you do … did … have a gift, then?'

'Gifts come at a price, Robyn.'

She stared at him, wondering what he meant by that.

'Hard work, sacrifice, loss.' He didn't stop there. 'Every weekend, evening, it was ice hockey practice. There was no time for anything else. Hockey, hockey, hockey.' He slammed his fist hard on the dashboard, making Robyn jump in surprise and making the van swerve.

David grabbed the steering wheel before they ran off the road into the snowy plains.

Robyn withdrew her hands from the front dashboard, where she'd braced in case the van skidded.

'And you thought I'd run us off the road!' She folded her arms and stared at him. She knew that was what he had been thinking when she'd insisted on driving his van.

David glanced at her sheepishly. 'Sorry.'

'I should think so!' Robyn replied, indignantly. She'd driven them all the way there, on a Snow Road she'd never travelled on before, in a van she'd never driven before, without incident – the stag notwithstanding.

Driving along in silence again, Robyn's expression softened. She was thinking about what he'd said about hard work, sacrifice, and loss. She turned to David, hoping he'd open up again about his past. She imagined that the injury, forcing him out of the game, must have come as a blow, especially when he was about to compete in the Elite Ice Hockey League. Wouldn't that make anyone bitter, and resentful, and change their feelings toward something they might have loved?

'You must have liked ice hockey once, to get where you did.'

'Yes. Once. Not anymore. Not for a long time.'

'How long?' Robyn wasn't sure she wanted the answer, not sure she wanted to know how long he had been wasting his life on someone else's dream.

'It doesn't matter anymore.'

They both fell silent, watching the road ahead. It wouldn't be long, and then they'd reach the end of the Snow Road and be back in Grantown-on-Spey, and well on their return journey to Aviemore.

Robyn glanced at David and felt disappointed that the conversation had ended. It seemed that just as suddenly as he had opened up about his past, he had clammed up. And he still hadn't answered her question – *what did Joe mean when he said it was like old times?* Had Joe been referring to the fight David had got into with his father? Somehow, she wouldn't be surprised. He sounded like a mean, selfish old man.

Robyn chanced another question. 'He doesn't seem resentful

or jealous, does he? Your brother, I mean.'

'Of me?' David said surprised. 'Why should he be? I mean, look at me – all washed up at twenty-six, with a busted knee and no career.'

Robyn stared at him. Perhaps he'd opened up a little too much. She'd certainly got a bit more than she bargained for. She imagined that next he'd be telling her his marriage had fallen apart, he was divorced, and he had kids.

Robyn thought she'd stop with the questions – for now.

'You know, my brother was lucky.'

'How so?' Robyn thought it would have been the other way around. David had had fame and fortune, his face in the papers, travel, a nice bank balance, she imagined, and a flashy car. She frowned at the thought of the flashy car that she'd driven into, which was, she imagined, a write-off. And what about a nice house and bank balance from all his years in ice hockey? Why was he living with his father? She hoped it was just a temporary arrangement while he found himself something more permanent.

'I watched him grow up doing all the things I longed to do. All the things *normal* kids do, like sleepovers with their friends, or just hanging out after school, going out on a Saturday night with their first date. With me, it was all practice, practice, practice.'

Robyn braced her hands on the dashboard, just in case.

She had a thought. 'Did he go to practice with you?'

'Who?'

'Your brother,' Robyn said. 'Did he go with you and your father?'

'Of course not.' The question took David by surprise. He looked at her as though she had just beamed down from another planet. 'Why would he?'

'Well, the reason I ask is that perhaps you've never put yourself in your brother's shoes.' She didn't mean to mock him, or to be unkind, but while David was busy feeling sorry for himself, she wondered if he had ever stopped to think about the situation from his kid brother's perspective. Had he felt left out and less important to his father because it was all about his big brother, and the game? It made her wonder. She asked, 'Where was Joe when your dad was taking you every evening and weekend to ice hockey practice?'

'Having a good time with friends, like I told you.' David was quick to answer, the envy in his voice unmistakable.

'But maybe he would have liked to have spent some time with his father. Don't you think he would have felt left out? I mean, it must have appeared as though it was all about you—' She stopped. She kept her eyes riveted on the road ahead, and thought she just might have gone a little too far. After all, what real business was it of hers – David and Joe's past? Except that she did care about David, and she cared about what hurt him. And things in his past had hurt him. She saw that his father had hurt him, and she hadn't realised until now how much it had hurt her – and now here she was, virtually telling David to shut up and stop feeling sorry for himself. She could feel her cheeks burning with embarrassment.

'And what makes you such an authority on my family?' David said, his voice rising in anger.

Robyn stared at him and suddenly felt an irrational fear over what might happen next. She couldn't explain it. She couldn't imagine that David would really suddenly pull the van over, jump out, race around to her side of the car, and pull her out, and have a huge row right in the middle of the road. And yet she had pictured it. She had no idea where that thought had come from.

She hoped to goodness it wasn't something from her past.

Of course, David did no such thing. He hunkered over the steering wheel, shaking his head and keeping his cool.

Unfortunately, Robyn didn't keep hers. At first she was going to apologise, and then she thought, *To hell with it. Why shouldn't I speak my mind?*

'You're mad at me because you realise that you've spent so long just thinking about yourself, you haven't even stopped to consider anyone else's feelings – like Joe's, for instance.'

'Are you and my brother like this now?' He put his forefinger over his index finger and held it up in front of Robyn's face.

She didn't even bother responding to that ridiculous question – she'd only just met Joe. She barely knew the man. In fact, she barely knew David. She said as much, adding, 'I'm only making an observation, from what you've told me – which isn't really all that much.'

'Well, I don't seem to recall you being that eager to talk about your past, your family.'

That shut Robyn up. She hadn't meant to cause an argument. But she realised she'd touched a nerve.

David shook his head. 'Just drop it, will you.'

Robyn looked at him in surprise. 'Me – drop it?'

He shifted in his seat, keeping his eyes on the road.

Robyn turned in her seat to face him. 'I seem to recall it was you who started it, talking about ice hockey leagues.'

'No,' David said, 'I seem to recall it was you who started it with that stupid question about what Joe meant by—'

Robyn interrupted. 'Yeah, and what the hell did that have to do with ice hockey? You didn't even answer my question.'

'Well, if you'd have let me finish without interrupting.'

'Interrupting what – someone feeling sorry for themselves? You're not the only one with problems around here, you know.'

David took his eyes off the road for a second to look at her. 'And what's that meant to mean?'

'Nothing.'

'No, come on. Tell me. What's your story is then? You don't talk about yourself much, do you?'

It was Robyn's turn to say, 'Let's drop it.'

'No, I want to hear what it is.'

'I said just drop it,' Robyn yelled.

'Fine.' David scowled at her and turned to look out of the window.

'Fine,' Robyn muttered under her breath.

They drove in silence back through the village of Grantown-on-Spey, where they'd started the evening, the crowd of people now dispersing as the car park in the village was emptying.

They continued on. As the van approached a bend in the road, David slowed down and changed gear. Around the bend, Robyn thought she recognised the place. He'd taken a different road back to Aviemore. Skid marks in the gravel were illuminated by the headlights as they came out of the curve in the road.

'Careful!' Robyn exclaimed as she glanced out of the passenger side window. She could just make out the cliff edge.

This was where it had happened – where they'd first met.

She turned to David. 'Why did you bring us this way back?' she said crossly. She didn't want to be reminded of the accident.

David slowed the car to a halt.

'What are you doing?'

'I thought I'd swing by the scene of the accident to see if you remember.'

'Remember what?'

'Anything.'

Robyn shot him a look. 'What are you talking about? Of course I remember the accident.' *Well, the aftermath, at any rate,* she thought.

'At first, I didn't think anything of it. In fact, it was really refreshing to meet a girl who wasn't self-absorbed, talking about herself all the time. And that suited me. I didn't want to talk about me either. But then it occurred to me, it's like you appeared out of nowhere. No family visited you in hospital. No friends. And here you are, with me today, instead of with your friends, your family on New Year's Eve.'

Robyn sat there in silence, not feeling inclined to tell him about her memory issues.

David finally asked the question that she had expected him to ask all along. 'What were you doing out here all alone on Christmas Day?'

Was that why he'd taken her there? To ask her that question?

'What were *you* doing?' Robyn retorted, deflecting a question she knew she couldn't answer. She stole a glance at David.

'Who have you been talking to?' he said, the guarded tone of voice unmistakable.

'What do you mean – *who have I been talking to?* I don't know many people in this town.'

Robyn winced. She wished she hadn't said that.

For some reason, that comment seemed to go over his head. David started the engine. 'I don't want to hang around here.'

'Well, at least that's something we agree on!' Robyn kept her eyes front and centre, wishing she hadn't seen that steep cliff edge as they took off again along the road. She willed David to keep his eyes on the road; one slip and they would both be down that embankment.

Just as they pulled back on to the road from the gravel passing place, too near the cliff edge for her liking, she caught sight of tyre tracks in the mud on the other side of the road, coming from the direction of the wood.

She stared at him. There had been something bugging her about the accident; specifically the photo of their mangled cars in the newspaper article. The odd angle of his car meant she was sure he couldn't have been travelling in the opposite direction. So where had he come from? Her eyes roved to the wood across the road as she thought about the tyre tracks. She looked at David. Were those his tyre tracks? If he hadn't been on the road, but in the wood instead, then it wasn't her who had run into him, losing control of her car as she approached the bend in the road, and driving into David coming in the other direction. That was what she'd been led to believe. It had been David, coming through the woods, accidentally driving into her as she rounded the bend on the road.

She frowned. That couldn't be true. Why would he have been driving through a wood, heading in the direction of the road, in the direction of the cliffs?

Robyn caught him rubbing his knee again as he drove. 'You didn't answer my question,' she said, narrowing her eyes, 'about what you were doing on this stretch of road on Christmas Day.'

'Neither did you.' It was a stand-off. They both sat in silence once more – all the way back to Gayle's

35

Robyn opened the front door. Gayle had given her a key, but the door was unlocked, so she guessed Gayle was still up, even though it was nearly one in the morning on New Year's Day.

She heard footsteps behind her as she walked in, and guessed David had followed her into the house. She didn't bother to look round to acknowledge him. Instead she called softly, 'Gayle?'

Gayle appeared in the lounge doorway, holding a glass of wine. 'Hey there! I didn't expect you back until much later … um, I mean earlier. Did you have a nice time?'

Robyn didn't want to answer that question. She wished David hadn't followed her into the house.

Gayle's gaze shifted to David. 'Oh, what happened?'

Robyn followed her gaze, glancing over her shoulder.

David stood forlornly in the hallway, dabbing at his forehead, which had started to bleed again. Robyn sighed, trying not to feel sorry for him. 'David needs a first aid kit,' she said matter-of-factly as she pulled off her coat. She threw her coat on the coat rack and headed for the kitchen. 'I'm going to make myself a cup of tea.' She caught Gayle's eye as she passed her, and the quizzical expression on her face. Robyn wouldn't have been surprised if

Gayle had guessed something was up; the atmosphere could have been cut with a knife.

She promptly went into the kitchen and put the kettle on, leaving Gayle to sort David out. With any luck, he would get the message and leave.

'Come into the kitchen and sit down,' she heard Gayle say in the hallway. 'I'll go and fetch the first aid kit.'

'No,' David said. 'Not in there.'

Robyn thought *good*. She walked over and shut the kitchen door, just to be sure he didn't change his mind and come in.

A moment later, the kitchen door opened.

Robyn whirled around, saying, 'David, I don't want to speak to … you.' It wasn't David but Gayle.

'I just came in to fetch the first aid box.'

Robyn dropped her gaze and busied herself putting a tea bag, milk and sugar in her mug while she waited for the kettle to boil.

Gayle swept into the room and rummaged in a cupboard, where she found a large green box with a big red cross on the front. She headed for the door. She paused and turned around. 'I take it the evening didn't go quite as expected?'

Robyn turned and eyed Gayle. She really didn't want to talk about it.

'Ok, have it your way. But sometimes it is better to talk about things. You know what they say – a problem aired is a problem shared.'

Despite everything, Robyn managed a wisp of a smile at another one of Gayle's quotes from the self-help books she so loved.

'There, you see.' Gayle smiled broadly. 'You're feeling better already, just at the thought of sharing.'

Gayle walked out of the door, but did a swift about-turn. 'David needs a nice cup of sweet tea while I deal with the gash on his head. He might need stitches.'

'I'm not making David a cup of tea!' Robyn said moodily. 'That gash on his head has got nothing to do with me.' Despite what she'd said after the fight, she'd changed her mind. David's relationship with his father had nothing to do with her.

'Is that a fact?' Gayle said flatly. 'Looks to me like someone's had their first lovers' spat.'

Robyn stared after her. 'I did not touch David!'

Gayle said, 'If you say so,' as she walked back to the lounge.

'Urrgh!' Robyn stamped her foot and picked up the kettle, which had just boiled. She wondered what David had been saying about her. She reluctantly made three mugs of tea, put them on a tea tray and walked into the lounge.

David looked up as she entered the room.

'Keep still!' Gayle grumbled as she placed two thin steri-strips over David's cut – the same sort of adhesive strips the hospital had used to dress Robyn's wound. She remembered what Gayle had said when she'd asked her what they were – for use on certain types of shallow wounds instead of stitches. She sighed in relief. It meant he wouldn't need a trip to A&E.

After applying the adhesive strips, Gayle carefully rolled a bandage around his forehead. She sat back and looked at her handiwork. Glancing at Robyn, she quipped, 'There! Now you two look like twins.'

Robyn's shot her a look.

David, who had been gingerly touching his bandage, stopped and looked at Gayle, his dead-pan expression saying he wasn't amused by the comment either.

Gayle looked at them both. 'No, you're right. That wasn't funny.' Even so, she sat there smiling at them.

Robyn set the tea tray down and picked up a mug. 'I'm tired. I'm taking my tea to bed.' She avoided David's eyes. 'Goodnight, Gayle. Happy New Year.'

Robyn walked over to the sofa with a mug of tea and stopped in front of David.

He looked up, surprised. His eyes never left hers as he took the mug.

Robyn stared at him, wondering if he was going to apologise about the argument; try and smooth things over before she went to bed. Whose fault was it, anyway? She'd only asked a question about the comment Joe had made – which he hadn't answered. Then he'd got all shirty when she'd asked him what he'd been doing on that road when they'd run into each other. But then she hadn't exactly been happy about David asking her the same question.

Secrets; that was what she realised their relationship was built on – secrets and, in her case, lies. Wasn't it about time she told David what was really going on with her before their relationship got serious?

Serious? Robyn thought. She looked at him. After the terrible way their first date had ended, there was no fear of that.

Unsurprisingly, David said nothing. She imagined he didn't want to start another argument.

Well, neither did she.

Robyn turned on her heel and handed Gayle her tea.

'Thank you, Robyn. Now, remember what I said, in the kitchen.'

A problem aired is a problem shared. Robyn nodded, but she didn't want to share; not with David there. That was why she was taking herself off to bed.

'Goodnight, Gayle.'

Robyn avoided David's gaze as she left the room, wishing she hadn't made him that cup of tea. She'd even dawdled for a bit, slowly spooning some more sugar into her tea from the sugar bowl she'd brought in on the tray, even though she didn't need more sugar; she just wanted to see if David said something, anything, to her before she left.

She thought that there was probably nothing worse that parting on bad terms – with anybody. What if something happened and you never saw that person again? How would it feel?

Despite those thoughts, Robyn had no intention of backing down and apologising first. She picked up her tea, glared at David, and walked out. She had the impulse to slam the door behind her, but she didn't. She would have, though, if Gayle hadn't been sitting in the lounge too.

She stopped for a moment outside the door, wishing that David would just go home. She expected he'd leave in a short time; perhaps when Gayle was satisfied he was okay and could drive.

Robyn was just moving away from the door when she heard Gayle say, 'David, you know, there's a rather lovely saying – a problem aired is a problem shared.'

Robyn turned around and stared at the door, her eyes narrowing. She knew Gayle's game. Gayle hadn't been able to get Robyn to tell her what was going on, so she was going to try and get it out of David instead.

She heard David say, 'Is that a fact?'

'Oh, yes. Now, would you like a biscuit with your tea?'

'Yes, I would, Gayle. Thank you.'

'Let me just go and get some.'

Robyn scooted off, up the stairs, being careful not to spill her tea. She was hoping that David *did* tell Gayle all about the evening – especially the fight with his father. Then at least Gayle would know she hadn't touched David. Well, she had. The colour rose in Robyn's cheeks when she thought about their kiss. Would he tell Gayle about that? Would he tell her about the row afterwards when Robyn wouldn't tell him what she was doing out late on her own on that country road on Christmas Day?

Would Gayle tell him why she couldn't answer that question?

Robyn walked into her bedroom and closed the door. She guessed she'd find out in the morning. At least by that time David would be gone.

36

Robyn rubbed her eyes. Chinks of light filtered through the heavy curtains at the window. She hadn't pulled them shut properly earlier that morning when she'd fallen into bed, exhausted and fully clothed. Her mug of tea sat cold and untouched where she'd left it on the bedside table, thinking she'd sit and drink it in bed in the early hours. She had thought the argument with David would have played on her mind, keeping her awake, but that hadn't happened. She realised that she must have fallen asleep sitting up, and that at some point, feeling cold, she'd crawled under the covers and promptly fallen asleep again.

Now, she was wide awake, feeling disconcerted. For a moment, she had to think what day it was. She was meant to be visiting Rose the day after New Year to start work on the interior design of her new house. She frowned when she realised what day it actually was. The same horrible day that had begun with an argument between her and David in the early hours.

But an argument is not how it started out, she remembered. Her New Year's Day had started in the highest village in the Cairngorms, with her clasping David's hand, singing *Auld Lang Syne*, and then enjoying their first kiss.

Yes, but look how it ended, she thought, shaking her head. Now she couldn't wait to put New Year's Day behind her. She decided that the next day, which she would spend with Rose, pushing all thoughts of David to the back of her mind, would be a better day. *Much better*. She managed a smile at the thought.

Robyn sat up with a start when she heard a faint knocking on her bedroom door.

'It's me – Gayle. Are you awake?' Gayle called in barely a whisper.

Robyn sighed in relief and relaxed. 'Yes, I'm awake.'

The doorknob turned, and the door opened. Gayle popped her head around the door, and grinned. 'There you are. Happy New Year!'

'Happy New Year,' Robyn chimed, even though she'd already wished Gayle a Happy New Year hours ago.

'Are we feeling better?'

Robyn actually felt in high spirits. She threw her arms wide stretching. 'Yes, much better.' Especially at the thought that David would be long gone.

'You're dressed already,' Gayle observed.

Robyn shook her head. 'Actually, I must have been so tired, I fell asleep in my clothes.'

'Yes, the eventful evening certainly caught up with you.'

Robyn's smile faded at that comment. That was when she remembered that she'd left Gayle and David talking in the lounge. What had he said? And more worryingly, what had Gayle told him?

Robyn remembered to breathe. What did it matter? After last night, she'd probably never see David again.

Even so, she had heard them chatting in the lounge when she closed the door behind her, and it was still on her mind. 'Last night

– I mean earlier, when I went to bed – did you mention to David about my memory issues?' Robyn motioned at her head.

'Of course not. I never betray confidences.'

Robyn knew she shouldn't have asked. She threw Gayle an apologetic look. She did wonder, though, what David might have confided in her. Gayle was one of those people who exuded calm, and she was so easy to talk to. She was a good listener, and gave people the inclination to open up to her.

Robyn thought that perhaps, instead of going back to hairdressing, Gayle should have considered training to become a counsellor instead. She could have swapped her role in nursing, looking after people physically, to helping people with their mental health instead.

'I'm making breakfast – come and join us.'

Robyn grinned. 'Fantastic. I am *so* hungry.' She swung her legs out of bed and exclaimed, 'Ouch!' clutching her head.

'Headache?'

Robyn nodded. 'Yeah.'

'I'll bet. You should have eaten something before you went to bed last night.'

'Why?'

'Helps when you drink too much.'

'I did not drink too much! I only had two bottles of beer. What has David been telling you?'

Gayle just smiled. 'Oh, before I forget.' She walked into the room with a kettle.

Robyn knitted her brow. 'What's that for?'

Gayle said, 'The boiler's on the blink again. I'm afraid that means no baths at the moment, so I brought up a kettle of hot water.'

'Oh.' Robyn glanced at the sink in the corner of the room. Although the sink would come in handy today, it would have to go, thought Robyn, if Gayle was going to have paying guests.

Gayle didn't know it yet, but her non-paying guest, Robyn, intended to do up the house – for Gayle and for her mum. It would make the most amazing guest house, and earn them lots of money. That was how she intended to repay Gayle back for her kindness and generosity, taking her in when she had nowhere else to go. The problem was that now, she didn't want to leave.

Thinking of guests as she watched Gayle cross the room and leave the kettle by the sink, Robyn wondered if Nick, the site manager from the housing estate where Rose lived, had arrived there yesterday evening, while she was out with David.

She was about to ask – she hoped Gayle hadn't turned him away – but she decided the question could wait. She needed to wash, and head downstairs for something to eat, hoping that helped her headache. She was looking forward to having breakfast with Gayle and her mum.

'I'll leave you in peace,' said Gayle. 'Come down to breakfast when you're ready.'

'All right.'

Gayle was just closing the bedroom door behind her when she paused, and said, 'I'm so glad you're here.'

Robyn smiled. 'Me too.'

She watched Gayle close the door, and then stood up. She looked at the heavy dark curtains. This place needed more light. The property had dark wood everywhere – the skirtings, dado rails, staircase, and the mahogany furniture. Although some of the wallpapered rooms were quite pretty, the wallpaper itself looked shabby and was peeling in places. The heavy velvety curtains throughout didn't help at all; they really aged the property.

Robyn couldn't do anything about all that just then, but what she could do was open those curtains and let in some natural light.

Before washing, and changing her clothes, she walked over to the heavy curtains, took one in each hand, and yanked them apart. The strong sunlight took her by surprise. It was later than she'd thought.

She immediately closed her eyes against the glare, standing in the window for a moment, feeling the warmth of the winter sun on her face. It felt wonderful. A new day was dawning, a new year, and Robyn couldn't think of any place she'd rather be than standing there in that house, holding the old worn curtains in her hands, soaking up the morning sunshine.

When she did open her eyes, she smiled at the view across the front garden. The grounds were quite extensive. Gayle had told her that the property had been the first one built at the end of the cul de sac, and so it had the prime corner position with more land than the others.

Although it was overgrown – Gayle's mum really could do with a gardener – Robyn could see past the overgrown hedgerows and weed-filled lawn to the sort of garden it could be, with perhaps a little wooden summerhouse sitting at the end of a perfectly manicured lawn, and colourful flower borders. The only thing she wouldn't change was the amazing backdrop of the snow-peaked Cairngorms.

And that was just the front garden. She could imagine what the back garden could be turned into with a little TLC, and a gardener.

Robyn was just turning to the sink when her gaze shifted just below her window to the stony drive outside the house. She blinked in surprise. *What is David's van doing here?* she wondered.

Her first thought was that he'd returned to make a delivery. She shook her head. On New Year's Day? Nobody should be working on New Year's Day; it was a bank holiday. But what if, after speaking with Gayle last night, she'd persuaded him to return and deliver some flowers as an apology?

'Well, I shan't accept them,' Robyn decided, folding her arms and pouting at the van for a full minute.

As she walked over to the sink, she thought it strange that Gayle hadn't mentioned he was back. Perhaps he wasn't. Maybe Gayle had given him a lift home in the early hours because she didn't think he should drive, so he'd left the van there.

That was it, Robyn decided as she washed and changed for breakfast.

37

Walking down the stairs, Robyn paused. She thought she heard two voices coming from the kitchen – Gayle's and a man's voice. She rounded the kitchen doorway to find two pairs of eyes on her.

'David!' Robyn stopped in the doorway. 'What are you doing here?' *Come to apologise,* she imagined. She slowly folded her arms.

'Oh, he never left,' said Gayle nonchalantly over her shoulder. She was standing at the Aga, cooking.

Robyn opened her mouth to say something, but the smell of fried breakfast stopped her in her tracks. Her mouth watered.

'Come sit.' Gayle beckoned at the table.

Robyn sat down in the chair furthest from David, aware she was being a bit childish.

If Gayle and David thought the same, they didn't say anything.

David said, 'I slept on the couch.'

'I told him we had plenty of spare bedrooms, but he insisted the couch was fine.'

'I didn't want to inconvenience anyone.'

Robyn frowned. 'I assumed that you'd left your van here, and Gayle had taken you home.'

Gayle set a plate down in front of him, with a full Scottish breakfast fry-up, and placed an affectionate hand on his shoulder. 'Honey, you weren't inconveniencing anyone. Stay as long as you like.'

Robyn's eyes went wide. She couldn't believe what she was hearing. *Stay as long as you like?* She frowned at both of them as though it was some sort of conspiracy.

'You said yourself you're not running a guest house,' Robyn reminded her. That brought Nick to mind. He wasn't there, sitting eating breakfast with them, and it was getting on now, almost mid-morning; she couldn't imagine he'd still be in bed.

'Well, I could be fast changing my mind.'

'Oh, really,' Robyn said, sarcastically. 'Then why isn't Nick here?'

'He's not here, because he left.'

'Already?' Robyn was so disappointed. 'I thought he'd like it here.'

'I do,' said David.

Robyn shot him a look before she turned her attention to Gayle. 'So, he only stayed one night?'

'Ah, I think we're talking at cross-purposes. He went jogging. That's what I meant. He left the house about an hour ago in his jogging gear. I spotted him in the hallway, fiddling with his phone, before he headed out, sticking those little wireless earbuds in each ear. Personally, that's the last thing I'd do on New Year's Day – go jogging.'

'Yep, me too,' said David, reaching under the table, rubbing his knee.

'So, wait, are you saying that he arrived yesterday, New Year's Eve, and he's staying on?'

'Oh, yes. He turned up after you guys left for the Hogmanay

in Grantown-on-Spey. It was a shame because I suppose he could have tagged along with you guys.' She paused, her eyes focusing in on David's bandaged forehead. 'Or maybe not. In any case, he doesn't really know anybody around here – his parents live miles away in Sussex. Or was it Surrey?' She shook her head. 'In any case, it's a long way away, so he spent the evening with me and my mother, seeing in the New Year. We had a lovely evening all together. Then he went to bed just before you guys turned up.'

Robyn smiled. She was so pleased to hear that Gayle and her mum had had company on New Year's Eve.

'I'm afraid we all missed breakfast with him this morning. He has a key to the house. I told him to help himself to breakfast, whatever he wants. He had muesli, I think, and even washed up his own dishes. He's such a nice young man – isn't he, David?'

'He's okay, I guess.'

Robyn looked at him. 'You met Nick?'

'It was earlier this morning,' said Gayle. 'We both saw him getting ready for his jog. You emerged from the lounge as I was walking down the stairs to put the kettle on. Didn't we look a pair?'

David rolled his eyes. 'Don't remind me.'

Gayle reminded him anyway. ''There Nick was, standing in the hall, jogging on the spot, setting up the music on his phone, getting ready for a run, all wide-eyed and bushy-tailed, raring to go, and you looked like you'd got out of the wrong side of the bed – oh, excuse me, sofa – with your hair wild and your clothes all astray.'

Robyn looked at him. He had slept in his clothes too.

'And there I was in my bathrobe and fluffy pink slippers, trudging down the stairs, yawning my head off.'

Robyn saw David frown. 'I used to be up with the lark, jogging, when I was training.'

'Yes – he's quite fit, isn't he?' remarked Gayle.

David said, 'Is that what you think, Robyn? That he's quite fit?'

Robyn stared at him. She knew what he meant when he said the word *fit*. Was that jealousy in his voice?

'How do you know him, anyhow?' David frowned some more. 'I thought you didn't know anybody round here?'

Robyn turned wide-eyed to Gayle, wondering what she'd told David. There had been an empty bottle of wine on the coffee table in the lounge; she'd noticed it when she'd glanced through the open doorway on her way to the kitchen. Just how much of that conversation could Gayle remember?

Gayle said, 'She met him when we visited Rose, one of my hairdressing clients. He's the site manager on the new housing development where Rose lives. Turned out he needed somewhere to stay while he works on the development, and Robyn knew just the place.'

Robyn winced. 'I'm sorry about that.'

David looked from Gayle to Robyn. 'Just the place?'

'She invited him to stay here.' Gayle smiled at Robyn. 'I'm so pleased you did.'

Robyn realised that after the previous night, seeing in the New Year with her new house guest, Gayle had had a change of heart. Robyn was so pleased too. And there she had been, thinking that Gayle had turned him away.

'Now, how about you, Robyn? Are you going to have a fry-up too?'

Watching David tucking into his breakfast, and wondering what he was still doing there, she realised she'd lost her appetite. She shook her head.

'Really?' Gayle looked at her. 'I thought you were hungry?'

David looked up. 'Are you okay?'

'Yes.' *No thanks to you.*

David pointed his fork at her across the table. 'You look kinda peaky.'

'I said I'm fine.'

Gayle turned to Robyn. 'Perhaps I'll take another look at that dressing, check things are still healing okay.'

'Will you check mine too? It was kind of itchy and hot last night,' said David.

'Well, you'd better get in line.'

Robyn did not want any more jokes about their matching bandages.

'I'll check Robyn's first, after breakfast.' Gayle turned to her. 'How about some toast?'

Robyn's mouth watered as she stole a glance at David's fry-up.

Gayle followed her gaze, and smiled. 'Are you sure I can't tempt you with something cooked? I have plenty. Even if it's just a teeny bit?'

Robyn's resolve crumbled. 'Oh, all right, if you're going to twist my arm.'

Gayle grinned, turned to a kitchen cupboard, picked out a large dinner plate, and put it in front of Robyn. She then reached for the frying pan and started filling up Robyn's plate. 'Just one slice of bacon?'

Robyn said sheepishly, 'I might manage two.'

'Would you manage a Lorne sausage and some haggis?'

Robyn licked her lips. 'Yes, I just might.'

A moment later, Robyn's plate was piled with mushrooms, baked beans, black pudding, and fried tomatoes too. She tucked in, catching David smiling across the table at her. He commented,

'Guess you're feeling better.'

'Oh, do shut up,' Robyn said with her mouth full.

Gayle stood with her hands on her hips, shaking her head and smiling to herself.

Robyn caught her expression. 'What are you looking so happy about?'

'Fairy godmothers,' said Gayle.

David gave her a double-take. 'Fairy – *what*?'

Robyn rolled her eyes and willed Gayle not to tell him about their conversation in which Gayle had said she thought she was playing matchmaker.

Gayle just smiled and didn't say anything more.

Robyn asked, 'So, did Nick mention what time he starts work tomorrow morning?'

Gayle replied, 'Ah, he's not in work tomorrow.'

'How come?' Robyn asked.

Gayle and David exchanged a glance.

Robyn looked at them. 'What?'

'It's a Scottish bank holiday the day after New Year,' said Gayle.

'Is it? I didn't realise. Oh dear. I thought I could get a lift in with him to start my new job.'

David put his knife and fork together on his plate. He picked up his last slice of fried bread. 'You've got a job?'

'Yes.' She looked at him. 'Why are you grinning?'

'I was just thinking that it's great you've got a job.'

''Why's that?' Robyn made her best attempt at sounding uninterested.

'Because that means you'll be staying around.' He pointed his fried bread at her. 'And I'd like that – very much.'

Robyn looked at him. Had he meant that as some kind of

apology for the previous night?

'Yeah, well, don't get too excited,' she mumbled, 'I probably won't have one after tomorrow if I don't turn up.' She didn't know how she would get to Rose's house to start work the next day, like she promised. She couldn't ask Gayle to drive her everywhere unless she could borrow the car. After her accident, she couldn't imagine Gayle would lend her the prized old Bentley.

David bit into his fried bread and turned to Gayle, who had sat down at the table to eat a slice of toast. 'Thanks, that was a great breakfast. There's nothing like home cooking. You know, I think I could get used to this.'

'Why – are you thinking of moving in?'

'Hmm, well … with breakfasts like this, I might just do that.'

Robyn looked at him. *Was he having a joke?*

David continued, 'I think you're on to something with the idea of a guesthouse. You'd do a roaring trade as a bed-and-breakfast.'

'But you haven't seen the state of the bedrooms,' Robyn butted in.

Gayle frowned. 'You said you liked the bedroom you're staying in. And you did a tour of the house. Your bedroom is no different to the others.'

Robyn pursed her lips and looked at Gayle sheepishly.

Gayle stared at her for a long moment and narrowed her eyes, shaking her head at Robyn as if to say, *I know what your game is.*

'I don't mind if the rooms are old-fashioned – if that's what you mean.'

'There are sinks in the room,' said Robyn.

'Really? What a good idea. That saves traipsing to the bathroom to clean your teeth.'

Robyn rolled her eyes. She was trying to put David off, but it wasn't working. She said, 'Haven't you got a home of your own to go back to?'

'Yeah – sure. Of course I have.'

Gayle said, 'I bet it's really nice – not like this dump.'

'It's not a dump!' cried Robyn, feeling quite protective of the old house all of a sudden.

'But I thought you just said …'

Robyn frowned at Gayle. 'Never mind what I just said.'

Gayle grinned. She was just having some fun with Robyn.

'I don't think this place is a dump either, Gayle,' David chimed in. 'Far from it. Okay, it might be a little … dated. But hey, it's got character, and it's in an enviable spot. And you've got famous neighbours.'

'Famous?' Robyn looked from Gayle to David.

Gayle said, 'Oh, you mean the wealthiest family in Scotland, with their holiday home in the next street.'

David nodded. 'That's right – the Rosses.'

'So sad, what happened to their daughter.' Gayle shook her head.

Robyn looked at them both. 'What happened to her?'

'Skiing accident, apparently. Up in the Cairngorms on Christmas Day. Very sad.'

'Skiing accident.' Robyn recalled that news bulletin she'd seen in the hospital soon after her own accident. She suddenly came over light-headed, as though she was going to faint.

'Are you okay, honey? You've come over awfully pale.'

'Yeah, I'm okay, I just feel a little heady. I have no idea why. May I have a glass of water?'

David darted out of his seat and poured her a glass of water from the tap. He passed her the glass and sat down opposite her, watching her intently as she gulped down the water.

Robyn put the empty glass on the table and wiped her mouth dry with the sleeve of her jumper. 'Sorry, I don't know what happened.'

'Are you sure you're okay?' David asked, concern in his voice.

Gayle stared at her intently too.

Robyn nodded. She looked at David. 'Are *you* okay?' He was running his fingers along the bandage over his eye. 'How's the …' Robyn pointed at his bandage.

'Gayle did a good job.'

Gayle sighed. 'I'm afraid you might be left with a small scar.'

'Hmm.' David thought about that. 'You know, I'd like a scar just above the eye.'

'Why?' Gayle and Robyn said in unison.

'Now, what I'm about to say mustn't go beyond …' he circled his finger to indicate the three of them, 'but you know those girly magazines I bring along for you, Robyn?'

'Which I don't read cover-to-cover, you know. I'm not shallow.' Robyn had no idea where that thought had come from. Reading women's magazines didn't make her anything of the sort.

David gave her an odd look, smiled and shook his head. 'Well, I wonder what that makes me. You see, I read in one of those magazines …'

Robyn laughed out loud. 'You mean to tell me that you've been reading those magazines too?'

'Sure, you know, just to pass the time while I'm waiting for the van to be loaded, and deliveries to arrive.'

She started to giggle.

'What's so funny?' David said in all seriousness. 'It's surprising, what us blokes can learn from those glossy pages – there's some good tips about women.'

'Oh, really.' Gayle turned and smiled at Robyn, raising an eyebrow. 'This I've got to hear.'

'Like the scar thing,' David continued. 'They say women find guys more attractive if they have a scar – or two.'

'I'll have two now – one here,' he pointed at his head, 'and one down here.' He lifted his leg, pointing at his knee.

Robyn and Gayle looked at each other and burst into a fit of giggles.

'What?' David held out his arms palms up on the table.

'Er, David,' Robyn reached over and clasped one of his hands. 'I suggest you stick to the guys' magazines.'

Gayle shook her head, smiling. 'Yeah, I agree. Who knows what sort of trouble you'll get yourself into otherwise.' Gayle got up from the table. 'Stick to sport or something,'

'I'm not much into sport at the moment,' David said quietly.

'What was that, honey?' Gayle said in a merry tone as she washed up the dishes.

David replied, 'It's nothing.'

Robyn stared at David as he turned her hand over in his, examining it.

She withdrew her hand slowly and put her hands together in her lap, leaving David's empty hand outstretched on the table.

'So,' David said, withdrawing his arm, 'what's this about you losing your job?'

She hesitated, not wanting to involve David in her problems.

'You don't have to tell me a thing,' he added.

Robyn looked at David, unsure whether he was being sarcastic, alluding to their row in the early hours of the morning. She decided to let it go; she didn't want to dredge all that up again.

Especially not the cliff thing; not in front of Gayle.

'I was meaning to ask Nick to give me a lift to Rose's tomorrow morning.'

'So, you need a lift to work?'

'Uh-huh.' Robyn didn't expect any offers from David; he'd probably be out on deliveries for this father.

Gayle said, 'Don't worry about tomorrow. We'll sort something out.' She turned to David. 'So, if your house is so nice, what are you wanting to stay here for?' She cast a gaze over towards Robyn. 'Oh, stupid question.'

David shook his head. 'It's not stupid at all. It's just that I have a permanent house guest.'

'You rent rooms too?' Gayle asked.

'No, nothing like that. It's my dad.'

'You live with your dad?' Gayle looked surprised.

'No, he lives with me. It was okay when I was off travelling all over the place for tournaments, just returning home to touch base. But now I'm there twenty-four seven, it really doesn't work.'

Robyn wasn't surprised in the least after she'd met him at the Hogmanay party. He was a horrible old man. 'So, tell him to go back to his own place.'

David sighed. 'Yeah, that would be a great idea if he had a place of his own to go back to. He got himself into a heap of gambling debts. Too proud to ask for my help, he lost the house. Then, of course, he had nowhere to go.'

'So, he came knocking on your door,' said Gayle. 'Couldn't you just buy him another house?'

'That was the plan. Then this happened,' he slapped his knee, 'and my career and my income went south. Now, all I've got is the house, and investments which pay me an income. Nothing like what I used to rake in, but it keeps my head above water while I figure out what I'm going to do next. I won't cash in that money just for him to gamble it away.'

'Good for you,' commented Gayle.

'So, I'm afraid I'm stuck with him.'

Now Robyn understood why he didn't want to go home. She wouldn't either, if she had to go home to someone like that.

She was staring at David, thinking of his predicament, when something suddenly came to mind – what Dr Jamieson had said about her memory loss and the possibility it was more likely psychological. She'd called it *selective* amnesia; the memories of her past, the people she knew, experiences she'd had were temporarily closed off to her, the theory being that the mind was choosing not to remember.

She recalled the doctor saying that it was more prevalent in children, but it was possible that adults could protect themselves in the same way a child could from some traumatic event.

Robyn thought of David's father and shuddered. She'd suddenly had a change of heart. She didn't want her memories to come back if there was someone in her past, like a boyfriend, just as mean and unlikeable as him. She blurted, 'I don't want to leave either!'

'Well, who says you have to?' Gayle said, smiling.

Someone out there, thought Robyn.

'Yes, don't leave,' David said, reaching for her hand across the table again.

38

'Who's leaving?'

Everyone turned in their seats as Nick walked into the kitchen, followed by Gayle's mum. She looked at them all sitting at the table and said, 'Where's my breakfast?'

'Oh, Mum, I didn't realise you were awake.'

'I'm always up with the lark – you know that.'

Robyn glanced at the clock on the wall. No one had the heart to tell her the time.

'And you are not going anywhere,' she said, walking over and putting her arms around Robyn, giving her a hug.

Nick agreed. 'Hey, I hope you're not leaving on my account. I thought there were enough bedrooms for me to stay too?'

Gayle said, 'Of course there are.' She looked at Robyn. 'You can't leave now.' She looked around the table. 'I'm going to need help running my new guest house. And don't forget, you've got a job to start tomorrow. One of us will drive you over there. Don't you worry about that.'

David said, 'And I still need to make it up to you after last night.'

Gayle's mum said, 'What happened last night?'

'Mum, come over and take a seat at the table. How about a nice fry-up to start the morning?'

She took a seat and peered at Robyn, then David. 'And why have you got matching bandages?'

David and Robyn exchanged a smile, ignoring the question.

Nick ignored it too. 'You know, I'm famished after that run. I don't suppose there would be enough for me to have some too?'

'Of course there is. Take a seat, Nick.'

He pulled out a chair next to Gayle's mum and was just taking a seat when an almighty howl reverberated around the house. It was like something out of *The Hound of the Baskervilles*.

Robyn nearly jumped out of her skin. Her heart pounding, she exclaimed, 'What the hell is that?'

She looked around the table, appearing to be the only one startled by the sound of a dog howling. No one else seemed at all phased by the terrible racket coming from somewhere in the house.

Gayle said, 'Go on, Nick – you'd better let her come in.'

Nick got up from the table, looking apologetic.

Gayle turned to Robyn. 'You haven't met the other new house guest.'

'What?'

At the door, Nick said above the din, 'She's the reason I got kicked out of the other bed-and-breakfast. Although he said he had holidaymakers booked in to stay, I guessed it was because of my dog. They said they welcomed pets. Not her – apparently.'

Robyn looked at him wide-eyed, thinking that with that sort of howl, who could blame them?

She was the only one on the edge of her seat, waiting to see what monster was about to walk through that door. Everyone else had clearly already met Nick's dog.

Nick said, 'She'll quieten down once I bring her in. She's just feeling left out – that's all. I left her in the lounge across the hall with a bone to chew. Guess she finished her breakfast already.'

Robyn moved around the table, and sat next to David.

He looked at her. 'Don't you like dogs?'

Robyn was sure she did. She just didn't think, by the sound of it, she'd like this one.

The howling stopped, and then she heard a dog barking excitedly instead.

'Here she comes,' commented Gayle. 'Put your tin hats on.'

Robyn caught David grinning. A second later, a large exuberant dog came bounding into the room. She skidded to a halt on the stone floor, head looking this way and that, tail wagging furiously, as though she didn't know who to say hello to first. She barked, then ran straight over to Robyn.

'Ah,' said David, 'She hasn't met you yet. Smart dog. She'll get extra fusses from the newbie.'

Nick sighed. 'Robyn, meet Olive.'

'Oh, my god, isn't she gorgeous?' Robyn gushed as the great big Old English Sheepdog put her large head on Robyn's lap, doleful eyes looking up at her. Robyn said, 'I think I'm in love.'

'Yep, that's the effect my big soppy dog has on most people,' commented Nick, 'once they meet her. Unfortunately, she's still a puppy, in a big dog's body. She's too much to leave with my parents while I'm away working, so she has to come with me. But not everyone wants this sort of dog in their guesthouse; she can be a problem.'

'Well, she's our problem now,' said Gayle affectionately.

'Here – girl!' Gayle called her over and fed her some scraps from the table.

Gayle gave her a fuss, then looked around the table. 'Has anyone got any plans today?'

Everyone shook their heads.

'Good. How about we take some hot chocolate in a flask, climb in the Bentley, and all go for a bracing walk around the loch together?'

Robyn loved that idea, and so did everyone else.

'Which loch?' asked David.

Robyn sat listening to David, Gayle, her mum, and even Nick, who was new to the area, but had visited some of the lochs already, deciding which one they'd like to visit that day.

She smiled as she looked around the old oak kitchen table at her new friends, her new life, and thought, *If getting my memories back means giving up all this, I don't want them back. I like things just the way they are.*

She felt happy there, safe. Dr Jamieson had said that something would trigger her memories – a familiar place, her belongings. But what if it wasn't those things that did it, but a familiar face … and what if that person came back into her life and took all this away from her, forcing her to go back to a life she was running away from?

Robyn's eyebrows shot up at that thought.

'Robyn – what is it?' David asked, noticing she was very quiet all of a sudden.

'I'm not going anywhere.' *If there is someone out there looking for me, they'll have to find me first*, thought Robyn, feeling defiant.

'Then you'll stay, here, with us?'

'Of course I will.'

She had a home, friends – they'd protect her. But protect her from what – from whom?

Robyn tried her best to ignore that thought. She looked around the table, convinced that the accident, and her selective amnesia, had happened for a reason. That was what Gayle said: *Everything happens for a reason.* Maybe one day, she'd find out the reason, but just then, she was happy – content just the way things were. She'd just have to cross that bridge when she came to it. But that bridge back to her memories, was, she hoped, in the very distant future, along with whoever might be out there waiting for her.

The Scottish Highlands Series continues in

The Secrets of the Glen

Paperback and Kindle eBook coming soon.

If you enjoyed *Winter in the Scottish Highlands* I would be grateful if you would leave a review on Amazon.

For further details about the author and her novels please visit the author's website.

www.elisedarcy.com

Also by Elise Darcy

The Sunrise Coast Series

New Beginnings at the Harbour Inn

The Secret of the Summerhouse

The Cottage by the Sea

The Guest House at Shingle Cove

The Houseboat by the Quay

Return to Willow Tree Cottage

The Bookshop of Memories

The Beach House

A Summer to Remember

The Living Apart Together Series

Living Apart Together

It Takes 2 to Tango

Dear John

Love on the Rooftop

Standalone Novels

Lola & The Man

A Mallorcan Affair

We'll Meet Again

The Villa in Sicily

Printed in Dunstable, United Kingdom

80632494R00201